To Charlie with love —
February 1975 —

Son of Giant Sea Tortoise

ALSO BY MARY ANN MADDEN

Thank You for the Giant Sea Tortoise

Son of Giant Sea Tortoise

Competitions from  Magazine

Edited by
MARY ANN MADDEN

THE VIKING PRESS / NEW YORK

For My Mother

Copyright © 1969–1975 (inclusive) by Mary Ann Madden
All rights reserved

First published in 1975 by The Viking Press, Inc.
625 Madison Avenue, New York, N.Y. 10022

Published simultaneously in Canada by
The Macmillan Company of Canada Limited

SBN 670–65727–1

Library of Congress catalog card number: 74–6850

Printed in U.S.A.

Contents

Preface	vii
Opening Line of a Bad Play	3
Closing Line of a Bad Play	11
What You Should Have Said/What You Said	19
Near-Misses	27
TV Guide Listings	39
Silly Definitions "C"	46
Odd Couples	54
Uncaptivating Captions	62
Nonsense Poems	68
Authentic Typos	76
Unfamiliar Quotations	83
Repunctuated Names	91
Four-Letter Words	98
Extract from a Best Seller	108
Modern Devil's Dictionary	115
Insipid Adages	122
Fractured Names	130
Bartlett Pairs	138
Word-List Poetry	146
Contrived Nomenclature	154
One-Letter Misprints	174
Flat Verse	182

Far-Fetched Fables	192
Bedwords	200
Classified Directory	208
Heavy-Handed Proverbs	215
Good News/Bad News	222
Short Stories	229
Conversation Starters	237
Conversation Stoppers	245
Film Promos	253
One-Letter Inserts	260
Gothic Novels	267
The Answer Game	275
The Newlywed Game	283
Biographies	292
Punned-Name Quatrains	299
Letters to Santa	307
Gossip Items	315
"The Bloated Cadaver of Poor Mrs. Hays"	322
Terrible Riddles	331
Greeting-Card Verse	338
One-Word Inserts	348
Repunctuation	356
Opening of a Bad Novel	363
Conclusion of a Bad Novel	370

☞ *Preface*

This book is a lot like the first one. I didn't write this one either.

But I would like to thank those who did. All the competitors. Those whose names we all recognize. And others, such as Jack Ryan, Monsignor McLees, Albert G. Miller, Virginia Feine, John Hofer, and Marilyn Crystal, whose names have become household words for reasons of health.

Again, I want to thank Stephen Sondheim.

For their patient help, thank you to Sheila Okun Edelman, Flavia Potenza, and Debbie Harkins at *New York* magazine.

Thanks to Herb Sargent for moral support and for allowing me to steal his ideas.

And last, I am grateful to Clay Felker, Barbara Burn, and the New York Knickerbockers for great editing and for hitting the open man.

—M.A.M.

Son of Giant Sea Tortoise

☞ *Opening Line of a Bad Play*

ACT I, SCENE 1: A studio apartment in mid-Manhattan.
TIME: The present.
At curtain rise, a buzzer sounds. SAMANTHA, an attractive if slightly bohemian girl of twenty-two, Xs to press the release. (A pause.) MRS. HEDLEY enters. A chic woman in her early forties, SHE SPEAKS: "So, my dear, this is the cozy retreat where my husband has spent so many happy hours...."

Above, the starting line for a brief run. Competitors were invited to supply the opening scene of an unpromising play.

Report. We left after the first act of the following:

ACT I, SCENE 1: The elegant library of a large English country estate. At rise, NIGEL, at forty-five devastating if disheveled, is pouring brandy as rays of morning sun bathe his face. Door opens. HELENA, forty, handsome and immaculate, stands at door. HELENA: "If you think, Nigel

Yewford Charnley, that you can lurch back here to Crenheim and the bosom of your family just because it is your daughter's wedding day, you must think again."

E. Klein, N.Y.C.

The curtain rises to reveal the Mayor of New York.

James L. Brooks, Los Angeles, Calif.

ACT I, SCENE 1: The interior of a log cabin in Kentucky. Time: A cold February night in 1809. At rise, the MAN (standing by a pot of boiling water, turns to the WOMAN on the bed and speaks, in a voice choking with excitement): "Nancy, you have given us a son!"

David Steinman, M.D., Scarsdale, N.Y.

ACT I, SCENE 1: An office in a large Midwestern city, Time: 1954. At rise, EZRA JOHNSON, an elderly lawyer in pince-nez, is reading to a small assemblage of bored people from the last will and testament of Caleb Jebediah Stone. " . . . And to my great-niece Miranda (*the group looks toward a simply dressed, lovely girl, sitting apart and quietly weeping*), I leave my family home, Blackthorn, on the condition that she spend one full night there alone."

Virginia L. Annich, Pennington, N.J.

(*the houselights fall*)
P.A. ANNOUNCER: "Ladies and Gentlemen! Shipstads and Johnson proudly present . . ."
(CRASH OF CYMBALS)
P.A. ANNOUNCER: . . . " 'TURANDOT' ON ICE!"

Bob Bradford, Chicago, Ill.

ACT I, SCENE 1: A small-town newspaper office. Time: Mid-thirties. OFFICE PERSONNEL are lazily looking at their day's endeavors. The door is slammed open. A YOUNG MAN enters, and stands rocking on the balls of his feet, a toothpick stuck in the side of his half-sneering mouth. Slowly tilting his hat to the back of his neck, HE speaks: "Tell your boss Scoops Harrigan is hear to show him something about the newspaper game."

Jim Marsh, Ashland, Ky.

ACT I, SCENE 1: A large sitting room in an English manor house. At rise, INSPECTOR SMYTHIES of Scotland Yard stands facing four men: GERAINT, a rejected suitor; ALDEN WHITLAW, an admirer of the deceased; MR. CARRUTHERS, a shy tutor approaching middle age, and CHALMERS, the gardener. A door (UR) opens and a man enters bearing a tray with a tea service. HE turns to audience and speaks: "I did it."

Arthur Penn, Philadelphia, Pa.

ACT I, SCENE 1: A cannon booms. A shaft of light illuminates CHAD, facing the audience (SR). CHAD: "Fowt Sumptah has been fahrd upon!" A second shaft of light illuminates WINTHROP facing audience (SL). WINTHROP: "Fowt Sumptah has been fahrd upon!" A third shaft of light falls on BUEL. BUEL: "Fowt Sumptah has been fahrd upon!" CHAD, WINTHROP and BUEL (*together*): "FOWT SUMPTAH HAS BEEN FAHRD UPON!!" (*blackout*) The orchestra strikes up "Dixie" as a shaft of light falls on the Confederate flag and the curtain rises on the new musical *Bellum*.

Stanley Gilson, N.Y.C.

No curtain. Lights up on a middle-aged man wearing business suit. HE speaks: "Good evening. Welcome to the theater. My name is Gaius Julius Caesar. Ah, I note surprise on some faces at seeing me in modern dress and without the laurel wreath with which artists are wont to depict me. But consider. Is your period of history so unlike mine? Are there not parallels which we might discover together if we tried? . . ."

Stephen Pearlman, N.Y.C.

6 / Son of Giant Sea Tortoise

ACT I, SCENE 1: Time: Now. Place: Kansas. CHORUS enters singing:
"The wheat is as neat
As an elephant's feet
And it looks like the sheep
In the meadow will bleat . . ."

Eileen Tranford, Dorchester, Mass.

ACT I, SCENE 1: A nineteenth-century upper-class English drawing room. At rise, a uniformed maid of advanced age is in the act of nervously dusting the furniture. SHE *soliloquizes:* "I hope the master knows what he's doing, bringing his new young wife into this house, and my poor mistress scarcely cold in her grave. It was wrong of me, I fear, not to have told everything to that nice man from Scotland Yard. . . ."

Msgr. A. V. McLees, St. Albans, N.Y.

ACT I, SCENE 1: Foyer of lavish town house. Doorbell *rings,* stodgy MILLIONAIRE opens door. Enter lovely YOUNG GIRL and filthy HIPPIE. GIRL: "Daddy, this is Lionel Nathanson, the leader of the demonstrations that are taking place in your bank and causing all your depositors to withdraw their money. Li and I are going to be married . . ."

Richard Baer, Beverly Hills, Calif.

ACT I, SCENE 1: The drawing room of LADY EXETER's magnificent English country house. LADY EXETER paces the floor nervously. SHE is naked. A BODY lies on the rug. IT is naked. There is a discreet knock on the door. The BUTLER enters. HE is naked. HE speaks: "Sherlock Holmes and Dr. Watson have just arrived, m'lady." HOLMES and WATSON enter. THEY are naked . . .

Ellen S. Ryp, N.Y.C.

ACT I, SCENE 1: The court of Queen Elizabeth I. Time: early 1600. As the curtain rises, ELIZABETH, in royal raiment, is speaking with her adviser, LORD BURLEIGH. She is clearly very angry. ELIZABETH: "Essex! Essex! Why am I forever plagued with his arrogance? His conceit shines more brightly than the panoplied splendour of our court! Bring him to me at once. (*long pause*) And leave us alone."

Ted Sennett, Closter, N.J.

ACT I, SCENE 1: Time: The twenties. The foyer in the home of three-quarters of a millionaire JAMES JONES. His wife SUE enters down a staircase center stage. In rushes their seventeen-year-old niece, MABEL. MABEL: "Oh, Aunt Sue! The gang is scooting down to Atlantic City for the weekend and going tea dancing at the Marlborough-Blenheim. May I go?" SUE: Maybe, maybe, Mabel."

Robert Barrie, N.Y.C.

(A large office; a balding, middle-aged man in a gray suit sits behind a large desk with the Presidential seal mounted in front, surrounded with barbed wire. A window behind him looks out at the Washington Monument. This is PRESIDENT DICK TRICKSON. HE rises, both arms above his head in the double-V salute). . . .

Martin Schlesinger, Brooklyn, N.Y.

ACT I, SCENE 1: Contemporary Park Avenue drawing room. When the curtain rises we find AGNES dressed in bridal gown at the telephone deep in conversation. AGNES: "Yes . . . Yes . . . Yes . . . No . . . No . . . No . . . I can't, Creg. You know I can't. You know I'm being married in an hour!" (The BUTLER and a MAID enter with big baskets of flowers. THREE MEN in overalls follow bringing in golden folding chairs.) "Ring off, Creg. I'll phone you as soon as . . ."

Catherine M. Delgado, N.Y.C.

ACT I, SCENE 1: A prison cell equipped with bunk beds and a lavatory. Time: The present. At rise, GUS, a con man, is lying on the top bunk reading a girlie magazine. MIKE, who is virile and twenty-seven, is sitting on the lower bunk reading a letter. His face hardens as HE finishes his mail. HE crushes the letter, stands, and speaks: "Ginger is two-timing me. I gotta get out of here!"

Betty E. Stein, Fort Wayne, Ind.

ACT I, SCENE 1: Vicksburg. Time: The Civil War. At rise: The smoke of battle still hangs over the scene. The signs of the terrible carnage over the stage: bodies of soldiers, horses' carcasses, wrecked artillery, etc. From stage right a lonely figure enters on horseback—it is GENERAL GRANT; he surveys the awful scene, dismounts, picks up a hand mike and sings . . .

Stan Lachow, Tallman, N.Y.

(Behind the scenes at a large theater. All is activity. STAGE MANAGER, followed by mousy ASSISTANT with clipboard, paces with agitation.) S.M.: Kids, kids, get a move on. (*pauses in front of set painters*) That's supposed to be blue, you numbskulls, not yellow! (*to* GIRLS *dancing*) Higher, kick higher! This is Broadway, not Podunk! (*to himself*) Why the hell did I ever let them talk me into doing this show?

J. Bickart, N.Y.C.

ACT I, SCENE 1: Office on Wall Street. Time: Present. At rise, LYLE and his secretary KAREN are embracing on the couch, which faces the window, in LYLE's office. The door opens which no one hears because it was thought to be locked, and in walks LYLE's MOTHER-IN-LAW—she waits —and quietly backs out the door which is *heard* as it closes.

Barbara Smith, N.Y.C.

ACT I, SCENE 1: Two stories of a brownstone on the "fashionable East Side" of New York. The lower floor includes the reception room and operatory of a dental office. The upper, while not a home, definitely is a house. It is early morning. At rise, DR. RUDOLPH KARTOOM, a Lebanese dentist, is at the telephone below, dialing. It *rings* above. LAURIE MOSCOWITZ appears from the rear, crosses to answer at the third ring. LAURIE: "Yes?"

Arthur Ash, Mount Vernon, N.Y.

ACT I, SCENE 1: Nighttime. A large office high in a midtown skyscraper. A solitary lamp etches the features of the seated BILL BREWSTER, fifty-three, gray-haired, as he slowly opens a drawer and then places a .38 Special on the desk top. After a long pause he pushes a button on his Dictaphone and begins speaking with great effort: "I guess you'll all say a man my age should have known better, that it was . . . but . . . perhaps I'd better start at the beginning. . . ."

Norman C. Ansorge, Ocean Grove, N.J.

ACT I, SCENE 1: A crashpad in the Village at twilight. A sitarist is grooving for the freaks. Enter a JUNKIE. JUNKIE: "Free love on the roof, sounds crazy, no?"

Alan Kroker, Oak Park, Mich.

ACT I: A dilapidated hotel ballroom in Dayton, Ohio. Time: A week ago last Friday. The room is decorated in Salvation Army Chic. Across the ceiling is a banner reading "Welcome Roller Derby Queens, 15th Anniversary Reunion." At the rise, STELLA and DOROTHY, both forty and plump, enter from opposite ends. STELLA staggers slightly, and DOROTHY *says* in a *loud voice*: "I see you still haven't learned to lay off the sauce."

Joel F. Crystal, Brooklyn, N.Y.

ACT I: A gunshot signals rise of curtain. The scene: a dingy two-room flat in Bayonne. ROSIE, an aging carhop, lies in a grotesque clump on bedroom floor (SL), revolver in hand. Silence for a moment. Then, footsteps on stairs.

JIMMY, athletic, young, bursts into front room (SR), throwing suitcase on floor. JIMMY: Rosie! I'm back! Got to the bus stop and changed my mind. *Rosie! Rosie? (X to bedroom.)* Promise me you won't laugh . . .

John Kavelin, Winston-Salem, N.C.

ACT I, SCENE 1: A studio apartment in mid-Manhattan. Time: The present. As the curtain rises, a buzzer sounds. SAMMY, a good-looking if slightly bohemian boy of twenty-two, Xs to press the release. (A pause.) MRS. HEDLEY enters. A chic woman in her early forties. *SHE speaks*: "So, my dear, this is the cozy retreat where my husband has spent so many happy hours . . ."

Marshall Karp, N.Y.C.

☞ *Closing Line of a Bad Play*

(They embrace.)
HEDLEY (exits left as SAMANTHA walks to center stage clutching her cat): "I guess it'll be just you and me from now on, Mittens."
CURTAIN.

Above, the final line of an unalluring play. Competitors were invited to submit one atmospheric but brief concluding line from a play destined to close out of town.

Report: Years from now, when we talk of this and we will . . . we'll remark the following: the *Allegory* or Pinter-Beckett-Ionesco "I wonder what that was all about" play; the *British-detective* "Who couldpossibly-have *dunit*"; *Dramas of Social Significance; Modern Morality Plays* of the new ambisexual freedom; *Plays for Peace*, often musicals, some hirsute, and some anachronistic: Elizabethan or Greek Classics hideously modernized. A kind of geographical classification evolved for others: the *Northern* homespun New England drammar narrated by the stage manager; the *Southern:* colorful plantation life "Auntie Bellum"; the *Eastern:* banal

Gotham life, the marital spat minus the Cowardly line; the *Western:* Hollywood beckons the farmerette. The most common fault: "punch lines" rather than *atmospheric* lines. We relished your nicely overwritten stage directions and authors' notes as we did the right-on *texture* of dialogue. But irresistible was just-plain-wretched-playwriting. Our thanks. Farewell. Exeunt omnes.

(The music fades as THE YOUNG JOANNA slowly dances off the stage. Spotlight returns to JOANNA (*following* THE YOUNG JOANNA *with her eyes. She shakes her head as if to clear it and turns crisply to* THE REPORTER): "Very well, young man, where do you want me to begin?"

J. Bickart, N.Y.C.

(OM, NEW-MAN, and MARY STUART don simple rayon-polyester masks broadly representing TRUTH, INCEST, JANSENISM, and ARLENE FRANCIS. THEY descend into the pit reading excerpts from *Mein Kampf* and a tuna-fish sandwich while assaulting the piccolo player . . .) ALL: "Why?" OFF-STAGE VOICE: "Why not?" CURTAIN.

Diane Davis, Huntington, N.Y.

(FOTHERINGILL falls. JEEVES reaches forward and pulls out the bloodied kitchen knife.) As HE carefully and oh-so-correctly wipes the knife clean, HE says (to the prostrate man): "Will there be anything else, sir?" CURTAIN.

Alan J. Glueckman, N.Y.C.

(CHARLES, GLENN, HANK, TONY, and SYLVIA are arranged DSR in symbolically grim death poses. THE OLD MAN and THE BOY enter as HELEN gags.) OLD MAN: "Who did it?" (THE BOY peers into the audience—his eyes move slowly down each row.) FADE OUT ON LONG TEN COUNT.

Anne Commire, N.Y.C.

Closing Line of a Bad Play / 13

THE PRESIDENT (as the whine of the atomic missile approaches the Oval Room, with anger, regret, weariness, fear and a certain "to hell with it" quality): "The fools. The goddam fools!" (Brilliant flash of light and VERY FAST CURTAIN.)

Rees Behrendt, N.Y.C.

(MARK ANTONY takes the lizard from CLEOPATRA and walks downstage . . .) HE turns: "If I've told you once, I've told you a hundred times . . . if it would have been a snake, it would have bitten you." CURTAIN.

Robert L. Edler, Jennings, Mo.

(SHE lifts her hand as in benediction, GINEVRA exits R as HILLARY fumbles with his prayer beads) HILLARY: "There isn't any second prize, ever, is there? . . ." CURTAIN.

Virginia Feine, Hartford, Conn.

(BETTY hangs up the phone. SHE *laughs quietly* and walks downstage): "I wonder why you never get a busy signal when you dial the wrong number?" CURTAIN.

Wallace Graham, N.Y.C.

(SHE stands weeping in the corner. The phone *rings*. SHE runs and picks it up.) SHE *shouts:* "Harry? Oh, I'm sorry, you have the wrong number." CURTAIN.

Harvey Chipkin. Rutherford, N.J.

(Then clutching the empty vial to her breast, RACHEL hurls the French telephone across the room.) RACHEL: "Ring, damn you ring!" (As the curtain slowly falls, RACHEL falls to her knees and vainly tries to hook the receiver on its stand.)

Gina Collins, N.Y.C.

(DAGMAR staggers from the bathroom door. A glass falls from her hand. SHE slumps onto the bed. Her speech is slow and grows less and less strong.) DAGMAR: "One

word, just one word of love from you, George, and . . ."
(Her body goes limp. The phone begins *ringing*. It *rings* ten times and finally stops. CURTAIN.)

Donald Wigal, N.Y.C.

(Four CAPTAINS bear the body of the PRINCE to the platform. COURTIERS and SOLDIERS enter dancing from left and right. FORTINBRAS, kneeling, faces them Upstage.) FORTINBRAS: "Gimme an H-A-M, gimme an L-E-T, yeah-h-h HAMLET!" CURTAIN.

Jack Ryan, N.Y.C.

(INSPECTOR FLINT crosses to U.C. door and holds it open. CONSTANCE picks up purse and gloves, throws coat over her arm as she crosses to him.) CONSTANCE (*at the door, smiling*): "I almost got away with it, didn't I, Inspector?" (They exit. CURTAIN.)

Elaine Anderson, N.Y.C.

As the door closes, RUBY gets up from the dressing table, walks around the room, quickly, compulsively touching the opening-night flowers, picking up RODNEY's picture, then, abruptly, putting it down again; the first opening strains of the overture can be heard in the distance. RUBY (*laughing bitterly*): "Everything! Yes, it's what I always wanted—you're right, Rod. At last I've got everything! (*She walks over to the dressing table, stares into the mirror and laughs again*). "I'm the happiest girl in the world!" CURTAIN.

Barnaby Sherman, N.Y.C.

LADY RALSTON: "Forsooth, Madam. He was a traitor and you are the Queen. Think not on him." (ELIZABETH remains silent, seated on her throne. SLOW CURTAIN.) This is the closing moment of this season's last play—an historical drama entitled *Elizabeth in Excess*.

Richard Helfer, N.Y.C.

Closing Line of a Bad Play / 15

(A VOICE is *heard* over the loudspeaker, announcing that the next stop, Elm Street, will be the end of the line.)
LAURA (*laughing ironically*): "Yes. The end of the line."
CURTAIN.

Carey B. Gold, N.Y.C.

(The young and uninhibited cast leaps from the stage to enthusiastically hug and kiss members of the audience as JOY strums her guitar and implores): "Don't hide/your love inside./Sing and shout/ Let it out!"

Scott Burnham, N.Y.C.

(DR. FREUD slowly stands, glass up-raised, and faces his colleagues): "A toast, gentlemen—to the Unconscious!"
CURTAIN.

David Steinman, M.D., Scarsdale, N.Y.

(All the guests have left the party except for EVE, who is putting on her wrap to go. She hesitates for a moment—looks at KEN as if to say something—then exits quickly.) (KEN is all alone holding a drink in his hand. HE walks stage right to baby grand piano, sits down, places drink on piano, and begins to play haltingly with one finger as HE *talk-sings*.) KEN: "I didn't know what time it was . . . (*continues to tinkle tune on piano*) . . . I'm wise, and I know what time it is now." (KEN takes drink from piano) . . . CURTAIN.

Gerald Perlman, Tarrytown, N.Y.

TIM (*stanches the flow of blood from his mouth, props his rifle up against the wall, staggers over to the corpse which has fallen through the door*): "Well, at least they didn't all get through, Mother—at least we stopped a few of them—at least I'll die knowing that much, won't I, Mother? (*Rolls the corpse over with the toe of his boot and sees its face for the first time. Softly*) Oh, dear sweet God in Heaven." CURTAIN.

Dan Greenburg, N.Y.C.

(Spot up on LARSON's portrait. AGON turns and holds his glass high.) AGON: "Father, will you not be satisfied until the last one of us is in the grave?" (The *portrait* falls to the floor with a *crash*. AGON's face transforms . . . there is the thinnest trace of a smile.) SLOW CURTAIN.

Tupper Saussy, Nashville, Tenn.

(MISS GIZZI clutches letter to her breast and stands up from behind the circulation desk. She removes her glasses and runs out of the library *exclaiming*):"I feel as happy as a kitten with its first mouse." CURTAIN.

Charles Renick, Providence, R.I.

MAURICE (*softly*): Tu mihi curarum requies, tu nocte vel atra lumen et in solis tu mihi turba locis.
DARLEEN: All right. CURTAIN.

Charles Gabel, Marquette, Mich.

(DEREK and MOLLY, holding hands, exeunt right. LEPRECHAUNS enter from behind trees, forming semicircle.) LEPRECHAUNS (*in unison*): "That's our tale, our evening's done,/And so good night to every one."

Barbara Allen, Ridgewood, N.J.

(Alone now, CRAIG and MAURICE regard each other silently across the luxuriously appointed room.) Then CRAIG (*crossing suddenly to the* OLDER MAN *and grasping his hands*): "Oh, Maurice, you've been right all along. Gay *is* good. Forgive me. I've been *such* a goose. . . ."

Angelo Papa, Trenton, N.J.

(Sound of ambulance driving off.) JUDITH (Xing from US window): ". . . and Partridge, tell cook there will only be three for dinner."

Alexandra Isles, N.Y.C.

HYDE-SMYTHE: "Inspector, for over thirty years I've been a respected and trusted burgher of this small village and

Closing Line of a Bad Play / 17

I give you my word that I shan't do anything rash but I plead with you, please unlock these handcuffs as we leave. I don't want the servants, the villagers, and my grandchildren to see me like this . . . a common criminal." (INSPECTOR hesitates and then unlocks handcuffs. They leave.)

Arthur Zigouras, N.Y.C.

(MONICA turns wheelchair to left, pulls gun from her lap robe, points it up at JEFFREY). MONICA: "No, Jeffrey. You are not going away with Annabelle. It is you and I who are going on a journey" . . . (She *fires*, JEFFREY crumples slowly to floor. Lights dim. Final curtain falls as second *shot* rings out.)

Kaky Dafler, Yardley, Pa.

(In surprise, CLAIRE lifts a string of perfectly matched pearls from her lobster thermidor.) GREG: "Happy anniversary, darling." CURTAIN.

J. Norton Banks, N.Y.C.

(JEANETTE exits, between TWO STORM TROOPERS. Silence for a moment, then, from offstage) JEANETTE: "Vive la France!" (The *sound* of rifle fire. ARMAND slumps into a chair). CURTAIN.

Mary Margaret Linn, N.Y.C.

(The dying ROCCO slumps back against the railing, his arms spreading out along its top in a Christ-like attitude; while BLIND NEWSDEALER has risen to his feet, one hand extended questioningly in front of him, as BOY enters from right). BOY: "It's time to go home, Grandpa Joe."

Oliver M. Neshamkin, M.D., N.Y.C.

(. . . and as the flames leap higher around NERO): "Ic-say ansit-tray oria-glay undi-may!"

Ellen S. Ryp, N.Y.C.

(THEY embrace. MITTENS the cat exits left as SAMANTHA walks to CS clutching her husband): "I guess it'll be just you and me from now on, Hedley." CURTAIN.

Pat Campbell, Syracuse, N.Y.

☞ *What You Should Have Said / What You Said*

---

1. "Why you ill-mannered, overbearing fossilized knave—you can't fire me, I quit!"
2. "Yessir. Thank you. I understand. Um, I'm awfully sorry. Can I get you anything while I'm out? I mean, you're welcome. That is, good-by . . . er . . ."

Above, The Beautiful and The Bad, or, 1. what you should have said, and 2. what you actually said. Competitors were asked to supply (in given order) one such pair of responses to any awkward social situation.

Report: It's very hard to think up new competitions, much less novel ways to report results week after week. I mean, after you take your first 165 best shots. . . . Anyway, *voici les* repeats: **1.** Watch where you're going. **2.** Excuse me. **1.** I have another pair at home just like them. **2.** Oh gosh, really? One brown and one black sock? **1.** I refuse to give up my freedom, my career, perhaps my integrity merely to become . . . **2.** I do. **1.** My, you're looking well. **2.** When's the blessed event to be? Oh, you're not? **1.** Unhand me. **2.** Here's my cash. Do you take Diner's Club? **1.** Take the watch please. **2.** It just happens that I'm a black belt myself . . .

After intimidation by landlords, office managers, teachers, waiters, butchers, cabdrivers, salespersons, even fellow travelers, many submitted: **1.** Yes. **2.** No. Or **1.** No. **2.** Yes. One final example: **1.** Thank you and goodnight. **2.** It's very hard to think up new competitions, much less novel ways to report results week after week. I mean, after you take your first 165 best shots . . .

---

1. The patina is nicely lustrous and no mistaking the Georgian gadrooning. But one cannot ever be too certain about the Bateman hallmark, can one? May I see one a bit more common by, say, De Lamarie?
2. Oh my gawd, for a *spoon?*

Al Gorisek, Cleveland, Ohio

1. I don't care if we *did* get permission from the president himself. This is dirty.
2. Let's see . . . Ellford . . . Ellman . . . Ah, here it is.

Richard Fried, Brooklyn, N.Y.

1. It's my wife! Ah! Thank God you're here, darling. But first, let me introduce you to Her Highness, The Princess Gloriana. Your Highness, this is my devoted wife. Dear, Her Highness does not speak. A mute from birth, hereditary, you know. I was able to be of some, ah, service to Her Highness and Her Cause. Thugs, looked like dacoits to me, were manhandling her outside this place. Notice how shocked the poor girl is? I stopped to help out a bit. Filthy swine ran away but the Holy Relic is safe, is it not, Your Highness, and that being so, my wife and I must be off. Bow low, dear, bow low and back

away for twenty paces as Her Highness retires. Retires, I say. Back away slowly, dear, and say farewell. You know I can never speak of this night again as I am sworn to the Silence imposed by the Order of the Holy Relic. Farewell, Your Highness and God Bless the Cause you serve! Back away, dear, that's it, bow low, say farewell.
2. Oh God, it's my wife! Er, this is Gloria from the office, dear. She felt faint after the party so we stopped at this motel and . . . I wish I were dead.

Jack Ryan, N.Y.C.

1. Chronological age is so unimportant. A youthful attitude is what counts. And besides, since women outlive men . . .
2. Thirty-six.

Lydia Wilen, N.Y.C.

1. You've sure got a lousy way of expressing yourself.
2. I think we're both basically saying the same thing.

Mary Cunningham, N.Y.C.

1. Where am I from, my dear? From Greenland's icy mountains. From India's coral strand. Where Africa's sunny fountains roll down their golden sand.
2. Ocean Avenue.

Marissa Piesman, Brooklyn, N.Y.

1. It's a pleasure meeting you, Mrs. Williams.
2. It's a pleasure meeting you, Mr. Williams.

Larry Laiken, Bayside, N.Y.

1. Tell him we're not hiring.
2. You say the President is calling from San Clemente about a job? Gee, that's pretty flattering, but I'm not sure I've got the right kind of experience.

Norton Bramesco, N.Y.C.

1. Living together is a fifty-fifty proposition, and I think we would both be more deeply satisfied if we shared the

responsibilities as well as the joys of our relationship. So I've drawn up a rough plan whereby on the days when you don't do the cooking you'll take care of the vacuuming and dusting while . . .
2. Dear, would you mind taking out the garbage?

Carol Diggory, Brooklyn, N.Y.

1. No, thanks. I'm a Bible salesman, too.
2. No, I don't have a Bible. Well, yes, I believe in God. Yes, I do like to increase my knowledge, but . . . No, I'm not afraid of it. Well, how much is it? All right, let me get my wallet.

Jonathan Fairbanks, Boston, Mass.

1. Just because we are presently adrift in a tumultuous sea of sexual promiscuity, misinterpreted female liberty, and abandonment of traditional ethnoreligious mores and other conventional modes of behavior is no reason to assume that I will leap blindly and wantonly into bed with every wolfish swain who wishes to take advantage of my elevated consciousnes and new bodily awareness with an offer of impersonal sexual relations.
2. Yes.

Ms. Randall S. Blaun, N.Y.C.

1. Your Rodin? No sweat. Pick anything from my collection.
2. Oh god, I was just standing talking to Seth, when I backed up a step and over it went. What can I say, Glynis? Well, let's make sure we get every single piece . . .

Arnold Rosenfeld, Dayton, Ohio

1. I have a B.S. in mathematics, an M.B.A. in economics and I *thought* I was applying for the position of financial analyst.
2. Only forty words per minute, but I'm sure if I practice . . .

Ms. Lyell Rodieck, N.Y.C.

What You Should Have Said / 23

1. Listen, it's my right knee! My throat is okay. My teeth are fine. I just had a checkup. But my right knee hurts like crazy since I fell off my bike and you can see that it's swollen. I swear, if you make me gag on that throat stick again, I'll strangle you with your stethoscope.
2. *Ahhhh...*

Eileen Tranford, Dorchester, Mass.

1. If you ever touch me again, I'll kill you!
2. Thanks—I needed that.

Mrs. Helen E. Baldassare, East Northport, N.Y.

1. You were rotten. The show was rotten. I came backstage only to avoid being ill in the lobby.
2. Flawless!

Carleton Carpenter, N.Y.C.

1. Thank you.
2. This award must be shared with so many people. A marvelous sound engineer, you know who you are, Jerry. An inspired...

Charlotte Laiken, Bayside, N.Y.

1. I'd love some, but I'm on a diet.
2. I'd love some.

Lil Wilen, N.Y.C.

1. Where's the fire? In the Governor's barbecue pit, officer. Big political clambake, heh-heh. Mustn't be late.
2. The fire? Er, oh. Uh, was I exceeding the...

George Fairbanks, Nutley, N.J.

1. Your cab is a pigpen—you're a slobbering cretin—and you drive like a Mongolian idiot! All you get is what's on the meter!
2. Here's ninety-five cents for the fare—and here's a dollar for yourself. Have a good day.

Albert G. Miller, N.Y.C.

1. Did I laugh? Sorry. Just remembering what Volodya said after the thirty-eighth publisher rejected *Lolita*.

2. Well, Christ, I'm not all that happy with it, either, and I have been doing a little tinkering here and there, kind of a limited rewrite as a matter of fact, so if you want me to, I can . . . Oh, oh, okay, then. Sure. Yeah, I guess send it back . . . what the hell . . .

George Malko, N.Y.C.

1. I haven't the foggiest idea who the hell you are. I detest being buttonholed like this, I'm in a big hurry and in no mood for guessing games.

2. Of course, I remember you! We must get together sometime—how about lunch?

Charles Librizzi, Atlantic City, N.J.

1. How did I make out on the morals charge? Quite well, actually. The decision was in my favor. They said it definitely was rape. She'll probably get off with a suspended sentence though . . . being a famous movie star and all that.

2. How did I make out on that morals charge? Come on, Carl, stop asking embarrassing questions every time we get on a crowded elevator. These people don't know that you're just kidding.

Daniel Weishoff, Brooklyn, N.Y.

1. Look, buddy, don't walk those dogs on my lawn; this isn't a public lavatory.

2. That's an awfully nice pair of Dobermans.

Mrs. Joel F. Crystal, Brooklyn, N.Y.

1. Forgive you? You rotter! Charlie—your best friend. He trusted you to look after his wife while he was away—and you . . .

2. Of course I understand. After all—Charlie and I . . . Well, remember when I said my sister had sprained her ankle and I went to the Cape for three days . . .

Lillian O'Brien, Poughkeepsie, N.Y.

What You Should Have Said / 25

1. The stork brought you.
2. Well, you see, dear, it's like this. The mommy has an egg inside her body. This egg is called an ovum. The ovum has to be fertilized. That's the daddy's job. Now, the daddy . . . No, wait, first I'd better explain about the ovaries. The ovaries . . .

Fran Ross, N.Y.C.

1. That's right, Fred . . . I told Tom you're a jerk because you *are* a jerk. . . .
2. Gee . . . Fred . . . No. I mean . . . Not me. Gee . . . maybe Tom thought I said . . . when I really meant . . .

Charles Zanor, Omaha, Neb.

1. Nice to meet you, Mr. Nagurski. I admire your play for the Green Bay Packers.
2. Did you hear the one about the Pole who had a date with a three-hundred-pound girl . . . ?

Alan Kroker, Oak Park, Mich.

1. Yes, that's he! That's the man! I'd recognize that face anywhere!
2. Well, er—I'm not quite sure, officer. I don't think the man who mugged me was quite so large and mean-looking.

David Grotenstein, N.Y.C.

1. You two must be sleepwalking . . .
2. What a nice surprise! Come in, you're just in time for Sunday breakfast.

Mrs. Anna Lambiase, Brooklyn, N.Y.

1. It's obvious that Stevens did not follow up on my memo dated August 6th requiring him to proceed with the shipment to the Cleveland plant.
2. How'd that happen?

Kathleen Jonah, Fairfield, Conn.

1. One-hundred-per-cent better looking? Are you telling me I looked that awful before? Maybe you'd better change your own hair.
2. Thanks. I wasn't too sure I liked it.
Mrs. Nell Carpenter, Washington, D.C.

1. Tell me, Mr. Vice President, how do you think the Redskins will do this year?
2. I know I've seen your face somewhere.
J. Bickart, N.Y.C.

1. If I don't get at least Honorable Mention, I'll cancel my subscription and sue.
2. Enclosed is my entry for Competition Number 162.
Michael P. Bazell, Smithtown, N.Y.

☞ *Near-Misses*

"A Man, a Plan, a Canal—Suez!"
             "Ethel Merperson"
"Butterflies Are on the House"

Above, Near-Misses—a would-be palindrome, a name, and a play title. Competitors were invited to list no more than three titles, names, aphorisms or the like, of a similarly just-off-the-mark nature.

Report: Since this is the third or fourth time we've run a "Near-Miss" contest, many entries that are old-hat to us (1775, 6-Up, and The United States of Vespucci, for example) were innocently new-hat to some recent converts. Less familiar repeats: *Last Fox Trot in Paris* (or *Bayonne*); *Jonathan Livingston Albatross* (or *Segal*); The World Swap Center; " 'Twas brillig and the slimy toads . . ."; *Bridget Loves Bernice; El Dr. Pepper Grande; Around the World in 2½ Months; The Maltese Bird;* "The Bronx? No, thank you"; *A Streetwalker Named Desire;* "Liza—with an S"; "Let's Hear That Once More, Sam"; *Start the Beguine;* and "One baby step for man. . . ." Saddest near-miss of all: Peace with Honor. No comment.

*Everything You've Always Wanted to Know About - - - **
** But Were Afraid to Ask.*
Philip Milstein, Dumont, N.J.

"I'd rather be right than Secretary of Health, Education, and Welfare."
"We hold these truths to be rather obvious . . ."
"Who knows what evil lurks in the hearts of men—perhaps we could ask Lamont Cranston."
Dan Greenburg, N.Y.C.

"I feel rotten, Egypt, rotten."
"And therefore never send to know for whom the bell tolls. It tolls for some dead person."
"It's nine-thirty, there's no one in the place except you and me . . ."
Robert B. Brown, N.Y.C.

"Yeah, *The New Yorker*."
Chuck of the Ritz.
Happy, Sleepy, Sneezy, Grumpy, Dopey, Bashful, and Neil.
Marshall W. Karp, N.Y.C.

"We who are about to die tip our hats to you."
"Though I've beat and I have flayed you,
    by the living God that made you,
    You're more than my peer, Gunga Din."
Richard J. Hafey, Morningdale, Mass.

Murray of Arabia
Ira S. Loeb, Jacksonville, Fla.

Cowpersons and Native Americans
Michael K. Stone, Richton Park, Ill.

"I answer to Ishmael."
"This was the winter of our socio-political-emotional unrest."
Ruth Dittman, Basking Ridge, N.J.

Zerox
>   John Jacobson, New Haven, Conn.

The Ups and Downs of the Third Reich
"Friends, Italians, Countrymen . . ."
>   Harry Elish, N.Y.C.

Lady Windermere's Air Conditioner
>   Shelia Katz, Brooklyn, N.Y.

"I got measured movement with uniform recurrence of a beat or accent, I got music, I got my man. Who could ask for anything more?"
"Yesterday, December 7th . . . or 8th . . ."
>   Douglas Bernstein, N.Y.C.

Les Brown and His Famous Musicians
>   Lawrence E. Grant, Whitefish Bay, Wis.

Tomorrow is the next day of the rest of your life.
>   Amy Kassiola, Brooklyn, N.Y.

Rebecca of Sunnybrook Agricultural Collective Number Seven
>   Jack Ryan, N.Y.C.

The Hunchback of Temple Beth-El
>   Anne Commire, N.Y.C.

Ravel's *Serape*
>   Barbara A. Huff, N.Y.C.

"I'm Gonna Shampoo That Man Right Out of My Hair"
>   Anita Greenberg, Jamaica, N.Y.

"I love Paris in the springtime / I love Paris in the fall / I love Paris in the summer, when it's hot / I love Paris in the winter, when it's not."
>   David Axlerod, N.Y.C.

"Lafayette, we are here, except for Harold."
"It turned out so right / For strangers in the night—
La la la la la . . ."
Elliott Shevin, Oak Park, Mich.

Barbara Streisand
"Onward Christian Soldiers / Marching as to cease-fire violations."
Ilene McGrath, Englewood, N.J.

Look at Your House, Angel
Tim Lewis, Fair Lawn, N.J.

"Yo ho ho and a bottle of Asti Spumante!"
Mark Dubowsky, Glen Oaks, N.Y.

Prometheus in Paperback
Joanna H. Spiro, Princeton, N.J.

Frank S. Fitzgerald
Josh Kates, Woodside, N.Y.

Jehovah's Bystanders
Bennet C. Kessler, Bayside, N.Y.

"Tomorrow, and the next day, and the day after that . . ."
Kathy Retan, Brooklyn, N.Y.

Exon
Mrs. John Winkler, Brooklyn, N.Y.

"There's No Business Like Being in a Stage Show"
Lois Winsen, Oak Park, Mich.

World War, Jr.
Harvey Chipkin, Rutherford, N.J.

Saran—Nature's spelled backwards.
Jesse Mittleman, Syosset, N.Y.

You're Correct If You Think So
Miriam Gurko, N.Y.C.

Aristotle, Looking at a Statue of Homer's Head
Morris Johnson, Bronx, N.Y.

Six Rooms River View
Allan Lehmann, Somerville, Mass.
Sal Rosa, N.Y.C.

Betty Davis
Daryl Warner, N.Y.C.

Mrs. Skeffington
Steve Wolfson, Forest Hills, N.Y.

George, Prince of Denmark
Whose Bell Is That Ringing?
The Story of Ulysses's Trip
Donald Inglett, N.Y.C.

The Person Delivering the Ice Has Arrived
Ellie Roche, Los Angeles, Calif.

"There was a senior citizen who lived in a shoe."
Mrs. John M. McNamara, N.Y.C.

"But I have promises to keep / And miles to go before I hit the hay."
Elaine Stallworth, Willow Grove, Pa.

Let the Spy Come In and Warm Up
Trudy Weinberger, Morristown, N.J.

Three Cents in the Fountain
George Fairbanks, Nutley, N.J.

"Peter Piper picked a bushel of pickled peppers."
George C. Grant, Milwaukee, Wis.

". . . and on the seventh day God crashed."
Larry Bielford, Croton-on-Hudson, N.Y.

"Allergy in a Country Churchyard"
John Norton, Columbia, S.C.

St. Urbain's Milkman

> Joel McCormick, Montreal, Canada

"Nothing is certain but death and the fund-raising activities of the Department of Internal Revenue."

> Fred Berg, Boston, Mass.

A June Twenty-First Dream

> Barbara Nolan, N.Y.C.

"In our opinion, Virginia, there is a Santa Claus."

> Robert W. Smith, Ithaca, N.Y.

Well, Maybe, Nanette

> Mrs. Robert Polunsky, San Angelo, Texas

There was a young lady of Twickenham / Whose boots were too tight to walk quickenham. / She bore them a while / But at last, at a stile, / She pulled them both off and threw up.

> Bernard Lovett, Hillside, N.J.

Banaczyk

> Jon Rich, N.Y.C.

"Listen, the Herald Angels Sing"

> Gary R. Ahlskog, N.Y.C.

"I love you more than yesterday and less than Wednesday."

> Alfred Shoenberg, N.Y.C.

Ozymandias-the-Pooh

> Bill Detty, Houston, Texas
> also: Rosie Falkenbloom, McLean, Va.

The Topless Horseman

> Norton Bramesco, N.Y.C.

"O what can ail thee, Knight-at-arms / Alone and palely hanging around? / The sedge has withered from the lake / And no birds make a sound."

> Miriam Weiss, N.Y.C.

"Once more unto the breach, everybody."
William Schallert, Pacific Palisades, Calif.

John the Episcopalian
Mel Taub, N.Y.C.

"The Beer That Made Milwaukee Well Known"
Lydia Wilen, N.Y.C.

"Friends, Romans, Countrymen, listen to me . . ."
"O brand new world, that has such people in't!"
Jack Easton, N.Y.C.

Blithe Spook
Rama Demac, N.Y.C.

Six Characters in Search of Another
Liselotte Laumann, Jackson Heights, N.Y.

The Big Scary Dog of the Baskervilles
Oliver M. Neshamkin, M.D., N.Y.C.

"I think I know whose woods these are . . ."
J. I. Durr, Philadelphia, Pa.

Donald Quixote of La Mancha
Howard Schain, North Bellmore, N.Y.

"Able was I until I saw Elba"
Helen Fechheimer, Glen Head, N.Y.

There once was a man from Nantasket / Who kept all his money in a basket / His daughter named Nan / Ran away with a man / And as for the basket—Nantasket.
" 'Tis better to have loved and lost than never to have loved *et al.*"

Joseph S. Brownman, Alexandria, Va.

"Give me liberty or kill me."
"Look! Up in the sky! It's a bird! It's a plane! Or else some third possibility as yet unnamed!" *
"Speak softly, but carry a cudgel or an ax handle or something."

Dan Greenburg, N.Y.C.
* also: *Peter Richards, N.Y.C.*

"A tramp walked up to me the other day and said, 'I haven't had a bite in two weeks.' So I kicked him."

T. E. D. Klein, N.Y.C.

"I have been faithful to thee, Cynara—sort of."
"I think, therefore I think I am."
"Brevity is the soul of a funny story, or a clever saying or anything of that kind."

William Schallert, Pacific Palisades, Calif.

"The pen is pointier than the sword."

Donald Elman, N.Y.C.

"Mother died today. Or was it father?"

Stephen Gelb, Brooklyn, N.Y.

"Friends, Romans, Countrymen, Ladies and Gentlemen . . ."
"The Charge of the Light Brigade to Experience"

Arnold Mendales, Bayside, N.Y.

"WHEATIES—The Breakfast of Honorable Mentions."

James M. Rose, White Plains, N.Y.

"My house shall be called the house of prayer; but ye have made it a den of alleged perpetrators of the robbery."—Matt. XXI, 13
Curtains in Venice

Joyce Terner, N.Y.C.

"There's No Business Like the Performing Arts Business"
"Wind, Sand, and Celebrities"

D. D. Ryan, N.Y.C.

"It's a lot better than the things I've done before, and I'm going to a really groovy place." —SYDNEY CARTON
The Man Who Became a Bug—KAFKA
David S. Litwon, Newark, N.J.

"Look for the Silver Interfacing"
Elaine Kendall, Princeton, N.J.

"In a divine, universal omnipotent being we trust."
M. Fordmant, Washington, D.C.

Nicholas II, Tsar of Some of the Russians
War and Negotiated Settlement
Gene Keesee, N.Y.C.

Nanny and the Teaching Assistant
Jack Riley, Los Angeles, Calif.

Lawrence Welk and His Cold Duck Musicmakers
Robert Blake, N.Y.C.

"I Saw Daddy Kissing Santa Claus"
Linda Neukrug, Brooklyn, N.Y.

How Much Does Glory Cost?
Judy Sprengelmeyer, Indianapolis, Ind.

"Tora! tora! tora! That's an Irish lullaby."
Michele Gerrig, N.Y.C.

"Fifty-four / Forty or Send Technical Advisers!"
John Kallir, Scarsdale, N.Y.

"A horse, a horse, what I wouldn't give for a horse!"
Andrew B. Schultz, N.Y.C.

Cary Gooper
Dennis Marks, N.Y.C.

"The rain on the Iberian Peninsula falls primarily on the prairie . . ."
Neil S. Atkinson, N.Y.C.

"I'd prefer being correct to being elected to the highest office in this land."

Joan M. A'Hearn, Saratoga Springs, N.Y.

"What, you haven't seen *Man of La Mancha* even wince?"

Wilfred S. Rowe, South Norwalk, Conn.

"You can't tell a horse by its color."

Sara E. Ward, N.Y.C.

"Ask not who that bell is ringing for . . ."

George Malko, N.Y.C.

"Come on out with your hands up or I'll make trouble for you!"

Oscar Weigle, Whitestone, N.Y.

"Jack Sprat would eat no cholesterol. . . ."

Rita Hailey, Hastings-on-Hudson, N.Y.

" 'Who touches a hair of yon gray head / Dies like a dog. Right on!' he said."

Nita Camp, Bronx, N.Y.

Dennis Hopper's Last Movie

Andrew Mezzetti, Flushing Meadow, N.Y.

Six Characters in Search of an Agent.

Tom Louis, Brooklyn Heights, N.Y.

"I dropped in. I saw. I conquered."

Bob and Susan Pilberg, Brooklyn Heights, N.Y.

"Let Go of My People!"

Alan Penn, Madison, Wis.

The Last of the Upper Hudson Valley Branch of the Algonquin Indian Confederacy

J. Evans, Bethesda, Md.

Guess Who's Staying for Breakfast!
A. Diane Raymes, Huntington, N.Y.

"Take thy beak from out my heart / and take thy form from off my door / Quoth the Raven, 'What's a door?' "
Peter M. Shane, Cambridge, Mass.

The Last Motion-Picture Entertainment
Larry Alson, N.Y.C.

"Monkey See, Monkey Ape"
Jack Rose, N.Y.C.

"When the moon hits your eye like a big pizza pie, that's annoying."
Mr. and Mrs. I. Perlman, Forest Hills, N.Y.

Bon Vivant Potato and Leek Soup
Mary Lynn Shapiro, N.Y.C.

"Whether thou goest, I will go!"
Rita Oakes, Drexel Hill, Pa.

"Baa, baa black sheep, have you any Dacron / polyester?"
Harvey Chipkin, Rutherford, N.J.

"An American in Paris, France"
Reeva Kacalanos, Woodside, N.Y.

Lieutenant Commander Kangaroo
John and Esel Rasor, Pittsford, N.Y.

Ivan the Disappointing
Oliver M. Neshamkin, M.D., N.Y.C.

"Never give a sucker an opportunity to compete on an equitable basis."
Dr. Sidney Groffman, Red Bank, N.J.

The Phantom of the New York State Theatre
Barry W. Cornet, N.Y.C.

"... that nature might stand up and say to all the world, 'this was a truly wonderful person.'"

Anne Kaufman, N.Y.C.

"What's the best chicken? Tuna of the Coop!"

Mrs. Edward W. Powell, Jr., N.Y.C.

"Better Read than Dad"

John Cunha, Islip, N.Y.

☞ TV Guide *Listings*

2 (Return) "Doris Day Show." This season, Doris is an Airline Pilot. Tonight's episode concerns a ticking package and other hi-jinx. co-pilot: Wm. Schallert.

4 (Debut) "Tenafly." New Jersey super cop investigates corruption in Bergen County. Mayor: Wm. Schallert.

11 (Rerun) "I Love Lucy." Ricky hires a redheaded bongo player who looks oddly familiar. Fred and Ethel can't find little Ricky. Cameo appearances by Claire Bloom, Wm. Schallert.

Above, "TV Guide" listings for the fall. Competitors were invited to invent typical summaries for two existing or imminent programs.

Report: A thicket of plots, many of them graced by the thud of plausibility. Most popular choices: Joe Gannon (Medical Center) SRO in the OR; Mary Richards (Mary Tyler Moore) with the inevitable old flame; and similarly, Richard M. Nixon making a guest appearance with Julia Child, cooking, of course, his own goose. Jim Phelps and the gang investigating Watergate (*Mission Impossible*); John-Boy Walton, Maude, and Carol Burnett do their respective things, while Lassie and her superhuman feats do their stuff. An unsparing look at the hilarity of P.O.W. life in *Hogan's Heroes* is almost matched by the fun *The Evening News* has reporting bombing attacks. For more of the lighter side, just send $5.95 for all three records or $8.95 for 8-track tapes. Take it from your Campari chief (whatever *that* means)—at the Pathmark Food Facts Hot Line, we're here to help you.

MANNIX. A grieving widow doesn't believe her husband's death was suicide. Mannix doesn't either and sets a trap for the murderer, with himself as bait.

CANNON. A grieving widow doesn't believe her husband's death was suicide. Cannon doesn't either and sets a trap for the murderer, with himself as bait.

Teresa Gerbers, Glenmont, N.Y.

THE JOE FRANKLIN SHOW. Interviews with business luminaries. Joe talks with Smiley Sumner, former key grip on *Gilligan's Island,* and Aldo Broncante, protégé of Louis Prima.

Charlie Laiken, N.Y.C.

AN AMERICAN FAMILY. In this episode, Pat lies on the sofa, calls Bill a "stupid ass," and watches Delilah comb her hair; Bill has a drink and talks over the phone to his accountant; Lance dyes his hair burnt sienna.

Edward Staub, N.Y.C.
John Hoffmann, Garden City, N.Y.

AMERICAN SPORTSMAN. Actor John Wayne hunts the endangered whitetail deer, ferret, and golden condor with nothing but a .50 caliber machine gun.

Carl Stewart, N.Y.C.

DAVID SUSSKIND SHOW. Susskind interviews six authors who have stopped using the spoken word for personal reasons.

Kirk Simon, Amherst, Mass.

TIMMY AND LASSIE. (Return) Timmy returns home and sells Lassie.

Richard Kaplin, Forest Hills, N.Y.

MY LITTLE MARGIE. (Repeat) If Margie doesn't impress their biggest client, Honeywell & Todd is set to fire Vera. So she dresses Freddy in women's clothes and invites everybody over for dinner. Which she burns. Clients: Ricardo Montalban, Fernando Lamas, Joseph Wiseman.

Staff of Bachelor *Magazine, N.Y.C.*

COLUMBO. A pro football superstar kills his wife in San Francisco while he is winning the game in Los Angeles. The police are baffled by the perfect crime—or is it? Columbo stops by the locker room after the game for an autograph.

Van Morrow, Jamaica, N.Y.

MOVIE—*Sclybishzmy* (1928). Polish silent classic about the battleship *Sclybishzmy* in peacetime.

Tina Fragale, Arlington, Va.

NBC REPORTS. Special: "The Impeachment Story So Far." For details see close-up opposite page. (*Untouchables* will not be seen tonight.)

Bradford Willett, Stevens Point, Wis.

THE FLYING NUN. En route to New York, Sister Bertrille gets caught in a holding pattern over Kennedy Airport and is late for Mass. Flight Controller: Paul Lynde. Father Vincente: Ricardo Montalban.

Don Gibbs, Omaha, Neb.

IRONSIDES. Chief Ironsides relentlessly pursues a criminal to an old five-story building, only to find the elevator out of order.

Jack Parr, Westland, Mich.

MISSION IMPOSSIBLE. M.I. forces stage the end of the world in a broom closet via electromagnetic gimmickry, hypnotic vapors, and disguises. The entire free world is saved from the clutches of a combine headed by a Central American dictator.

Marilyn Cooper, Rye, N.Y.

TUESDAY MOVIE OF THE WEEK. Tolstoy's *War and Peace* in two segments. Tonight Part I: "War." (90 min.)

Peter Meltzer, N.Y.C.

THE ANDY GRIFFITH SHOW. Aunt Bee is determined that this year she'll win the ribbon for the best pie at the county fair. Opie decides to help her.

Ken Trombly, Silver Spring, Md.

THE AMAZING KRESKIN. (Return) The first show of the new season deals with how amazing it is that Kreskin has returned.

Joan Wilen, N.Y.C.

COLUMBO. . . . Columbo uses an ashtray.

Jonathan Suna, Freeport, N.Y.

THE NEW PERRY MASON. Perry is attacked by a mysterious sniper in a wheelchair.

Elizabeth V. Powell, Orlando, Fla.

BOLIX. (Debut) A physically intact, but mentally unstable, private eye discovers the power to cloud men's minds by blundering.

STAR TREK. The Enterprise becomes embedded in styrofoam.

Joseph Dubey, M.D., Great Neck, N.Y.

CAPTAIN KANGAROO. The Captain learns a card trick from Mr. Greenjeans. Also: a demonstration of muscle power; how the President is elected; the value of a good friend. (60 min.)

Jonathan Fairbanks, Boston, Mass.

ADAM 12. Officers Reed and Malloy rescue a cat from a tree and then prevent a nuclear holocaust.
Denis Mullaney, Whitestone, N.Y.

BRIDGET LOVES BERNIE. The Steinbergs give a dinner party for two of their classmates—Rabbi O'Reilly, a former Catholic, and Sister Sydell, a nun who converted from Judaism. When an argument ensues, peace is restored by a small Chinese girl who lives next door.
Norton Bramesco, N.Y.C.

EL SHOW DE ESTA NOCHE. Jack Paar con Dodie Goodman, Hugh Downs, y José Melis. Invitados especiales: Alexander King, Geneviève. (B & W)
David Axlerod, N.Y.C.

JEOPARDY. In this special anniversary show, Art Fleming and three undefeated champions make the shocking discovery that Don Pardo is a robot.
Bob Leighton, Roslyn Heights, N.Y.

THE DICK CAVETT SHOW. Dick discusses Marlon Brando with Jimmy Breslin, Chita Rivera, and Harry Reasoner.
MASTERPIECE THEATRE. "The Diary of Samuel Pepys." Chapter 768. April 28, 1663, is dramatized. Pepys goes to his office and stays there all morning. (R)
Carol Guilford, N.Y.C.

ROADRUNNER SHOW. Hapless coyote, in repeatedly frustrated attempts to capture and eat bird, is mangled, crushed, poisoned, drowned, suffocated, blinded, incinerated, dismembered, disemboweled.
Sylvie Charier, Paris, France

OWEN MARSHALL. (Return) With Owen busy seeking a zoning variance, Jess must singlehandedly conduct a title search.
ABC MONDAY NIGHT FOOTBALL. Howard Cosell, Don Meredith, Frank Gifford, and, oh yes, a football game.
Don Beschle, N.Y.C.

(2) CBS SPORTS. Football doubleheader. New England Patriots vs. Kansas City Chiefs at Kansas City followed by Miami Dolphins at Green Bay. Then Pro-Am Golf Tournament from Palm Springs; A.A.U. swim meet from Coral Gables; U.S.A.-U.S.S.R. weight-lifting match from Leningrad; Melrose Games, Track and Field from The Garden; N.Y. Knicks vs. Bullets from Baltimore; Little League Baseball finals from Sioux Falls, South Dakota; National Arm Wrestling Championship from Gila, Arizona; China-Tibet Wrestling from Ulan Bator (satellite); Word Series Highlights (tape) and pre-season N.H.L. Hockey, Rangers at Chicago (until conclusion). (4, 5, 9, 11, 13) WATERGATE.

Jack Ryan, N.Y.C.

ALL IN THE FAMILY. Scarcity of beef causes Archie to call Mike a fish-head.

Alan Levine, Amityville, N.Y.

TWILIGHT ZONE. Ventriloquist Lance Madison defies the warnings of The Diamond Karma, a secret society, only to find himself gradually shrinking while his dummy, Kokomo, keeps growing.

Bill McDonald, Concord, Me.

FRENCH CHEF. Julia Child prepares fresh electric eel. (Last of the series.)

Jonathan Abrams, Brooklyn, N.Y.

ALL IN THE FAMILY. Archie is upset when he discovers that Gloria is bisexual. Mike defends her. Edith doesn't understand.

Eileen Tranford, Dorchester, Mass.

THE BRADY BUNCH. Peter tells all his friends he knows Roman Gabriel personally. The former L.A. Rams star appears briefly as himself.

Bruce Karp, Flushing, N.Y.

AN ARMENIAN FAMILY. (Debut) Aram and Zabelle Sarsakian and their four children, Harout, Vasken, Arax, and Mary, prepare for the annual bazaar at the local church.

Alex Sahagian-Edwards, M.D., N.Y.C.

FATHER KNOWS BEST. Cathy, thinking she is adopted, runs away from home. Betty is rejected by the college of her choice. Jim asks a client home for dinner without telling Margaret.

Suzanne Siegel, N.Y.C.

COLUMBO. Two old friends who've made good pose a problem for Columbo: which of his boyhood chums murdered Tippi Longstreth (Blythe Danner), Main-Line-heiress-turned-actress—the brilliant director with the cynical smile (John Cassavetes) or the hard-eyed lawyer-in-a-hurry (Ben Gazzara)?

Fran Ross, N.Y.C.

MASTERPIECE THEATRE. "Edward R." Five-part saga of the five-month reign of Edward V. Tonight, Part I, "The First Month." Host: Alistair Cooke.

THE TWILIGHT ZONE. Homer's neighbors think him a harmless eccentric. However, when he invents a time machine which brings people from the past to Elm Street, they change their minds.

Joel F. Crystal, Brooklyn, N.Y.

MEET MONMOUTH COUNTY. The Mayor of Red Bank discusses housing problems with host Don Resler.

NASSAU COUNTY TODAY. The Mayor of Oceanside discusses housing problems with host Ron Desler.

Bunny Daniels, Hewlett, N.Y.

THIS IS YOUR LIFE. Ralph surprises Martin Bormann in Buenos Aires . . .

Dick Elkind, Forest Hills, N.Y.

☞ *Silly Definitions "C"*

CATASTROPHE—Award presented to Most Unusual Couple at Animals' Masqued Ball, 1974.

Above, another extract from our fractured dictionary. Competitors were asked to invent a suitably silly redefinition for an existing word beginning with the letter "C."

Report: A big batch. And a fearful symmetry among entries defining words with these prefixes: car, can, con, cab, cop, cap, cu(e), and crypt. The *methods* for redefinition were, basically, twofold: 1. Onomatopoeia, and 2. Syllable-by-syllable translation. Most successful was the felicitous combination of these approaches. Herewith the repeat section: CICATRIX: tired of Watergate; COPULATION: the gendarme explosion; CIRCUMSPECTION: physical for Israeli Army; CARNATION: Detroit as an independent city-state; CIRCUMFERENCE: meeting of Round Table knights; CHARLATAN: French sun oil; CHAMPAGNE: fake ache; COFFEE: Camille; CHINCHILLA: triple-decker ice-cream cone; CONDOMINIUM: ineffectual birth control or short sentence by magistrate; COPULATE: admonition to tardy policeman; CRITERIA: snackshop for losers; CANDID: vacuum-packed ego; CONNOTATION: prison graffito; CEREBRATION: Japanese festival; CATARACTS: luxury cars;

Silly Definitions "C" / 47

CANTALOUPE: must marry formally; CRIBBAGE: Infancy; COUNTENANCE: landlord's census; CACCIATORE: popular U.S. pastime 1776–83; CASTRATE: critique of or twofers for performers; COVENANT: unwanted guest at witches' picnic; CAMELOT: Middle Eastern division of Kinney Parking; CANTILEVER: request for divorce. Best left to the imagination, definitions for: CACOPHONY, CLAPTRAP, and CHESTNUT. Also excluded: certain, um, inappropriate choices. I just don't find CARCINOMA a funny word, however redefined. In all, a comely cumulate conglomeration of C notes.

CHLORINE: unfeatured swimmer in a water-show spectacular.

E. C. Harrison, N.Y.C.

CLICK BEETLE: Linda Eastman McCartney.

Paul Morse, Brooklyn, N.Y.

CROCODILE: publicity release from the Irish National Telephone Company.

Fred Berg, Boston, Mass.

CARRION: a series of madcap British films.

James M. Green, M.D., Livingston, N.J.

CHEETAH: Bette Davis's pet cat.

David Allen, Ithaca, N.Y.

CRASS: the sound of breaking plastic.

Roy G. Saltman, Bethesda, Md.

CUSPIDOR: one of the horsemen at the start of a bullfight who enrages the bull by vigorously snapping a set of hand-held dentures.

George Fairbanks, Nutley, N.J.

CRÊCHE: the scene of a Jewish accident.

Henry Morgan, Truro, Mass.

CALCULUS: **1.** method of computation first discovered embedded in plaque of teeth of Copernicus, now 33-per-cent obsolescent due to Crest and regular professional check-ups: **2.** the capital of Poland.

Maurice Katz, N.Y.C.

CACKLE: sound emitted when milk is poured onto a bowl of Chicken Krispies.

Emily Karp, N.Y.C.

CENTENARIAN: 10 Deutsche marks; the so-called "Nazi dime."

Jack Ryan, N.Y.C.

CONJUNCTIVITIS: disease brought on by reading too much Harold Robbins.

J. Bickart, N.Y.C.

CAROTID: An abandoned vehicle on a major artery.
*J. Winterkorn, J. Gelfman
Anatomy Dept., Cornell University Medical College, N.Y.C.*

CURFEW: a mongrel on the endangered species list.

Lydia Wilen, N.Y.C.

CURDLE: canine star of the popular TV series, able to leap tall buildings in a single bound.

Ruth Brewster, Hillside, N.J.

COWL: experimental breed of Ungula-Avis: low milk production; grazes at night.

Daniel C. Rosenthal, N.Y.C.

CHANNEL: new perfume created by Louis of Detroit.
Robert C. Brown, Sedalia, Mo.

CLONE: perfume mixed in a test tube.
Iris Bass, Brooklyn, N.Y.

COTILLION: a million billion trillion zillion.
Ruth Ellen Proudfoot, N.Y.C.

Silly Definitions "C" / 49

CHIROPODIST: **1.** any of the disciples of Fred of Chiropod, who was nyah-nyahed to death in 1478 for his heretical views on penmanship; **2.** a Freddist.

Dan Greenburg, N.Y.C.

CYCLONE: the act of referring one's analyst.

Mobil Room 361, N.Y.C.

CASTIGATE: a stone's throw from Washington, D.C.

Linda Segal, Endwell, N.Y.

CORACLE: a wise or inspired utterance by a crow, rook, or raven.

Bettina Glaeske, N.Y.C.

CLEMENCY: sub-rosa purchase of Presidential real estate.

Linda J. Kern, Midland, Mich.

CHECKMATE: one married only for his or her money.

R. M. Lustgarten, N.Y.C.

CRIMSON: *coll.*, calling family to table for borscht and sour cream. See SOUPÇON.

Henna Arond Zacks, Brooklyn, N.Y.

CITRONELLA: a young girl whose fairy godmother turned her into a small French car.

Marshall W. Karp, N.Y.C.

CAMOUFLAGE: to engage in sadomasochistic behavior with a dromedary.

Stephen Sadowsky, Poughkeepsie, N.Y.

CUCKOOPINT: a small, crazy person.

Phyllis Kelly, Locust Valley, N.Y.

CATENOID: a form of mental disorder characterized by delusions of being a feline.

Jack Neal, N.Y.C.

CYBERNETICS: a set of moral standards for trimming hair around the ears.

Jack Paul, Brooklyn, N.Y.

CYCLIST: Who's Who at Bellevue.

Edith Watson, Berkeley Heights, N.J.

CLAQUE: a timepiece that goes "tick-taque."

Mrs. Joel F. Crystal, Brooklyn, N.Y.

CURSORY: a handbook of imprecations and oaths.

Phyllis Taub, Brooklyn, N.Y.

COBALT: a dual citizen of Latvia and Lithuania.

Fran Ross, N.Y.C.

CLOISTER: a celibate mollusk.

Carol Drew, Palisades Park, N.J.

CANCAN: a toucan.

Evelyn Nethercott, N.Y.C.

CHIROPRACTIC: gung-ho fraternity man.

Gwen Pettit, N.Y.C.

CROCODILE: what the bride walks down wearing a crooked smile.

Linda Quirini, Providence, R.I.

CERVIX: Roman dinner for nine.

Claire Martinson, N.Y.C.

CROSSTALK: #!+*#/?&#!

Stanley Stone, Oceanside, N.Y.

COWBOY: the bad guy in an American Indian movie.

Felicia Young, Tipp City, Ohio

Silly Definitions "C" / 51

CORUSCATING: the big finale of the Ice Capades.
Gloria Rosenthal, Valley Stream, N.Y.
Mort Mergentheim, New Rochelle, N.Y.

CHANSON: Oriental detective's assistant specializing in waiting in the car.
Irwin Vogel, Brooklyn, N.Y.

CREPE DE CHINE: egg foo yong.
Sal Rosa, N.Y.C.

CYCLOPEDIST: **1.** one-eyed foot doctor; **2.** a one-footed giant.
Jay McDonnell, N.Y.C.

CACHINNATION: a country ruled by the military (no laughing matter).
Sidney Shore, N.Y.C.

COD: supreme deity of aquatic mammals.
Irv Teibel, N.Y.C.

CONTRARIWISE: advertising slang for balky client.
Walter Murphy, Madison, N.J.

COWARDLY: *Brit.*, not quite bovine.
Sandra Steinberg, Teaneck, N.J.

CONTEST: polygraph.
Mrs. B. J. Krintzman, Worcester, Mass.

CREMATORY: a cow.
W. H. Richardson, Peace Dale, R.I.

CANARD: a subspecies of the yellow-bellied Washington warbler.
A. Meremagi, Mount Vernon, N.Y.

CLASSICAL: an ice-cream pop large enough for thirty children.
Hank Weintraub, Stamford, Conn.

CHICANERY: Rum producer on the shore of Lake Michigan.

      Kate Johnson, Rumson, N.J.

CAMPHOR: Bette Midler's mink coat.

      Zale Koff, New Rochelle, N.Y.

CHIMNEY: scene of Claustrophobic nightmares.

      Larry Laiken, Bayside, N.Y.

CHEEK: well gobbed.

      John Hofer, Southboro, Mass.

CARBUNCLE: **1.** a nearly-identical nephew; **2.** brother of your mother's carburetor.

      1. *Carol Milano, N.Y.C.*
      2. *Bunny Daniels, Hewlett, N.Y.*

CHAUFFEURS: group-discount theater tickets.

      Florence Decker, Woodhaven, N.Y.

CASHMERE: pocket money.

      Jackie Pollock, Williamsville, N.Y.

CRITERION: a long prehistoric period of widespread lachrymal activity now cited as true proximate cause of Noah's flood.

      N. T. Altshuler, Newport News, Va.

CANTILEVER: singing soap commercial.

      Gilbert Melnick, M.D., West Orange, N.J.

CLAVICHORD: warring tribe which overran Eastern Europe in fourth century under the leadership of the ill-tempered and dreaded Fugue.

      Harold Brewster, Hillside, N.J.

CHAMPION: person who is eaten at breakfast.

      John L. Vogelstein, N.Y.C.

COMPETITION: democratic method of selecting French aristocracy.

Janet A. McDowell, N.Y.C.

COMPETITOR: a clever fellow who can't afford a one-year subscription to *New York* Magazine.

Gary Forman, N.Y.C.

☞ *Odd Couples*

Cashmere Bou and Danny Kaye
Hello and Salvador Dali
Parallelo and Katharine Graham

Above, odd couples. Competitors were asked for up to three similarly improbable pairs.

Report: A competition for Improbable Pairs was first set some years ago—so some excellent entries (Hotsie and Giorgio Tozzi, for example) were innocently repeated. Others of merit making a comeback: Ella & Allen Funt; A Jury of One's & Jan Peerce; Gorgon & Emile Zola; Paul & Yogi Berra; Oompah & Jack Paar; Camel & Mel Ott; Sorcerer's & Paula Prentiss; Run of & Agnes De Mille; Chili Con & Art Carney; Import & Howdy Doody; Moonlight & Frank Sinatra; Little White & Chou En-lai; Honi Soit Qui Mal Y & Lily Pons; Where's & Manuel de Falla; Tops & José Iturbi; Knee & Mercedes Benz; Foot & Clare Luce; Anna & Billy Graham; Turkey & Nevil Shute; Queen & Michael Faraday; Tippy & Albert Camus; Brica & Georges Braque; Fool's & Elliott Gould; Madison Square & Rumer Godden; Subway & J. R. R. Tolkien; Chip & Thelonius Monk; Socket & Regis Toomey; Galloping & Eydie Gorme; Kim & Yoko Ono; Simple & John Simon; Gay D. & Tom Seaver; Grin & Rona Barrett; Rolla & Gen. George Custer; Para & John Keats; Cotton

& Mahatma Gandhi; Gesund & Horace Heidt; Midas & Marcus Welby; Sang & Sigmund Freud; Dementia Prae & Tricia Cox; Moo Goo Gai & Peter Pan; Hold The & Virginia Mayo; Shubert & Muhammad Ali; Berry & Sid Caesar; Spa & J. P. Getty. New for this competition, but abundant nonetheless: Jonathan & George Segal; Laser & Abe Beame; Neosyn & Nora Ephron; Gunga & John Dean; Theater & John Marchi; Balder, Slap, or Bangla & Sam Dash; Chicken Allah & Billie Jean King, and Tood & Felipe Alou. A spiffy and fructiferous crop for the fecund time around.

Nobody Loves A and Clifton Fadiman
Roman and Kay Kendall
Zip-a-dee and Carol Doda
Erna and Bernard Lovett, Hillside, N.J.

Dennis and José Jiménez
John Michael Stein, Fort Wayne, Ind.

A, B, C and Ruby Dee
1, 2, 3, 4, 5, 6, 7, 8 and France Nuyen
Do, re, me, fa, sol, la and Marshal Tito
Jack Paul, Brooklyn, N.Y.

One for the money, two for the show, three to get ready, and Elena Verdugo
Miles Klein, East Brunswick, N.J.

It's Tough to Get and Miguel de Cervantes
Hi Hans and Jascha Heifetz
Wag and Jean Anouilh
Joan and Lydia Wilen, N.Y.C.

Did You Ever and Haile Selassie
P. A. Vanterpool, Saskatoon, Sask., Canada

Monday Morning and Gil Blas
Sesame and Eva Marie St.
Kawa and H. H. Munro

John Hofer, Southboro, Mass.

The Afternoon of A and Robert Vaughn
Vas You and Virginia Dare
Gone But Not For and Rumer Godden

Harold and Ruth Brewster, Hillside, N.J.

Whistler and Tommy Smothers
Jockey and F.A.O. Schwarz

Mrs. B. J. Krintzman, Worcester, Mass.

Yukon and Kateri Tekakwitha

Rev. Vincent P. Gorman, Bronx, N.Y.

Japanese Skin and Henry Clay Frick
Mazel and Sonny Tufts

Eileen Kopec, New City, N.Y.

Northtua and Harold J. Laski
Po and Minerva Pious
Gay and John Barth

Max Dixon, Westminster, Md.

O Sole and Darius Milhaud*
Finicu and Trygve Lie
Finicu and Bert Lahr

Frank Jacobs, N.Y.C.
* Joshua Daniels, Hewlett, N.Y.

Syllo and Shirley Chisholm
Glockens and Norman Vincent Peale

Martin E. Healy, Sag Harbor, N.Y.

Doin' What Comes and Maurice Nadjari

Michael G. Gartner, N.Y.C.

Odd Couples / 57

Pussin and Earl Butz
Dawn Shirley and Enoch Light
Daniel Robins, Syosset, N.Y.

Jacques Ze Giant and Ruby Keeler
Arthur Weller, Interlaken, N.Y.

Maples and Wyatt Earp
Bobbi Harwyn, Cedar Grove, N.J.

Nota and Jack Benny
I'll Cry To and Wellington Mara
Mrs. Frances F. Doyle, Schenectady, N.Y.

Baked Al and Mary Lasker
Ira M. Lechner, Arlington, Va.

Canadian and Ken Monte
Donald H. Comras, N.Y.C.

Chrysanthe and Somerset Maugham
Eve Gelofsky, Verona, N.J.

Selfs and Sam Ervin
Paul I. Jacobs, Princeton, N.J.

The Andromeda and Gordy Strachan
Phyllis Grossman, University City, Mo.

The French Con and Richard Nixon
Overtime and I. M. Pei
Premarital and Morris Sachs
Donald Baerman, New Haven, Conn.

Marcello Mastroi and Tugboat Annie
Reflections in a Gold and Louis Nye
Robert Heller, Brooklyn, N.Y.

Heidi and Bruce Ho
Navy and Cat Ballou
Helen Russo, Poughkeepsie, N.Y.

Atlantic and Frank Gorshin
> Nick C. Malekos, N.Y.C.

Haydn and Alexei Kosygin *
Human and Brendan Behan
Copaca and Junior Bonner
> Ruth Ellen Proudfoot, N.Y.C.
> * Jim Milton, San Francisco, Calif.

Dolores Mai and Jean Shepherd
> L. J. Smith, San Francisco, Calif.

Hugh Gotterhaf and Moss Hart
Polly Esther and Joseph Cotten
> Barrios, Schuyler & Uniti, N.Y.C.

Standing and Daniel Inouye
> Nella and Alan Silverman, Rockville, Md.

Pepper and Mickey Rooney
> Karen Schnabel, Massapequa, N.Y.

Elephant and Herman Wouk
> Myles Lavelle, Stony Point, N.Y.

Wella and Martin Balsam
> Frank McAteer, Maplewood, N.J.

A. Nonnie and Mickey Mouse
> Gino Dente, N.Y.C.

Yellow Subma and Jim Ryun
> Carol O. Bander, Bronx, N.Y.

Afro and Fulton J. Sheen
> Larry Laiken, Bayside, N.Y.

How to Succeed in Business without Really and Tom Tryon
> M. Borowka, Mineola, N.Y.

Odd Couples / 59

Ken Tuck and José Iturbi
Guido Scarato, N.Y.C.

Yugosla and Pancho Villa
Christine Mulak, Providence, R.I.

Upand and Abou Ben Adem
Kanga and Madelyn Rhue
Estelle Sell, St. Paul, Minn.

I and Fifi D'Orsay
Keith Blake, Gloversville, N.Y.

Hothouse and Jack Palance
Jonathan Abrams, Brooklyn, N.Y.

Deepth and Kyle Rote
Jim Milton, San Francisco, Calif.

How Dry and Omar Khayyam
Thomas Cadogan, Glen Burnie, Md.

Two Cases of Corn Flakes With One and John Cassavetes
Sam Bassin, Brooklyn, N.Y.

Call Me and Perle Mesta
Carol Jacobs, Princeton, N.J.

Genghis Khan and Immanuel Kant
Melvin Bender, N.Y.C.

Viva and Mervyn LeRoy
Larry Kiss, N.Y.C.

Perspa and Hopalong Cassidy
William Cole, N.Y.C.

Hey, Ma, the Chicken's and Sam Peckinpah
David F. Dean, Grand Rapids, Mich.

Mrs. and Fra Lippo Lippi
Latissimus and Tommy Dorsey

        Jack Ryan, N.Y.C.

Spinal and Albert Anastasia
Antidisestablishmentaria and Barbara Nessim

        Norton Bramesco, N.Y.C.

Chopin and Mischa Auer

        Irwin Vogel, N.Y.C.

Ecclesi and Billy Sol Estes

      Claudia B. Goldberg, Little Neck, N.Y.

Sauce Bay and Desi Arnaz
Ring Around The and Maria Callas
Come Heller and Hiawatha

      Elaine Stallworth, Willow Grove, Pa.

Chef Boy and Andy Hardy
Slop and Willie Hoppe

       Maria Conti, Pawtucket, R.I.

Lola and Birch Bayh

        Mel Taub, N.Y.C.

Bengal and Mario Lanza

       Alan Levine, Amityville, N.Y.

One Fell and Herbert Bayard Swope

      Joel F. Crystal, Brooklyn, N.Y.

1. Dot and Anwar Sadat
2. Who The and Anwar el-Sadat

       1. *Maurice Varon, Bronx, N.Y.*
       2. *Doris Fields, Old Brookville, N.Y.*

Jimmy The and Edvard Grieg
Hebrew University and Thomas A. Kempis
Mental and Hilaire Belloc

      Eileen Tranford, Dorchester, Mass.

Born and Lautrec, Toulouse
Lakenan Barnes, Mexico, Mo.

Vita and Claude Monet
Mary Lynn Gottfried, N.Y.C.

Roto and Walter Reuther
Patricia Friedmahrr, New Orleans, La.

Nope and Alan Arkin
Colleen Newman, N.Y.C.

Tippe Ca and U Nu
Glorios and Nguyen Cao Ky
Alan Kroker, Oak Park, Mich.

Stoplook and Sonny Liston
L. J. Horwitz, Bronx, N.Y.

They're Fattening But and Sholem Aleichem
Shawai Talia, Washington, D.C.

Pen and Nell Gwynne
Pericles Crystal, Brooklyn, N.Y.

Csonkas — Screaming Yellow and Larry
Ronald Robins, Atlanta, Ga.

Billy Jean King Plays Tennis Better than and H. L. Mencken
Michael Deskey, N.Y.C.

Da and Msgr. McLees
Peter J. Katz, Hastings-on-Hudson, N.Y.

President and Richard Nixon
J. Bickart, N.Y.C.

☞ *Uncaptivating Captions*

---

1. PRESIDENT TO DELAY TURNING OVER TAPES
2. SLIGHT TREMOR ATOP MOUNT EVEREST—FEW INJURED

Above, uncaptivating captions. Competitors were invited to invent two predictable, uninformative or uninspiring headlines for a newspaper item of past, present or future.

Report: In a litter of DOG BITES MAN news items, the following reprints appeared: HENRY VIII (or ZSA ZSA) TO WED; BURTONS SPLIT; MAYOR PLEDGES TIMES SQUARE CLEAN-UP; UNION SEEKS WAGE HIKE; FOOD PRICES UP; LINDSAY-ROCKY FEUDING; RAINFALL AVERAGE FOR '73, STATES REPORT; PHASE 24 ANNOUNCED; EASING OF MARIJUANA LAWS URGED; EXPRESSWAY TIE-UP—TRAFFIC DELAYED; L.I.R.R. BEHIND SCHEDULE; SUN TO RISE AT 5:40 A.M.; END OF WORLD PREDICTED; PRESIDENT TO WEEKEND AT CAMP DAVID; CANDIDATES OPPOSE FARE RAISE; AARON HITS NO. 734; CON ED ANNOUNCES RATE HIKE; POWER CUT; STASSEN TO RUN; BISHOP TO SUB FOR CARSON; JERSEY POL INDICTED; SINATRA TO RETIRE; BERT PARKS WILL HOST PAGEANT; NETWORKS ANNOUNCE FALL

PROGRAMS; JULIE DEFENDS FATHER; BEAME WINS; METS DROP TWO; POPE URGES PEACE. And, sadly, PEACE TALKS CONTINUE. Also, a late bulletin: "COMPETITION EDITOR IMPROVING, WORKING IN CLAY," REPORTS SUNNY HAVEN CHIEF. Hoping you the same.

EVERETT DEDICATES GETTYSBURG CEMETERY: BRIEF REMARKS BY PRESIDENT

"THIS TIME I'VE FOUND TRUE LOVE"—LIZA
Michael K. Stone, Richton Park, Ill.

WILSON TO REPRESENT NIXON
Mrs. Clara H. Leville, Albany, N.Y.

MOVIE STAR REVEALS FUTURE ENGAGEMENTS ON MERV GRIFFIN SHOW

CHAIRMAN OF BOARD ADMITS HE LEFT ELEMENTARY SCHOOL TO BECOME NEWSBOY
Zena Trett, N.Y.C.

JEHOVAH'S WITNESSES AT STADIUM
HOUK TO STICK WITH LYLE
Jay Hoster, Columbus, Ohio

DALE CARNEGIE ON WHITE HOUSE ENEMIES LIST
Alan Levine, Amityville, N.Y.

NETWORK CANCELS THE NEW DON RICKLES SHOW
NETWORK CANCELS THE NEW TIM CONWAY SHOW
Lydia Wilen, N.Y.C.

600 FRIENDLY CAMBODIANS ACCIDENTALLY KILLED IN U.S. BOMBING

MANKIND ITS OWN WORST ENEMY STATES U.N. PRESIDENT
Louise Mowder, Bedminster, N.J.

P.O.W.'S DOG REMEMBERS MASTER AFTER 5 YEARS
Bill Detty, Austin, Texas

MANY OPENINGS FOR WHITE HOUSE JOBS

TRANSIT TALKS BREAK DOWN
> Sidney Abrams, Brooklyn, N.Y.

NANCY SEAVER ATTENDS METS GAME
> Pericles Crystal, Brooklyn, N.Y.

PORT AUTHORITY PLANS 4TH METROPOLITAN AREA JETPORT
> Dorothea H. Scher, N.Y.C.

POLICE FIND NO MOTIVE FOR SLAYING
> Joseph A. Kaselow, Glen Rock, N.J.

GREEK ELECTION RETURNS NOT YET IN
> Stanley S. Passo, Bronx, N.Y.

G.O.P. INCUMBENT FAVORED IN IOWA GUBERNATORIAL CONTEST
> Sumner Rosen, N.Y.C.

DIPLOMATS IN LONDON FOR CORONATION

BILLY GRAHAM PRAISES NIXON
> James Fechheimer, Glen Head, N.Y.

FIRES IN ROME FAIL TO HALT VIOLIN CONCERT

QUEEN HELPS SOLVE FRENCH BREAD CRISIS
> Judith R. Goldsmith, Woodmere, N.Y.

LT. MARK PHILLIPS TO MARRY
> James Chotas, N.Y.C.

GENERAL LEE SEES "LIGHT AT END OF TUNNEL"
> Joel Morris, Teaneck, N.J.

D.A. TERMS CAPONE "GANGSTER"
> Albert G. Miller, N.Y.C.

Uncaptivating Captions / 65

LOCH NESS MONSTER SIGHTED

LANDSLIDE VICTORY FOR MARCOS
Kenneth and Casey O'Brien, Fair Haven, N.J.

CLAIMS EVEN THO' HE TOOK MONEY, HE DID NOTHING WRONG
Al Schreiber, Springfield, N.J.

MISSING PERSON APPEARS FOUND IN AFRICA
Frances V. Killpatrick, Scarsdale, N.Y.

$2,000,000 WEEKLY PAYROLL CHECK ISSUED TO SUPERMARKET CLERK AS RESULT OF FIRST COMPUTER ERROR SINCE 1993. PAY SHOULD HAVE BEEN $1,500,000
Jack Paul, Brooklyn, N.Y.

PLATYPUS IN BRONX ZOO REFUSES TO MATE
Vera Leeds, N.Y.C.

CRONKITE TO COVER APOLLO LAUNCH
Dr. R. J. Reiss, N.Y.C.

OAKLAND A'S TO MOVE TO CAMDEN

900,000 YOUTHS FLOCK TO ROCK CONCERT
Maris Conti, Pawtucket, R.I.

DUBUQUE MAN SETS WORLD RECORD IN ROCKING-CHAIR MARATHON
Susan Kingdon Fields, Rumson, N.J.

CALVIN COOLIDGE DEAD
Kathleen Cotter, Providence, R.I.

MAILER DISCUSSES SEX IN INTERVIEW
Robert Verini, Albany, N.Y.

KING CLAUDIUS WEDS DOWAGER QUEEN

EX-PRIEST SUSPECT IN WITTENBERG CHURCH-DOOR VANDALISM
Dita Greene, Sayville, N.Y.

HIGH COURT TO HEAR REDISTRICTING CASE
         Emanuel Frankel, N.Y.C.

PIG BORN AT BRONX ZOO

WIDOW LEAVES ESTATE TO CAT

DEAD RECLUSE HAD ¼ MILLION
         Tom Morrow, N.Y.C.

STUDY URGES WELFARE REFORM

STUDY URGES ELECTION REFORM
         Barry Morris, Teaneck, N.J.

MILLIONS LOSE SLEEP AS CLOCKS ARE RESET

NOTTINGHAM SHERIFF TO SEARCH FOREST FOR MISSING LOCKSLEY HEIR
         Martin H. Israel, Brooklyn Heights, N.Y.

MILITARY COUP IN BOLIVIA
         Linda Quirini, Providence, R.I.

C.I.A. DENIES INVOLVEMENT IN MILITARY COUP IN BOLIVIA
         Elsie Angell, Greenville, R.I.

LINDSAY EXTENDS CITY'S APOLOGY TO BELGIAN DIPLOMAT FOR CENTRAL PARK ASSAULT

MID-DAY CHECK OF GARMENT CENTER FINDS ILLEGAL PARKING RAMPANT
         Irving Steinberg, Lakewood, N.J.

WOMAN GIVES BIRTH TO QUADS: USED FERTILITY DRUG
         Thomas Cadogan, Baltimore, Md.

LIZ: I LOVE HIM
         Ms. Gene Winslow, Florham Park, N.J.

KING TOLD DARK AGES WILL CONTINUE
         Joel F. Crystal, Brooklyn, N.Y.

"NO SUBSTANTIVE ADDENDUM" HIGH LEVEL "CREEP"
MEMBER REVEALS
> *Rosemarie Williamson, Basking Ridge, N.J.*

ALL KING'S HORSES AND MEN HAVE HEARTY BREAKFAST
> *Peter Griska, N.Y.C.*

G.M. ANNOUNCES '74 PRICE INCREASE
> *L. J. Horwitz, Bronx, N.Y.*

3-PART DIVISION OF GAUL ANNOUNCED BY CAESAR
> *George Reiss, Houston, Texas*

MOVIE STAR BREAKS PHOTOG'S CAMERA

COUNTDOWN ON ASTROS STARTS AT 7 A.M.
> *Patricia Maybruck, N.Y.C.*

BUTZ PREDICTS CHERVIL SURPLUS
> *John Hofer, Southboro, Mass.*

MARTHA TALKS
> *Joel Weber, Elmhurst, N.Y.*

FIRE CHIEF SAYS PENN C. NEGLIGENT
WOOLWORTH HEIRESS TO WED
> *Philip Hathaway, N.Y.C.*

WORK ON ST. JOHN THE DIVINE COMPLETED: SERVICE HELD
> *Bessie A. Gladding, Gasport, N.Y.*

POLAROID UNVEILS NEW CAMERA
> *Sue Wolf, Hollywood, Fla.*

BONAPARTE FAULTS AIDES FOR WATERLOO
> *J. M. Riordan, Laguna Beach, Calif.*

COMPETITOR SUES I.B.M.
> *Dan Cunningham, Salt Lake City, Utah*

☞ *Nonsense Poems*

"No Pig Should Go Sky Diving During Monsoon"

Above, the first line of a nonsense poem. Competitors were invited to supply three appropriate lines to conclude the quatrain.

Report: Since these results speak eloquently for themselves, we've only one or two specific observations. Occasional scanning problems aside, "immune," "simoom," "ruin," even "tune," do not, strictly speaking, rhyme with "monsoon." And with a rasher of entries (heh, heh) we had to be strict. In all, a nice lot of nonsense, refreshingly free of predictable allusions to the police, and much of it clever and sense-making. Now you know the wurst.

No pig should go sky diving during monsoon
For this isn't really the norm.
But should a fat swine try to soar like a loon,
So what? Any pork in a storm.
Herb Sargent, N.Y.C.

No pig should go sky diving during monsoon;
It makes for a huge crashing boar
And scatters raw pork chops as far as Rangoon
And bacon o'er San Salvador.
David Grotenstein, N.Y.C.

No pig should go sky diving during monsoon,
It's risky enough when the weather is fine.
But to have a pig soar when the monsoon doth roar
Casts even more perils before swine.
Charlotte Curtis, N.Y.C.

No pig should go sky diving during monsoon
Without donning a puncture-proof rig.
A rain-shrouded steeple unlit by the moon
Could transact quite a poke in a pig.
Wilson A. Shelton, N.Y.C.

" 'No pig should go sky diving during monsoon'
"Is a line I'll forget," declared Barrymore Ribb.
"Worry not," replied Barbie the script girl, too soon
For on opening night little Barbie cued Ribb.
Mrs. Janet Herron, Cincinnati, Ohio

No pig should go sky diving during monsoon
He sows a strange seed in his folly:
Some chap in his garden discovers, next June
He's reaping a hock, but no holly.
Mrs. Elinor C. Beason, Capitol Heights, Md.

No pig should go sky diving during monsoon
Said Timothy Leary one evening at noon.
(I'd have won with this poem, but it ended too soon.)
Diane Davis, Huntington, N.Y.

No pig should go sky diving during monsoon
Unless he has practiced, or lives in Kowloon
And he knows how to samba; or, if none of these
He must have permission from Dom De Luise.
Mrs. Edward W. Powell, Jr., N.Y.C.

No pig should go sky diving during monsoon
Though his debts may be far in arrears
For whether he lands on the earth or the moon
His hocks are still over his ears.
T. A. Kenney, Camillus, N.Y.

No pig should go sky diving during monsoon
If he's lacking enough savoir-faire
To croon, while he bounces 'twixt earth and the moon
"They call me The Mass in the Delicate Air."
                                    Rita Halley, N.Y.C.

No pig should go sky diving during monsoon
To start a quatrain with? Don't be such a loon!
Might as well ask me to close with the phrase:
"The bloated cadaver of poor Mrs. Hays"!
                                    Jack Rose, N.Y.C.

No pig should go sky diving during monsoon
To get her poor doggie a bone;
Next day the New Orleans *Times-Picayune*
My little green shack in Athlone.
                                    Albert G. Miller, N.Y.C.

No pig should go sky diving during monsoon
No pig should go sky diving during monsoon
No pig should go sky diving during monsoon . . .
Besides, he got his parachute stuck in his bicycle chain
  on the way to the airport.
                                    Robert Harrington, Boston, Mass.

No pig should go sky diving during monsoon
For his chute will collapse like a rubber balloon
And down on the ground, midst the rain and the smog,
The natives will live it up high on the hog.
                                    Alice M. Yohalem, N.Y.C.

No pig should go sky diving during monsoon
Leave us hear no last porcine hurrah
'Twould encourage that kid with his adenoidal croon
To wit: "More Park Sausages, Ma!"
                                    David G. McAneny, Rumson, N.J.

No pig should go sky diving during monsoon
No dives should go pig skying during sun moon

No sky should go monsooning during pig dives
And ice cream and cold cream are awful with chives.
Michael Sage, N.Y.C.

No pig should go sky diving during monsoon
But don't let the bad weather faze ya
Take Laos by June, then we'll land in Rangoon
As we Vietnamize all over Asia.
Robert Emmett, N.Y.C.

No pig should go sky diving during monsoon
Oy! what a rhyme to contend with
It's crasser, it's gauche-er, it's not even kosher
And I really don't know what to end with.
Miles and Judith Klein, East Brunswick, N.J.

No pig should go sky diving during monsoon
Terra firma should be their demand
For the firmer the terror, the firmer the boon
To live off the fat of the land.
Mrs. Arthur Armour, Seagate, N.Y.

No pig should go sky diving during monsoon
The season is much to be dreaded
But warn as I will, they go jump to it still
What can we expect? They're pig-headed!
Peter Haas, N.Y.C.

No pig should go sky diving during monsoon
With a Trotskyite glued to his knee
Unless he has read half of *Darkness at Noon*
And three-quarters of Merleau-Ponty.
F. J. Abbate, Moorestown, N.J.

No pig should go sky diving during monsoon
Especially over New York
It's frightening how lighting plus swine could balloon
The high price of barbecued pork.
Sally Latham, Chattanooga, Tenn.

No pig should go sky diving during monsoon
Unless he should chance to enjoy it
As I enjoy humming *Au Clair de la Lune*
Whenever I drive through Detroit.

Joseph E. Clonick, N.Y.C.

No pig should go sky diving during monsoon
Save maybe in Westchester County at noon.
For then if the poor thing should suddenly die
We'd have a nice sandwich. To wit: Ham on Rye.

Ann Lipman, N.Y.C.

No pig should go sky diving during monsoon
When in Rangoon on the first day of June
Before the new moon of a cold afternoon.
Otherwise, it's okay.

Roy Franklin, N.Y.C.

No pig should go sky diving during monsoon
We were grateful for this sage advice.
But would have preferred its arrival (last June)
In the cookie and not the fried rice.

Anne K. Siviglia, Yonkers, N.Y.

No pig should go sky diving during monsoon
All cats should avoid foreign missions;
The dog should stay clear of the man in the moon . . .
And I should resist competitions.

Arthur J. Cunningham, N.Y.C.

No pig should go sky diving during monsoon
Could he know to what fate he'd be blown.
Desert? Lush jungle? Maybe golf on the moon?
Or a Fun City "No Porking" zone!

Keith Blake, Gloversville, N.Y.

No pig should go sky diving during monsoon
Without credit cards, passport and visa.

He may find that he's landing in downtown Rangoon
Though his Sty Diving School's back in Pisa.
Rosalie Lewis, Woodside, N.Y.

No pig should go sky diving during monsoon
Nor in weather that's fine, nor at time of full moon
For if God wanted pigs to be doing such things
He'd have given them raincoats, umbrellas—and wings.
Christopher Curtis, N.Y.C.

No pig should go sky diving during monsoon
Like Porky, who's subject to jokes.
If he met his demise in monsoon or typhoon
The obit would read: "Th-th-th-that's all folks!"
Joan Wilen, N.Y.C.

No pig should go sky diving during monsoon
A dog should not roller skate with a baboon
An elephant's place is not in a cocoon:
that's the end of this poem—not a minute too soon.
Olga and Joseph Wettenstein, Bronx, N.Y.

No pig should go sky diving during monsoon
Or surf-boarding in a sirocco.
A pig's tender hide, if not weathered too soon
Makes fine imitation morocco.
Ethel Strainchamps, N.Y.C.

No pig should go sky diving during monsoon
The Mandalay Jumping Club proved it one day.
Braving lightning and winds they took off for Rangoon
And landed, feet first, in a Charles Lamb essay.
S. E. Coon, N.Y.C.

No pig should go sky diving during monsoon
For rain makes a chute rip asunder.
A porky who tries it will learn all too soon;
A wet little pig knuckles under.
Elizabeth Reiss, Brooklyn, N.Y.

No pig should go sky diving during monsoon
No rabbit go skin diving during typhoon.
I know of a pig and a rabbit who did once
And all I can say is good-by and good riddunce.
David Scoggins, N.Y.C.

No pig should go sky diving during monsoon
Because from the rain, he might turn a pork prune;
He should stay on the ground—and take a long breather.
(No sky should go pig diving, at that time, either.)
Bill Becker, Urbana, Ill.

No pig should go sky diving during monsoon
Spake the quarterback (sneak) at the U. of Rangoon
"A wrinkled condition results from downpours
And passing that pigskin produces low scores."
Joan and Jack Seltzer, Forest Hills, N.Y.

No pig should go sky diving during monsoon
This is the name of my favorite toon;
I think it's unique, and you'll like it too
The new record of it is done by "The Who."
Iris Weiss, Rego Park, N.Y.

No pig should go sky diving during monsoon
But I know of one who dove into a spoon;
He now rests inside—and please pardon the phrase—
The bloated cadaver of poor Mrs. Hays.
Frank Jacobs, N.Y.C.

No pig should go sky diving during monsoon
Nor pole vaulting munching a stale macaroon
He should cut out martinis, Scotch, bourbon, and rye
And clean his apartment—it looks like a sty.
Marian Soloway, West Orange, N.J.

No pig should go sky diving during monsoon
Unless there are cows jumping over the moon

At least as consumers are waiting to drown
While beef's going up, they'll see pork going down.
    Math Coffee Room, University of N.C., Chapel Hill

No pig should go sky diving during monsoon
The old roller derby queen told me in June
Just then the Bay Bombers ran over her head
"What does it mean?" I begged, but she was dead.
    John Hill, Kansas City, Mo.

No pig should go sky diving during monsoon
Says his ne'er-do-well brother Fong-Sen
For No-Pig inherited papa's estate
And poor old Fong yens for the yen.
    Myla Bookbinder, Peekskill, N.Y.

No pig should go sky diving during monsoon
No storm, then should blow on a cross-eyed baboon
In consequence, apes reject Smyrnean figs
And nuts who write quatrains on sky-diving pigs.
    Eileen Tranford, Dorchester, Mass.

☞ *Authentic Typos*

---

26 Quit School Jobs in Drive on Oklahoma City Deviates

OKLAHOMA CITY (UPI) July 11. Curtis Harris, attorney for Oklahoma County, said today that 26 teachers . . . had resigned as the result of a six-month investigation of alleged homosexual activity. . . . "If evidence substantiates the charges, the person is asked to design," he said.

Above, the genuine article—an authentic if excerpted clipping from "The New York Times." Competitors were invited to submit one example of fortuitous typographics from any "bona fide" journal.

Report: Yes, folks, these are the jokes. And they're all *bona fide*. Guaranteed. So much for authenticity. Now, as for what's actually printable—or reprintable—that is a hearse of another color. Sometimes black, sometimes blue. A smuttering of rest-room humor (the wit that turns public to pubic, for example) and a smattering of just plain bathetic taste: excerpts from news items on the war, murder cases—obits, even. Whereas the variety, even the antiquity of submissions was remarkable, equally remarkable were the similarities: some verbatim, most inevitable duplications from recent news items. Among these repeats: the ad for "Dr. Atkins's now-fiction best seller"; the "prostitutes incarcerated for several lays" (both from the hapless *New York Times*); from a *Hartford Courant* advice column: "Do not pour cold water into hot pants . . . ," and the ill-starred item re the Tricia Nixon wedding-cake decorations. (Ask a friend.) A few typos cropped up from *New York* magazine. Ridiculous. Relieve me, it can't happen her. ETAOIN SHRDLU.

THE NEW YORK POST
(Headline) ALLEN'S GOAL: END ILLITERCY IN U.S.

Edith B. Panzer, Yonkers, N.Y.

THE SARASOTA (FLA.) HERALD-TRIBUNE
She has more than 200 wild parakeets in her yard, which eat about 100 pounds of bird feed a week, and a dog and a cat.

Sharon K. Cover, Sarasota, Fla.

THE OSHKOSH (WIS.) DAILY NORTHWESTERN
Mrs. Richard Nixon will wear a slim, pastel blue princess dress . . . it is made of blue georgette over blue crepe for a two-ton effect. . . .

Mr. and Mrs. Alex Doering, Oshkosh, Wis.

THE PHOENIX (ARIZ.) GAZETTE
The grup is made up of . . . Al Bentley on electric bass and vocals and Ed Allen on drugs and Mike David on piano . . .

Michael Schwartz, Scottsdale, Ariz.

THE NEW YORK POST
Even in such a bad TV show, one has to pick out a bright spot. That would be Susan George, playing the trumpet whom Hyde drove out of her mind.

Hannah Brown, N.Y.C.

THE NEW YORK TIMES
Charming, spacious homelike 1-rm apts. Modern, kitchenette. Hotel service. Weekly rats available.

Terry Davis, N.Y.C.

THE GREENWICH (CONN.) TIMES
Kittens would like loving home. One month old. Also do typing at home. Call etc.

Mary Ann Sanders, Bridgeport, Conn.

THE SYRACUSE (N.Y.) POST-STANDARD
(Headline) EYE PROBLEMS OF MINORIETIES.

Mrs. G. K. Moe, Barneveld, N.Y.

THE NEW YORK TIMES
New evidence that some cases of manic-depressive illness can be a team of scientists from the Columbia-Presbyterian Medical Center here.

Linda Levy, Lawrenceville, N.J.

THE NEW LONDON (CONN.) DAY. POSTING NOTICE
On and after this date, I the undersized, will not be responsible ...

Jane Cable, Old Lyme, Conn.

THE DAILY NEWS (N.Y.)
The drug gained the reputation among users as a sexual stimulant, but is usually prescribed in small dosages for Assistant District Attorney cases of amnesia or depression.

Alfred Thuemmler, Whitestone, N.Y.

THE WRITERS GUILD OF AMERICA, EAST, NEWSLETTER
Our Annual Writers Guild Awards your garment in the East River which your Guild will make available for that purpose on the night of March 16th.

Albert G. Miller, N.Y.C.

THE JERSEY JOURNAL
Eleanor Steber opens her American music concert . . . with "With Pleasures Have I Passed My Days," by Francis Hopkinson, a singer of the Declaration of Independence . . .

Muriel Greenberg, Jersey City, N.J.

THE DELAWARE COUNTY (PA.) DAILY TIMES
. . . James H. Baxter, 65, a *Daily Times* employee in the typographical department, was talking about his retirement Saturday. Typographical department, was talking about his retirement Saturday.

Joseph Biscontini, Media, Pa.

THE PHOENIX (ARIZ.) GAZETTE
Dear Heloise: When I bake a cake and use a boxed cake mix I always make good use of the box. I save the box until I've mixed the cake and put it in the oven. Then I clean up all the mess, egg shells, etc. and put it in the box and toss it in the garage.

—Mrs. T.R.
Debora H. Schwartz, Scottsdale, Ariz.

THE STATEN ISLAND (N.Y.) ADVANCE
Garage Sale. . . . Baby and other things. Saturday March 10.

Sam L. Haynes, Staten Island, N.Y.

THE ALLENTOWN (PA.) CALL-CHRONICLE
"Night of the Living Dead" . . . A gruesome horror thriller, amateurish, low-budgeted and nasty. A group of people find refuse in a farmhouse: the dead return to life and perpetrate all manner of evil.

J. F. McNichol, Montoursville, Pa.

THE EASTCHESTER (N.Y.) RECORD
". . . D'Agostino can feel all the voters some of the time. He can feel Celestino and his cohorts all of the time. But

he cannot feel all the voters all of the time. Very truly yours, etc. . . ."

Linda Waill, Eastchester, N.Y.

THE WASHINGTON POST

For two years the People's Drug Store . . . has had a sign reading: Shoes or sandals must be worn in this store while shopping. Trank you. PEOPLE LAUGHED. "At first people used to laugh at the sign," said manager Leonard Demino, "but now they don't. . . ."

Mimi Cantwell, Washington, D.C.

THE LIBERIAN AGE

You may win $1,000 (One thousand) dollars cold cash and a plague. Your sex, colour or religion is no barrier. Write now. The Committee will visit you.

Harold Lentzner, Washington, D.C.

VARIETY

All of the 42nd Street theatres and most of the Broadway houses employ house guards, that is, uninformed private cops, to deal with their off-screen violence.

Richard J. Dillon, Milwaukee, Wis.

THE ATLANTA (GA.) JOURNAL

Julie wore a buttercup yellow double knot dress . . . Her chest hair falling to her shoulders was caught up with an orange and yellow yarn bow . . .

Pat Bramlette, Phoenix, Ariz.
Jill Schoenbach, N.Y.C.

THE CHICAGO SUN-TIMES

AREA AGAIN IN ALERT FOR TORNADOES. Tornado watches, for the senond emening in a row, kept Chnego erea res dents on the r toes bmonday.
Forenastes seidstightly cooter air moving nto the area set sp cond tions that made tornadoes poss ble.

Several funnets in the erea, mostly southwest of the

nity, were reported Sunday night. None naused demage.

The zeather bureau said Monday's coot font would not Monday's cool front would not be enough to reduce temperatures much on Tuesday.

Irene A. Harner, Kathleen, Ga.

THE PHILADELPHIA INQUIRER
(Photo Caption) Maestro Eugene Ormandy congratulates Miss Lena Louise Hale on her 98th birthday . . . Party honoring Miss Hale was held in the bathroom of the Academy.

Mrs. Jay Kayser, Doylestown, Pa.

THE ALBANY (N.Y.) TIMES-UNION
(Headline) WATERGATE SPY TESTIFIES. Thought It was Legal, Bugger Claims.

Carol R. Richards, Albany, N.Y.

THE MIDDLETOWN (N.Y.) TIMES HERALD RECORD
The All Time Classic "GONE WITH THE WIND" Clark Gable. Janet Leigh.

Chris Emanuel, Middletown, N.Y.

THE NEW YORK TIMES
The decision to revive the controversy was taken by Max Ritter of the United States, who succeeded Jan De Vries of the Netherlands as the federation president after the Olympics, and by Abe of Japan, the new secretary.

Susan Bachelder, N.Y.C.

THE YONKERS (N.Y.)HERALD STATESMAN
"I come from a political family," she said. Her brother Parliament," she says. The couple also both love northern Westchester, which is now in the House of Lords, and altogether, "16 members of our family have served in Mrs. Hayward prefers to Long Island describes as "real country, like England."

Thomas E. Louis, Dobbs Ferry, N.Y.

THE HERMITAGE (MO.) INDEX

Funeral Services were held . . . for (a) long time resident of the Urbana community. He was well known as a stockman and farmer and an active community servant. A large crow attended.

Faculty Lounge, Warsaw High School, Missouri

☞ *Unfamiliar Quotations*

"Hi, I Want You Should Say Hello To My Better Half. . . ."
—AMY VANDERBILT

Above, an extract from "Unfamiliar Quotations." Competitors were asked to select any well-known personality of past, present, or fiction and attribute to him or her an atypical remark suitable for this anthology.

Report: In a mixed mailbag the quotedest quotes were as follows: profanity from Shirley Temple, Doris Day, or Billy Graham; "Drat" from Lenny Bruce; Ms. Garbo or Howard Hughes having an open house; Ms. Hollander having a closed one; Archie Bunker: "Black is beautiful"; John Simon raving; Sherlock Holmes baffled; Julia Child ordering at McDonald's; Mr. Nixon: "I'd rather be right than . . ."; George Scott's acceptance speech; Sydney Carton: "This is probably a dumb idea . . ."; Jack Benny: "Keep the change"; George Washington with various denials re the cherry tree (the best one: "See, there was this huge beaver . . ."); Sinatra praising Cheshire; Carry Nation: "Set 'em up!"; Madalyn O'Hair: "God Bless You"; lovelorn advisers telling us to get lost; Ralph Nader: "What's good for G.M. is good for . . ."; a definite "No!" from Marv Albert and Molly Bloom; and from Nasser: "Oy." I know what he means.

That's her, my last one, painted on the wall—
And don't she look like she's alive and all
And like, you know, she's giving you the eye?
She'd go for you and I or any guy.

—ROBERT BROWNING
Sally Brainin, N.Y.C.

"Open wide, please." —MARK SPITZ
Phillip Minoff, Oceanside, N.Y.

"No thanks." —EGON and DIANE VON FÜRSTENBERG
David Cassidy, Purdys, N.Y.

"No, wise guy, I'm plugging Aqueduct."

—HESTER PRYNNE
Steve Brody, Yorktown Heights, N.Y.

"Hello, young lady, my name is Rumpelstiltskin."
Jack Ryan, N.Y.C.

"I don't get it." —ED MCMAHON
Elaine Stallworth, Willow Grove, Pa.

"WeeeeeO! How A & P prices have changed!"

—JACQUELINE ONASSIS
Donna Prince, N.Y.C.

Man, I dig your whole physique,
And your kisses make me weak;
Without you I'm up the creek,
'Cause I love you, love you, love you, baby!

—COLE PORTER
Phyllis Taub, Brooklyn, N.Y.

"We'll do it in its proper period with no gimmicks and an all-white cast." —JOSEPH PAPP
Richard Fithian, N.Y.C.

"The funniest thing happened to me on the way to the White House. I was walking because I do not choose to run. 'I do not choose to run.' Get it? Ha ha ha. Well, who do I bump into but Charlie. Charlie Who. No, Charlie Dawes. You know, my Vice Prez. Yep, good old Charlie G. Told him he should've been working because the business of America is business. Pretty good, eh? So you know what he said to me? Well, you'll never know because he never got a chance to get a word in edgewise. Ha ha ha. And furthermore I told him . . ."
—CALVIN COOLIDGE
Jack Paul, Brooklyn, N.Y.

"A ballplayer named Who is on first base. Another ballplayer named What is on second base . . ."
—BUD ABBOTT
Miles Klein, East Brunswick, N.J.

"I don't think that's so funny." —QUEEN VICTORIA
Bob Kenney, N.Y.C.

"Mind your own beeswax." —MARY WORTH
Toby Smith, N.Y.C.

"Well, what do you *think* happened?" —JOE FRIDAY
Carol Drew, Palisades Park, N.J.

"De foot bone connected to de ankle bone, de ankle bone connected to de shin bone, de shin bone connected to de knee bone . . ." —HENRY GRAY
Gloria Ullman, Los Angeles, Calif.

"I'm putting my nose to the grindstone."
—NANETTE FABRAY
Jack Schindler, Brooklyn, N.Y.

"Two's company, three's a crowd."
—TINKER and EVERS
William W. Robinson III, Yardley, Pa.

"Fools' names and fools' faces
Are often seen in public places."   —TAKI 183
Joyce Harrington, Parkersburg, W. Va.

"Let me put it in the form of a parable . . ."
—RICHARD M. NIXON
Mrs. Clara Leville, Albany, N.Y.

"Oh, leave me alone."   —VICTOR VITO
Robert Blake, N.Y.C.

"My autograph?"   —MARTIN ABZUG
Marshall W. Karp, N.Y.C.

"Now is the time for all good men to come to the aid of their party."   —JOHN CONNALLY
Richard Effman, Hollis Hills, N.Y.

. . . "And if you gentlemen want something more direct from him along this line, I can arrange for him to fill you in—on the record if you like . . ."   —RONALD ZIEGLER
William Delaney, Alexandria, Va.

"You have to kick it to get it started."
—WERNHER VON BRAUN
William H. Lee, Chanute, Kans.

"My wife, I think I'll keep her."
—HENNY YOUNGMAN

"Do you have change for a dollar?"   —KRESKIN
Math Coffee Room, University of N.C., Chapel Hill

"Gentlemen, this week we shall focus our discussion on exponential and logarithmic derivation."
—MATH COFFEE ROOM, UNIVERSITY OF N.C.
Irving Steinberg, Lakewood, N.J.

Unfamiliar Quotations / 87

"What did you say? I wasn't paying attention."
—JOHN BARTLETT
Alan Kroker, Oak Park, Mich.

"So what's the story?" —GIOVANNI BOCCACCIO
James M. Green, M.D., Livingston, N.J.

"We'll give it all we've got." —WINSTON CHURCHILL
Betty Stein, Fort Wayne, Ind.

"The sky is falling." —ISAAC NEWTON
Benji K. Green, Livingston, N.J.

". . . let me ask you this: did you by any chance eat pizza or green apples before you went to bed?"
—SIGMUND FREUD
Teresa Gerbers, Glenmont, N.Y.

"A big sister is someone you admire, someone you confide in . . ." —JOAN FONTAINE
Don Gibbs, Omaha, Neb.

"Our CBS election night coverage will begin just as soon as all the votes have been counted."
—WALTER CRONKITE
Anthony Gray, Closter, N.J.

"Oh, sorry, that one's not for sale."—THOMAS HOVING
Mary Sharaf, Brooklyn, N.Y.

New Jersey.
Yessirree. —OGDEN NASH
Jay B. Hoster, Columbus, Ohio

"What took you so long?" —PENELOPE
Pericles Crystal, Brooklyn, N.Y.

"If it means risking my life, count me out."
—NATHAN HALE
Judith R. Goldsmith, Woodmere, N.Y.

"Nah, it was probably the wind . . ." —HAMLET
Phina Grinberg, N.Y.C.

"I'm Barbara. Respect me." —NATIONAL AIRLINES
Patricia Cusick, N.Y.C.

"That's the stupidest name I ever heard." —JULIET
Gail Kmetz, Tenafly, N.J.

"I was born in this city; I was raised in this city; and I have worked in this city. Responsibility and involvement are my lifeblood. That is why I want to be your Mayor."
—ISHMAEL
John P. Rorke, Summit, N.J.

"Good morning!" —COUNT DRACULA
Dodi Schultz, N.Y.C.

"I find this contest both entertaining and instructive."
—CASEY STENGEL
Anita Beenk, N.Y.C.

"What was all that racket last night?"
—FRANCIS SCOTT KEY
Sam Bassin, Brooklyn, N.Y.

"Your name, sir?" —DIOGENES
Rose Abrams, Brooklyn, N.Y.

"You shouldn't have." —HOWARD COSELL
Jerry Richman, Washington, D.C.

"Can you tell me the price of the dress in the window?"
—JACQUELINE ONASSIS
Mavis Harcourt, N.Y.C.

"Most assuredly." —GARY COOPER
Armand Atella, Ridgewood, N.J.

"Gentlemen, presently we shall approach the castle in which my father resides."   —TONY CURTIS
John Hogan, Glen Rock, N.J.

"Oh, gosh, Fatima, how are the other girls dressing?"
—GOLDA MEIR
Elena Brunn, N.Y.C.

"Adam and Eve on a raft, hold the mayo!"
—ANDRÉ SURMAIN
Dan Greenburg, N.Y.C.

"Miss Jane, I should like to present my simian . . ."
—TARZAN
Tom Morrow, N.Y.C.

De gustibus non est disputandum.   —DR. PEPPER
Donald Wigal, N.Y.C.

"Roses are red, violets are blue,
And you know what, Roxanne? I love you."
—CYRANO DE BERGERAC
Leah Fineberg, N.Y.C.

"Secretary Rogers will now read the minutes of the last meeting."   —RICHARD M. NIXON
Justin Kodner, Cranbury, N.J.

"This third one I don't think we have to take too literally."
—MOSES
Joel Fram, N.Y.C.

"Help!"   —SUPERMAN
Brenda Gustin, N.Y.C.

"First, we'll need plenty of boiling water . . ."—PRISSY
Rees Behrendt, N.Y.C.

". . . and a large can of *Raid,* please."
—GREGOR SAMSA
Judith Klein, East Brunswick, N.J.

"If one is unable to endure the oppressive, insufferable temperature exacerbated by appliances maintained for just such a project, one should hastily withdraw from those environs." —HARRY S. TRUMAN

Mike Leifer, Valley Stream, N.Y.

☞ *Repunctuated Names*

Kitty-car Lisle—Hosiery material impervious to transient pets.

Above, a familiar name redistributed and redefined. Competitors were asked to provide a definition for a well-known name altered by repunctuation.

Report: An enormous batch. And funny, we thought, albeit tainted by the dreaded (and ineligible) more-than-one-entry-per-contestant. Tsk, tsk. Now, then. If there were recurrent faults, they were these: **1.** The selection of the too-obvious name, as: Messrs. Nixon and Kissinger (variations on the latter we leave to your imaginations —*hint:* chickens and bussing figured heavily). **2.** Names mangled rather than merely repunctuated: misspelling, deliberate or otherwise; added or deleted letters, etc. **3.** Names redefined but *not* repunctuated: *Dinah Shore*—Leave the boat for supper. **4.** Names only slightly redistributed, leaving, for example, the entire last or first name unsullied. *Harvey Korman*—Pukkah in the Marines. **5.** Names transformed by onomatopoeia only. And so forth. Of the repeats, a meager sample herewith: *Betted Avis*—

Wagered on Number 2; *Edsull Ivan*—Extinct Russian car; *Flee Bailey*—Bond jumper; *Elke sommer*—hot weather analgesic; *Batmaster Son*—Baseball scion; *Artlink Letter*—Painters' chain mail; *Mar Tin Gabel*—Cat on hot roof; *Don, Rick, Les*—Village trio; *Or Son Bean*—Chinese soup; *Judith and 'er Son*—Israeli-Cockney act. Anthropoids: the *Dustinhoff Man, Ingmarberg Man, et al*. First-name admonitions on the order of: Char, Pat, Mar, Bet and Bar. *Einstein* done as an equation. And the competition editor done to a turn.

JOHNNY-MAT: "HIS"—Bachelor's bathroom accessory *
* see also: COTTON-MAT: "HER"

Jack Rose, N.Y.C.

"ER . . . MA BOMB! ECK!"—Last words of absent-minded French anarchist upon opening a package that was returned for additional postage.

Fred Berg, Boston, Mass.

UTAH AGEN—Former dancer in Texas Guinan's club.

Mungen Gumbee, Bryn Mawr, Pa.

MAR, GAR, ET MEAD—Roman goddess of Anthropology, Women's Studies, and Brewing.

Lucinda Biese, Plymouth, Mass.

MA EWE ST.—Main thoroughfare of the sheep-worshiping Montywoolleys, and site of the famous Lamb's Club.

Erna Lovett, Hillside, N.J.

SAMMY D. AVIS, JR.—The second-best entertainer in the U.S.

Gary Blake, N.Y.C.

LA NATURNE®—Face creme of the stars.

Charles Almon, Brooklyn, N.Y.

STANLEY-KU BRICK—Prompting device for Polish actors.
Elaine Stallworth, Willow Grove, Pa.

JOHN PHILIP SO (U.S.A.)—G.I. of American-Korean descent.
Frank Morse, N.Y.C.

BE, LA, LU, GO, SI—The quintonic musical scale of ancient Palindrome.
Rosemarie Williamson, Basking Ridge, N.J.

CHAR LESB RONSON—Smoking accessory for gay maid.
Rees Behrendt, N.Y.C.

FRANK LOVE! JOY!—Marquee on Times Square.
Arnold N. Panzer, Short Hills, N.J.

A GNESMORE HEAD—Bust by the obscure sculptor, Gnesmore.
Abyna Jean Snyder, N.Y.C.

BETH-EL LESLIE—The Scarlet Pimpernel's synagogue.
Anne Moss, Croton-on-Hudson, N.Y.

GENE-HACK MAN—A cab driver by heredity.
George Hatch, Jr., N.Y.C.

ERNES, THE MING-WAY—Sea pheasant prepared in ancient Chinese manner.
Paul Dunkel, N.Y.C.
Susan Schubach, East Hills, N.Y.

WALT W. HITMAN—Dispenser of poetic justice.
Anthony Gray, Closter, N.J.

FORD-MAD OXFORD—British community dominated by American car-fanciers.
James Fechheimer, Glen Head, N.Y.

C/O LE PORTER—How to address the tip you neglected to leave when you checked out of your Paris hotel.
Rorri Feinstein, Bayside, N.Y.

A RIST O'PHANES—A bracelet of deceptions.
>Florence Lowenkron, Roslyn Heights, N.Y.

LIZABETH'S COTT—'Ollywood bedd.
>M. Sullivan, Cincinnati, Ohio

VIN CENT-PRICE—The cheapest drink in town.
>Michael Schiffrin, N.Y.C.
>Don Gibbs, Omaha, Neb.
>Kathleen Ganim, Weehawken, N.J.

TO N.Y. PERK-INS—Sign indicating where magazine employees spend coffee-breaks.
>Renée Katz, Bronx, N.Y.

ALEX AN'DER BELL—German children's story.
>Donald Wigal, N.Y.C.

BUS BY BERKELEY—How to avoid getting caught in a demonstration.
>Dava Grayson, Brooklyn, N.Y.

KAHLILGI BRAN—Indian health food cereal.
>Jacqueline Fogel, Jamaica, N.Y.

CHIC OMAR X—Fashionable militant tentmaker.
>Ruth Brewster, Hillside, N.J.
>Brian Watson, N.Y.C.

GEORGE, BAL' AN' CHINE!—Your Honor, meet the wife!
>Arthur Kober, N.Y.C.

ROBE: RT., RED, FO'RD—to convey "Robe" (full dress with decoration), a Naval signalman uses right-hand flag only, keeping the left close to the body . . .
>Jack Ryan, N.Y.C.

T.S. ELI! (O.T.)—Biblical gibe.
>David E. Diener, Irvington, N.Y.

TO: MS. WIFT—Office memo to woman of indeterminate marital status.
Paul H. Coladarci, Haledon, N.J.

BOB BY FISCHER—A new car from Detroit.
Lee Naiman, N.Y.C.

WILBURM ILLS—A House Blight.
L. P. London, Glen Rock, N.J.

BENJAMIN'S POCK—Childhood disease characterized by a single lesion.
Dodi Schultz, N.Y.C.
John Chervokus, Briarcliff Manor, N.Y.

PATRICIAN IXON—High-test gasoline.
Norton Bramesco, N.Y.C.

JAMES B. O. SWELL—Sparkle Plenty's high-class uncle.
J. Bickart, N.Y.C.

"PIKE: SPEAK!"—The Bishop's widow has yet to hear from him.
Walter Rossmassler, Jr., Flourtown, Pa.

BILLBOYD—A Brooklyn signboard.
Jill Tanner, N.Y.C.

MICKEY-SPIL LANE—Short, tavern-lined street where the bartenders are unscrupulous but palsied.
Rosemary S. Jung, Berwyn, Pa.

MARK T.W.A. IN—Control tower instruction at Kennedy Airport.
Joseph J. Romm, Middletown, N.Y.

ALP A CINO—A Swiss coffee treat.
Arthur Zigouras, N.Y.C.

R.I.P. TO R.N.—Requiem for a Nun.
Gajda, N.Y.C.

GALI, LEO! GALI, LEI!—Hawaiian greeting.
Maria Montero, Tarrytown, N.Y.

"GA., L.I., LEO"—M-G-M movie distributed in limited areas.
Sam Bassin, Brooklyn, N.Y.

BENJA MIND (ISRAELI)—A Mideastern hallucinogenic.
N. D. Kutin, N.Y.C.

WILLIAM'S LOAN COFFIN—Casket rental company.
Christopher E. Smith, Maplewood, N.J.

DON ALDO CONNOR—Irish Godfather.
Math Coffee Room, University of N.C., Chapel Hill

LOU IS XIV—Comment on Justice Brandeis a year after his bar mitzvah.
Ellis Schein, Reading, Pa.

DO NAME CHE—Señora Guevara decides son's nomenclature.
Judith Klein, East Brunswick, N.J.

ARION ASSIS—Neo-Nazi gang of high-school drop-outs.
Henry Hirschberg, Bayside, N.Y.

RA QUEL WELCH—The Egyptian god of crushed grapes.
Norma Mostowitz, Brooklyn, N.Y.

MAX BEER BOHM—Cheap drunk.
Peter Meltzer, N.Y.C.

MAX: I'M ILL. IAN.—Regrets, cannot attend Beerbohm soirée.
Harry Watts, St. Louis, Mo.

EL MERRICE—Notorious night club in El Barrio.
Joyce Harrington, Parkersburg, W. Va.

ISAAC'S TERN—Seagull belonging to Abraham's son.
Mitch Darer, Hohokus, N.J.

PET ULAC LARK—Domesticated bird of genus Ulac.
Laura Ost, N.Y.C.

DO NADA MS.—Liberated Puerto Rican housewife.
Marcy Losapio, Scarsdale, N.Y.

GEORGE, MAC? GOVERN?—(No explanation needed.)
Ernst T. Theimer, Rumson, N.J.

"LADY? GOD, IVA!"—That was my wife.
Liana Giuntini, Elmhurst, N.Y.

FRA, N.C.O.—A military monk.
Frank Scully, N.Y.C.

EFRE/MZIM
BALI/STJR—C.I.A. Message.
Michael Deskey, N.Y.C.

CYNE WULF—Type-casting of Lon Chaney, Jr.
James M. Green, M.D., Livingston, N.J.

SAN TACLA, U.S.—A resort for gifted children.
Mrs. R. Nivison, Little Silver, N.J.

WAR D BOND—Early World War II investment.
Gene Fishman, N.Y.C.

HIPPO CRATES—Cartons used for shipping large animals.
Ann San Fedele, N.Y.C.

"BEBEREB!" "O! ZO?"—Conversation between a Dutch gentleman and the frog he has just discovered in his bed.
Mark Lawrence, N.Y.C.

☞ *Four-Letter Words*

Love Poem

Above, four-letter words. Competitors were asked to compose two quatrains of appropriate terse verse.

Report: Poems tender, touching, timely, tepid, witty, crafty, sensual, even brief—of love sacred, profane, even heterosexual. A few of you had trouble handling grammar attendant on "thou," or contracted "you are" as "your." Legitimate contractions ("can't," etc.) and spelling ("rime") were admissible. Others weren't. Were not. While amusing, verse such as "Rose sare redv iole tsar . . ." didn't strike us as strictly within bounds. As for repeats, many realized the potential of "Into each life . . ." and Jack Plus Jill With Pails Sans Pill. But O! Mores! the slew of entries citing Mr. Segal's *chef* hors d'oeuvre failed to note that his first name is spelled Eri*ch*. Drat. Laud Each Poet/Work Went Well/Even When Some/Folk Can't Spel.

Nice rich Wasp Hugh (Kent, Taft, Yale, crew),
Cool, tall, lean, lank exec Chem Bank,

Four-Letter Words / 99

Woos, wins chic Char (Dana Hall, Bryn Mawr),
Trim, glib, cute wife, once with Time-Life.
East side co-op, Glen Cove next stop.
Club, kids, cars, vino, golf, gals, gout, Reno,
Long hair, teen riot, boob tube, blah diet,
Grim tale, stay wise: true love soon dies.

Lesley Perrin, N.Y.C.

That time
That tear
That girl
That year.
This time
This tear
That girl
This year.

Ted Kennedy, Brooklyn, N.Y.

Joan made love with Pete, then Paul,
Sven, Stan, Chas, Kurt, Sean, then Saul,
Brad, Greg, Jack, John, Jeff, Hank, Bill,
Dave, Dolf, Rolf, Duke, Luke, Fred, Phil,
Andy, Alan, Adam, Stew,
Ivan, Joey, Oren, Hugh,
Zeke, Nick, Dick, Rick, Rock, Jock, Josh,
Mary, Tony . . . MARY? Gosh!

David G. McAneny, Rumson, N.J.

John dear. Mail call.
We're fine. All's well.
Bill runs. Bob's tall.
Ruth eats. Anne fell.
Your chum, Stan Gray,
From work, made life
Real nice. He'll stay.
DEAR JOHN. Your wife.

Arthur Penn, Philadelphia, Pa.

Hate Dick? Hate Veep?
Hate John? (Plus wife?)
Hate pigs, G-men, Army life?
Come lift your fist!
Come wave your sign!
Come bomb!—Come join
Your hate with mine.

        Dennis Marks, N.Y.C.

Nick digs Gert; Gert digs Rick
Anne digs Burt; Burt digs Nick
Jean digs Curt; Rick digs Fran
Fran digs Myrt; Nate digs Anne.
Kate digs Dean; Curt digs Kate
Dean digs Jean; Myrt digs Nate
What kick next will stir this clan?
Wait four days till they meet Stan.

        Frank Jacobs, N.Y.C.

Your eyes
Your ears
Your lips
Your nose.
Your neck
Your legs
Your hips
Here goes.

        Bruce Feld, Bronx, N.Y.

What made mild Mort Sahl hate guns?
What will make Joan Baez sing?
What made Babe Ruth slam home runs?
Also, what made Bert Lahr king?
What gave Muni that much guts?
What runs "hawk" away from "dove"?
What once made Will Hays make cuts?
Love Love Love Love Love Love Love

        Harold Stone, N.Y.C.

... Love lady slim.
Love aged hags.
Love what ever.
Send free mags!

C. R. Mann, Arlington, Va.

Till fake turn real
Till fool turn wise
Till head turn heel
Tell your love lies.
Till nays turn ayes
Till book turn bell
Tell your love lies
They work well.

Willard Espy, N.Y.C.

Gary, Mary, both from Erie
Meet. Alas! Poor dear sick Mary.
(Mary ails with beri-beri.)
Gary yens. Fair Mary wary.
Lust from evil, wily Gary.
Fear from poor pure lost lamb Mary
Gary wins. Beds maid from Erie.
Exit Mary—hara-kiri.

Richard A. Rosen, M.D., Mount Vernon, N.Y.

... Your book
Came late.
This Anne
Don't rate.

Mrs. Anne Thompson, N.Y.C.

Leda, lose that icky swan
Shoo that bird away
Love like mine won't come anon
Sack Zeus, baby, pray.
Just like Cain left Abel, dear

Show that fowl your dust
Take this chap that eyes thee here
Know pure love from lust.

Albert G. Miller, N.Y.C.

Once Dad's live ball game star
Soft hair, warm eyes (Paul, nine)
"Best pals" they were back then
Long easy days, life fine.
Away, drug shot, lone wolf
Long hair, lost soul, lean face
(Paul, nine plus nine this year)
Paul, come back here, home base!

Louis Williams, Pompano Beach, Fla.

Fran can't
Stay here
Love won't
Come easy.
We'll talk
Some more
She's only
Gone home.

Paul Karchawer, N.Y.C.

That face less soul
That hand like nose
With four flat eyes that lied
That said
"Grok Spoo Noom Ooon
Grok Ilov eyou June"
Sure wish that Gurk from Mars
Were dead!

Paul Eden, N.Y.C.

. . . This pert, pink, pint-size runt
With wide eyes, can't hate, can't hurt.

Pigs have God's gift, love—know
They have been born ugly . . .

Joan H. Verner, Long Lake, N.Y.

. . . Pill will
Plan clan
Miss this
Lots tots.

John Sheehan, Baldwin, N.Y.

This tale will show
That love once bold
Like days that glow
Must soon turn cold.
This kiss won't last
This urge will slow
When she's gone past
With your best beau.

Herb Rovner, N.Y.C.

Both have woes
With each one's clan
They name some rose
They plot, they plan.
Many will know
This love duet
Dead girl, dead beau
Romeo and Juliet.

Joan Wilen, N.Y.C.

Name? Jill.
Jack. Hill.
Pail, Fill?
Sure will!
Atop hill.
Kiss till . . .
Hope Jill
Took pill.

David Scoggins, N.Y.C.

Deep blue eyes
Hair like silk
Ruby lips
Skin like milk.
Love your mind
Love your soul
Love best your
Huge bankroll.

Judy and Miles Klein, East Brunswick, N.J.

Drop that wine
Stop that song
Lest your life
Last less than long.
Take your girl
Down some long lane
Find that love
Still tops sham pain!

Robert B. Pearsall, N.Y.C.

". . . Feed your cold, Mama. Have more Chow Mein."
(Whom else will sons help than Mama with pain?)
"More food can't hurt. Pass some rice," Mama said.
Then, alas! Alan Hays eyed poor Mama dead.

Stephen Gelb, Brooklyn, N.Y.

Love, when your eyes, more blue than gray
Pert oval face, your soft long hair
—That halo flow less dark than fair—
Flow into view, smog goes away.
They lift this mind, soul, body, wing
Them into Eden, sift with gold
Dull city dust, make pale hope bold
Turn sigh into song, clod into king.

D. H. Fitzgerald, N.Y.C.

Some love
Some don't.

Some can't
Some won't.
Some love
Some hate.
Some flee
Some wait.

Rosemary Bascome, Shelter Island, N.Y.

Eyes that show pain
Flow with warm rain.
Arms once held true
Life gone, days blue.
Snow blow, rose grow
Time heal, face glow.
Sing bird this song
Love can't hide long.

Kathleen M. Scott, Brooklyn, N.Y.

"Ship Sank, Oily Mess," said news item, Tues.
Over gold sand slid foul lime ooze.
Bird-Girl avid eyed, sees torn inky hull
Runs down from hill, hugs tame baby gull.
Arms rock oily babe, hand rubs muck from tail
Tiny bird hops, can't soar, even wail
Can't open taut wing, can't flee, even rise
Late news lead: "Girl, with gull love bird dies."

B. W. O'Brien, Ridgewood, N.J.

... Once, when lass knew lad's last name
She'd seek, next have, then hold thru life
She'd wear pink silk, she'd sigh, sing soft
Talk like pure maid, love like true wife.

Keith Blake, Gloversville, N.Y.

Dear Gael: Hail food!
Fine fare your wish.
What fits each mood—

Snob menu, junk dish.
Don't cook *chez vous*
With mate ever roam.
Next type *pour nous*
Your true love poem.

       Mike Nickolay, N.Y.C.

Love thee
Many ways
Well over
Just four.
Then when
We're dead
Many, many
Many more.

       Angelo Papa, Trenton, N.J.

Love isn't that keen when seen from afar
With wild life, love sits like some evil *bête noir*.
What rare news when mare gnus from zoos find *amor*!
Make your vows that more sows will deem love just some
 boar.
When male bees make love, they fade away fast
Your dodo made none—left this vale ages past.
Sole puma near Yuma, lone roan roam your glen
Love only taps man's kind; let's each sing, "Amen."

       Norton Bramesco, N.Y.C.

... This love poem blue
Seeks love anew
Like Boys sans Band;
Phil Roth sans hand.

       John H. Mershon, Atlanta, Ga.

"Cads must lose
Hero wins,"
Mom's book says.

"Down with sins."
Dull Bill lost
When that word took
Jane just read
Dad's dear book.

Sharon Reilly, N.Y.C.

Life grew from your love.
Your eyes made mine glow like sun's rays.
Time flew fast
Like that bird with aims lost.
Then fall came
Life died.
Soft rain wept
When your love went away.

Debbie Baron, Ossining High School, N.Y.

Girl died
Shed tear.
Gal's year?
Year five.
Plus five
Plus five
Plus five
Plus five.

Jacklin VanMechelen, Derwood, Md.

What! Only just four?
With love like mine
Will need much more
Must pack each line.
Your rule—such pith
Sure don't help none
Just can't work with
Good Lord! We're done!

William Cole, N.Y.C.

Extract from a Best Seller

"Congratulate me, Salvatore," said my brother as he kissed me. "I just got a new contract...."

Above, an extract from an imaginary, albeit trendy, novel. Competitors were asked for a poignant one-sentence excerpt from an imminent best seller.

Report: Less fiction than nonfiction, and less of heaven than earth. Subject matter varied. But not much. Lunar exploration; Sexuality, homo and trans; Women and/or blacks as President, men as housewives; Current politics, Presidential candidates, Ping-Pong and the radical right-on left; Celeb bios; Memoirs of World War II personnel; Confessions of fallen women; World War III or the environment causing the end of the world (score: Nuclear Holocaust 100 per cent—Population Zero); Bedside reading on the order of *The Sensuous Android;* and Ira Levin/William Blatty devilry. In brief, an assortment which was not, with notable exceptions, time-capsule fodder.

"I'm a law-enforcement officer, and I'd like to tell you about some of the most unforgettable alleged perpetrators I've ever met."

Ed Butler, N.Y.C.

Extract from a Best Seller / 109

"By June 1943, we controlled all German spies in England, and M5 was feeding information to them which they radioed to Berlin; however, Allied espionage agents in occupied Europe were once again controlled by the Gestapo, who forced them to send false information to London, information which was monitored by *our* German agents in Britain, who, nevertheless, continued to transmit actual secrets to the German High Command through the duplicity of Section Chief M5, actually a double agent —whether theirs or ours, I haven't the foggiest idea."

Jack Ryan, N.Y.C.

" 'It's Saturday and I'm busy,' said the Rabbi, 'but if you can keep the suspect under surveillance until sundown I'll be happy to take the case.' "

Lewis S. Marks, Brooklyn, N.Y.

"It's crucial to start the four years off right, the Egyptian Ambassador thought as he entered the Oval Office, and then he beamed with inspiration: 'Mazel tov, madame,' he murmured."

Richard Walter Hall, N.Y.C.

"If men are willing to pay, I'm willing to sell."

Jonathan Abrams, Brooklyn, N.Y.

"I leaned back, imagining what Jonah Ross might say if he knew that now, at the very moment of his begging me to save his foundering empire, the woman waiting in my bed upstairs was his own beautiful young bride of three months."

J. Bickart, N.Y.C.

" 'Gentlemen,' said the exiled general, 'if the Englishman in the Foster Grant shades could pass himself off as a movie star's possessed, twelve-year-old daughter and drive a Jesuit exorcist to defenestration just for laughs, codewise speaking the day of the Hyena has dawned!' "

Rees Behrendt, N.Y.C.

"That swollen shape whom I once called brother glared at me when I shouted the incantation and moved toward me, shuddering and groaning as it slumped to the floor, dead as his promise, his hands a few inches from my outstretched paw."

Arthur Zigouras, N.Y.C.

" 'Get into the moon rover,' they ordered. 'Don't try any funny moves and don't bother trying to call Houston.' "

Toby Smith, N.Y.C.

" 'Congratulations, Mr. Ph.D. in German literature,' Al said, handing me the *Times*' want ads when I returned home from the ceremonies."

Paul A. Garcia, Ph.D., Gambier, Ohio

"As little Angela spat obscenities and kicked the doctor in the groin I thought, What the devil has got into this sweet child?"

Jack Rose, N.Y.C.

" 'It's a pleasure to be here, Madame President,' the Chilean Ambassador said, only to have Genevieve retort: 'It's *Ms.* President, Mr. Santiago, and you needn't assume I'm married merely because of my pregnancy.' "

Henry Slesar, N.Y.C.

"Remembering the heart-stopping excitement of the game he had once played so well, Rabbit could still recall vividly being under the gun and wondered if Farmer Brown or the others still played at lettuce-stealing with the neighborhood kids. . . ."

William Jeanes, Jackson, Miss.

" 'We've only been in it one day,' the command pilot reported to ground control, 'and already the paint is starting to peel.' "

Burns Copeland, N.Y.C.

"'Please stop clicking that awful camera at me,' she said, pushing me into the shrubbery."

Charles K. Robinson, Kearny, N.J.

"Believing that she had dismissed all of us for the night, the First Lady turned toward the shadowy figure behind the curtains and said, 'It's safe now.'"

Elaine Stallworth, Willow Grove, Pa.

"At first glance, the courtship rites of the tuna fish may seem a far cry from today's teen-age proms—but recent findings of biologists suggest that, in fact . . ."

T. E. D. Klein, N.Y.C.

"At that point Garbo offered me an organic onion and began to tell me her story."

Andrew and Renée Herz, N.Y.C.

"'Charge! Charge, you demonic offal,' sobbed Margo as the delegates stared curiously into the den."

Wallace E. Knight, Ashland, Ky.

"'We loved your new play,' said the Queen as she snuggled closer to the bearded playwright recumbent on the royal bed, 'but why must both Romeo and Juliet die?'"

Joel F. Crystal, Brooklyn, N.Y.

". . . and although I didn't have my first cigarette, my first drink, my first shot of dope, or my first lover until I was thirteen, I knew that time and nature could overcome the retarding influence of a girl's backward parents and I would yet attain the freedom, maturity, and experience of my younger friends. . . ."

Jack Paul, Brooklyn, N.Y.

"'Chrahst in the foothills!' yelped the Senator in his Mississippi drawl. 'If mah daddy's dyin' words was true, it means ah'm an effin' nigra!'"

Albert G. Miller, N.Y.C.

" 'Don't be too hasty, Bishop,' Monsignor Harkin pleaded. 'At least speak to Father Acker's wife.' "

D. K. Dann, Fort Lee, N.J.

"The congressional hearings on scrapping the Supreme Court were daily growing more divisive; the much-heralded trip to Bali was threatening to become a tourist's nightmare; the astronauts were littering the moon with breakfast food; the Russians wanted Alaska back; the Joint chiefs were still partying in Vegas; and from his bedroom window an angry but resolute man in his fifties could see on this rainy morning in May a throng of protesters on Pennsylvania Avenue burning David Susskind in effigy."

George Fairbanks, Nutley, N.J.

"My shrink told me I had 'latent hostile proclivities generated by severe pubescent repression,' and that in order to achieve an emotional plane consonant with the societal ethos I must release the strangle hold of these psychic inhibitors—so I shot him."

Rosemarie Williamson, Basking Ridge, N.J.

"As the new lieutenant turned away from the stubborn squad he thought to himself, 'I wonder who will get me, the Cong or these guys.' "

Marilyn Marcosson, Flushing, N.Y.

"The astronaut placed his hands on the thought-translator: 'Since when have you Martians been recycling your own . . . people?' "

Ellis Schein, Reading, Pa.

"No more inward, downward, surging, *ugly* . . . she knew at last she had found happiness, with Solange."

James Elward, N.Y.C.

Extract from a Best Seller / 113

"As the celebrity-presenter nervously ripped open the envelope, darling Esther put her hand on mine and in a raspy-from-too-much-Scotch whisper, she assured me, 'It got best set, best costumes, best lighting, best actor, best actress, best director, best music and lyrics, best book—how can it miss as the year's best musical?' "

Lydia Wilen, N.Y.C.

" 'Seems we're in a bit of luck, sir, it's the doomsday device all right,' said Sergeant Kelly as he ran his hand along the configuration, '. . . though I'm afraid that the radiation off the dial of my watch has just activated the triggering mechan . . .' "

J. M. Riordan, Laguna Beach, Calif.

"As a small book fell into the enveloping petals below, he laughed softly, and said, 'You look very natural among Ohio peach blossoms, Soo-ling.' "

M. Sullivan, Cincinnati, Ohio

" 'It's fourth and goal, Lord!' he shouted above the pounding waves. 'Just open up the middle and I'll take it from there.' "

Louis Sabin, Milltown, N.J.

"One night, early in 1943, while I was preparing his favorite meal—sauerbraten and liver dumplings—my hands began to tremble and my heartbeat thundered as I suddenly realized that I was not simply a head chef; I held the power of life and death over *der Führer*."

Marvin Goodman, N.Y.C.

"From atop the diving board the spectacular view of the California shoreline set off an equally delightful view of his three friends' wives sunbathing below and David wondered which one he would end up with tonight."

Mona Good, Brooklyn, N.Y.

". . . It was a marvelous house for a giant duck—Wallace quacked happily over the walnut paneling, as I knew he would. . . ."

J. A. Zogott, Brooklyn, N.Y.

" 'You made a fortune by selling your *what?*' "

Rose Abrams, Brooklyn, N.Y.

"Oh, oh, oh, oh, oh . . ."

Angelo Papa, Trenton, N.J.

" 'Well, congratulations,' I chuckled as I returned his kiss, 'you get an offer from Hollywood and I get a pretty good contract myself.' "

Eileen Tranford, Dorchester, Mass.

☞ *Modern Devil's Dictionary*

---

conservative: n. a liberal who has just been mugged.

Above, an excerpt from a modern "Devil's Dictionary." Competitors were asked to select one common word or phrase and invent for same a brief redefinition which is of present-day sociopolitical relevance.

Report: What with events being so current and all, emphasis lay more on the political than the socio. And "Watergate" was defined nearly to death. Samples: WATERGATE, *n.* bug sanctuary (see WATERBUG and RAID; see also ELEPHANT'S EAR). Next in popularity was LIBERAL, *n.* a conservative who has just been **1.** bugged **2.** drugged and/or **3.** jugged. A few familiar quotations sounded Wilde, or Pope-ish (Papal, if you will). But decidedly *déjà vu:* MARRIAGE, *n.* the last refuge of the roué, or PEDESTRIAN, *n.* a man with three cars, a wife, and two teen-age children. Jokes, certain puns and the like did not seem ironic enough, lacking a kind of Mort Sahl ring. And a few definitions were simply not couched in dictionaryese: BROTHEL, *n.* home is where the tart is. In all, a first-rate assortment. Special thanks to Grade 3, Columbia Grammar School, N.Y.C., for their acuity.

ANTEDILUVIAN, *adj.* pertaining to the state of affairs in Washington, D.C., before someone opened the watergate.
James M. Green, M.D., Livingston, N.J.

BUG, *n.* a tiny device refuting the contention that those in power do not listen to the people.
Jack Paul, Brooklyn, N.Y.

REPUBLICAN, *n.* a species of elephant you can lead to the watergate but cannot make remember.
Jenny Krasner, Melville, N.Y.

OXYMORON, *n.* a self-contradictory statement—such as Army Intelligence.
Catherine Vivona, N.Y.C.

CRIME, *n.* the thing that President Nixon has taken out of the streets and brought into the White House.
Grace S. Harris, Pittsburgh, Pa.

EGOTIST, *n.* a man who looks in the index of the Bible to see if his name is mentioned.
George Oppenheimer, N.Y.C.

WATERGATE, *n.* **1.** five elevators and twenty-two stories. **2.** power to the peep-hole.
1. *Michael Campain, N.Y.C.*
2. *Jim Sheridan, Teaneck, N.J.*

APOCALYPTIC VISION, the amazing ability to see Watergate clearly from the White House.
Judith Anne Newell, Houston, Texas

PEACE FEELER, *n.* promise of only alternate-side-of-the-street bombing.
Albert G. Miller, N.Y.C.

VETO, *n.* the final stage of a congressional bill for social welfare.
James Fechheimer, Glen Head, N.Y.

PHASE II—PHASE III, *n.* phase to phase with adversity.
Berton Greenberg, Hoboken, N.J.

BOYCOTT, *n.* phase IV.
Jeffrey R. Mann, Flushing, N.Y.

DOLLAR, *n.* eighty-six cents.
Leslie J. Solove, Lancaster, Pa.

WAGE INCREASE, what a legislator must have to enact wage-control laws.
Michael Schreiber, Brooklyn, N.Y.

ACTOR/ACTRESS, *n.* an interim occupation for political aspirants.
Teresa Gerbers, Glenmont, N.Y.

LIBERAL, *n.* a radical who has got a job.
Martin Helgesen, Malverne, N.Y.

REACTIONARY, *n.* a liberal who has just been mugged, then jailed for using an unauthorized weapon upon his attackers.
Dr. Martin Horn, N.Y.C.

POLITICIAN, *n.* an unsuccessful statesman.
Ruth Salit, N.Y.C.

SOCIALIST, *n.* a Communist with two children.
Erwin H. Ezzes, N.Y.C.

DIPLOMAT, *n.* a sophisticated gossip.
A. Abramowitz, Washington, D.C.

AMBASSADOR, *n.* nonresidential Presidential campaign contributor.
Msgr. A. V. McLees, St. Albans, N.Y.

CIVIL WAR, conflict between factions of the same country with one side aided by U.S. troops.

> *Judy Mostowitz, Brooklyn, N.Y.*

PRISON, *n.* low-income housing.

> *Liana Giuntini, Elmhurst, N.Y.*

COMMUNIST, *n.* **1.** a person who lives on a commune. **2.** a person who looks like he is living on a commune.

> *Math Coffee Room, University of N.C., Chapel Hill*

UNDER-REACHER, *n.* a collector of Rod McKuen first editions.

> *Elaine Stallworth, Willow Grove, Pa.*

HAWK, *n.* a person with no sons, brothers, or husband between the ages of eighteen and twenty-six.

> *Cookie Gray, Closter, N.J.*

POLITICAL BOSS, *n.* the leader of any political group which opposes you.

> *Steven D. Cooper, Brooklyn, N.Y.*

FUTURE SHOCK, *slang.* Election Day 1976.

> *Robin Corey, Manhasset, N.Y.*

COMEDIAN, *n.* a TV newscaster having a high Nielsen rating.

> *Amy S. Mann, Flushing, N.Y.*

SEGREGATIONIST, *n.* a disciple of Thomas Jefferson (1743–1826) who holds that all men are created equal but separate.

> *Mel Taub, N.Y.C.*

TOKEN, *adj.*, *n.* **1.** woman or black in corporate management. **2.** small slotted piece of brass required for descent into hell.

> *John W. Kunstadter, N.Y.C.*

OBSTRUCTIONIST, *n.* a prominent elected official who does not want to know how he became one.

Jerome Majzlin, Howard Beach, N.Y.

NONDISCRIMINATORY, *n.* holding no prejudices (except for fags).

Andrew Mezzetti, Flushing Meadow, N.Y.

WARMONGER, *n.* another mother for peace (P.O.W. slang).

Fran Ross, N.Y.C.

REPUBLICAN, *n.* one reappointed to the I.R.S.

Mary D. English, Stamford, Conn.

SUSPECT, *n.* an alleged perpetrator.

Raymond M. Holmes, Tarrytown, N.Y.

PERPETRATOR, *n.* N.Y.C. Police team referring to members of society not in uniform.

Stephen Pfeiffer, Brooklyn Heights, N.Y.

EAGLETON, *n.* (see ALBATROSS)

Lloyd Dyer, Oakland, N.J.

PENTAGON, *n.* five sides with a single view.

Steve Brody, Yorktown Heights, N.Y.

ESTABLISHMENT, *n.* **1.** a select group to which no one will admit belonging. **2.** a) *obs.* them. b) us.

1. *William Cole, N.Y.C.*
2. *Larry Laiken, Bayside, N.Y.*

PRE-MARITAL SEX, *obs.* (see MARRIAGE)

Stanley Stone, Oceanside, N.Y.

CATEGORICAL DENIAL, prelude to COMPLETE CONFESSION.

Esther Fraenkel, N.Y.C.

PORNO, *n.* a not-quite-round football (*political*), with varying degrees of inflatability and an unpredictable bounce.

Mark Lawrence, N.Y.C.

GIRL, *n.* female employee age sixteen to sixty-two usually prefaced in male corporate structure by possessive pronoun "my."

Marilyn Francis, Livingston, N.J.

FATHER, *n.* (see MOTHER)

Carol Kanzer, Flushing, N.Y.

PERSON, *v.t.* to supply with personnel, as barricades, telephones, etc. "See how the surly Warwick persons the wall!" *Shak.*

Barbara A. Huff, N.Y.C.

GOVERNOR, *n.* a body for limiting speed.

Lorena M. Akioka, Athens, Ga.

LIBERAL PARTY, Rockefeller's center.

Alice M. Yohalem, N.Y.C.

MCCARTHYISM, *n.* endorsing a likely loser for political office.

Peter Meltzer, N.Y.C.

AID TO NORTH VIETNAM, to feed the hand that bites you.

Walter H. Rossmassler, Jr., Flourtown, Pa.

HARDHAT, *n.* someone able to resist the new even as the old caves in on him.

Carleton Carpenter, N.Y.C.

EXECUTIVE PRIVILEGE, a defensive block by the owner of the club.

Mike Sage, N.Y.C.

SECRETARY OF STATE, *n. obs.* (see PRESIDENTIAL ADVISER)

Richard Fried, Brooklyn, N.Y.

DEAN'S LIST, Presidential aides who did not make the grade(s).

Allan G. Sperling, Rye, N.Y.

WOMEN'S LIB, an attempt to have the hens rule the rooster.

H. H. Hart, Margate, N.J.

INOPERATIVE STATEMENT, a lie that no longer works.

William Schallert, Pacific Palisades, Calif.

REQUIREMENT, *n.* something needed by a minimum daily adult.

Jane M. Collins, N.Y.C.

☞ *Insipid Adages*

He who takes a pill in a darkened room
Trusts a faithful horse to a drunken groom.

Above, an insipid adage. Competitors were asked to compose a two-line rhymed maxim of minimal distinction.

Report: The "He who . . ." form of our example proved to be a bit too popular. A few maxims neither scanned nor rhymed. (We have no rhyming reason for printing the last entry, we simply liked it.) Many adages seemed very distinctive, indeed. Those that did not ranged from the subliminal to the absurd. We've embroidered the following on our tea cozy:

When bulbuls roost in ginko tree
Our fairy queen in danger be.
Albert G. Miller, N.Y.C.

The fool may laugh but the scholar will nod his head
When surprised by burning lava in his bed.
Jack Ryan, N.Y.C.

She who takes a pill in a darkened room
Trusts nothing to a drunken groom.
Robert Speiser, Philadelphia, Pa.

He who fights not and runs away,
Hopes to get amnesty some day.

Nick Scoyni, Montauk, N.Y.

I cried because I had no Guccis,
Then I met a girl who had no Puccis.

Oliver M. Neshamkin, M.D., N.Y.C.

Standing on your head makes a smile out of a frown,
But the rest of your face will be upside down.

Jack Labow, N.Y.C.

All Honorable Mentions, mark my word—
The good men do is oft interred!

Rita Oakes, Drexel Hill, Pa.

If winning contests brings content
One entry only should be sent.

Mrs. Eugene Colmes, Longmeadow, Mass.

Poems are made by fools like me
For an *Encyclopedia of World History*.

D. Grayson, Brooklyn, N.Y.

An unwashed peach is full of fuzz
For beauty is as beauty does.

Ellis Schein, Reading, Pa.

Don't sit under an apple tree,
If you're allergic to D.D.T.

Abram Kadner, D.D.S., Hampton Bays, N.Y.

Where birth control ends and sorrow begins,
A slip of the knife makes a vas deferens.

Richard Baer, Beverly Hills, Calif.

The sire of sage advice, it seems,
Is not success, but broken dreams.

Roger Klorese, Brooklyn, N.Y.

Keep a turkey in the straw
And darken my doorstep nevermore.
Martin Schwager, Bronx, N.Y.

Who walks in the rain in the nude on a bet
Will find, if it rains, that his back gets all wet.
Fred Berg, Boston, Mass.

You must remember this,
A fist is not a kiss . . .
Susan E. Cornet, N.Y.C.

Mohair does not a camel make,
Nor candles on a birthday cake.
Helen M. Ghegan, Freeport, N.Y.

He who sleeps from dawn to dusk
Puts the elephant before the tusk.
Andrew and Renée Herz, N.Y.C.

A broom that is new will sweep away
That penny saved for a rainy day.
Peter Howard, N.Y.C.

Men seldom show dimples
To girls who have pimples.
Michael K. Stone, Matteson, Ill.

The mighty sultan's scimitar
Is no match for a motorcar.
Elliott Shevin, Detroit, Mich.

A bombing a day,
Keeps peace away.
J. Clarke, Long Island City, N.Y.

She who kisses a frog, while out of sorts,
Tho' expecting a prince, may instead find warts.
Jacqueline Fogel, Jamaica, N.Y.

Insipid Adages / 125

As a goatherd learns his trade by goat,
A writer learns his trade by wrote.
>Barry W. Cornet, N.Y.C.

Scoop and bag ordinance number 110
To justify the ways of dogs to men.
>C. R. Geisst, Fort Lee, N.J.

If it pour before seven
It has rained ere eleven.
>Dodi Schultz, N.Y.C.

Late to bed and early to rise
Puts dark rings beneath the eyes.
>Dr. S. Traunstein, Jackson Heights, N.Y.

'Tis better to have seen *Godfather*'s gore
Than never to have stood on line before.
>Barbara Siskind, Rego Park, N.Y.

Rent not an enclosure
With northern exposure.
>Larry Laiken, Bayside, N.Y.

Many men who speak with forked tongue,
Had silver spoon in mouth when young.
>Mrs. Anna Lambiase, Brooklyn, N.Y.

The farmer with a bootblack son resigns
Himself to making hay while the son shines.
>Mel Taub, N.Y.C.

Who downs his liquor by the case,
May some day need a friend at Chase.
>Patrick Beary, Jamaica Estates, N.Y.

See a moose?
You're on the juice.
>Danny Hirschfeld, White Plains, N.Y.

He who sows his field with oats
Will never be the butt of goats.
>> Judith R. Goldsmith, Woodmere, N.Y.

Thunder in May;
April is away.
>> Ruth Dittmann, Basking Ridge, N.J.

An arrow shot into the blackened night
Will appear at dawn: a shaft of light.
>> Mike Leifer, Valley Stream, N.Y.

Since the maker of the boat
There's little need for cars that float.
>> Babbie Mallery, N.Y.C.

An orchestra doth not sound sweet
Without a fiddle in second seat.
>> Charles C. Dahlberg, M.D., N.Y.C.

If a nurse takes her doctor for a mate
In an oft cold bed she'll lie and wait.
>> Richard C. VanWiebe, Fort Wayne, Ind.

A man who turns green
Has eschewed protein.
>> Lisa McNear Carlson, Studio City, Calif.

A nun who's adept at karate chops
Is *persona non grata* in porno shops.
>> J. F. O'Connor, Washington, D.C.

Do not clog the intellect's sluices
With bits of knowledge of questionable uses.
>> Kaky Dafler, Yardley, Pa.

He who thinks a Ms. is as good as a Mlle.,
Paves his way down the primrose path to hl.
>> Eugene Paul, Grand View-on-Hudson, N.Y.

Insipid Adages / 127

A girl who kisses on the first date
Often has trouble with her weight.
Mrs. Joel F. Crystal, Brooklyn, N.Y.

Be brief in all ways;
We live but few days.
Michael Schreiber, Brooklyn, N.Y.

He who spends a storm beneath a tree
Takes life with a grain of TNT.
Bennett Zucker, Laurelton, N.Y.

He who finds a rabbit adrift at sea
Never takes sugar in Darjeeling tea.
James Chotas, N.Y.C.

Sightseers touring devastation by flood
End up stuck in the mud.
Ruth K. Adams, York, Pa.

Curry a dog, comb a chicken,
Simmer the soup lest it not thicken.
Dan Greenburg, N.Y.C.

In the soccer match of war
Ask not the goalie for the score.
Maurice Katz, East Hampton, N.Y.

Dire warnings of woe are heard gloomily
By despots all full of contumely.
George Fairbanks, Nutley, N.J.

Gardens not tended
Are seldom splendid.
Msgr. A. V. McLees, St. Albans, N.Y.

He who considers his own voice dearer
Resembles the fly who walks on a mirror.
Shirley Rosenthal, Lawrenceville, N.J.

If you're bored and feeling sloppily,
Play Monopoly.

> *Robert A. Steiner, Westfield, N.J.*

Far duller than a serpent's tooth
It is to spend a quiet youth.

> *Hank Volker, N.Y.C.*

He who has a shady past
Knows that nice guys finish last.

> *Rosemarie Williamson, Basking Ridge, N.J.*

He who writes verses with masculine rhymes
Is a chauvinist pig, out of touch with the times.

> *E. C. Pier, Whitingham, Vt.*

Steal a pig, pay the piper;
Have a baby, clean the diaper.

> *Jeff Forster, Lancaster, Pa.*

Like winter snow on summer lawn,
Time past is time gone.

> *Angelo Papa, Trenton, N.J.*

A man who fishes for marlin in ponds
Puts his money in Etruscan bonds.

> *Jonathan Abrams, Brooklyn, N.Y.*

To swim in June
Is to swim too soon.

> *Bernard S. Zarrow, Pompton Lakes, N.J.*

He who would have a wrist watch must two things do
Pocket his watch and watch his pocket too.

> *J. G. Richards, San Francisco, Calif.*

He who thinks Band Aid is help for the band
Takes off his glove and says, "Pardon my hand."

> *Ronnie Nathan, Great Neck, N.Y.*

The breath, once inhaled joyously,
Must subsequently exhaled be.
> *George D. Vaill, Bethany, Conn.*

Be not too quick to push the knob "Close Door"
Full elevators show you every floor.
> *Ron Harvie, Montreal, Canada*

If the curfew does not ring tonight and the moon shines on La Jolla
Means not that we have enemies, just a little paranoia.
> *Eileen Tranford, Dorchester, Mass.*

He who makes up adages for others to peruse
Takes along a rowboat when going on a cruise.
> *Richard D. Savitsky, N.Y.C.*

He who prosties his wit in *New York* Mag
Would pinch his poor mother's last Hefty bag.
> *Anne Commire, N.Y.C.*

How sharper than a hound's tooth
It is to have a thankless serpent.
> *Ross Heller, Washington, D.C.*

☞ *Fractured Names*

Well-dressed Indian suffering from hives
—NATTY BUMPPO
Press agent for a 1930s musical—ROBERTA FLACK

Above, excerpts from a Dictionary of Fractured Names. Competitors were asked for definitions for two actual names.

Report: One brief comment before the "repeats" list. (This was a huge entry.) To wit: the onomatopoetic definition proved funnier and apter than the too-literal one in almost all instances. JACK CARTER—a Brink's Truck, for example is derived too closely from the original meaning of the name. (Same for Taylor, Newman, *et al.*) Now. Most popular repeats: A Scrooge; NOËL COWARD; a lion: CHRISTIAN HERTER; a dieter: TAB HUNTER; hirsute logician: HARRY REASONER; outdoor washroom: W. C. FIELDS; change for same: JOHNNY CASH; Monday—rivet: TUESDAY WELD; murderous Latin jewel thief: RUBY KEELER; Wm. the Conqueror's armorer: NORMAN MAILER; a transvestite: TOM TRYON, and a London paddy wagon: BOBBY VAN. (You may readily see the pattern that emerged from such names as Bobby, Gene, Ethel, John, and Norman.) In agonizing quantity: constable trawling Thames: BOBBY FISCHER; Latin trumpeter: ROMAN GABRIEL; Italian winter Olympics: ROMAN

POLANSKI; French podiatrist: LE DUC THO; judge in vulgarian contest: MARK SPITZ, and Confessor for N.C.O.S: SARGENT SHRIVER. And many more too humorous to mention.

The Greek Goddess of Temperature
                          —MELINA MERCOURI

A morbid fear of toilet tissue   —DRED SCOTT
                   David G. McAneny, Rumson, N.J.

Leo Durocher's brother   —FRA LIPPO LIPPI
Oyster with an overbite   —PEARL BUCK
                       Albert G. Miller, N.Y.C.

Four days and four nights   —CURT FLOOD
Transit system to upper-class elf resort community
                           —LIONEL HAMPTON
                         Rees Behrendt, N.Y.C.

Scarlett O'Hara's order to her jeweler
                         —SELMA DIAMOND

Sound from a very, very sick ocean
                           —SIMONE SIMONE
                         Howard Haines, N.Y.C.

Polysaturated theory   —FATS DOMINO
Cottontailed emperor   —PETER NERO
                       Neil O'Brien, Bronx, N.Y.

Child's toy priced at $3,000 and featured in the Neiman-Marcus Xmas catalogue   —STIRLING SILLIPHANT
                         Peter Howard, N.Y.C.

Famous Irish pinking-shears murderer
                           —MICK JAGGER
                         Ed Weiner, Camden, N.J.

Most recent Copenhagen patient   —VIRGINIA BRUCE
Ed Leslie, New Orleans, La.

Manager of carnival on East Side I.R.T.
—LEX BARKER
David Grotenstein, N.Y.C.

A short-fanged snake which frequents dry grass
—NIPSY RUSSELL
Hank Levinson, N.Y.C.

What do you say to a large, menacing tarantula
—BIX BEIDERBECKE
Edith Abrams, Brooklyn, N.Y.

Cabin in the sky   —CELESTE HOLM
Belle Stein, N.Y.C.

Hair style created by board of directors of a bank, all of whom happen to be named George
—GEORGES POMPIDOU
Fred Berg, Boston, Mass.

Owner of residential building in Greenwich Village
—GAYELORD HAUSER

Italian sterility rites   —VASCO DA GAMA
Allan B. Smith, N.Y.C.

The first man in America   —ADAM WEST

A re-cycling crusader   —RIN TIN TIN
Harvey Chipkin, Rutherford, N.J.

Oscar winner making *brief* acceptance speech
—GERMAINE GREER
Roger Darin, N.Y.C.

Biblical figure whose excellent sea legs became legendary.
—NOAH DIETRICH
Dita Greene, Sayville, N.Y.

Statement received on first of month after you buy a bison   —BUFFALO BILL
Milton Herman, Mount Vernon, N.Y.

Folding bed with Hi-Fi   —AUDIE MURPHY
H. M. Kinzer, N.Y.C.

A social climber   —TONY NEWLEY
Elena Brunn, N.Y.C.

Dark-complexioned heiress to dinnerware fortune
   —OLIVIA DE HAVILAND

Feverish Irish beauty   —SCARLETT O'HARA
Judy Kass, N.Y.C.

Cathy in *Wuthering Heights*   —HEATHER ANGEL
Dorothea H. Scher, N.Y.C.

Tenant award to nicest landlord   —OSCAR DE LA RENTA
Valerie Lenza, Staten Island, N.Y.

Model-T milk truck   —LIZZIE BORDEN
Jill Blauner, N.Y.C.

Cat fight   —TOM MIX
Hedley Burrell, Bethesda, Md.

A two-month, $10,000 round-the-world cruise
   —DOC HOLLIDAY
Sherry Selden, N.Y.C.

Brutal collector of cranial bones   —MENASHA SKULNIK
Toby Smith, N.Y.C.

Very tiny French general   —NINA FOCH
William J. Butvick, Woodhaven, N.Y.

An upholsterer   —SOPHIE TUCKER
Carol Kanzer, Flushing, N.Y.

Command to intelligent dog   —REX REED
Benjamin Ivry, Fresh Meadows, N.Y.

134 / *Son of Giant Sea Tortoise*

Home for aged tennis players —PANCHO VILLA
                                          Gary Blake, N.Y.C.

Offenbach revival —DUSTIN HOFFMAN
                                       Anne Layton, Bayside, N.Y.

Revolutionary new soft drink —ABBIE HOFFMAN
                          Michael A. Gentry, West Caldwell, N.J.

Person who marks up cost of summer furniture
                                      —JUNE PREISSER
                                        Gretchen Rennell, N.Y.C.

Part-time Oriental detective —QUASIMODO
                                        Cameron Huff, N.Y.C.

Costly Austrian amphitheater —MAXIMILIAN SCHELL
                            Steven Gerber, Bridgeport, Conn.

Tree planter from Northern Ohio
                                        —GROVER CLEVELAND
Tree planter from Northern Ohio who drinks brandy
                     —GROVER CLEVELAND ALEXANDER
                      Lawrence E. Grant, Whitefish Bay, Wis.

Slogan for the French Foreign Legion recruiting office
                                              —JEAN ARP
                                      Mary Lambert, St. Louis, Mo.

An honest elf —FRANK FAY
                                        Ellen H. Bradley, N.Y.C.

Garbled World War II message received by German Intelligence —TRUMAN CAPOTE
One-legged Confederate general —PEGGY LEE
                          Earle Field Maricle, St. Louis, Mo.

Drive-in chain for rabbits —WARREN BURGER
                          Lois Rose, Cleveland Heights, Ohio

Six-foot invisible Arab hero —LAURENCE HARVEY
R. A. Haines, Edison, N.J.

Aural alchemist —GOLDA MEIR
Robert S. Cook, Jr., N.Y.C.

A lawman, for example —E. G. MARSHALL
Mike Hickey, Richmond, Va.

Academy Award-winning cow —OSCAR HOMOLKA
Berne Baker, Los Angeles, Calif.

Placard carried by child at "Lindsay for President" rally in Midwest —JOHNNY UNITAS
Marion E. Slabas, N.Y.C.

Black-owned peanut butter company —SCIPIO AFRICANUS
Philip J. Rosino, Poughkeepsie, N.Y.

Ivy League Mafia chief —DON CORNELL
William Blow, Edison, N.J.

Lighthouse keeper doubling as mortician —AMBROSE BIERCE
Arthur Penn, Philadelphia, Pa.

God Is My Co-Pilot —ROGER ANGELL
Harry Feldman, Brookline, Mass.

English gossip columnist —LADY CHATTERLEY
Amy Spencer, Coventry, R.I.

Service for jousting enthusiasts who do not wish to buy their own equipment —LANCE RENTZEL
Eliott Shevin, Oak Park, Mich.

Order to Irish bartender —PHYLLIS MCGINLEY
Kit Hurley, N.Y.C.

California gentile —FRANCISCO GOYA
I. M. Richlin, San Gabriel, Calif.

English panhandler —BOB HOPE
J. F. O'Connor, Washington, D.C.

A devotee of Walter Cronk —WALTER CRONKITE
George Malko, N.Y.C.

Golf course on the San Andreas Fault
—SHECKY GREENE
Francesca Cash, Brooklyn, N.Y.

Member of N.Y. underworld, best known for her role in the "Dutch Connection" —MOLL FLANDERS
Judith Newell, Houston, Texas

Cigarette-lighter burns —ZEPPO MARX
Anita Siner, Washington, D.C.

Arabian dish named for local hero
—LAWRENCE KASHA
Tom Morrow, N.Y.C.

Film editor for late showing of *Sunset Boulevard*
—NORMA SHEARER
C. Robert Kocheck, Perth Amboy, N.J.

Former great defensive tackle for the N.Y. Giants, who has now become relevant —GERMAINE GREER
Charles Hurd, New Vernon, N.J.

First sign of spring in the Bronx —JEROME ROBBINS
Phyllis Kelly, Locust Valley, N.Y.

Mascot of Royal Mounties, trained to lower and store flag —FERLIN HUSKY
Harvey Kelly, N.Y.C.

Old record player —VICTOR MATURE
TV dinner served on religious days
—GLORIA SWANSON
Dolores Dolan, N.Y.C.

Spanish pretender to the Tibetan throne
—FERNANDO LAMAS
Richard H. Thorns, N.Y.C.

Amusing Spanish nobleman —DON HO
Louis B. Raffel, Phoenix, Ariz.

French espionage agent stationed in Edinburgh
—FRANCIS SCOTT KEY
Lois Winsen, Oak Park, Mich.

Once-wealthy nobleman, now reduced to manual labor
—ERLE STANLEY GARDNER
Mike Cocca, Montclair, N.J.

Dental school student working as hamburger carhop
—MACDONALD CAREY
Martin W. Helgesen, Malverne, N.Y.
Elaine Stallworth, Willow Grove, Pa.

(Polish witticism) The device that opens all doors in the hotel is not interesting —BORIS SPASSKY
Dan Greenburg, N.Y.C.

☞ *Bartlett Pairs*

"As the King Said, Divide the Living Child in Two...." —KINGS 3:25

"Say the Secret Woid and Divide 100 Dollars." —GROUCHO MARX

Above, a Bartlett pair. Competitors were invited to provide two authentic familiar quotations, unexpectedly if appropriately coupled.

Report: Inseparable and oft insuperable—the classic quotation (Shakespeare, let us say) coupled with current TV commercials. Chiefly, Alka-Seltzerisms. Other repeaters: *The Godfather,* the Bible, and the President (not necessarily in that order). Generally, humor derived from the anachronistic. And, who's to say that's wrong? I mean, what was so great about our own example, right? These, to mention a few, were a damn' sight better:

" 'Twas brillig, and the slithy toves/Did gyre and gimble in the wabe;/All mimsy were the borogroves,/And the mome raths outgrabe." —LEWIS CARROLL

"If you do not itemize deductions and line 18 is under $10,000, find tax in Tables and enter on line 19. If you itemize deductions or line 18 is $10,000 or more, go to line 46 to figure tax."
—FORM 1040, U.S. TAX RETURN, 1971

Michael Schreiber, Brooklyn, N.Y.

"Now glow'd the firmament/With living sapphires; Hesperus, that led/ The starry host, rode brightest, till the moon,/Rising in clouded majesty, at length/Apparent queen, unveil'd her peerless light,/And o'er the dark her silver mantle threw." —J. MILTON

"Say good night, Gracie." —G. BURNS
Anne Commire, N.Y.C.

"There be three things which are too wonderful for me, yea four which I know not: The way of an eagle in the air; the way of a serpent upon a rock; the way of a ship in the midst of the sea; and the way of a man with a maid."
—PROVERBS 30:18-19

"It was a horrible experience. Can you believe that a man can walk into your bedroom, take over, and pull the phone out of the wall? I just couldn't take it any more. . . . [They] threw me on a bed and stuck a needle in my behind." —MARTHA MITCHELL
Mary Sutton Smith, Rochester, N.Y.

"My particular grief is of so flood-gate and o'erbearing nature that it engluts and swallows other sorrows."
—OTHELLO

"Good Grief!" —CHARLIE BROWN
M. Sullivan, Cincinnati, Ohio

"He goes in there for half an hour and gets a lot of flabby and fairly dumb questions . . ." —JOHN EHRLICHMAN

" 'I have answered three questions, and that is enough,'/ Said his father. 'Don't give yourself airs!/Do you think I can listen all day to such stuff?/Be off, or I'll kick you downstairs.' " —LEWIS CARROLL
Elaine Stallworth, Willow Grove, Pa.

"We shall never understand each other until we reduce the language to seven words." —KAHLIL GIBRAN

"Doc, Grumpy, Sleepy, Happy, Bashful, Sneezy, and Dopey."
—SNOW WHITE
Jack Ryan, N.Y.C.

"My own position is well known. I am opposed to busing for the purpose of achieving racial balance in our schools. I have spoken out against busing scores of times over many years. And I believe most Americans—white and black—share that view. But what we need right now is not just speaking out against more busing, we need action."
—RICHARD M. NIXON
(*Speech,* March 16, 1972)

"I hate it. But I use it twice a day."
—LISTERINE COMMERCIAL
Tim Weinfeld, Westminster, Md.

"I never met a man I didn't like." —WILL ROGERS

"Ladies and gentlemen, the President of the United States."
—TELEVISION ANNOUNCER
Rosemarie Williamson, Basking Ridge, N.J.

"That feller runs splendid but he needs help at the plate, which coming from the country chasing rabbits all winter give him strong legs, although he broke one falling out of a tree, which shows you can't tell . . ."
—CASEY STENGEL

"Let me make one thing perfectly clear."
—RICHARD M. NIXON
John F. Keppler, Fresh Meadows, N.Y.

"With all my worldly goods I thee endow."
—BOOK OF COMMON PRAYER

"A fool and his money are soon parted."
—AMERICAN PROVERB
Jack Labow, N.Y.C.

"For whither thou goest, I will go; and where thou lodgest I will lodge." —BOOK OF RUTH, 1:16

"I'm Ruth. Fly me to Miami."—AIRLINE COMMERCIAL
Celia Krapkoff, N.Y.C.

"But soft! what light through yonder window breaks? It is the East, and Juliet is the sun."
—ROMEO AND JULIET

"Go west, young man."   —HORACE GREELEY
Arnold Diamond, Rego Park, N.Y.

"Sir Ralph the Rover tore his hair."
—ROBERT SOUTHEY

"And, see! No more tangles!"   —JOHNSON & JOHNSON
Bernice Kline, Brooklyn, N.Y.

"Youth is wholly experimental."
—ROBERT LOUIS STEVENSON

"And so to bed."   —SAMUEL PEPYS
Kathy Mansfield, Cliffside Park, N.J.

"I beheld the wretch—the miserable monster whom I had created."   —MARY SHELLEY, *Frankenstein*

"I never knew so young a body with so old a head."
—MERCHANT OF VENICE
Mrs. Joel F. Crystal, Brooklyn, N.Y.

"I'm nobody, who are you?"   —EMILY DICKINSON

"I'm Nobody's Baby."   —POPULAR SONG
Catherine V. Poulin, Brooklyn, N.Y.

"Go to grass."   —JOHN FLETCHER

"You may all go to pot."   —OLIVER GOLDSMITH
J. F. O'Connor, Washington, D.C.

"In the same hour came forth fingers of a man's hand, and wrote over against the candlestick upon the plaster of the wall of the king's palace; and the king saw part of the hand that wrote." —DANIEL 5:5

"Kilroy was here."   —WORLD WAR II GRAFFITO
Mrs. June Beattie, South Hadley, Mass.

"Daddy, Daddy! I only had one cavity!"
—CREST COMMERCIAL

"Frankly, my dear, I don't give a damn."
—GONE WITH THE WIND
Anne Hord Lehmann, Memphis, Tenn.

"Uneasy lies the head that wears a crown."—HENRY IV

"Brush your teeth twice a day, see your dentist twice a year."   —AMERICAN DENTAL ASSOCIATION
Louis Kleinman, Louisville, Ky.

"I do not choose to run."   —C. COOLIDGE

"Don't Drink the Water."   —WOODY ALLEN
Jack Rose, N.Y.C.

"Euclid alone has looked on Beauty bare."—MILLAY

"Ere the blabbing eastern scout/The nice morn on th' Indian steep,/From her cabin'd loop-hole peep."
—MILTON
Math Coffee Room, University of N.C., Chapel Hill

"What is the question?"   —GERTRUDE STEIN

"To be or not to be: that is the question."
—WM. SHAKESPEARE
M. S. Seacat, N.Y.C.

"In Boston they ask, How much does he know? In New York, How much is he worth? In Philadelphia, Who were his parents?"   —MARK TWAIN

"On the whole, I'd rather be in Philadelphia."
—W. C. FIELDS
Mrs. Anna Lambiase, Brooklyn, N.Y.

"The little dogs and all, Tray, Blanch, and Sweetheart, see, they bark at me." —KING LEAR

"I don't get no respect." —RODNEY DANGERFIELD
Lou Seeger, Port Washington, N.Y.

"I am dying, Egypt, dying."—ANTONY AND CLEOPATRA

"Th-th-th-th-th-at's all, folks!" —PORKY PIG
Toby Smith, N.Y.C.

" 'Optimism,' said Candide, 'is a mania for maintaining that all is well when things are going badly.' "
—VOLTAIRE

"I have a plan to end the war."—RICHARD M. NIXON
Mrs. Barbara Solomon, Brooklyn, N.Y.

"No more that Thane of Cawdor shall deceive our bosom interest; go pronounce his present death, and with his former title greet Macbeth." —MACBETH

"Would *you* like to be 'Queen for a Day'?"
—JACK BAILEY
Toby Hecht, Bronx, N.Y.

"Consider the lilies of the field . . . they toil not, neither do they spin." —MATTHEW 6:28

". . . With a little bit of luck, someone else will do the bloomin' work." —MY FAIR LADY
Eileen Tranford, Dorchester, Mass.

"Good king of cats. . . . Will you pluck your sword out of his pilcher by the ears? Make haste lest mine be about your ears ere it be out." —ROMEO AND JULIET

"Hmmm. Guess I'll pull my finicky act some other time."
>—MORRIS THE CAT
>*Carole Conroy, Morrisville, Pa.*

". . . Eye of newt, and toe of frog,/Wool of bat and tongue of dog,/Adder's fork and blind worm's sting . . ."
>—MACBETH

"I can't believe I ate the whole thing."
>—COHEN & PASQUALINA
>*Mona Abramesco, Brooklyn, N.Y.*
>*Kenneth Popler, Brooklyn, N.Y.*

"And God rested on the seventh day from all the work He had made."   —GENESIS 2:2

"You deserve a break today . . ."
>—MCDONALD CORPORATION
>*William J. Kaan, New London, Conn.*

". . . E is for her eyes with love-light shining . . ."
>—H. JOHNSON, SONGWRITER

"$E = mc^2$"   —ALBERT EINSTEIN
>*Albert G. Miller, N.Y.C.*

"I never spoke with God/Nor visited Him in heaven/Yet certain am I of the spot/As if the Checks were given."
>—E. DICKINSON

"Kennedy Bars Any Spot on 1972 Ticket."
>—HEADLINE, THE WASHINGTON POST
>*Dan Rosenthal, Washington, D.C.*

"A baby is an inestimable blessing and a bother."
>—MARK TWAIN

"That's why it's time for a change."
>—THOMAS E. DEWEY
>*Jim Leeds, N.Y.C.*

"The pen is mightier than the sword."
—E. G. BULWER-LYTTON

"Ink-a-dink-a-doo." —JIMMY DURANTE
Harvey Chipkin, Rutherford, N.J.

"I regret the necessities of war have compelled us to bomb North Vietnam. . . . And let this also be clear: Until [their] independence is guaranteed there is no human power capable of forcing us from Vietnam."
—LYNDON BAINES JOHNSON

"Let it work. For 'tis the sport to have the enginer/Hoist with his own petar." —HAMLET, III, IV
Steven Tagashira, Bronx, N.Y.

"Fire in each eye, and papers in each hand,/They rave, recite and madden round the land."—ALEXANDER POPE

"The Battle of Competition." —KARL MARX
Msgr. A. V. McLees, St. Albans, N.Y.

Word-List Poetry

☞

Quicksilver   Umbrella   Nixon
Impair   Polish   Fawn   Clone
Chastise   Herb   Dismember

Above, a word list to bemuse the poet. Competitors were invited to select five words to be contained, in any order, in six lines of verse rhyming ABAB CC.

Report: Love poems, hate poems, pretty poems, nasty poems, poems grotesque and joyous, picaresque and sad. Recipes. Good poems and bad poems. And political! Some poems used fewer than five words (not okay)— some more than five (okay we suppose). Puns seemed fair as in "Dismember is leaving de party." So did splitting up words—" 'Quick, Silver,' said the Clone Ranger." Fella/umbrella was consistently unresisted. Sad to say, so was dismember/remember—again, the dreaded identity, not rhyme. Special thanks to many very young readers for very good work. We wish more space were allotted to print their poems and lots more. Lots.

He rode through town upon a fawn
Dismemb'ring an umbrella.
A youngster asked, when he was gone,

"Was that a Polish fella?"
"No, that was Nixon," his father said.
"Forget you saw it. Go back to bed."
                    Doug Hundley, Beverly Hills, Calif.

Rain on my umbrella—quicksilver drops
Run down my cheeks, impair my sight.
An outcast from the bright, no one stops
To hear my soul dismembered on this night.
Chastise me not while my heart's heaped with sorrow.
Nixon shone today, and I grieve for tomorrow.
                    Leslie Schweitzer, South Orange, N.J.

Our pet baby doe was allowed to run free
Till the herb-eating rascal dismembered some leeks;
She was chastised and tied to a hook in a tree,
But this morning I woke to my wife's woeful shrieks:
"My umbrella leaf plant! And my pansies! Oh, look—
Some silly damn fool's left the fawn off the hook!"
                    Lou Seeger, Port Washington, N.Y.

When my umbrella strikes a Polish fawn,
As through the woods of Cracow I meander,
'Tis not to chastise this unwitting pawn
Of Lenin's heirs, I act. NO! My Neander-
Thal impulse stems from brooding on November.
'Tis Nixon, not the fawn, my thoughts dismember.
                    Hugh Wheeler, Monterey, Mass.

Joan, with Q on every tile,
Used twelve to make IMPAIR;
Herb, in his quicksilver style,
Stacked CHASTISE on one square;
And so it was, amid the babble
That we mastered Polish Scrabble.
                    Frank Jacobs, N.Y.C.

Once armies wasted Asia's soil.
Now Nixon sends, as if gone wild,
Quicksilver planes with bombs to foil
Regrowth of tree, herb, rice, and child.
Yet fawning Congressmen avow
It's far too late to chastise now.

J. Bickart, N.Y.C.

"Herb Clone?" said Nixon fearfully,
"I don't believe I've met him!"
"It's Klein," an aide said cheerfully,
"It's easy to forget him!"
His thoughts impaired, his mind a blur,
"Chastise me not, I remember her!"

Bruce Kahn, Putney, Vt.

Mrs. Malaprop dismembers
Having had such fawn before!
Spiked herb tea and glowing embers
Sketch strange shapes upon the floor.
Ghosts impair, both large and smallish,
Gliding o'er the gleaming polish.

Rosemarie Williamson, Basking Ridge, N.J.

A Polish chemist made a fawn
From quicksilver and a secret herb;
And by the nineties, labs will spawn
Test-tube babies, claims a blurb.
So come 2000, when alone
And craving company, just clone!

Elliott Shevin, Detroit, Mich.

Your spirit's impaired, I know, and though
O'er your ev'ry need I meekly fawn,
I chastise you for passed fish stew, so go
To the tasty feed and linger long.
And polish it off, you'd better hear that,
Or tomorrow you'll wake up dismembered, dumb cat!

Sidney Lawrence, Berkeley, Calif.

My mistress's nails were polished like the sun,
Her eyelids sparkled like quicksilver.
Her chastised hair was piled in a bun,
A ringlet of crepe fawned upon her finger.
  Imagine her anguish, picture her pain,
  Without an umbrella, caught in the rain!
William Berliner, Woodmere, N.Y.

Jack's bride was quite busy at changing his home:
Dismembering bookshelves and chastising rugs,
Impairing the gloom with her bright polished chrome,
Pouring herb-flavored milk into rum-seasoned mugs,
Instinctively strangling what threatens a wife:
Jill killed her arch rival: Jack's old, careless life.
William F. Lanahan, Brooklyn, N.Y.

Meet your antagonist, polish your rhetoric,
Turn to quicksilver each elegant phrase;
Reason, not fawning, will help turn a better trick,
If you chastise you can balance with praise.
There must be an end to it some way, somehow,
So please, Mr. Nixon, get on with it now!
Marion Adams, Indianapolis, Ind.

The nun, an Ursuline, her steps impaired
By age, her mind, quicksilver once, now slow,
Its polish lost, with few bright fragments spared,
Takes black umbrella, convent gloves,
To seek an herb named in the ancient themes,
A promised cure for age, dismembered dreams.
Gerelyn Hollingsworth, St. Louis, Mo.

A Nixon clone we did create
Of bodies dismembered by shell and flak
Of Agnew's polished words of hate
And impaired justice for poor and black.
The clone replaced Dick in '72.
The country didn't notice, did you?
Arthur Zigouras, N.Y.C.

For oft, when on the couch I lie
In mind impaired, in heart chastised,
The resident Freud, with polished eye,
Dismembers me. I'm analyzed!
And then my brain with Nixon fills,
And dances with the daffodils.

Oliver M. Neshamkin, M.D., N.Y.C.

WORD ASSOCIATION
Umbrella—rain
Polish—shoes
Dismember—pain
Chastise—blues
River—flow
Nixon—go!

Joy C. Russack, N.Y.C.

Crab grass, long my favorite herb
For polishing off an acorn mousse,
Does not impair nor does it curb
My appetite for lilac juice.
Dismembering a luncheon clone,
I wonder why I eat alone.

Nita Savitz, Douglas Manor, N.Y.

My friend Herbie wears a tie,
His shoes are polished, chin is bared;
Chastises me when I get high,
Says my genes will be impaired.
He'll vote for Nixon, I've no doubt.
My friend Herb is sure far out.

Ilene McGrath, Englewood, N.J.

Sir Neville, the fawn, impaired by blind trust,
Held his umbrella shut tight in the rain.
Au contraire Sir Dick Nixon, who feels himself just,
As he makes legend his license of pain.

Parasol unfurled
To dismember the world?

Marty Ross, New Hyde Park, N.Y.

The quicksilver falls, the outlook is rain—
No umbrella will offer protection.
The Reds in Hanoi must be chastised again
So Nixon can win re-election.
Let Kissinger polish his latest lie . . .
Aggression is native, like apple pie!

John Kallir, Scarsdale, N.Y.

Polish your quill, for time,
Quicksilver fawn to power,
Impairs the poet's rhyme
To mark the tyrant's hour.
If bullets no longer tear, bombs do yet dismember.
With more shame than days, poets!
 Write for November!

Charles W. Soffel, N.Y.C.

True happiness is like an herb;
Its polished leaf one must impair,
Dismember, and the whole disturb
To bring its latent scent to air;
Quicksilver, then, in being known,
The corpse is left, the spirit flown.

Suzanne Spadola, N.Y.C.

The Masked Rider sprinkled his body with clone,
And said to his horse, "Let's go have us some fawn."
Unlike other Rangers, dismember's been Lone.
But that's not the way it'll be from now on.
"It's better to travel impairs, so they say.
Let's find a companion . . . Quicksilver, away!"

Jack Labow, N.Y.C.

'Twas noontime and the quicksilver clone
Did dismember in the shade,
All moldy was the rotten bone
And the umbrella was afraid.
"What does it mean?" asked Nixon. "I implore—"
"It means," said Henry, "they want to end the war."

Michael Siegel, Brooklyn, N.Y.

ODE TO WESTERN UNION
Impair was spelled repair; and fawn changed to fain.
Clone was alone; and herb became here.
Irate, I grabbed my umbrella and ran through the rain,
To complain—mad, insane I screamed in their ear
Upon losing control I did passionately swear.
"Sir, your mother likes sailors and your daughter's a where."

Richard Morris, Bridgeport, Conn.

Why chastise a wooden duck?
Or polish the edge of a cliff?
Why dismember a green Mack truck?
Or fawn in front of a stiff?
Why chew an umbrella? Are you daft?
Or is your purpose escaping the draft?

Alan Levine, Amityville, N.Y.

You were a fawn, running between quicksilver raindrops when I found you,
Your face, flower white beneath the umbrella of your scented hair
I had no charm against you then, herb, clove and incense, a witch's brew
That would, in time, my only heart impair.
I must remember, if we ever meet again,
How dangerous it is to find love in the rain.

J. K. Sapinsky, N.Y.C.

Pigs who go skydiving during monsoon
Ought to alter their sty-flying ways
Lest they end up dismembered, or in a lagoon,
Impairing the progress of poor Mrs. Hays.
Such wit as above, plus "The Nixon I've Known"
Hail from my guidebook: "The Sensuous Clone."
Diane Davis, Huntington, N.Y.

☞ *Contrived Nomenclature*

Lovely Houlihan—Irish-Hawaiian Dancer
Sleepy Harlow—Peroxide-blond Dwarf
Lilli Putt—Miniature Golf Pro

Above, contrived nomenclature. Competitors were invited to submit up to two invented names with apposite occupations.

Report: You are all very silly, I'm proud to say. *Et maintenant, les* repeats: JUSTIN CASE: Insurance Salesperson; PAUL BEARER: Mortician; CLAIRE VOYANT: Seeress; NATALIE CLAD and DELLA WEAR: Fashion Plates; WALTER WALL: Carpet Magnate; WANDA LUST: Travel Agent; SY "METHA" COHEN and EMIL NITRITE: Druggists; GLUTEUS MAXIMUS: Hip Emperor; BERTHA D. BLUES: Jazz Singer; LOIS CARMEN DENOMINATOR: Math Teacher; JACQUES STROPPE: Athlete; AGNES DEI, GLORIA MUNDI, MIA CULPA, and BARBARA SEVILLE: Actress/Models; AL FRESCO, POLA and YOGI BARE with their Indian son, RUNNING BARE: Streakers; GERRY MANDER: Politician; WARREN PEASE: Jurist; BESSIE-MAE MUCHO: Singer; DAWN SHIRLEY LIGHT: Lyricist; CLAUDE TIBBETTS: Lion Tamer; ELDER BERRY WEIN: Clergyman; MARIAN HASTE: Divorcée; NOLA CONTENDERE: Attorney; ROSE HIPS: Health-faddist/Stripper; SAL MONELLA: F.D.A. Inspector; PHIL O'DENDRON: Horticulturist; AUGUSTA WIND: Weatherperson; FREDA SLAVES: Militant; POLLY GRAPH: Policewoman; BERTHA VENETIAN: Gondolier; SEYMOUR GLASS: Window Cleaner; NOAH MOSS: Rolling Stone; GOLDA LOX: Deli owner; MAUDE LYNN and WELLA BAWLSOME: Sob Sisters; PERRY O'DONNELL: Dentist; and BILL and EMERY BORED: Disciples of Anouilh.

TOM PERDUE—Author of *Remembrance of Chickens Past*.

Hank Levinson, N.Y.C.

MÈRE D'ALORS—Concierge.

Rebecca Knapp, Cambridge, Mass.

JIM PEACH—Follower of Jack Hughes.

Stephen Bennett Yohalem, M.D., N.Y.C.

GEORGE SANK—Backstroke Champion of Poland.

Bernard Lovett, Hillside, N.J.

KNUDE ROCKNE—Coach of the First Varsity Streaking Team.

Erna Lovett, Hillside, N.J.

FLASH BORDEN—Notorious Streaking Milkman.

George Fairbanks, Nutley, N.J.

RUDOLPH BINGO—Impresario in the Basement of Our Lady of Victory.

Margaret M. Sauer, Riverdale, N.Y.

HERMAN DERANGE—Emotionally Disturbed Cowboy.

Raymond S. Kauders, N.Y.C.

GEORGE WASHINGTON CARVEL—Inventor of Peanut-Butter Ice Cream.
Hank Volker, N.Y.C.

HAROLD SQUARE—Conservative Buyer for Macy's.
Bruce Karp, Flushing, N.Y.

RORY BOREALIS—Film Star.
Toby Smith, N.Y.C.

AVA RICE—Acquisitive Actress.
Michael York, London, England

MATT JERSEY—Jazz Pianist from Trenton.
Nita Schroeder, Bedford Village, N.Y.

"LUCKY" OLSEN—Frankie Laine's Songwriter.
George E. Ward, N.Y.C.

KAREN FEADING, M.D.—Pediatrician.
Marie Berler, Syosset, N.Y.

MADAME LA FORGE—White House Executive Secretary.
Merrill P. Roseman, N.Y.C.

DON R. (GAY) APPAREL—Transvestite.
Jack Ryan, N.Y.C.

SAVANNAH FUMA—Cambodian-born Pollution Controller in Georgia.
L. J. Horwitz, Bronx, N.Y.

EMERALD AISLE—Usher, Abbey Theatre.
Charlotte Laiken, Bayside, N.Y.

UMBILICUS—Roman Naval Attaché.
Daniel F. Melia, Berkeley, Calif.

CASSIUS KETCHIKAN—Lean and Hungry Alaskan Wrestler.
Michael Schreiber, Brooklyn, N.Y.

Contrived Nomenclature / 157

DONNA HATCH—Toastperson.

Harold T. Miller, Plainfield, N.J.

RED BHUTANS—Himalayan Revolutionary.

Mobil Room 361, N.Y.C.

MC CORMACK REAPER—Inventive Brother of Jack the Reaper.

Warren Kask, N.Y.C.

PENNY LOAFER—College Co-ed, Pi Beta Phi.

Bob Issacson, San Francisco, Calif.

VINNIE VITO VICI—Jet Set Gigolo.

Nina Levy, Monsey, N.Y.

PAPA DOPOULOS—Gift-Bearing Haitian Dictator.

Robert Barrie, N.Y.C.

TERRY YAKKY—Talkative Japanese Chef.

Robert J. Blake, N.Y.C.

HEIDI FOKES—Country Radio Announcer.

J. and D. Hobbing, Berkeley, Calif.

FRANK X. POSAY—Muckraking Reporter.

Msgr. A. V. McLees, St. Albans, N.Y.

SNOOKY RANSOM—Leading Moneywinner on Kidnaping Charts.

Lee Rostal, N.Y.C.

JENNY FLEX—Y.W.C.A. Calisthenics Director.

William M. Goff, N.Y.C.

HEINZ ZEIT—German Historian (Follower of Forsyte).

N. W. Polsby, D. Bell, and P. Seabury, Berkeley, Calif.

JUAN FORDERODE—Mexican Bartender.

Richard Cagan, N.Y.C.

VERA SIMILITUDE—Broadway's Most Sought-after Understudy.

Irma E. Reichert, N.Y.C.

LEO TARD—Dimwitted Dancer.

Ellen Cohn, N.Y.C.

LEIGHTON PRINTZ—Police Fingerman.

Lee Greene, Briarcliff Manor, N.Y.

SAAB SISTERS—Swedish Car Dealers.

Donald E. Biederman, Garden City, N.Y.

PHIL MOON and M. T. ARMS—Hollywood Songwriters.

Florine McCain, N.Y.C.

LIZ S. TROTTA—Feminist-Nudist Sulky Driver.

John Weil, N.Y.C.

ST. IGNATIUS PAYOLA—Patron Saint of the Record Industry.

Robert A. Wilson, Texas

HICK JACKET—Manufacturer of Denim Shrouds.

Elaine Stallworth, Willow Grove, Pa.

ABRACA DEBORAH—Vanishing Cream Salesperson.

Sam Bassin, Brooklyn, N.Y.

REYNOLDS RAPP—Manufacturer of Aluminum Door Knockers.

Arthur J. Cunningham, N.Y.C.

BABE GOERING-GOERING KAHN—Star Home-Run Hitter, German League.

John J. Coniglio, Brooklyn, N.Y.

DIEM TZE—Vietnamese Centrist Politician.

Glen A. Ruzicka, Towson, Md.

Contrived Nomenclature / 159

DEB U THANT—First Woman's Secretary General of U.N.
Fred Strickhart, Irvington, N.J.

PATTON PENH DING—Inventive Oriental-Quaker General.
Joan Wilen, N.Y.C.

NGO DEM GUDH—Vietnamese Politician.
Elizabeth A. Widenmann, N.Y.C.

PERRY PHRASTIC—Latin Teacher.
Emanuel Landau, Teaneck, N.J.

HARDY HARHAR—Down-at-the-Heels Comedian.
Mr. and Mrs. James Davies, Princeton Junction, N.J.

VINCE LUMBAGO—Coach, Green Bay Backers.
Roy Hoffman, Forest Hills, N.Y.

THE PRONETOPOPOVS—Short-tempered Russian Skaters.
Marc Judson, Stanford, Calif.

DRED SCOTT FITZGERALD—Author of *Black Is Beautiful and Damned.*
Earle F. Maricle, St. Louis, Mo.

GRACIE MANSION—Famous Madam of the Eighties.
Ben Wickham, N.Y.C.

OZ CARMEYER—Sleight-of-Hand Frankfurter Producer.
Dodi Schultz, N.Y.C.

MARK DOWNS—Purveyor of Discount Tranquilizers.
Jerry Wachtel, Columbia, Md.

PERRY TORTE—Forensic Pastrymaker.
Fran Ross, N.Y.C.

BAMBI DEXTROUS—Transvestite Exotic Dancer.
Ross Becker, Newtown Square, Pa.

DONNY OZYMANDIAS—Fallen Rock 'n' Roll King.
Baylor Board of Old Trustees, Chattanooga, Tenn.

MILES TOUGEAU—Circuit Poet.
>*Irene McInerney, West Lafayette, Ind.*

CANDY BERGMAN—Sweet-toothed Film Director.
>*Irwin S. Epstein, Spring Valley, N.Y.*

CORLESS ARCHER—Sloppy Bowperson.
>*George Malko, N.Y.C.*

PETER SALT—Secretariat's Veterinarian.
>*Laura Wilson, Dallas, Texas*

TANTE PIS—Eccentric Relative of Well-Known Belgian Mannequin.
>*Jack Rose, N.Y.C.*

HERB HENRY NEWELL—City Redevelopment Chairman.
>*Bill Thurston, Danbury, Conn.*

ELKE PONE—Author of *South German Cooking—Is It a Crime?*
>*Ruth Brewster, Hillside, N.J.*

JUAREZ HILL—Spanish Pacifist.
>*Ken Fritz, Los Angeles, Calif.*

GUY WIRE—Western Union Messenger.
>*David Laiken, Bayside, N.Y.*

PERRY MUTUEL—N.Y.R.A. Attorney.
>*R. Valeriani, Washington, D.C.*

SEAN LAMB—Victim of Con Artist.
>*W. R. Richardson, Peacedale, R.I.*

SHAUN TELL—Third Grader with Arrow, Apple.
>*Roger McMillan, Orinda, Calif.*

C. C. SPOT—Author of Children's Books.
>*Virginia Herzfeld, Linden, N.J.*

MONTY VIDEO—Latin TV Star.
> David M. Hart, N.Y.C.

DEAN JOHN—Head of the Department of Plumbing.
> Jan Zerby, Amherst, Mass.

LADONNA MOBILOIL—Chairperson, Italian Petroleum Industries.
> Allan G. Sperling, Rye, N.Y.
> C. M. Addiego, Bayside, N.Y.

MONTE CELLO—Conductor, Catskills Philharmonic.
> Ed Donath, Peekskill, N.Y.

ROLAND ROCK—Confused Musician.
> Jean Devine, Baldwin, N.Y.

TELLY FOTOS—Greek News Photographer.
> M. Greenberg, Bronx, N.Y.

ARI KARI—Greek-Japanese Shipbuilder with Suicidal Bent.
> Stanley Stone, Oceanside, N.Y.

LENNY PROUST—Stand-up Memory Expert.
> Fred Danzig, Eastchester, N.Y.

GROUCHO LENIN—Revolutionist with a Sense of Humor.
> Allen Balla, New Hyde Park, N.Y.

MOCK SPITZ—Animal Impersonator.
> Richard S. Weiner, N.Y.C.

HAYDN ZEKE—Reclusive Mountain Musician.
> Sylvia Baumgarten, Far Rockaway, N.Y.

"LOX" NESS—Secret Agent for the F.D.A.
> Harold Brewster, Hillside, N.J.

WILL KOMMEN—Captain, Lufthansa Airlines.
> Joe Schaffner, Alfred, N.Y.

HUCKLE BERRIGAN—Jesuit Friend of Tom Sawyer.
>*Elsie Angell, Greenville, R.I.*

EUNICE X. DENHAM—Designer of Mod Clothes.
>*Rowland Barber, Beverly Hills, Calif.*

CRRIE NTION—Occuption, Proofreder.
>*Barbara B. Talley, Burnsville, N.C.*

HUAN EN TRI—Competition Editor, *Saigon* Magazine.
>*Edward Steinberg, Silver Spring, Md.*

GLUTEUS MAXIMUS—Roman Rear Admiral.

WLADYSAW SIMON—Pole Faulter.
>*John Coniglio, Brooklyn, N.Y.*

N. "LOCO" PARENTIS—Crazed Baby Sitter.

ARCH DIOCESE—Playful Papal Legate.
>*Jack Ryan, N.Y.C.*

MADMAN POMPADOUR—Used Car Salesman Turned Avant-Garde Hairdresser.

FLUNKY BROADWAY—David Merrick's Right-Hand Man.
>*Lyn Semels, Riverdale, N.Y.*

GEORGE BLIMPTON—Dilettante Zeppelin Pilot.
>*Ilene McGrath, Englewood, N.J.*

PASCAL LAMB—Physicist and Free-lance Kosher Butcher.

SALLY FOURTH—Queen of Poland.
>*Dan Greenburg, N.Y.C.*

DON VITO PAN—Fairy Godfather.
>*Sy and Ruth Kaplowitz, Parsippany, N.J.*

RICHARD REFUSE—Tired, Poor, Tempest-Toss'd Immigrant.
>*Margot Howard, N.Y.C.*

Contrived Nomenclature / 163

THINKER BELLE—Rodin's Mistress.
Jan Leighton, N.Y.C.

BUSBY BURPEE—Director Gone to Seed.
Helene Arthurs, Keansburg, N.J.

GOWER OF PISA—Italian Choreographer.
PASTOR AL SWEET—Country Priest.
Laura DeMarco, Bronx, N.Y.

MAHATMA KILOWATT—Passive Resister.
Martin J. Levine, Teaneck, N.J.

WINNIE THE POOR—Former Prime Minister Seeking Employment.
Mrs. Frances Erenburg, Rutherford, N.J.

MONTGOMERY ROBERTS—Ward Healer.
Michael Wooly, Alexandria, Va.

MONTGOMERY WEIRD—Transylvanian Department Store Executive.
HOME, JAMES—Self-Employed Chauffeur.
Bill Blanchard, N.Y.C.

PRINCE VALIUM—Calm Hero of Middle Ages.
JULIUS SEIZURE—Military Man with Cardiac Symptoms.
Ellen and Rolf Korstvedt, Tappan, N.Y.

VANCE BEAUJOLAIS—Iowa based Food and Drink Writer.
M. Bender, N.Y.C.

HOWES BAYOU—Louisiana's Official Greeter.
LAZAR BEAM—Israeli Optical Scientist.
Ellis Schein, Reading, Pa.

CONNIE FRANCES MACK—Soprano Truckdriver.
Stephanie J. Marks, Northampton, Mass.

LUKE HOMEWARD—Angel.

SANFORD R. BROCHURE—Real-Estate Agent.
Joan H. Priore, Coram, N.Y.

HANS ORFF—Touchy German Composer.
J. Bickart, N.Y.C.

JUDGE M. COHAN—Actor/Referee.
Mrs. S. Lipchonsky, Flushing, N.Y.

MILES TOGO—Night-Shift Cabdriver.

AYN PEA—Reactionary Tea Merchant.
Charles C. Dahlberg, M.D., N.Y.C.

HY CHAPARRAL—Jewish Cowboy.
Michael S. Bennett, Evanston, Ill.

GITTEL LONG—Jewish Cowgirl.

GITTEL LITTLE—Free-Love Advocate.
Bob Rose, Bloomfield, N.J.

"POP" SMEAR—Elderly Gynecologist.

"BABY" REBOZO—Midget Clown.
Marshall and Emily Karp, N.Y.C.

"BOOTS" DEBUSSCHERE—Dribble Puss.

POPE ADOLF—Benign Despot.
John M. Scott, Philadelphia, Pa.

FERMI LABUSH—Close-Mouthed Atomic Scientist.

TENNYSON D. DE DEEP—A Whale of a Poet.
Anne Law, Rowayton, Conn.

ADOLPH LITTLER—Argentine Golf Pro.

FLORENCE OF ARABIA—Elmhurst Bnai Brith Defector, now U.A.L. Leader.
Walter Marks, N.Y.C.

FANNY FORMER—Retired Girdle Fitter.

MA FIAT—Head of Stolen Sports Car Syndicate.
S. Steven Siporin, Los Angeles, Calif.

PRETTY ASA PITCHER—Good-Looking Jewish Gunga Din.
Arthur Weller, Interlaken, N.Y.

O'TIMON DE RIVER—Irish-Athenian Homeseeker.
James Fechheimer, Glen Head, N.Y.

HELEN BACK—Lady War Correspondent.

MAUREEN CORPS—Mistress of the Military Strip.
Martyn T. Denlea, N.Y.C.

ROBINSON CARUSO—Singer/Man Friday.

LIZZIE STRATA—Zero Population Specialist.
Frank Colangelo, Bronx, N.Y.

BRILLIANT-SAVARIN—Demanding French Coffee Connoisseur.

ANN RAND—Author with Identity Crisis.
Patricia Redis, Flushing, N.Y.

VENAL VEDA VICHY—World War II Collaborationist-Prostitute (Living in France with Roman Background).

SYBIL WRIGHTS—Militant Prophetess.
Jack Sydow, Seattle, Wash.

SOSUMI ARETI—Waiter in Japanese Delicatessen.
Paul Desmond, N.Y.C.

BOSTON CARMEN—High-Tea Cigarette Girl.
John Chantler, Detroit, Mich.

MERLE OBERAMMERGAU—Passionate Actress.

TALLY RAND—Diplomatic Fanhandler.
The Dorenkamps, Worcester, Mass.

CHIEF RED DOG—Kansas City's Indian Linebacker.

BUCK SKIN—Star of Western Nudies.

Louis S. Pryor, New Canaan, Conn.

A. ROSE CONPOLLO—Andalusian Cook.

Sue Antman, Evanston, Ill.

HADASSAH GARDENGROW—Chairwoman, Israeli Memorial Forest Fund.

"COMMUNITY" SINGH—New Delhi Municipal Recreation Director.

Judy Tetzlaff, Evanston, Ill.

RHINO NEAL—African Big-Game Hunter Who Never Says He's Sorry.

PEARL E. SHELLS—Ukulele Player for Lovely Houlihan.

Jim Milton, San Francisco, Calif.

"PA" DEDEUX—Father of Twins.

SIMPER FIDELIS—A Loyal Friend You'd Like to Be Rid of.

Molly Yonderhill, N.Y.C.

ELEPHANTS GERALD—Pachyderm Jazz-Singing Group.

BERNARD MALAMUTE—Dog Story Author.

Bradford Willett, Ingleside, Calif.

VIDA MINH—Vietnamese Baseball Player.

MIDAS WELBY—Incredibly Wealthy Physician.

Linda Lashbrook, Fanwood, N.J.

"NO GOOD" DIDI—Failed Girl Scout.

RALPH NADIR—Consumer Advocate with Low Standards.

Alice Brickner, Bronx, N.Y.

ZERO MOTEL—Fiddler on Roof of Holiday Inn.

AQUILINE ONASSIS—Big Bird of the Jet Set.

Melvin S. Alpren, West Orange, N.J.

Contrived Nomenclature / 167

ARISTOTLE CONSENSUS—Democratic Dark Horse.

MARK TWANG—Bluegrass Musician.
>Paul D. Hoekstra, Oakland, N.J.

YEGGS BENEDICT—Monk Turned Safecracker.
>Jerry and Cynthia Dantzig, Brooklyn, N.Y.

"EGGS BENEDICT" ARNOLD—Betrayer of Secret Recipes.

SANTA BERGER—Father Chanukah.
>William Schallert, Pacific Palisades, Calif.

STANLEY KOFF—Intellectual Hockey Star.

JOHN DARM—The French Connection.
>Betsy Holland Gehman, Middletown, Conn.

RORY BOREALIS—Eskimo Film Star.

DAMON DE LA RENTA—Hispanic Landlord.
>Jack Rose, N.Y.C.

GYPSY MOTHRA—Outsize Exotic Dancer.
>Cal and Fran Ackerman, Teanack, N.J.

CLARK KANT—Mild-Mannered Philosopher.*

ABBA EGAN—Irish-Israeli Detective.
>Barbara Schlesinger, N.Y.C.
>* Similarly: Lewis Bart Stone, N.Y.C.

DOLLY LAMA—Tibetan Matchmaker.

NEVA MOORE—Raven Trainer.
>Fred Cline, N.Y.C.

MONTE AZUMA—Vengeful Japanese-Mexican Importer/Exporter.

JEROME WOODLAWN—Underworld Authority, Well-Connected in Bronx.
>Mal Goldenberg, Plainview, N.Y.

JEWELS LA VERNE—Fortuneteller.

JANE, HENRY, AND PETER FONDUE—Kurdish Entertainers.
>Asa J. Berlin, State College, Pa

HUGO IGO—Secret Service Man.

ROSE N. KRANTZ—Stern Gilder.

JACK BLACK—Dealer.

MINNIE MAX—Game Player.

FAY STEW—Nixon Economic Adviser.
> *Math Coffee Room, University of N.C., Chapel Hill*

KODIAK ARREST—Heartless Mountie.
> *Jeanne Scholz, Madison, Conn.*

HALF GAYNOR—Movie Star and Former Olympic Diving Champ.
> *Kaky Dafler, Yardley, Pa.*

TENNESSEE FALSE—Playwright Impersonator.

BUNKER HULL—Bigoted Secretary of State.
> *Harvey Chipkin, Rutherford, N.J.*

CARMEN VERANDA—Latin-American Porch Singer.
> *Mr. and Mrs. Hal Marc Arden, Shelter Island, N.Y.*

MADISON SQUARE CARDIN—Unimaginative Wisconsin Designer.

CUPID BOW—The "It" Reindeer.
> *William Jeanes, Jackson, Miss.*

CHARLIE CHAPLAIN—Religious Tramp.

DITA BEERED—A Grand Old Partygoer.
> *Richard Fitzgerald, Malvern, Pa.*

BJORN FREE—Norwegian Lion Tamer.

ELSA VANDERBILT—Social Lioness.
> *Anthony L. Morgan, N.Y.C.*

TORTILLA FATS—Mexican Pool Shark.
> *James Chotas, N.Y.C.*

RON GORILLA—Tree-Dwelling Photographer.
> *Eric A. Stone, N.Y.C.*

WESTMINSTER ABBEY—English Love-Lorn Columnist.
"TWOFER" TEE—Theatrical Golf Pro.
>
> *Rita Halley, Hastings-on-Hudson, N.Y.*

JACQUES HUGHES—District Attorney.
>
> *Mary Lynne Shapiro, N.Y.C.*

LAURA INERTIA—Lady Physicist.
>
> *Aben Rudy, West New York, N.J.*

JIMINY CROCKETT—King Cricket of the Wild Frontier.
HAILE GOLIGHTLY—Small-Town Girl Who Made Good as Empress.
>
> *Marvin Goodman, N.Y.C.*

DEUS X. MACNAMARA—Attempted Savior of the Vietnamese People.
SAM SPAYED—Defective Detective.
>
> *John Hellegers, East Setauket, N.Y.*

SITTING BULK—Obese Indian Chief.
TUESDAY SUNDAY—Actress Who Married Preacher's Nephew.
>
> *Jonathan Abrams, Brooklyn, N.Y.*

SESAME STREET—Belly-Dancing Legal Secretary.
LES S. MOORE—Minimalist Painter.
>
> *Amy Kassiola, Brooklyn, N.Y.*

RON DELAY—Poetic Train Dispatcher for the Long Island R.R.
RUSHIN' BARE—Chronically Late Stripper.
>
> *Joyce Terner, N.Y.C.*

MAGDA CARTA—Budapest Garbagewoman.
MONA LOA—Hawaiian Torch Singer.
>
> *Frank Jacobs, N.Y.C*

PACHY SANDRA—Elephant Seeress.

LAVA LAVA—Samoan Soapmaker.

Fran Ross, N.Y.C.

CLOUD RAINES—Comanche Actor.

ION PAISLEY—North Irish Chemist.

Jay Folb, N.Y.C.

BURKE SPEERIDGE—Distinguished Linesman.

Msgr. A. V. McLees, St. Albans, N.Y.

PATTY O'FURNITURE—Irish Lawnchair Maker.

HAIFA SIXPANTS—Israeli Tailor: "Trousers for Every Day in the Week."

Frances V. Killpatrick, Scarsdale, N.Y.

IVAN HOE—Russian Farmer.

SIR ADOLPH CONAN DOYLE—Right-Wing Propaganda Writer.

Louis de la Foret, New Orleans, La.

PRINCE VARIANT—Japanese Royal Deviate.

K. Kobayashi, Bronx, N.Y.

NOBEL S. O'BLEAGE—Irish Authority on International Protocol.

SUE K. ACKEY—Harvard Professor of Home Economics and Noted Japan-Watcher.

Raymond Maher, Bronx, N.Y.

BOO MERINGUE—Much Married Baked Goods Heiress.

Charles Almon, N.Y.C.

NIXON CRANNIES—Politician Who Hides Things..

Edwin R. Apfel, N.Y.C.

WRIGGLY FIELD—Belly-Dancing Member of Chicago Mercantile Family.

Albert G. Miller, N.Y.C.

TY TANIC—Esther Williams' Leading Man.

BUNNY HOP—One-Legged Starlet.
> *Marilyn Madderom, Brooklyn, Heights, N.Y.*

JACKSON HIDES—Queens County Schizophrenic Furrier.
> *Paul Nobel, N.Y.C.*

ZIPPA DE DOODAH—Southern Stripteuse.
> *Joseph Duchac, N.Y.C.*

MARK THIRTY—Obituary Writer.

LUKE WARMER—Glove Manufacturer.
> *George Fairbanks, Nutley, N.J.*

SHERLOCK HOMES—House Detective.
> *Kenneth Malkin, Hillsdale, N.J.*

YOKO ONUS—Oppressive Multimedia Artist.

CORBETT MONICKER—Eponymous Comedian.
> *T. P. Edwards, N.Y.C.*

GOWEST YOUNGMAN—Job Counselor Given to One-Liners.
> *Karen N. Dakan, Sarasota, Fla.*

PRETTYBOY FREUD—Well-Adjusted Hoodlum.
> *Leslie Wheeler, Lakewood, N.J.*

OLIVER DE PLACE—Dickensian Playboy.
> *Jan Parkinson, Kansas City, Mo.*

AMBER LIGHT—School-Crossing Guard.
> *Ann Sigmund Cahn, N.Y.C.*

SLAPPY ROCKEFELLER—World's Richest Clown.
> *Richard C. Van Wiebe, Fort Wayne, Ind.*

HUGH HEFFER—Male Chauvinist Cow.

JOHN V. KINSEY—Mayor of Sex City.
> *O. Grassel, Woodside, N.Y.*

GAUCHO MARX—Left-Wing Argentine Cowboy.
Toni Marco, Brooklyn, N.Y.

MODEL HOLMES—Comely Real-Estate Agent.
BANG LA DESH—Moslem Stripper.
Jack Labow, N.Y.C.

MANDRAKE ROOT—Web-Footed Male Cheerleader.
Jules D. Grisham, Brooklyn, N.Y.

MOUSIE TUNG—Disney World Ping-Pong Player.
BURNEY REYNOLDS—Year's Hottest Male Model.
Sharon Isch, Washington, D.C.

RUMPLE SUITZKIN—Sloppy Elfin Tailor.
JOHN OCTOGENARIAN—Elderly Armenian.
R. K. Jones, Harrington Park, N.J.

COLE STU NEWCASTLE—Unemployed Porter.
Erna Lovett, Hillside, N.J.

"ROBBER" DUCKIE—Godfather's Tub-Mate.
Mrs. Michael Zales, Greenwich, Conn.

COZY NOSTRA—Comfortable Sicilian Family Man.
Myron H. Milder, Omaha, Neb.

IRIS HADRIAN—Roman Emperor's Blond Sister.
FRIEDA UNESCORT—German Lady Who Travels Alone.
Tom Morrow, N.Y.C.

PNOM DE PLUMH—(Penh name of) Cambodian Writer.
Maurice Varon, Bronx, N.Y.

PITHECANTHROPUS ERECTOR—Prehistoric Toymaker.
PRAYING MANTILLA—Spanish Evangelist.
Byron E. Fox, N.Y.C.

MANNY "HAPPY" RETURNS—Tax Counselor.

JUMPING G. HOSOFAT—Weight Watchers Skydiver.
B. and O. Katz, N.Y.C.

DEGAS VU—Painter You've Already Seen.

TRUMAN KAPUT—"Finished" Literary Haberdasher.
Barbara P. Alpren, West Orange, N.J.

HORATIO ALGAE—Rags-to-Riches Botanist.

RANDEE MC NALLEE—She Put Minsky's on the Map.
Rosemarie Williamson, Basking Ridge, N.J.

HELGA HUGHES—Female Impersonator.
Charles Douglas, N.Y.C.

☞ *One-Letter Misprints*

"Why Can't a Woman Be More Like a Mat?"
"The Old Wives' Sale"

Above, familiar phrases changed in meaning by a one-letter misprint. Competitors were invited to alter, by one-letter substitution, an aphorism, title, slogan, proper or product name, line from a song, or the like.

Report: For no apparent reason, three distinct, not to say disparate, themes were reprised: homosexuality, animals, and antiwar. We've run this contest before. Therefore, many worthy but familiar efforts innocently submitted by recent converts were ineligible. Among them: "Nobody knows the trouble I've been"; *Love's Labours Cost;* He who hesitates is last; "I never let a man I didn't like"; "Thou shalt now . . ."; and "Let me make one thing perfectly clean." New but also duplicated: *The Art of French Hooking; The French Confection;* Gun City; Women's Lip; and "A miss is as good as a male." Herewith the most-often-used substitution (you supply the appropriate aphorism): wife/life; nose/rose; way/lay; honey/money; sweet/sweat; leap/leak; union/onion;

soul/soup; goy/boy: raven/maven; bush/bust; Mr./Ms.; make/fake; lover/loser; feel/feed; far/fat; whore/where; brothel/brother; cover/covet; and prey/pray. Occasional derelictions: the addition or deletion (rather than substitution) of a letter or a change based on punctuation. Generally, we preferred the aptly altered *aphorism* to the simply switched *word*. Ah, but then, as so many of you observed, the mass of men lead wives of quiet desperation.

"They call the wino Maria"

Robert Blake, N.Y.C.

"Look, stranger—there ain't enough room in this gown for the two of us."

Dan Matics, Chattanooga, Tenn.

Lie Down in Harkness

Robert Bianchi, N.Y.C.

Chock Full O' Nuns—The Heavenly Coffee

Fred Cline, N.Y.C.

"You said you loved me; or were you just being kind? Or am I losing my mink?"

David Mann, Bronx, N.Y.

Caution: Misuse of the pills contained herein could prove fetal.

Roland Brave, Baltimore, Md.

"Boss, You Is My Woman Now"

Alice M. Yohalem, N.Y.C.
Janet Davidson, Los Angeles, Calif.

"There are fairies at the bottom of my warden"

James Fechheimer, Glen Head, N.Y.

"Take my wand, I'm a stranger in paradise"

Ford Hovis, N.Y.C.

"They call her frivolous Hal, a peculiar sort of a gal"
Corinne Latta, N.Y.C.

"Et tu, Bruce?"
Jay McDonnell, N.Y.C.

The Loveliness of the Long-Distance Runner
Donald Weisel, Rego Park, N.Y.

"Buck, Be a Lady Tonight"
Carey B. Gold, N.Y.C.

"I think I am failing in love"
Alissa Abrams, Brooklyn, N.Y.

Punch and Judo
Sylvan H. Greene, Wyncote, Pa.

"Miss Otis regrets she's unable to lynch today"
Betsey Ansin, Leominster, Mass.

"But the poet of them all is the one that is called the card of Stratford-on-Avon."
Marjorie C. Silverman, N.Y.C.

"Men seldom make passes at girls who wear Blasses"
Paul Elliott, N.Y.C.

". . . I was the product of a dating mother . . ."
Richard H. Freeman, Summit, N.J.

"I'm just mild about Harry"
Anne Wiedre, Brooklyn, N.Y.
Alfred N. Greenberg, N.Y.C.

"What fight through yonder window breaks?"
Patricia Miller, N.Y.C.

"I Dream of Jeannie with the Light Brown Heir"
M. Johanna Miller, Brooklyn, N.Y.
Rose Fagin, Huntington Woods, Mich.

"Sumer is icemen in"
Martin E. Healy, Sag Harbor, N.Y.

Had Amy lately?
Christopher Curtis, N.Y.C.

Rome wasn't built in a bay.
Richard Bredhoff, Brooklyn, N.Y.
Jack Schindler, Brooklyn, N.Y.

"Workers Arise! You have nothing to lose but your chairs!"
Rowland Barber, Beverly Hills, Calif.

Six and the Single Girl
William Schallert, Pacific Palisades, Calif.

"In Xanadu did Khubla Khan a stately pleasure dame decree"
Mrs. Thalia Stern, Miami Beach, Fla.

"Anyone who mates dogs and babies can't be all bad"
Jan M. Abrams, N.Y.C.

Gladys Knight and the Pigs
Joseph Duchac, N.Y.C.

"Where on the duck my captain lies / fallen cold and dead"
Sari Teichman, Miami Beach, Fla.

"Faster than a speeding pullet . . ."
S. L. Schlesinger, Larchmont, N.Y.

Unsafe at Ant Speed
John R. Driskill, Maryville, Tenn.

"I have nothing to offer but blood . . . sweat and bears"
Judith Christian, N.Y.C.

You can't make a silk purse out of a sow's oar
Carol Rosen, N.Y.C.

To Each His Owl
>> Pani Kolb, New Orleans, La.

"Make it one for my baby and one more for the toad"
>> H. Slavitz, N.Y.C.
>> Tom Morrow, N.Y.C.

Love me, lave my dog.
>> Marion Briggs, West Tisbury, Mass.

"We have met the enemy and they are curs"
>> Christian A. Zabriskie, N.Y.C.
>> Russell W. Annich, Jr., Princeton, N.J.

The Autobiography if Howard Hughes
>> Rees Behrendt, N.Y.C.
>> Stanley D. Chess, East Meadow, N.Y.

"I think, therefore I um"
>> Ken Wolff, Bronx, N.Y.

Ill the News That's Fit to Print
>> Leo Taubes, Teaneck, N.J.

Who says a good newspaper has to be bull?
>> Joel F. Crystal, Brooklyn, N.Y.

"You say potato and I say potuto"
>> Dennis Brite, N.Y.C.

"Little Things Mean a Tot"
>> Lois K. Geller, N.Y.C.

Rolls-Royce: The Bust Car in the World
>> David Cobb, Toronto, Canada

Helen Girley Brown
>> Susan Ferla, Providence, R.I.

"We Three Mings of Orient Are"
>> Mrs. Barbara Payne, N.Y.C.

"Population, when unchecked, increases in a geometrical patio"

Henry Henegar, Chattanooga, Tenn.

Trivia Nixon

Sheila Ffolliott, Philadelphia, Pa.

Legalize Pat

Ed Schultz, N.Y.C.

Where there's a will there's a wad

Valerie Lenza, Staten Island, N.Y.

The Lisp of Adrian Messenger

Barbara B. Carroll, Forest Hills, N.Y.

The Gang That Couldn't Thoot Straight

Toby Smith, N.Y.C.

Let's Score Jessica to Death

Paul Desmond, N.Y.C.

"Don't scoot until you see the whites of their eyes"

Paul Weiss, Washington, D.C.

"The Surrey with the Fridge on Top"

Charlotte Curtis, N.Y.C.

"A stag danced and I was born"

Walter Broadstreet, N.Y.C.

"Those Wedding Bills Are Breaking Up That Old Gang of Mine"

Teddy Huxford, Skaneateles, N.Y.

Bus Stop—Go Standing

David E. Diener, Irvington, N.Y.

"Parking is such sweet sorrow"

Steve Brody, Yorktown Heights, N.Y.

Beverly Sills, Cal.
D. Young, N.Y.C.

"Please don't walk about me when I'm gone"
Larry Lederman, N.Y.C.

An Oily Child Is a Lonely Child
Maurice Varon, Bronx, N.Y.

Klopman—a man you can lead on.
Fr. William J. O'Malley, Rochester, N.Y.

"Stone walls do not a prison make nor iron bars a cafe"
Miles Klein, East Brunswick, N.J.

Dime Is Money
Max Zigas, Bronx, N.Y.

When you live in New York you need all the hemp you can get
Jack Rose, N.Y.C.

"Hark, Hark, the Nark . . ."
Morton A. Rauh, Yellow Springs, Ohio

Judge not, that ye be not jugged
Gerald R. Dorman, Brooklyn, N.Y.

Happily even after
M. S. Arentzen, Brooklyn Heights, N.Y.

"Little Miss Muffet sat on a buffet eating her curds and whey"
S. Musso, West Hempstead, N.Y.

Fiddler on the Roof—starring Nero Mostel
Sherman Davis, N.Y.C.

Would You Buy a Used War from This Man?
Mrs. Barbara Wolf, Portland, Me.
Vivien Friedman, N.Y.C.

Tet and Sympathy
> Susan Fishman, N.Y.C.

". . . My country right on wrong"
> V. Johnston Cooper, Cumberland, Md.

There's a Fort in Your Future
> Eileen Hall, Tarrytown, N.Y.

"I sing of arms and the ban"
> Trudy Drucker, Newark, N.J.

War End Peace
> James H. Hughes, Fresh Meadows, N.Y.

Amerika.
> Elaine Nissen, Brooklyn Heights, N.Y.

☞ *Flat Verse*

I met him in the east, and twice he brought me flowers.
We walked alone and often. Sometimes we walked for hours.
We stopped to sip May wine. He undertipped the waiter.
And then, of course, came the divorce. But that was some time later.

Above, uninspired poetry. Competitors are invited to submit a sample of Flat Verse, which may rhyme as well as scan, but should be "essentially uncontroversial and devoid of any trace of emotion." Limit 8 lines.

Report: Flat Verse. Yes. Well. Neither Henry Gibson nor Henrik Ibsen; a kind of Miniver Cheevy poem prevailed. Almost all were "flat" enough—but many poems managed enough tone for respectability. And some proved humorful—Ogden Nash *manqué*—which hardly qualifies as "devoid of emotion." Others, political poems, let us say, seemed to violate the "uncontroversial" rule (we wanted uncontro verse). And what else? Poems of Beckett-y blackness. Poems old, poems new. Poems borrowed, even blue. Greeting-card rhymes. Poems about

Flat Verse / 183

writing poems, winning this Competition or nonsense poems. Childish poems. Poems not merely bad-bad, but silly-bad. And, as we said, poems entirely too *good*. Still, the flat majority seemed marvelously mediocre and provided the following snacks for thought:

Who could have left their laundry in the drier next to mine?
Of who they are, or where they've gone, there isn't any sign.
The drier's stopped revolving and the drum is now inert;
The clothes are lying in a heap without a trace of dirt.

Fred Berg, Boston, Mass.

Bees are always busy flitting,
Sipping buds and sucking blossoms.
Never do we see them sitting
Placidly like cats or possums.

Albert G. Miller, N.Y.C.

I run the computer for a large corporation
(One of the biggest companies in the nation).
The computer does payroll and accounts receivable—
It calculates so fast it's unbelievable.
I just punch the cards, the computer reads them in,
And it automatically knows where to begin.
The computer room is quiet and air-conditioned too.
Don't you think computing is the job for you?

J. Bickart, N.Y.C.

My mail's addressed to "resident,"
Which happens to no President,
Perhaps because their pictures go
On postage stamps with paste below.
Not that I do seek their fame,
Just letters that will bear my name,

Which, better still, my child should do;
Would not call it "resident," would you?
Michael Schreiber, Brooklyn, N.Y.

My husband likes to say *banal*
While I pronounce it *banal*.
I say it rhymes, not with *canal*,
But properly with *anal*.
Rollie Hochstein, Tenafly, N.J.

I was changing the litter in the cat's dirt box
The night you called to ask
If you could borrow my brother's socks
And I said yes and resumed my task.
The following day the cat's fur fell
All off when you returned the socks
And some other things you borrowed as well.
Fur's not heir to such natural shocks.
Nick Knebels, Philadelphia, Pa.

No longer will large spectacles disgrace
What otherwise would be a pretty face.
No longer is there any need to cry
Putting hard lenses in the eye.
Surely he must be judged as one of men's
Great benefactors who discovered the soft lens.
Leo Taubes, Teaneck, N.J.

"I know why you're confused," said she. "My uncle married twice.
You're thinking of his second wife, the former Helen Brice.
The one that I was speaking of I know you'll recollect—
We met her at that dinner for her son, the architect.
Her eldest son, that is, of course; the younger one's in law.
That evening he was sitting with a girl from Omaha. . . ."
Kate Schreibman, Corona, N.Y

Flat Verse

A few weeks ago, I forget just when,
My favorite summer reruns, like *Gentle Ben,*
Were canceled for some party in Miami.
TV Guide now warns us that coming soon
Some other folks'll howl at that Miami moon
And I'll never know what happened to Tabatha's Grammy . . .

Ann Park, San Francisco, Calif.

Not seeing each other for ages, they lunched but a month ago.
They walked a few blocks to a restaurant, then went to a fashion show.
Returning by way of a taxi, whose driver had slightly gray hair,
They sat by opposite windows, each eating a chocolate eclair.

Pama Hoopes, Greenville, Del.

One night as I lay drowsing in bed,
A noisy scuffle disturbed the quiet;
A horrid scream, enough to wake the dead,
Someone thinking of murder had decided to try it.
I thought of moving, yawned and rolled over instead,
"I'll read it in the *News* tomorrow—if I buy it."

Blossom Nicinski, N.Y.C.

That day you won the sulky race, and slept for several hours,
Miss Wright was in her garden here, attending to her flowers—
Installing stakes for hollyhocks, transplanting bits of rue,
And picking twenty daffodils she later gave to you.
Eleven years have passed since then, and you are thirty-three—
Four times a dad, a college grad—in fact a Ph.D.

You own three cars, a twelve-room house beside
   Manhasset Bay.
According to the *Weekly News,* Miss Wright has moved
   away.
                    James Fechheimer, Glen Head, N.Y.

He checked in with a blue suit in his case.
Unpacking it, his large hands were adept.
He lay down after having washed his face,
And woke up early, realizing he'd slept.
                    Lesly Bradley, Floral Park, N.Y.

She began to undress like a stripper at work,
As he watched with cool fascination.
As she started her dance,
He gave one more glance,
And got off at the 14th Street Station.
                    Sidney Abrams, Brooklyn, N.Y.

Out of West End Avenue, he came.
Out of East End Avenue, she came.
By Fate, on Fifth they neared a meeting,
Paused then passed without a greeting.
He, Gabe Pressman's dentist, and
She, a girl whose mother used to know Alice Faye,
Once.
                    Jack Ryan, N.Y.C.

"My uncle's farm was near a creek;
We went there ev'ry other week.
My constant pal was the bulldog, Lad;
(One August a heat-wave drove him mad.)
Last night I had a fuzzy dream:
I saw the house beside the stream;
A flock of ducks perched on a gray log.
And then my view was obscured by fog."
                    Elaine Stallworth, Willow Grove, Pa.

I spent most of the day having my daughter
And was thirsty when it was done.
Finally they brought me some water.
Fortunately he hadn't wanted a son.
She was kind of small although all right
But soon they had to take her away.
My Mom got a chance to tell me that night
What happened on *General Hospital* that day.

       Maxine Troop, Decatur, Ga.

Lord Nelson asked his analyst:
"Why must this chilling dream persist?
I'm standing in Trafalgar Square
In nothing but my underwear."

       Annie Aronson, N.Y.C.

He always said he would
Join the Foreign Legion
If ever I would leave him.
I did.
First came Ingrid, then Enid,
Juanita, Carmen and Anna Marie.
We reconciled for a while
Me and this man of mystery.

       Mrs. A. Cook, Astoria, N.Y.

Perched along the windy edges
Of their narrow cliffside ledges,
Bonaventure Island's birds
Squawk out raucous avian words
At the motor-driven launches
From which tourists—on their haunches,
With binoculars to eyes—
Stare at them birdwatcherwise.

       S. Brainin, N.Y.C.

"What are the most beautiful and flowing words you
 know?"

He asked me in a most serious manner.
Thinking words of love, I asked him back.
He said. "Monongahela, Susquehanna."

        Laurie Lidz, N.Y.C.

A-waiting for an omnibus
I tarry at the stop,
A-fing'ring of the silv'ry coins
Which soon I hope to drop
Into the dank receptacle,
Coin-hopper at its top.

       E. M. Schneider, Woodhaven, N.Y.

That summer we made marzipan
And braided each other's hair
The horizon was our only gate
And our ceiling was rarefied air
Then you went back to the plumber's trade
With plungers, snakes and lye
And I —
But that was yesterday.

       Arthur Weller, Interlaken, N.Y.

Today, it is raining.
Last Tuesday, it wasn't.
On some days it rains, and
On some days it doesn't.

        Dodi Schultz, N.Y.C.

Got into Rock. Tried Esalen.
Did Women's Lib. Thought about Mattachine.
Found the answer. No longer a lost 'un—
I came to Oxford and I'm rereading Jane Austen.

       Dorothea H. Scher, N.Y.C.

Here is the dish with scalloped edge,
Adorned by nut-brown pears and grapes.
Small berries lightly circle o'er the rim.

Flat Verse

Across it lies the long bread knife
And the gas station's gift fork.
The tomato's crater-like top is abandoned
With a silent tea bag and cigarette butt;
All lie among the dried flakes of tuna.
Alice Barron, Staten Island, N.Y.

The sun came up to start the day,
And everything was bright.
The sun went down and all was gray,
I figured it was night.
Sharon Cumberland, Winter Park, Fla.

In the U.S.A. the President
Is head of the whole government
And that is why we must respect
The man the voters all elect.
And if you did not vote for him
That is no reason to be grim.
For, after all, he's all we got
And one should be a patriot.
Phyllis Taub, Brooklyn, N.Y.

We met one rainy morning and the evening was the same
I never got his number and I never knew his name.
I saw him Sunday breakfast for poached eggs and day-old bread
He kissed my cheek with coffee, I went home and went to bed.
I saw him Tuesday evening for two hours of TV
He ate potato chips and dip which was all right with me.
On Friday of the second week he kissed me on the head
Since Johnny Carson had the flu I guess we went to bed.
Toby Devens Schwartz, Baltimore, Md.

Bernard is our puppy all fluffy and cute
At four in the morning we wish he was mute.
R. and J. Eisner, N.Y.C.

In moonlit skies, stars were glowing.
Throughout the camp, bugles blowing.
Tid-da-did-da-da, tid-da-did-da-da,
Tid-da-did-da-da, tid-da-DAH-da.
If Murphy's ears had heard it right,
There was a sound of reveille by night.
       Arthur Ash, Mount Vernon, N.Y.

The flag that flies, unfailing, over each
United States Post Office, comes to teach
That every single letter which we mail
Will reach its destination without fail.
       Cal and Fran Ackerman, Teaneck, N.J.

The sea was calm; the day was fair.
The lifeguard squinting in the glare,
Observed me from his stilted chair.
I wondered what had brought me there.
       E. C. Pier, Whitingham, Vt.

My husband died in September, the same day I lost my
 job.
I was quite upset, I remember, he was kind though some-
 thing of a slob.
I was a good wife, I did my best.
I got the job through a civil-service test.
       Teresa Gerbers, Glenmont, N.Y.

Hamlet was a prince of yore;
His tale well-known near 'n' far.
He found Ophelia quite a bore,
And argued with his ma 'n' pa.
       Dr. Myron Leiman, Mineola, N.Y.

Winter starts to splinter and soon departs.
Spring is a buck and wing and love throws darts.
Summer is a bummer when insects bite.
Fall is a clarion call both day and night.

There are many reasons
Why we have four seasons.

                        B. C. Spellman, N.Y.C.

"That's my last duchess painted on the wall,
Looking as if she were alive.
She's not."

                        Larry Laiken, Bayside, N.Y

☞ *Far-Fetched Fables*

Dick Whittington becomes involved with warring factions of a Chinese secret society. Members of the society take his pet as a hostage. Whittington reports the abduction to the police, who ask: "What's the matter, Tong got your cat?"

Above, a far-fetched fable and its mangled moral. Competitors were invited to submit a brief story including and clarifying a punned, spoonerized, or otherwise mutilated aphorism, title, or the like.

Report: It was fun judging this one. Well, almost. A big batch, and a rewarding one. However, we beg your indulgence for a litany of old complaints: to wit: **1.** *Multiple entries* from individual competitors. **2.** Entries exceeding the *50-word limit*. **3.** Gratuitous and often wretched rhymes offered as puns, i.e., "A curd in hand is worth two in the mush." **4.** *Lame spoonerisms* with incomplete syllabic transpositions (perhaps best defined as "snooperisms"). **5.** Abstruse anecdotes relying on *invented names*, i.e., "The beer that made pitcher Mel Famey walk us." **6.** *Misconception of the original aphorism,* clearly boding ill for the mangled version. **7.** And most regrettable: *Stale material.* Need we, now, in our dotage, state "original" in our instructions? Most duplications derived from these timeworn near-fetched tales. A sampling: boyfoot bear with teak of Chan; furry with the syringe on top; no tern unstoned; wait 'til the nun signs, Shelly. New to us this time but too numerous to special-mention: Love means never having to save your sari; carp to carp walleting and the Callous Dough Boys. The majority of entries? We thought them nifty. But for this and future comps a hint: grab the first well-known phrase (or name, or whatever) that comes to mind—and forget it.

An impressionable New England college girl dropped out of school to live with a handsome young man whose main attraction was his smoldering dark gaze. Within six months she was abandoned and heartbroken—a situation which, in retrospect, came from loving not Wellesley but two eyes.

Helen K. Weil, Larchmont, N.Y.

Prince Souvanna Phouma of Laos is offered his own talk show on television. He joins the American Federation of Television and Radio Artists, but the show bombs. The Prince then lands a job in a shaving commercial. He becomes this country's best-known AFTRA shaving Laotian.

Richard Valeriani, Washington, D.C.

When Walt Disney created his famous Mickey, he also created Minnie, of whom we have heard little in recent years. Disgruntled at being cut off from her rightful share of fame and fortune, she is calling her new book *Diary of a Had Mousewife.*

Mark Lawrence, N.Y.C.

Erich Maria and his three brothers attended a small country school in Germany. One wintry day their father's carriage broke down, so neighbors came to pick up the children. Finally only Erich remained shivering outside. A teacher watching from the window said: "That last Remarque was uncalled for."

Oliver M. Neshamkin, M.D., N.Y.C.

Ravi Shankar, in New York for a concert, returned to his hotel to find it in flames. As he ran toward it, a beautiful woman flung herself into his arms. Rushing on, he cast her aside, exclaiming: "A woman is only a woman, but a good sitar is asmoke."

Paula A. Franklin, N.Y.C.

The captain of the *Bounty* kept a talking bird as a companion. A sailor, reporting aboard, thought he recognized the bird as one he'd befriended and named Bert, while shipwrecked on a tropical island. Approaching the bird he remarked, "Hail to thee, Bligh's parrot! Were thou never Bert?"

Don Koenig, Bronx, N.Y.

Louie was happy to have rented an apartment to the Parisian couple, but upon the pair's arrival a series of burglaries occurred. As he plotted to catch the man in the act, Louie's neighbors announced the startling news: "It was the French tenant's woman, Lou!"

Bonnie Helschen, Brooklyn, N.Y.
similarly from: Richard C. Letau, Alexandria, Va.

One of King Arthur's men was returning to court with a gift for the king—a sheep and two gulls. When they all became ill, he wrote this note explaining his tardiness: "Ewe and the knight and the mews sick."

Joan M. A'Hearn, Saratoga Springs, N.Y.

Titania awakens after slumbering in a botanical area of her kingdom to find a strange creature lying near her.

After asking its name, she sends a message to Oberon stating: "There's a Bottom in the garden of my fairies!"

Mike Olton, Los Angeles, Calif.

"I've invented a portable stove for use in automobile campers. It even has an automatic timer, so your frankfurters won't get burned." "What do you call it?" "A Clockwork Car-Range."

T. E. D. Klein, N.Y.C.

... the handsomest man in the world was but a lowly floor scrubber. Hundreds of women rushed to hug him as he went about his work. To keep them away, he hung up a sign which read: "Please Don't Squeeze the Charman."

Anne Miller, Teaneck, N.J.

Plans for Jonathan's new comedy album were announced at a press conference by a recording company executive as he introduced his star: "This is the Winters of our disk intent."

Lydia Wilen, N.Y.C.

The German Academy of Arts and Sciences holds a beauty contest. Berthold wins the title: "BRECHT—BEAUTIFUL HERR."

James M. Rose, White Plains, N.Y.

Wily Spartan boy, from family of notorious unbelievers, steals savage fox, conceals animal under cloak, next to his skin. Thief arrives home, removes fox from hiding place, revealing his own unclawed, unbitten skin. His father exults: "Down with superstition! There are no foxholes in atheists!"

Bennet C. Kessler, Bayside, N.Y.
similarly from: Arnold Horwitt, Weston, Conn.

At the medical outpost, a native was brought in with a cleanly fractured leg. The assistant applied a leech. When the doctor arrived, he scolded: "Never give an even break a sucker."

Jack A. Kasman, Yonkers, N.Y.

When Patrice Lumumba went to visit the Prime Minister, the driver took him to Number One Downing Street. Realizing the error, the occupant brought him back to the driver and said: "Take Lumumba from One to Ten."

Arnold R. Breuer, Dobbs Ferry, N.Y.

The Federal Trade Commission director and a staff lawyer discuss the pending case against an antacid TV commercial. As the director outlines the government's strong case, the young attorney stands, pounds his fist and says, "I like it." The director points his finger at him. "Like it! You'll try it!"

Edward Schneider, Akron, Ohio

Attending a lecture on the works of the Bard, René Descartes was called on by the eminent lecturer to name Will's favorite meter. "Spondaic" was his reply. The professor shook his head, whereupon M. Descartes was heard to remark: "I think, therefore, Iamb."

Adrian A. Durlester, N.Y.C.

Bought up by unscrupulous land developers, Hunter Rock, one of the most beautiful vistas along Lake Success, was destined to become a combination McDonald's/Puppy Palace/House of Blondes. The question on the minds of local townspeople was "Will Hunter Rock Spoil Success?"

Ellen Wisoff, Brooklyn, N.Y.

Manny, the modish creative director, was proud of his curly, shoulder-length locks. But snarls and tangles made combing a painful problem. "Try a brush, instead," advised a friend. "After all, with hair like yours, a man's comb is his hassle."

Gary Moore, N.Y.C.

President Nixon and his family were in Peking when Mrs. Nixon noticed that Checkers was missing. After the disappearance was reported to him, President Nixon informed local authorities. He was told not to worry; the dog was at a game factory where workers were making Checkers Chinese.

David M. Kaufman, Bronx, N.Y.

Bing Crosby likes to prepare gelatin pudding alone. You are not to disturb him when Der Bingle Jells.

Alissa Abrams, Brooklyn, N.Y.

The scene: a dance studio in Warsaw, Isadora was rehearsing with Stanislaw, whom she preferred to all his compatriots. "Don't you adore this piece about the beat beat beat of the tom tom?" she said. Then she leapt—to the strains of "Night and Day." Her favorite Pole caught her.

James Fechheimer, Glen Head, N.Y.

Where Vaughn Monroe lived as a child, a group of men formed a walking club. Because their wives objected, they often wore disguises while walking. Little Vaughn took delight in pointing them out, crying, "There go striders in disguise."

Judith Klein, East Brunswick, N.J.

Arthur Murray's own story: How I went twelve rounds with heavyweight Muhammad Ali to the tune of the Sabre Dance in the musical prizefight of the century and how I won by the simple expedient of punching him to the beat.

Duncan G. Steck, N.Y.C.

At a recent cocktail party in Saigon, a well-known ABC newscaster was asked to introduce Premier and Mrs. Thong Von Gnow to Ambassador Huang Ben Nu. He is reported to have said, "Good evening, I'm Roger Grimsby. Here Nu the Gnows."

Judd S. Levy, Livingston, N.J.

Keenan Wynn's appearing on Broadway. After the matinee, he goes to a French restaurant for dinner. Suddenly, his agent dashes in screaming he's late for the evening performance. Casually, Keenan says, "As soon as I finish this fish." Angrily, his agent barks, "What's it gonna be, Wynn— plaice or show?"

Rita Oakes, Drexel Hill, Pa.

Viking's lovely daughter languishes uncourted on Norse shore, smoking family's salmon catch. Countless admirers back off, remembering runic warning that salmon-smoking can be injurious to health. Finally, ardent suitor defies legends, woos and wins maiden. They live happily ever after, murmuring: "Love laughs at lox myths."

David De Porte, Slingerlands, N.Y.

Count Dracula's henchmen get tired blood. They desert him. A ghoul and his fold are soon parted.

Clark Smith, Baltimore, Md.

Once upon a time a family of beavers wanted a pond of their own, so they would catch smaller animals, cuff them into unconsciousness, and toss their limp bodies into the stream, thus damming with faint preys.

Anthony Gray, Closter, N.J.

Goneril (ten) and Regan (eight) organize a kids' baseball team. But on the day of the big game they slip in Tom Seaver and Vita Blue. The other team squawks angrily: "Little Lears have big pitchers!"

Joan T. Nourse, N.Y.C.

Dr. Watson sensed that the great detective had overstepped the bounds of prudence in this encounter with Moriarty, but due to the seriousness of the confrontation, felt it was nothing to right Holmes about.

John Gardner, Rowayton, Conn.

Tibet and Holland arrange, for the second time, to trade cattle for birds. This becomes known as the New Yak-Stork Exchange.

Doug Hoylman, Staten Island, N.Y.

One day, an ex-track-and-field star, having long made good as a bank president and made whiskey on a hillside, left home forever. Knowing she was irreplaceable, her husband told everyone: "With all her vaults, I love her still."

Paul Elliott, N.Y.C.

Dr. Spooner had a sister who married a mortician named Bappy. Once a week it would be Bappy's turn to drive the hearse. His wife, who lisped, would remind him: "Happy Birthday."

Mrs. David Goldstein, Glen Ellyn, Ill.

☞ Bedwords

---

kisSPLAnter – 1. An effusive greeter (esp. So. Calif., U.S.A.); a clutchdarling, a sardissitter. 2. One who raises or cultivates the flowering kissplant. 3. A peanut fancies. Obs.

Above, (with acknowledgments to James Thurber's "bedwords" *) our own four super-ghost letters which form the nucleus of an invented word, plus definition(s) for that word. Competitors were asked to invent and define a word containing the four contiguous letters, SPLA.

Report: Who would have thought? Thousands of entries, and nearly all of them first rate. Certain base phrases were bound to recur in so large a group; among the most popular: asp, ass, cusp, cuss, esp, grass, latch, lisp, mess, ms., plaud, plain, plait, plane, (s)platter, and wasp. It followed that even the cleverest definitions were duplicated verbatim—for example: WASPLAND: Plymouth Rock or Middle America; ASPLADY: Cleopatra; MSPLACE: the Barbizon Hotel for Women. Limited space prevented our crediting all the "similarly froms," so we settled for a mere sampling of your abundant wit. In a case of special

---

* *Thurber Country*, Simon and Schuster.

merit (Jack Ryan, N.Y.C., below) we overlooked lengthiness staggering even for the O.E.D. Ruled out were definitions not couched in dictionary lingo and those where stress and therefore meaning changed in mid-word. Which brings us to our own definitions: LISP, Use of: Often, esp. when pert. to homosexuality, deemed not funny. Substitution of L for R and R for L: (see Jokes, Ethnic) usually confused by entrant; former is Chinese, latter Japanese, by our lights. Or rights. Generally, however a splandid assortment.

DUCKBILLEDSPLATYPUS—egg-laying mammal so short it is often accidentally trod upon.

Oliver Katz, N.Y.C.

SPLAG—(shpläag), *n.*, pl., the splaggies. (A.S. splagat, a ggarthe or similar farkle = D. splage, a word or momfret = Icel. splague, the common curlew = G. splach, identity papers = Celt. splash, whisky.) Orig., a typical spawl or wiven, but now refers to the ordinary nurdle or similar grond. I. *Heral.,* an escutcheon bearing an invisible farole or transparent plagent to confuse the villain. II. *Theol.,* that dogma that deals with general principles and espouses the tenet that man is composed of body, soul and yeast; any Trappist carnival. III. *Geol.,* noting or pertaining to rich ore and the land adjacent to it, esp. belonging to others. IV. *Polit.,* the former National Assembly of Serbia or the former khedive of Clifton, N.J. V. *Obs.,* a sowern or blind pig (as Chaucer, *Canterbury Tales,* "Ffloke cithern and vertheth in sowern and splag.") VI. *Pathol.,* a somewhat mild pediatric condition of the lower extremities ("a dose of the old splag."; Motley's *Rise of the Dutch Republic.*) VII. Any Incan beaker, Jewish month, obscure part of a cathedral, minor Scandinavian goddess, word in Low German, a popular name for the thane of Crawford, So. Dak., and collectively, all S.E. Asian turpentine gatherers. VIII. *Arch.,* an edifice constructed entirely of marzipan. IX. A casual gesture of contempt made by placing knees on buttocks and grimmacing humorously, or any such merry gesture, viz. (". . . the splag was cast towards Genghis Khan by his late vizier, known to history as 'Timor of a Thousand Deaths.'" De Quincey, *Revolt of the Tartars.*) X. *Naut.,* any irregular rippon, snard, or other riculette used by carlmen and flagans for waining, hence, in general, any fannion, whord or steapsin used in foc'lin'. XI. Sexual congress with palm trees or the avoidance of such. ("Prince Albert observed wryly that the Pathans prefer a woman for childbearing, but he was not amused at their excessive splag." Parkman, *The Oregon Trail*). The family name of King Zog of Albania and, to some extent, a sect of roach worshippers.

Jack Ryan, N.Y.C.

s.p.l.a.d.—**1.** World War I aeroplane of Polish design, whose appearance over the Eastern Front in 1916 is thought to have contributed to the collapse of the Russian Army. While seven of the unusual planes were built and flown, none was ever landed successfully. **2.** Hence, the onomatopoeic *splád,* sugg. the sound of a crash esp. into mud. *See also:* SPLADRON: KRAKOW ESPLADRILLE.

William Schallert, Pacific Palisades, Calif.

PARKLESPLANTY—young female character in an unsuccessful detective comic strip.

Dan Greenburg, N.Y.C.

RASPLAT—**1.** older woman given to the wearing of heavy tweeds; a Bestgranny, *Obs.* **2.** *M.E.,* the placket on a hair shirt.

Donald Cromley, N.Y.C.

TRESPLASH—**1.** to swim in forbidden waters; to sin-paddle. **2.** uninvited or forcible entry of an occupied bathtub; the throwing of soap into an occupied bathtub. **3.** unwarranted violation of moral and social rules of water polo.

John Leo, N.Y.C.

ESPLANATION—The medium's message.

James Vonnell, Austin, Texas

AVUNCUSPLAR—*M.E.*, to threaten a knave with your mother's brother.

Kathy Erskine, East Hampton, N.Y.

CUSPLAW—one who evades action by the skin of his teeth.

Rees Behrendt, N.Y.C.

CUSPLAZY—**1.** slothful about brushing after meals; molarlax, fangsluggish, pearly-poky. **2.** too indolent to take careful aim at the spittoon; gaboonreckless.

Albert G. Miller, N.Y.C.

RESPLATE—**1.** struck with overwhelming nausea upon discovering a foreign body in one's food: "He sat resplate after spying the beetle." **2.** a shallow dish used as repository for unpalatables of the nature of sweet potato (or yam) peelings, spent corn cobs, small fish bones and the like. **3.** to repeat the splating process. *Arch.*

William Jeanes, Jackson, Miss.

MANISPLANDER—**1.** to build by committee. **2.** to embrace on a high and windy hill.

Karl Levett, N.Y.C.

ESPLANADA—a public walkway along an unscenic beach in Spain.

D. Kotteb, N.Y.C.

SUPERCALIFRAGILISTICESPLALAODOCIOUS—unsuitable Nanny, *Eng.*

Mrs. Peter Reich, Pasadena, Calif.

CLASPLAWYER—**1.** an inveterate plaintiff; a suithanger; a courtplasterer. **2.** one excessively fond of attorneys. *See antonym:* KILLAWYER (Shak.)

Henry Slesar, N.Y.C.

GASPLAYER—**1.** atmospheric level closest to earth having low oxygen content. **2.** a member of power company's repertory theater group. **3.** an unattended child; a handburner.

James and Nancy Lynn, N.Y.C.

WASPLASH—**1.** reactionary attitude of Am. minority group: blacklash; papacynic, Semiticritic. **2.** to birchbark.

Catherine V. Poulin, Brooklyn, N.Y.

WASPLADY—Batman's mother.

Ellie Spielberger, N.Y.C.

WASPLADYKILLER—John V. Lindsay.

Lawrence Pollock, Williamsville, N.Y.

WASPLACK—Inability to assemble a quorum at D.A.R. meetings.

Rochelle Weiner, Flushing, N.Y.

WASPLANDSMAN—a friend from the old country who has changed his name.

Bernie Katz, N.Y.C.

RASPLANILLA—**1.** a coastal city of Surinam. **2.** the organ between the spleen and the pancreas.

Monroe F. Schwenk, Jackson Heights, N.Y.

CHUTZSPLAW—a boorish, loud-mouthed relative by marriage.

Sidney Abrams, Brooklyn, N.Y.

CUSSPLACER—typographer specializing in ! ! ! * * * - - -. *Obs.* **2.** compulsive user of four-letter words.

Gil and Iris Melnick, West Orange, N.J.

DISPLAYBOY—**1.** an apprentice window decorator. **2.** an open-faced chest of drawers. **3.** a blind date, *colloq*. **4.** ancient wind instrument used for virtuoso passages. *Arch.*

Gerald Blank, New Rochelle, N.Y.

ANTIDISPLANTABLISHMENTARIANISM—opposition to the withdrawal of popular support or the deprivation of a privileged position of an established plant or tree, esp. the pine tree on Dec. 26.

Rita and David Kaufman, Bronx, N.Y.

GRANTSPLATTER—**1.** wanton allocation of research funds. **2.** an Indian rain god.

Pamela Ann Memishian, Arlington, Mass.

DISPLAYLET—Short underworld drama.

Math Coffee Room, University of N.C., Chapel Hill

THREECENTSPLAIN—**1.** blank postage stamp having low production costs. **2.** a postinflation fountain drink.

Daniel Cohen, N.Y.C.

DYSPLASTIC—**1.** dyscapable of being molded, folded, extruded, or mutilated; unsculpturalistic. **2.** one having chronic ductile indygestion.

Mary D. English, Stamford, Conn.

BASPLAN—a welfare program, wherein the low-income group goes on basrelief.

Barbara Alpren, West Orange, N.J.

GURSPLAZT—*Colloq.*, a word used to describe the first audible sounds made when waking from sleep, popularized by Dagwood Bumstead in early 1940s. (*See also:* BGYWISRQULFX).

David Grotenstein, N.Y.C.

QUACKSPLAQUE—the diploma of a disreputable physician.

Ina Weidman, East Meadow, N.Y.

HOSPLANOON—one who faithfully follows nurse, intern, doctor serials on daytime television.
E. Oliver, N.Y.C.

PASSPLAID—*Scot.* **1.** Ancient clan law instituted by Robert the Bruce transferring the right of inheritance to the female line in the absence of male issue. **2.** any secondhand garment; a hand-ye-down.
Susanna Lesan, N.Y.C.

ASPLAWN—a snake in the grass.
Diane Davis, Huntington, N.Y.

ASPLAUSE—venomenal response.
Ernest W. Stix, St. Louis, Mo.

ASPLAMONY—**1.** (corrupt. of Anc. Egy. asplamammy) act of mistakenly holding an object close to one's bosom. **2.** *Law.* in divorce proceedings, the monies awarded for the support of the family boa constrictor.
James M. Green, M.D., Livingston, N.J.

ASSPLADISTRA—girdle pin worn by Eng. monarchs who followed Ethelred the Unready.
John P. Rorke, Summit, N.J.

HOSSPLAYER—one who poses as a fabricator of carts; sp., a danblocker.
R. M. Neudecker, White, Plains, N.Y.

OBITSPLANTSKY—**1.** *Russ.,* a deceased ballet dancer. **2.** *Pol.,* foliage that dies quickly without sunshine.
Kenneth G. Geisert, Ridgewood, N.Y.

TOSPLAI—**1.** a topsail which has become entangled and confused, probably due to the action of a storm. **2.** to throw about with abandon.
Michael Sage, N.Y.C.

MSPLANET—third runner-up in the Msuniverse contest.
Bette-Jane Raphael, N.Y.C.

MSPLANTAGENET—Eleanor of Aquitaine.
Barbara A. Huff, N.Y.C.

☞ *Classified Directory*

Dolly Llamas—Stuffed Toys
Esprit Décor—Interiors

Above, extracts from our new "Classified Directory." Competitors were asked for a congruous listing for a firm doing very small business.

Report: Aside from some confusion with Fractured Names, listings ranged from arcane to apt. Some so apt, in fact, as to exist. (There *is* an Esprit Décor—and doing very nicely, thank you.) Small-businesspersons might consider seriously some of the below-mentioned. For the nonce, we will concentrate on the proliferation of worthy "repeats": EDIFICE WRECKS: Demolition; FRANK 'N STEIN: Beer and Hot Dogs; FREUDIAN SLIPS: Lingerie; GOLDA MEIR: Jewelry; HAIR APPARENT: Toupees; YUM KIPPER: Fish; LOXSMITH: Delicatessen; AD HOCK: Pawnbrokers; JEB MAGRUDER: Party Favors; COUP DE GRACE: Lawnmowers; CAVIAR TEMPTER: Seafood; RAISIN D'ÊTRE: Health Foods; CHARGE D'AFFAIRES: Credit Card Caterers; LONDON DERRIERE: Corsets; SURELOCK HOMES: Security; TOOT SWEET: Music Lessons; HAVANA GILAS: Exotic Pets; and S. LIVINGSTON: Encounter Groups. All in all, a batch of equally winsome entries sponsored no individual prizes this week, but congratulations to all.

SAUNA BERNADETTE

> *G. Gene Gentry, N.Y.C.*

JOHN BROWN'S BODY & FENDER REPAIR

> *Tom Anderson, La Jolla, Calif.*

3.14159+ : Pies

> *Math Coffee Room, University of N.C., Chapel Hill*

BETA THETA—Pies

> *Laura Cowman, Columbus, Ohio*

TEE AND SYMPATHY—Golf Lessons

> *J. Bickart, N.Y.C.*

O TEMPURA, O MORAYS—Japanese Seafood

> *Eve Gelofsky, Verona, N.J.*

HUMAN KINDNESS—Dairy

> *Thomas C. Galyon, Richmond, Va.*

LAWN ORDER—Gardeners

> *Barbara Mackowiak, Chicago, Ill.*

MARCHI DI SOD—Florentine Landscaping

> *Dodi Schultz, N.Y.C.*

DAVE THE BUSHER—Landscaping

> *David Kristol, Newark, N.J.*
> *Joel W. Caesar, Englishtown, N.J.*

STEP IN WOLF—Costume Rental

> *Janis Brodie, N.Y.C.*

SHOEMAKER & ROONEY—Small Business Consultants
FINC COLLEG—Finishing School

> *Staff of* Bachelor *Magazine, N.Y.C.*

LEDGER DOMAIN—Accounting

> *Mona Abramesco, Brooklyn, N.Y.*

CHARMING, INC.—Prints
> Lora W. Asdorian, Springfield, Va.

VAULTS OF THE FLOURS—Silos
> Ellen Jackson, Brooklyn, N.Y.

OAT CUISINE—Grain & Feed
> Arnold M. Berke, Springfield, Mass.
> Mary Connelly, N.Y.C.
> Betty Cornfeld, N.Y.C.

LIBERTY VALANCE—Draperies
> Robert Anthony, Laurence Harbor, N.J.

PROPER GANDER—Geese Importers
> David Wolff, East Meadow, N.Y.

HEAVEN FOR BID—Auctioneers
> Richard A. Schwartz, New Haven, Conn.

DEMENTIA PEACOCKS—Crazy Quills
> Bernard Lovett, Hillside, N.J.

POINT OF NO RETURN—Pens, All Sales Final
> Anita Gerber, Brooklyn, N.Y.

THE WIZARD OF VASE—Urn Repair
> Alan C. Hochberg, Forest Hills, N.Y.

CHACONNE A SON GOUT—Music to Order
> Charles Israels, N.Y.C.

LAST GASP—Shockingly Mod Shoes
> Walter A. Kilrain, Schenectady, N.Y.

ENTENTE CORDIALS—Wines and Liqueurs
> Mrs. Eva Edmands, Bronx, N.Y.

DAYLIGHT SAVINGS—Part-time Banking
> Stephen D. Tannen, Lynbrook, N.Y.
> Dave Gordon, Pittsburgh, Pa.

BO'S ARTS—Handiwork by Vagrants
>	*Walter Barrett, Englishtown, N.J.*

APOLOGIA PRO VITA SUA—Herring
>	*Barry Fisher, Livingston, N.J.*

CALF 'N' COOLAGE—Frozen Meats
>	*Jack BenAry, Brooklyn, N.Y.*

FÊTE ACCOMPLI—Party Planners
>	*Kathleen R. Grilley, Madison, Wis.*
>	*David S. Greenberg, N.Y.C.*

FATE ACCOMPLI—Expert Crystal Gazing
>	*Judith Kohl, Leonia, N.J.*

THE EMOTIONAL OUTLET—Psychiatric Clinic
>	*Robert S. Barnes, N.Y.C.*

AGAIN, NATURALLY—Finance Company
>	*M. Kelly, Jr., Perth Amboy, N.J.*

BAA NANAS—Shepherds
>	*Bonnee Waldstein, N.Y.C.*

CAMEL LOTS—Bargain Caravans
>	*Bobbie Patrick, Staten Island, N.Y.*

AD INFINITUM—24-Hour Media Service
>	*Jerry Fields, N.Y.C.*

STAR DREK—Memorabilia
>	*Jerry Richman, Washington, D.C.*

HOWE'S BAYOU—Shore Resort
>	*Frances Larson, Guilderland, N.Y.*

NICK OF THYME—Herbs & Spices
>	*Thomas Nethercott, N.Y.C.*

DEUTSCHLAND UBERALLES—Imported Workpants
>	*Tom Wolf, N.Y.C.*
>	*Renée Katz, Bronx, N.Y.*

HELL'S KITCHEN—Regional Cuisine
          Sandy and Dean Behrend, Kendall Park, N.J.

BOLT UPRIGHT—Theatrical Hardware
          Bill Tchakirides, Jackson Heights, N.Y.

OCTOPUS, INC.—Holding Corporation
          Peter Szilagyi, Jr., N.Y.C.

SECOND-HAND ROES—Bargain Seafood
          Rosemarie Williamson, Basking Ridge, N.J.

AUTO DA FEY—Juice Bar (div. of Horn & Hardart Corp.)
          Cassie Roessel, N.Y.C.

DE FOREST PRIME VEAL—Butchers
          Fred Morrison, Whitestone, N.Y.

DYE-IT CONCHES—Decorative Sea Shells
          Mark Lubroth, Melville, N.Y.

O'NEIL & PRAY—Hymn Books
          Howard Rosenblum, Brooklyn, N.Y.

A LEASH 'N' FIELDS—Kennel
          Ronny Borrok, Riverdale, N.Y.

PRINTS OF WHALES—Mammalian Fine Arts
          Jenny Krasner, Melville, N.Y.
          Elizabeth Robbins, N.Y.C.

MAISON DIXON—Georgia Château-Bottled Wine
          Marilyn Crystal, Brooklyn, N.Y.

EMANU-EL CELLAR—Underground Synagogue Tours
          Richard Fried, Brooklyn, N.Y.

HEAR HERE—Records, Tapes, etc.
          Robert E. Kroll, Evanston, Ill.

HEAVENLY QUIRES—Stationers to the Clergy
          Alison Watt, Wayne, Pa.

KANGAROO COURT—Australian Dating Service
> H. H. Gifford, Philadelphia, Pa.

CHOU EN LAI—Food and Lodging
> Diane Kovacs, Roslyn, N.Y.

MIA CULPA—Hairshirts
> Donna Ricca, Brooklyn, N.Y.

MORT TITIAN—Still Lifes
> Mark S. Andrews, N.Y.C.

APRES NOUS—Flood Control
> Tom Morrow, N.Y.C.

GNU FACES—Taxidermists
> Arthur Cornfeld, N.Y.C.

EYE OF KNUT—Scandinavian Occult Shop
> Bill Schwartz, Los Angeles, Calif.

CAWS CÉLÈBRE—Exotic Birds
> Joyce V. Eggert, Lafayette, N.J.

SUEY GENEROUS—Chinese Restaurant
> Lester E. Rothstein, Great Neck, N.Y.
> Susan and Peter Pouncey, N.Y.C.

SKULL DUGGERY—Archaeologists
> J. S. Botelho, Alexandria, Va.

DEJA VIEUX—Antiques
> Phoebe W. Ellis, Millwood, Va.

RICH'S CREASES—Pants Pressed
> Ellen K. Danzig, Eastchester, N.Y.

FIAT LUX—Imported Cars & Soap
> Mrs. S. S. Klein, North Caldwell, N.J.

TINY TIERS—Bunk Beds for Tots
> Saul Immerman, Fonda, N.Y.

CREPE SUZETTES—Paper Dolls
>   *Irma Malcolm, Teaneck, N.J.*

SUNNY AND SHARE—Florida Condominium
>   *Linda Quirini, Providence, R.I.*

DEAD WRINGERS—Antique Washing Machines
>   *Stephen Lax, Millburn, N.J.*

PRIMAL CREAM—Dairy Products
>   *Catherine Arenella, N.Y.C.*

LOUIS CANS—French Preserves
>   *Michael Snowday, N.Y.C.*

FORMAL D'HYDE—Leather Tuxedos
>   *Arthur J. Lohman, N.Y.C.*

SAVOIE FARE—North Italian Cuisine
>   *Ransom Wilson, Hoboken, N.J.*

YANGTZE GO HOME—Take-Out Chinese Food
>   *Howard Pasternak, Brooklyn, N.Y.*

CHEZ STADIUM—Ticket Agency
>   *Henry Wagner, Verona, N.J.*

NIXON & CO.—Lyres
>   *Elaine and Raymond Mansbach, Bronx, N.Y.*

☞ *Heavy-Handed Proverbs*

"Old Age Is Not Always a Cure for Adolescence."

"A Man with No Toes Can Still Feel the Cold."

"The Largest Square Has But Four Sides."

Above, heavy-handed proverbs. Competitors were invited to submit up to three maxims or aphorisms, the truth or value of which are as egregiously self-evident.

Report: It is a poor judge who cannot award a prize. The simplest contests are oft the hardest won. Much of this lot was like, heavy, man. The Tree of Life, The Barkless Dog, The Clock Without Hands, Sunrise, Sunset. You know, like heavy. Certain proverbs held truths we thought to be meaningless rather than self-evident. And many funny entries were only that—funny. Jokes. Humor, it was felt, should come from the *haimish* (however heavy-handed), old country *style* of the maxim rather than from a punch line. Of necessity, some entries sounded a bit like Near-Misses. That seemed fair. Nonoriginals did not. Repeated among these: "It is better to be rich and healthy than to be poor and sick"; "Sterility is not hereditary"; and (ugh) "Death is nature's way of telling us to slow down." Duplicated also were switch endings combining two axioms: "A bird in the hand is the better part of valor." But, listen, do we have to tell *you?* Even the boldest zebra fears the hungry lion. A tree need not be tall to bear fruit. The surest road to . . . oh, forget it.

Deprive a mirror of its silver and even the Tsar won't see his face.
In the house of a hangman, extinguished candles shed no light.
A leaking garden hose sometimes wets the gardener.
Linda H. Heinze, N.Y.C.

Eleven fingers are better than none.
The man who has no opinion will seldom be wrong.
No one knows what the dinner was after the plates have been washed.
Michael Sage, N.Y.C.

'Tis nae th' waiter cooks th' food.
To build the tallest building, dig a deep foundation.
He who reaches for the sky oftimes stands upon a soapbox.
Dan Greenburg, N.Y.C.

He who does not have fins cannot call himself a fish.
A wise man sees more from a mountaintop than a fool sees from the bottom of a well.
A live Indian can eat more pemmican than a dead wolf.
Fred Berg, Boston, Mass.

Man's horizons are bounded only by his vision.
To play the game, one must buy the ball.
Unemployment does not guarantee leisure.
Ed Coudal, Park Ridge, Ill.

To criticize the incompetent is easy; it is more difficult to criticize the competent.
Even light takes a decade to travel ten light-years.
If neither animal nor vegetable you be, then mineral you are.

Math Coffee Room, University of N.C., Chapel Hill

If thine enemy wrong thee, he is not yet thy friend.
If at first you don't succeed, you have failed at the outset.

Albert G. Miller, N.Y.C.

You can't get pears from an apple tree.

Leo Taubes, Teaneck, N.J.

Life teaches the wise man more lessons than it does the fool.

Lewis S. Marks, Brooklyn, N.Y.

A king's castle is his home.

Paul Elliott, N.Y.C.

A man's appearance diminishes long before his desires.

James F. Mulligan, Jr., Bridgeport, Conn.

He who would be king, needs have a queen for a mother.
Blue skies mean fair weather.

Alice M. Yohalem, N.Y.C.

It is easy to follow the straight path if the road has no winding.

J. H. Dorenkamp, Worcester, Mass.

Being right means never having to say you're sorry.

Cynthia Dantzig, Brooklyn, N.Y.

A cynic may know much but he does not know how to believe.

Paul Weiss, Washington, D.C.

Plus ça change, plus c'est la chose différente.

James H. Hughes, Fresh Meadows, N.Y.

Whether you ignore a pig or whether you worship that pig from afar, to the pig it's all the same.
The deaf man may speak and the dumb man may hear, but the blind man may do both.

Eric Thompson, Brooklyn, N.Y.

A bald sage is wiser than a bearded fool.

Aben Rudy, Brooklyn, N.Y.

If there is no wind, row.

Nancy Asch, Great Neck, N.Y.

No sun ever rose that did not first set.

Luise Putcamp, Jr., Stamford, Conn.

It is the wise bird who builds his nest in a tree.
The man who is tired will find time to sleep.

Edward W. Powell, Jr., N.Y.C.

Success is just another form of failure.

Jack S. Margolis, Los Angeles, Calif.

Even paranoids have real enemies.

Matthew S. Watson, Washington, D.C.

The wise shepherd never trusts his flock to a smiling wolf.

B. Sherak, Larchmont, N.Y.

You can't be an Airedale if you are a Bouvier des Flandres.

Fred Cline, N.Y.C.

The poor man seeks only a crumb, then finds that he still hungers.
The most noble dog can only bark.

Burt and Karen Siegel, Bronx, N.Y.

Even a hawk is an eagle among crows.

Howard A. Lederer, N.Y.C.

Heavy-Handed Proverbs / 219

Before a man is born, he is conceived.
The mind is father to the thought.
> *Rev. Francis Gorman, Distrito Federal, Venezuela*

A man becomes a great leader only if he has followers.
> *Ruth Carey, Oak Ridge, Tenn.*

One does not pursue butterflies with a sledgehammer.
> *Harvey West, Austin, Texas*

A procrastinator puts off until tomorrow the things he has already put off until today.
> *Adam Remez, Mount Vernon, N.Y.*

Without walls, there would be no need for doors or windows.
> *Judy Sprengelmeyer, Indianapolis, Ind.*

Many pages make a thick book.
Every purchase has its price.
> *Beth Rogers, N.Y.C.*

It is not necessary to fall into the well to know its depth.
It may be said that noisy barrels are also easier to carry.
> *Stephanie J. Marks, Northampton, Mass.*

Greed cannot exist when there is nothing to want.
> *George Malko, N.Y.C.*

A bowl is always hollow no matter what its contents.
> *Julia Percivall, N.Y.C.*

A dwarf's heart is as big as a giant's.
> *Tom Morrow, N.Y.C.*

You can't grow a rose by planting an onion.
> *Cheryl M. Hoffman, Ithaca, N.Y.*

One doesn't have to be a horse to judge a horse show.
> *Roger L. Winters, Cambridge, Mass.*

Without the peach, whither the nectarine?
Do not look to the peaceful man for cudgels.
Elliott Shevin, Detroit, Mich.

Sins of omission are seldom fun.
Rees Behrendt, N.Y.C.

Dark night must end the brightest day.
Msgr. A. V. McLees, St. Albans, N.Y.

It is never too late to ask what time it is.
A woman who thinks she's beautiful usually is.
Henry Slesar, N.Y.C.

A bad writer makes a bad book.
Charles K. Robinson, Kearny, N.J.

Even the smallest candle burns brighter in the dark.
Martin Gross, N.Y.C.

The early bird catches the early worm.
Sidney Abrams, Brooklyn, N.Y.

Lightning never strikes twice at the same time.
Elaine Stallworth, Willow Grove, Pa.

When the tree falls there is no shade.
Richard P. Widdicombe, White Plains, N.Y.

With someone who holds nothing but trumps it is impossible to play cards.
Better to sit all night than to go to bed with a dragon.
Peggy Bussey, Greenwich, Conn.

The tallest tree is rooted in the ground.
HEOP Office, Dowling College, Oakdale, N.Y.

Men who make wars do not often die in them.
Laura Sternkopf, Kennett Square, Pa.

Heavy-Handed Proverbs / 221

Many have carved their initials in the Tree of Knowledge, a few have even plucked its fruit, but none has ever changed the fragrance of its flower.
> *Richard A. Rosen, M.D., Mount Vernon, N.Y.*

If you must climb the ladder of success, watch out for the boots of the man above you.
> *Herbert Wasserman, Harrison, N.Y*

A sandwich tastes better with two slices of bread.
If you don't know which way is north, sunrise and sunset look the same.
> *Mr. and Mrs. Joel F. Crystal, Brooklyn, N.Y.*

I used to feel sorry for myself because I had no shoes until I met a man who was dead.
> *John R. Christiansen, Princeton, N.J.*

The lowest rung upon a ladder is a step up for the tallest man.
> *Oscar Weigle, Whitestone, N.Y.*

Mistakes are oft the stepping stones to failure.
A book never opened is a book never read.
> *Rev. Vincent P. Gorman, Bronx, N.Y.*

The loudest bark rids not a dog of his fleas.
> *George Fairbanks, Nutley, N.J.*

Seek not the fruit of the Tree of Life unless you are willing to rake its leaves.
> *Richard J. Hafey, Morningdale, Mass.*

To a falling man it's the last foot that's important.
A splendid effort does not always win recognition.
> *Michael Deskey, N.Y.C.*

A proverb like this need not win a prize.
> *Linda Castro, Staten Island, N.Y.*

☞ *Good News/ Bad News*

AIRLINE PILOT TO PASSENGERS: "I have good news and bad news. First, the bad news: we're lost in an impenetrable fog. Now, the good news: we're one half hour ahead of schedule . . ."

Above, a familiar joke in a familiar format. Competitors are invited to submit one original piece of Good News/Bad News (either order—any topic).

Report: "Greetings." There's fire, flood, famine, pestilence, disease, death, a fare increase, staggering bills, frozen wages, stock declines, job loss, divorce, alimony, multiple births, Red China in the U.N., the war is accelerating and your subscription's expired. And now for the *bad* news. *Our* bad news consisted of sifting the staggering numbers of *un*original repeats—see clue in entry from H. Sargent, N.Y.C., below. Others as follows: Surgeon to Patient: "Bad News: We amputated the wrong leg; Good News: The other leg's improving." Castaway to Friend: "Bad News: There's nothing to eat but lizards (*sic*); Good News: Plenty of lizards." College Dean to Parent: "Bad News: Your son's a homosexual; Good

News: He's been chosen Homecoming Queen," or, "He's living with a doctor." Prison Guard to Inmates: "Good News: Today we change underwear; Bad News: Kowalski, you change with Ryan; Smith, you change with . . ." And so forth. Or in the words of Baby Leroy, "Chaqu'un à son goo."

PRINCE CHARMING (*to* CINDERELLA): "Good News: The glass slipper fits you perfectly. Bad News: I just found this big toe in the grass . . ."

Germaine Sande, N.Y.C.

"Judging by your splendid background and extensive experience, you are exactly the person we need to head up our new multidivisional advertising department. By the way, our board chairman was wondering if by any chance you happen to be of Jewish ethnic extraction, not that it matters. . . ."

Fred Berg, Boston, Mass.

Bad News: "The captain wants to go water skiing."
Good News: "I'm not going to tell this joke again . . ."
Herb Sargent, N.Y.C.

MAYOR JOHN V. LINDSAY (*to his staff*): "I have good news and bad news. First, the Good News: I am going to run for the office of the President of the United States. Now, the Bad News: So is Paul Newman . . ."

M. S. Arentzen, Brooklyn Heights, N.Y.

Good News: "The photographs came out perfectly . . ."
Bad News: "Your wife will be able to recognize both of you."

George Malko, N.Y.C.

Tape-recorded message to Jim Phelps of *Mission: Impossible*: "Good morning, Mr. Phelps. The envelope you are now holding contains goods news and bad news. The Good News: A letter from the Finance Company approving your personal loan upon receipt of a reference from your employer. The Bad News: A letter to the Finance Company in which the Secretary disavows any knowledge of you. Good luck, Jim."

Mrs. Anna Lambiase, Brooklyn, N.Y.

"First the Good News: The rope we were going to use to hang you was found to be defective. Now the good noose . . ."

Math Coffee Room, University of N.C., Chapel Hill

EMCEE (*to* AUDIENCE): "Good News: Our speaker tonight is going to show you how to improve your memory vastly, just as he showed me. Now, the, uh, there was one other thing. Well, never mind; let's get on with it . . ."

Stephen Dickman, Brooklyn, N.Y.

AGENT (*to* WRITER): "Good News: G. P. Putnam's Sons loved your manuscript; absolutely ate it up. Bad News: G. P. Putnam is my cocker spaniel."

Paula Diamond, N.Y.C.

TV ANNOUNCER: "Ladies and gentlemen, first the Good News: The man who predicted the world would suddenly end today has been proven to be an escaped mental patient. Now, the Bad N— . . ."

Jack Paul, Brooklyn, N.Y.

"*Hee Haw* will not be seen tonight in order that we may bring you the following special address by the President of the United States."

Barry W. Grant, N.Y.C.

VISITOR (*to* PRISONER): "Bad News: You've been indicted on twenty-eight counts of rape and assault with a deadly weapon. Good News: I got you booked on *Cavett*

Thursday, and Random House is willing to go $150,000 for the hardcover advance."

D. Kotteb, N.Y.C.

OTHELLO (*to* DESDEMONA): "Bad News: I've discovered your infidelity, and you must die. Good News: I found that handkerchief you lost . . ."

*Ellen S. Ryp, N.Y.C.
similarly from H. Ruppenthal, Milwaukee, Wis.*

MAN (*to* WIFE): "Bad News: There's a 600-pound Yorkie at the door. Good News: He says he used to go to camp with Muffin."

Dan Greenburg, N.Y.C.

OPPENHEIMER (*to* TRUMAN): "Good News: We've completed our experiments with the thermonuclear device. Bad News: It works."

Mackie G. Westbrook, Milwaukee, Wis.

Good News: "President Nixon is planning to visit China." Bad News: "He's coming back."

*Stephen Young, Whitestone, N.Y.
Jay Livingston, Kingston, N.J.*

A. G. BELL (*to* WATSON): "Good News: We've succeeded with our design of the telephone. Bad News: I can't get a dial tone."

James M. Green, M.D., Livingston, N.J.

MARGARET MEAD (*to* AMERICAN ANTHROPOLOGICAL ASSOCIATION): Good News: I've completed my study of the fully initiated fight-leaders of the Kangel River area of the Upper Wahgi Valley of Central New Guinea. Bad News: I have fleas."

Perry Palmer, Eastchester, N.Y.

August 14, 1971. "Honey! I got the raise! Effective September 1! Let's go out and buy that new car tonight!"

August 15, 1971. "Ladies and gentlemen, the President of the United States..."

Maxine Mays, Buffalo, N.Y.

AD MAN (*to* CREATIVE STAFF): "Good News: Nine out of ten people interviewed loved our new campaign. Bad News: The tenth person interviewed was the client..."

Dan Conaway, Memphis, Tenn.

EIGHT-YEAR-OLD (*to* FATHER): "The Good News is that you can fix it..."

Robert Rackear, North Miami Beach, Fla.

CAPTAIN (*to* CREW): "Bad News: Enemy torpedoes have inflicted heavy damage on our engine room. Good News: The movie for tonight is *Hollywood Cavalcade* with Don Ameche and Alice Faye."

James T. Aspbury, Jr., Brooklyn, N.Y.

AIDE (*to* KISSINGER): "Good News: The President is happy with your arrangements for his trip to China. Bad News: The shirts came back with too much starch."

Sally Champlin, N.Y.C.

Good News: "Contrary to what you may believe, machines are not replacing man in industry."
Bad News: "This is a recorded message."

Faith Reisman, Chicago, Ill.

RENTAL AGENT (*to* APARTMENT SEEKER): "Good News: I have an apartment for you. Bad News: José Greco lives upstairs..."

Cornelius J. Foley, Williamsville, N.Y.

SNOW WHITE (*to* SEVEN DWARFS): "Good News: I'm madly in love with a dwarf. Bad News: His name is Smelly."

Tom Morrow, N.Y.C.

Good News: "I finally got the mink coat I said I'd do anything for. Bad News: I can't button it."

Eileen Tranford, Dorchester, Mass.

SOCIAL CLIMBER (*to* SPOUSE): "Good News: We've been asked to the party of the year. Bad News: Do you still have your maid's uniform?"

Sandra Schnyder, Waverly, Pa.

STAGE MANAGER (*to* UNDERSTUDY): "Bad News: Your favorite uncle died at dawn. Good News: So did the star..."

Jay McDonnell, N.Y.C.

Good News: "Yes, Virginia, there is a Santa Claus." Bad News: "But the Easter Bunny..."

Mary Lynn Shapiro, N.Y.C.

PRESS AGENT (*to* BROADWAY PRODUCER): "Good News: John Simon raved. Bad News: ... and ranted."

Rees Behrendt, N.Y.C.

Good News: "Your wife just remarried: your alimony payments stop." Bad News: "She married your boss and you're fired."

Arthur J. Greenbaum, N.Y.C.

Good News: "Your violin is a Stradivarius dated Cremona, 1701." Bad News: "It and our appraiser are missing."

Larry Alson, N.Y.C.

Good News: "I dreamed last night someone walked over my grave." Bad News: "My God! I'm dead!"

Ruth Simon, Forest Hills, N.Y.

MASOCHIST (*to* SADIST): "I have good and bad news. The Good News is that I have Bad News..."

Jerry Goodman, Great Neck, N.Y.

ZEUS (*to* AESCULAPIUS): "Bad News: By Jove, I have a splitting headache. Good News: It's a healthy girl!"

David Sosland and Eva Barron, Teaneck, N.J.

RON ZIEGLER (*to* NIXON): "Good News: John Mitchell is divorcing Martha. Bad News: He's marrying Bella Abzug."

Ross Yockey, N.Y.C.

ACROBAT (*to* PARTNER): "Allez-Oop!/Ooops, Allie!"

Howard Leichter, Warren, N.J.

Bad News: "My daughter married a (drug) pusher." Good News: "He's a good provider."

Jan Shannon, Rego Park, N.Y.

Good News: "I read here that Nixon is willing to debate vital issues on TV." Bad News: "The paper is dated 1960."

Patricia Kerman, N.Y.C.

STRANGER (*at door*): "Good News: I have a cashier's check for you for $1 million. Bad News: My name is Michael J. Anthony."

Liliane Tanenbaum, Brooklyn, N.Y.

Good News: "You have won First Prize on New York's Competition number 97. Bad News: "Your prize is *A Century of College Humor.*"

James I. Campbell, Seneca Falls, N.Y.

☞ *Short Stories*

"I grew up ripe, unready, glutted with the grass-clean salt smell of summer in that old house, I had met few strangers . . ."

"I never saw her again."

Above, the first and last sentences of a short story. Competitors were asked to provide the opening and concluding lines from a single piece of urbane short fiction.

Report: An abundance of first-rate openers and closers, not all of them, how you say, urbane. A few repetitive *structural* patterns emerged: verbatim first and last lines; concluding sentences resembling rather a second, follow-up line (or at least the wrap up of a hopelessly short story); and entries containing more-than-one-sentence-per-opener-or-closer. Duplication of *content,* however evocative or provocative, ran to: Science Fiction; the Failure/Success story (often the ruthless captain of industry) beginning "I was just a kid with a dream . . ." and concluding ". . . the envelope, please"; Romance and Heartbreak: "Our eyes met across the room . . ." and "I walked away in the rain"; Tales Ending in Divorce, Insanity or Worse(?). Perhaps our instructions seemed oblique, since a startling number of actual quotes, complete with sources, appeared. We had not thought it necessary, after lo these ninety-odd competitions, to include the word "parody." We hope that among the excellent offerings below we have not, please God, printed a few such *bona fide* lines, innocently submitted *sans* source. It will come as a shock (it did to us) but, you see, we're just not entirely familiar with *all* urbane short fiction. Ah, well . . .

"When I was eight, I hid behind the radiator when my maiden aunt played Chopin, the sentimental tears splashing down my collar: hovering on the edge of some profound, exquisite beauty whose full and terrible meaning would not become clear to me for many years to come."
"Yet they tell me, too, that Bartok died on Central Park West."

Faith Davis Humphreys, Boston, Mass.

"Until I met her I had made it a practice never to go to bed with women whose husbands I knew."
"And then he slapped me on the back; harder than necessary, I thought."

Laurence Miller, N.Y.C.

"Being both absent-minded and legally blind without glasses—which I never wear (more of that later)—I forgot to pick up the girl on the Long Island Railroad (though I had emphatically meant to—she was quite gorgeous, though fuzzy) and instead tripped onto the lap of Joanna R. while vainly attempting to get out of my seat and off the train before the doors closed at my station."
" 'Neither do I dig you a bit,' I squinted."

Joel Gross, N.Y.C.

"Whether my spiritual discipline had been forged in the hearth of Irish Catholicism or was coolly chiseled from the granite of self-meditation, I knew that it set me uniquely apart from that rowdy bunch of would-be novitiates who shared that autumnal bus ride to Sts. James and Joseph Seminary."
" 'That's the whole story, pal,' I said, pouring my lone customer one on the house. 'Turn them upside down and they all look alike.' "

Kit Hurley, N.Y.C.

"Arnold wore his hair parted on the side and looped across his forehead like a curtain opening on an empty stage. . . ."
"He'd have walked away, flipping his cigarette on her Moroccan rug, but he didn't smoke."

Patricia Miller, N.Y.C.

"I rocketed around the corner on my skateboard, portfolio under one arm and the other fending off dowager strumpets, the topcoat wind molding the maroon double-knit to my tennis-firm body, and the keening whine of freedom, just behind me, matching my Uptown speed."
"The rest of the way was downhill."

E. F. Coudal, Park Ridge, N.J.

"She was one of those extremely complex women: bright, beautiful, with high-cheek-boned sophistication and long legs, and the darkest, most alluring eyes I had ever seen . . ."
"Of course, she got custody of the children."

Anton E. Peeters, N.Y.C.

"Often he had heard the story from Baba Sonia: how his great-grandfather, Reb Yitshak of Loivitch, had led the villagers, with their cattle, horses, and chickens, away from the plague to safety, and Life, and how years later, when his great-grandfather's hair was like snow, those same people reviled him as though he was *trayf*."

" 'They're killing me at Screen Gems,' he muttered bitterly as his chauffeur gunned the Mercedes down La Cienega."

Jess Korman, N.Y.C.

"My husband's lawyer arrived promptly at eight, an owlish caricature with small, close-set eyes magnified by thick, tortoise-shell glasses riding on an ample pointed nose, all perfectly placed above a thin-lipped smile designed to advertise past legal accomplishments and present general supremacy."

"He was smiling in a new way now, and he winked as he tripped over the threshold on the way out."

William N. Finn, Augusta, Me.

"Having survived a war and two wives, it seemed absurd now to find myself flying into emotional fragments because of a stranger's remark in a bar."

"I wondered what Ann had had for dinner."

Jo Ann West, Cheverly, Md.

" 'The Churl-in-the-puce-greatcoat,' as my father called him, was, I discovered early, an Englishman and therefore to be despised."

"That autumn Irish night, shivery in my pajamas, I knew what the others did not: that it was the object of our fun and malice who had carried my little brother's body out of the fire and (it was his style) departed."

Raymond O'Kane, Bronx, N.Y.

"It wasn't the old RHinelander 4 number, but a meaningless series of digits, that her stepson in Rye had reluctantly given him."

"Shrugging faintly, he turned from the gallery window and walked toward Madison murmuring, 'The bitch never could paint worth a damn.' "

Barbara Allen, Ridgewood, N.J.

"There she was, waiting, a fugitive from the forties, seated in a large sedan chair, situated in a corner of the lobby littered with potted palms—as I approached her, I wondered how I would broach the subject...."
"The elevator ascended—I headed for the nearest bar."

Sybil Cooke, Furlong, Pa.

"I was reading the evening news when I saw it: 'Omes, Allyn, thirty-two, on October 9, 1968, of Smith Street, Greenport, Conn.; beloved daughter of—'; Mass was next morning several towns away, and I had no way to get there, even if I wanted to . . . which I didn't."
"I wish I could tell her that."

Andrea Ackerly, Manorville, N.Y.

"We lived in a third-floor apartment on Maple Street in St. Louis, on a block which also contained the Ever-ready Garage, a Chinese laundry, and a bookie shop disguised as a cigar store . . ."
"I hold my breath, for if my sister's face appears among them—the night is hers!"

Haig Keshishian, Richmond, Ind.

"The new five-gallon tank stood gleaming on the window sill, waiting only water and a suitable piscine inhabitant —surely not another torpid goldfish or a banal guppy."
"I can even tie a very presentable cravat with my left hand."

Fred Berg, Boston, Mass.

"Marriage, a wearily belated plunge, foundered after two years on my sixtieth birthday (a devastating coincidence), thus initiating my intensive verbal therapy with Dr. Dahlkuntz, age thirty-four and twice divorced, with a Zurich degree below her Warhol and an erotic cluster of freckles at the base of her amber neck like a naughty friction rash from the yanking of an opal pendant on its silver cords while gamboling in her cleavage."

"The fact of her third, entered with such appalling equanimity, and my second suddenly ignited my contained anxiety at sixty-two (the time of my social security), setting off a fine angina, no doubt abetted by the exit numbers on the freeway as my mind jiggled with permutations throughout our Dahlkuntz-driven journey to her selected mecca, grubby Niagara Falls."

William Pitts, Woodmere, N.Y.

"On those rare occasions when she visited him, they walked in a garden that was more a memory of things as they had been than a current landscape, and it occurred to him that the pock-marked, decayed stone benches were charming as Greek ruins only when she was there."
"He greeted the police with more wonder than surprise, and asked them calmly if they were concerned with a recently committed sin, or one he had perpetrated in some previous existence."

Annalee Gold, N.Y.C.

"The chrome and Lucite accessories of his penthouse reflected the many facets of his personality like some magnificent diamonds."
"And using for a spoon a piece of rusted metal which had no doubt fallen from the trestle overhead, he scraped out the last few rancid morsels of food, and wept aloud when he saw his soiled, distorted reflection at the bottom of the bean can."

George A. Hatch, Jr., N.Y.C.

"In Vermont they are fond of saying that until a man has reached a certain undefinable age, has tasted the rarity and purity of life in all its pungency, has learned the sorrow of building bridges when he could have forded the stream, has broken his knuckles repairing his neighbor's barn, only then can he know the simple, placid joy of watching the robins dig for worms . . ."

"I boarded the train, clutching the briefcase to my breast like a triumphant thief and feeling older than I had ever felt before."

Norman R. Wallis, Chicago, Ill.

"There is, perhaps especially in those of us who would make a point of denying it, an aura of anticipation surrounding the beginning of any New Year . . ."

". . . then, inevitably, the orchestra struck up the first notes of 'Auld Lang Syne.' "

William A. Hafey, Avon, Conn.

"The moment he leaped out of bed that sultry, sunless, simmering Sunday, Alain Trenton ('Lally,' as his ex-sister-in-law called him) knew with the sudden, sick certainty of his naked gut that something was about to happen, and to happen fast."

"Someplace a door slammed shut."

Bel Kaufman, N.Y.C.

"She could hear the strident voices and high-pitched laughter even before she reached the long corridor which led to the College Parlor, where her classmates had gathered to celebrate their twenty-fifth reunion."

"No one, not even Nancy, who had brought them together, remembered to ask her about Harry."

Mrs. Judith R. Goldsmith, Woodmere, N.Y.

"Aliens came at him, wielding carrots."

"Yes, Mother, I want to marry Carl."

Si Dunn, Denton, Texas

"I must tell of the terrible and ruinous thing that happened to Harry Clarke, of the fate that overtook and destroyed him when he was only thirty-two."

"I see him around town occasionally; he drives a white Jaguar and is often accompanied by a well-dressed blonde."

John Vachon, N.Y.C.

"When I was in my junior year at Thomas Jefferson High School in Elizabeth, N.J., I hung around a lot with a fellow named 'Chuck' Murphy who was really good on clarinet and who had a tape recording of every record that Benny Goodman, Artie Shaw, and Woody Herman ever made."

"I heard he finally got a job with New Jersey Bell."

George Fairbanks, Nutley, N.J.

☞ *Conversation Starters*

"Fifty Lumps Please, and Hold the Cream. ..."

Above, a Conversation Starter. Competitors were invited to submit a one-line attention-getter designed as an invitation to further colloquy with a stranger.

Report: Stranger is right. A very strange lot indeed. A few of our old complaints recurred: **1.** multiple submissions from the same individuals (perhaps the welcome presence of many new competitors explains this rule-stretching); **2.** the imitation of the tone or setting of our own example ("Tuna on dogwood, to go"), and **3.** flagrantly ancient ploys: "Only one earring, Miss?" A smattering of *déjà* views and a smuttering of rest-room humor. But the prevailing fault was the use of jokes-per-se, as in Jackie Vernon's "Pardon me, but have you seen a Congressional Medal of Honor anywhere around?" For some reason, deformities and communicable (if not social) diseases were popular, as were: travelogue dialogue ("Didn't we meet at ———?"), Martian words, strange pets, and the old switcheroo, as in: "Your slip is not showing" or "Pardon me, *sir,* but your slip is showing." Other arresting (some literally) approaches: offers of Park Avenue duplexes for $125 per month; tow-away warnings: "Would you please hold (or watch) my —— for me?"; "You're stepping (or sitting) on my ——"; and "You're a dead ringer (speaking of Quasimodo) for so-and-so." Ah, well. What can you say about a twenty-five-year-old joke that dies? Not much. After sifting through so many bizarre conversational attempts, some of the more prosaic come-ons seemed apter and more disarming. At least *we'd* answer the following:

"I am Daniel Ellsberg."
Sam Bassin, Brooklyn, N.Y.

"Of course she's very graceful on stage, but you know those are not really her own hands."
Howard Newman, N.Y.C.

"That cobra isn't getting enough air!"
Peter Stone, East Hampton, N.Y.

"I Am Who Am."
Don de Nicola, Brooklyn, N.Y.

"Oh, a Maltby puzzle; would you please hand me that pen?"
Ralston Hill, N.Y.C.

"Hello, my name is Spartacus Bernstein."
Spartacus Bernstein, Brooklyn Heights, N.Y.
Special mention: Peter Pussydog, N.Y.C.

"I've heard so much about you from your twin."
Ellen S. Ryp, N.Y.C.

"I don't care what time it is, and I have a match . . ."
Marc Melvin, N.Y.C.

"Is that Miss or Mr.?"
N. Newgent, Washington, D.C.

"Pardon me, but does that phone work?"
>> Joan Wilen, N.Y.C.

"Is 'hold-up' one word or two?"
>> John Walker, San Luis Obispo, Calif.

"Take me to Bedford-Stuyvesant, driver. . . ."
>> Barbara Metsky, Washington, D.C.

"Excuse me, is this the ten-items-or-less line?"
>> Josephine Burns, Jersey City, N.J.

"Boy, it's a good thing you don't happen to be superstitious."
>> Rees Behrendt, N.Y.C.

"Taxi! Gracie Mansion, please."
>> Robert Emmett, N.Y.C.
>> Harvey Chipkin, Rutherford, N.J.

"Main floor . . . watch your pocketbook."
>> Mary Conte, North Miami, Fla.

"Could you direct me to the nearest convent or pawnshop?"
>> Tom Morrow, N.Y.C.

"Hey, man, need any spare change?"
>> Raymond Kauders, N.Y.C.

"If you live on West 87th Street between Central Park West and Columbus, I think I may once have been your cat."
>> Dan Greenburg, N.Y.C.

"Excuse me, did you drop this newt?"
>> Molly Yonderhill, N.Y.C.

"You're standing on my tail."
>> George Malko, N.Y.C.
>> Similarly from: Marsha Levy, Brooklyn, N.Y.

"Pardon me, but if that's a fall, I believe you're wearing my hair."
                                    D. Kotteb, N.Y.C.

"Hey, did you hear about atomic radiation?"
                                    Peg Biagiotti, Brooklyn, N.Y.

"I wish I knew how to stop making money."
                                    Paul Weiss, Washington, D.C.

"As an economy measure the elevators in our building run down only."
                                    Edith H. Coogler, Atlanta, Ga.

"Are you here alone, or should I start with your mother?"
                                    N. Bayer, Ruston, Va.

"I understand you were an adopted child."
                                    Joseph T. Rigo, N.Y.C.

"Great Caesar's ghost, my good man, but you're the spitting image of Bjorn Andresen."
                                    Arthur Weller, Interlaken, N.Y.

"She says she's really getting into midgets . . ."
                                    Mrs. A. German, Amherst, Mass.

"There once was a man from Dundee . . ."
                                    Eleanor Barry, Rocky Hill, Conn.

"Do you speak English?"
                                    Jane Milbrath, Cullowhee, N.C.

"You're flat again . . ."
                                    Charles Renick, Jr., Great Neck, N.Y.

"You have been in Afghanistan, I perceive."
                                    S. S. Smith, Cooperstown, N.Y.

"Oh, my God, I left my baby on that bus!"
                                    Grant M. Waldman, N.Y.C.

"Two doors to the left, but I don't use their bathroom any more."

Hedley Burnell, Washington, D.C.

"Of course, my father's the only Orangeman in the whole of Belfast who's actually orange."

Laurence M. Pretty, N.Y.C.

"Perhaps you noticed the rash on my hand when we were introduced. . . ."

Arnold Rosenfeld, Dayton, Ohio

"Have you heard about Luchino Visconti's death in Venice?"

Laura Donenfeld, N.Y.C.

"Abaft the barnacle lies an overstuffed lazarette."

Charles M. Lane, North Haven, Conn.

"Excuse me, your mustache is missing."

Barbara Cates, N.Y.C.

"I'd like to return this defective Bible."

John S. Sherman, Jr., Morris Plains. N.J.

"Would you mind holding this match while I pour the kerosene over my head?"

Miles and Judith Klein, East Brunswick, N.J.

"Have you a hypodermic needle I might borrow for a few minutes?"

Elaine Stallworth, Willow Grove, Pa.

"Excuse moi, quelle heure est Rona Barrett sur ici?"

Anne Commire, N.Y.C.

"As I was just saying to my friend Howard Hughes . . ."

Andrew and Renée Herz, N.Y.C.
Similarly from: Michael Deskey, N.Y.C.

"Madam, you may think it's all very funny, but my hyena doesn't."

Chuck Suttoni, N.Y.C.

"I don't know about you folks, but I've got to work tomorrow."

Carol Petras, N.Y.C.

"Do you happen to have a roller-skate key?"

Ted Heyman, Chicago, Ill.

"My dog lies about her age."

Carla Rich, N.Y.C.

"Again last night he left his shoes in the refrigerator."

Gloria Ullman, Los Angeles, Calif.

"I was at a small get-together the other night and right in the middle of . . . 'Sha-Boom, Sha-Boom,' who should walk in but Diane Varsi . . ."

Rita Oakes, Drexel Hill, Pa.

"Quick, if you value our national security, take this attaché case and meet me under the Biltmore clock in twenty minutes."

Marshall W. Karp, N.Y.C.

"Oh, *you're* the one that's Nixon."

Louis de la Foret, New Orleans, La.

". . . perhaps a cup of arrack in the ashrack of your humble arriviste."

Bob McLaughlin, Bronx, N.Y.

"Yes."

Brenda F. Gustin, N.Y.C.

"Aren't the walls unusually perpendicular with the ceiling?"

Margaret Cherol, Hanover, Pa.

"I probably shouldn't mention this, but—oh, never mind."

Ruth Ellen Galper, N.Y.C.

"What did the witch do to turn you into a frog in the first place?"

A. S. Cappelli, Providence, R.I.

"This is very important, my life is at stake, I'm going to embrace you . . . for God's sake just act natural."

James S. Kirby, East Longmeadow, Mass.

"I hope you have Blue Cross coverage."

Marilyn Crystal, Brooklyn, N.Y.

"I'd like two tickets for *Oh! Calcutta!* Friday evening, one in the front row and one in the balcony . . ."

Donald Elman, N.Y.C.

"Pardon me for staring, but you are the image of my wife before the operation."

Susan Schneider, Scarsdale, N.Y.

"You're lucky John Simon doesn't know you."

Joel F. Crystal, Brooklyn, N.Y.

"While rape and pillage are to be deplored, I must say . . ."

Rev. Vincent P. Gorman, Bronx, N.Y.

"Why is everyone singing 'Nearer My God to Thee'?"

A. J. Stein, N.Y.C.

"Pardon, sir, but when that pay phone rings would you answer and say you are speaking for Cornelia?"

Herbert C. Holt, Woodstock, Vt.

"So, what's the story?"

Alan Fox, Little Neck, N.Y.

"I don't wear underwear in the summertime . . ."
Richard Van Wiebe, Fort Wayne, Ind.

"What do you mean you're somebody's grandmother—I left my wolf here!"
Bonnie Stein, N.Y.C.

"There's something you must try with a stuffed owl and cantaloupe halves in a water bed."
Norton Bramesco, N.Y.C.

"I'm trying to think of a conversation starter for a *New York* Magazine Competition . . ."
Ilene McGrath, Englewood, N.J.

☞ *Conversation Stoppers*

"My Sister-in-Law's Cousin Is Totie Fields's Accountant..."

Above, a Conversation Stopper. Competitors were invited to supply one similarly uninviting line, guaranteed to doom further colloquy.

Report: A reasonably hefty entry. Some good news, some bad, but all of it prodigiously boring. (A new outcropping of more-than-one-entry-per-contestant: desist, please.) Typical were the following categories: Obvious facts or ancient news: "Have you heard about Lindsay's party switch?" Arcane data: "Did you know that this is National Maritime Elephant Week?" Pictures of, facts about, the kiddies or pets. Deprecating remarks about the person addressed. Admission of a communicable disease or unsavory habit. Gratis advice asked of a doctor, lawyer. Lengthy dental or medical reports. Boasting of subculture status. Talk of food (recipes), home furnishings, etc. Details of TV shows, home movies, travel plans. Insurance sales pitches. "When I was your age . . ." "Heeeere's Johnny!" and "I just entered (or I've never won) the *New York* Magazine Competition." In other

words, a group so painstakingly mesmeric that we . . . .
zzzzzz . . .

"My friends are kind enough to find this story amusing . . ."

Joanne Vance, N.Y.C.

"We've been meaning to have you folks over for dinner but we've had a lot of other social commitments lately . . ."

Barbara Allen, Ridgewood, N.J.

"I have a friend who's a colored fellow."

Mrs. Curtis Stein, Fort Wayne, Ind.

"We've got to tell you about this apartment we looked at . . . you enter here, and . . ."

Jess Korman, N.Y.C.

"I'm actually primarily a housewife, but I also dabble in poetry; mostly iambic pentameter."

Dan Greenburg, N.Y.C.

"Ladies and gentlemen, the President of the United States."

Mike Leiderman, Schenectady, N.Y.

"I don't think that's a bit funny: I have a great deal of admiration for the Polish people."

Adrien Patrick, New Orleans, La.

"How does the word-of-mouth thing get started if you don't advertise the book?"

Elaine Kendall, Princeton, N.J.

"Excuse me, I heard that you're deaf."

Barry Poskanzer, N.Y.C.

"Stone deaf, can't hear a thing, was it important?"

James Hickman, N.Y.C.

"Did you know that Lana Turner's eyebrows never grew back?"

Edward J. Walker, N.Y.C.

"Well, after today all of us will have twenty-four hours fewer to live."

E. Thurston, N.Y.C.

"Such is life."

Joan Beisel, Elmhurst, N.Y.

"The worst accidents happen right in your own home—my friend tripped over a vacuum cleaner cord and broke her hip in three places..."

Mary Lampel, Jamaica Estates, N.Y.

Well, Nixon is a devoted father."

Ronna Stoloff, Rego Park, N.Y.

"Actually, I'm working on a history of the American Liquor Industry."

Nora Ephron, N.Y.C.

"I was on television once."

George Kozarevic, West New York, N.J.

"I teach economics."

K. Harrison, Professor of Economics, Potsdam, N.Y.

"Do you know a game called 'Bore Back'?"

David E. Cassidy, N.Y.C.

"Yes, but they don't do it that way in the South."

Paul Ruben, Dayton, Ohio

"In my opinion Abe Beame was a better budget director than a controller."

Richard M. Rosen, N.Y.C.

"Nothing really: the same old thing."
Charles K. Robinson, Kearny, N.J.

"Yes, we've met before, but you don't remember me."
Angela Veneto, Cambridge, Mass.

"You stay here, I'll go and get help."
R. James, N.Y.C.

"For God's sake, will somebody please tell me how to gain weight?"
Vince Buscemi, Bayside, N.Y.

"I never dream."
Gisella Baumann, Astoria, N.Y.

"The trouble with me is I'm hard on shoes."
John D. Grant, N.Y.C.

"The bird tipped the water dish in his cage and now the paper's wet. . . ."
Hilda Benfer, Elkhorn, Wis.

"And here is our Pomeranian; say 'Good morning' to the nice man, poochums."
Barbara A. Huff, N.Y.C.

"I hear the air was unacceptable today. . . ."
Ed Schultz, N.Y.C.

"Yes, I picked it up in Bloomingdale's last week when I was in New York."
Mrs. Phyllis Kelly, Locust Valley, N.Y.

"I wish I could remember the punch line of the one about . . ."
Dolly H. Hecht, N.Y.C.
Rosemary Wells, Croton-on-Hudson, N.Y.
Nelda Davies, Montclair, N.J.

"My shrink encourages me to talk about my divorce . . ."
Lydia Wilen, N.Y.C.

Conversation Stoppers / 249

"I wouldn't say you look like Kathleen Freeman if I really didn't mean it."

James Kuslan, Hamden, Conn.

"I think Father O'Leary fell asleep during my confession last Sunday."

Virginia Page, Guilford, Vt.

"This is my seventh glass of water today on the Stillman diet."

Linda Hanrahan, N.Y.C.

"I think someone else is on the line."

Michael Ulick, N.Y.C.

". . . you may remain silent . . . you have the right to counsel . . ."

Ronald Litowitz, N.Y.C.

"I used to date Kate Smith."

David Grotenstein, N.Y.C.

"I wish I knew someone with a nice big apartment who could take care of our orangutan for a few weeks while we're in Majorca. . . ."

Fred Berg, Boston, Mass.

"I'm getting out of New York."

Bob Kenney, N.Y.C.

"Wasn't it terrible what happened to Mary, Queen of Scots?"

Harold Luhrs, N.Y.C.

"It really turns me off when people knock Edward the First."

Nancy Bloom, N.Y.C.

"Mother said you were a pretty girl when you were young."

Darthy Craft, Gallatin, Tenn.

"The man I'm going to marry loves Wonder Bread."
Susan Scher, Albany, N.Y.

"I always eat the same lunch at the same place with the same people every day."
Tom Morrow, N.Y.C.

"I don't know what made you think that I take the pill."
Judy Zuckerman, Elmhurst, N.Y.

"Yes, my daughter has become the bride of Dr. Frankenstein, and I've cut her off without a cent; he's a Jew, you know."
Albert Weiner, Albany, N.Y.

"I attend Emerson College. . . ."
Jeffery Ofgang, Emerson College, Boston, Mass.

"Lately I've dah this crazy egru to say yreve third word sdrawkcab."
Msgr. A. V. McLees, St. Albans, N.Y.

"Guess who I saw on the street today—Fletcher Knebel."
Norman C. Ansorge, N.Y.C.

"Life is a stone that sits by the bushes."
J. Economos, Scarsdale, N.Y.

"Yesterday I saw my first sunrise."
Paul Weiss, Washington, D.C.

"I still know the whole thing by heart: 'On my honor, I will try . . .'"
Elaine Stallworth, Willow Grove, Pa.

"Cat got your tongue?"
Gary Levine, Merrick, N.Y.

"I wanted to create something with my own two hands, so I bought this afghan kit at Woolworth's."
Helen Shaffer, Chambersburg, Pa.

Conversation Stoppers / 251

"Okay, now, are you ready for one that will really date you?"

Bob Hervey, Albany, N.Y.

"During the bomb scare I went out and bought a couch."
Janet Jakubowski, N.Y.C.

"By the way, your check came back. . . ."
Gary Blake, N.Y.C.

"Jean, this girl in my office, she's a scream, well . . ."
Kit Hurley, N.Y.C.

"Oh, man, am I turned on! You know, no, I mean—it's . . . you know, it's like, real heavy, you know?"
Mill Herndon, N.Y.C.

"Pardon me, I seem to remember the Forum Theatre being located here in the Vivian Beaumont . . ."
Bob Shepard, Passaic, N.J.

"Bats are the only kind of bird I don't like."
Peter Hollander, N.Y.C.

"Well, I guess Nixon is doing the best he can."
Michael Margolis, N.Y.C.

"So *this* is where you young people spend your afternoons!"

Ruth Ellen Galper, N.Y.C.

"I heard you were a good conversationalist."
Ann Lehmann, Eads, Tenn.

"Let f be a function of a complex variable . . ."
Math Coffee Room, University of N.C., Chapel Hill

"I think my mouse is dead."

Barbara Friedberg, N.Y.C.

"I had a couple of awfully good meals at a restaurant out West this summer, but I forget now what we ordered . . ."
James Fechheimer, Glen Head, N.Y.

"I see where this week's *New York* Magazine Competition is number ninety-three."
Bill Becker, Urbana, Ill.

☞ *Film Promos*

"In the Eyes of the World, Their Love was Illicit, but Theirs Is a Story You Cannot Forget . . ." (No One Will Be Seated After the Picture Begins.)

Above, typical promotional copy for an unnamed film. Competitors were asked to submit provocative copy for an unspecified but sure-fire box-office-hit film.

Report: SEE! the wonderful results of this competition! SEE! Contestants without shame. HEAR! the editor laugh! Most duplication derived from types of films rather than verbatim copy. Exceptions ran to: "Makes Myra Breckinridge Look like Snow White"; "X Is Back and Y Has Got Him (or Her or It)"; The Lone Survivor of a Nuclear Holocaust—*Or Was He??*" Drug flicks were rated Rx. Parenthetical notes advised "Adults admitted only if accompanied by teen-agers," "A registered nurse will be on duty in the theater lobby," etc. We X-rated entries obviously describing a particular film, and those containing endorsements by critics. The use of real actors' names seemed extraneous—again, there were exceptions. Be it hard- or soft-sell, tastiest was the "sounds-just-like-an-ad-I-can-hardly-wait-to-see-the-movie" copy. Yet we couldn't resist a few out-and-out jokes. In all, a snappy assortment. Please do not reveal the beginning to your friends. . . .

JACKIE ACTS!

William Mathewson, N.Y.C.

"Motion pictures come and go. Some are great, some are brilliant, but rarely does the president of a motion-picture company have the opportunity to endorse his own product. I now have that opportunity . . ."

Anne Hormann, New Haven, Conn.

A Secluded Girls' College Offers Quite an Education.
DeeDee—Campus Queen—with a pillow for a crown?
Paige—What *had* happened in Portugal?
Dorey—A nice girl? Or a good one?
Kay—The redhead. She always had an extra toothbrush. Then came DUDE.

Lois Spencer, Purchase, N.Y.

A town in flames . . .
An abandoned kayak . . .
And the heart of a great dog.

Jean Houston, Chapel Hill, N.C.

For Some It Will Be the Story of a Boy and a Dog.
For Others It Will Be More.
Rated: **GP** For those who think it's the story of a boy and a dog.
    X For those who think it's more.

Barbara Lindberg, N.Y.C.

Neither the child, nor the call girl, nor the dog, nor the Pope . . . could forget the man they called Bad Betty.

Daniel J. Moriarty, N.Y.C.

Speed Was His Life, but She Was His Soul.

Robert Corsi, N.Y.C.

He thought that he had reached the very peak of his manhood, but then he met—Lyla . . .

Iris Temple, Flushing, N.Y.

Her ways of getting information from a man were different from the Gestapo's!

Warren G. Harris, N.Y.C.

Tender Love in the Bitter Cold! A Film as Big and Broad as Russia Itself. . . .

Anthony J. Sousa, N.Y.C.

Who thought he existed—let alone could be captured?

Steven and Judy Kunreuther, N.Y.C.

Makes the Seven Deadly Sins Look Like the Corporal Works of Mercy!

Rita Oakes, Drexel Hill, Pa.

"Madman" "Misfit" "Psychopath" and more! What will you call Mr. Souhlim?

Charles Almon, N.Y.C.

One man held the key to the new horror that threatened to engulf the world. They had to find him—*and Time Was Running Out!*

Eleanor McKernan, Guilford, Conn.

Why did Ellen lie to the F.B.I. about the President? You won't sleep for weeks after you find out!

Phil Young, Glen Ellyn, Ill.

The Sadistic Film That Shocked Hitler!

James Fechheimer, Glen Head, N.Y.

Iguana or man . . . who can say? But he was destined to become President . . .

Susan Aronson, Philadelphia, Pa.

At Last, the United States Supreme Court Has Ruled You Have a Constitutional Right To See This Film!
>George Haber, Brooklyn, N.Y.

What two World Wars ripped apart, only her lips could bring together . . .
>Roderick Cook, N.Y.C.

Corinne—women may condemn her and men may adore her, but all will envy her.
>Joyce Terner, N.Y.C.

Everyone in town knew Selena—some knew her intimately.
>Arthur Weller, Interlaken, N.Y.

Yesterday I Was Jeffrey. Today I Am Beverly. Witness My Story Before You Judge Me.
>Anthony Visconti, Cambridge, Mass.

Charlton Heston IS God.
>E. Hulick, N.Y.C.

In order that we might bring you this motion picture, the Mann Act has been violated.
>Robert Clark, Cincinnati, Ohio

They Lived a Lifetime in Twenty-four Crowded Hours!
>Gertrude Radin, N.Y.C.

From the glory of the Great White Way . . . to Prison Bars!!!
>Peter Howard, Los Angeles, Calif.

She rode a thousand miles—to kill a man she'd never met. . . .
>Knox Burger, N.Y.C.

He drank for a hobby. He killed for a living. Men feared him. Women desired him. He took what he could get—and he could get what he wanted.
>Ed Craig, N.Y.C.

It took guts to film! Have you the guts to see it?
> *Charles Hollerith, Jr., N.Y.C.*

The motion picture that could change your life . . . Or save it!!!
> *Salli Madden, Massapequa, N.Y.*

They met in the DMZ! An American Nurse. A Viet Cong Soldier. A Love Story as different as the war that brought them together!
> *Joyce Elbert, N.Y.C.*

If we told you the ending, you could never sit through it!
> *Robert A. Wilson, Dallas, Texas*

There were four men in her life. One to love her. One to marry her. One to take care of her. And one to kill her.
> *Bonnie MacDougall, N.Y.C.*

Stripped of all but pride, he fought his way from the torture chamber of the Inquisitor to the bedchamber of the Queen.
> *Don Morrison, N.Y.C.*

They met strangely in the plum-blue dusk of Paris. They melted into each other's arms, into each other's lives. Waiting . . . watching . . . was the man he was sworn to kill.
> *Laurence Miller, N.Y.C.*

The Book They Said Could Never Be Written Has Become the Movie They Said Could Never Be Filmed.
> *David Rothenberg, N.Y.C.*

With this single film, Lima becomes a major movie capital.
> *Janet Murray, N.Y.C.*

She liked men—men liked her. The story of a girl in today's world. At fifteen she knew it all. At sixteen, she was still learning.
>
> *Zvi Ribalow, Cambria Heights, N.Y.*

Money Does Different Things to Different People.
>
> *Sue Bugden, Boston, Mass.*

They were only Roman slaves, never invited to the nightly orgies, until from their ranks came one man . . .
>
> *Spartacus Bernstein, Brooklyn Heights, N.Y.*

He was a man of letters. He was a man of affairs. Until that one letter from that one affair destroyed him . . .
>
> *Michael Greer, N.Y.C.*

It's the Duke again—roaring, raping, screaming, marauding, and bayoneting his way into your hearts. (Rated **G**)
>
> *H. Bert Aronson, Philadelphia, Pa.*

At last it can be told. The passionate true-life story of a pre-teen-age romance. (No one under eighteen admitted.)
>
> *Mrs. Lillian Cherensky, Metuchen, N.J.*

This is the ONE picture you MUST see ALONE!
>
> *Frank Maguire, N.Y.C.*

If you scoff at the powers of darkness, DO NOT SEE THIS FILM ALONE!
>
> *Martin Gross, N.Y.C.*

. . . Creatures so frighteningly real you will think they have stepped out of the screen. (No seating in the first eight rows.)
>
> *Harvey Chipkin, Rutherford, N.J.*

No one will be allowed to leave his seat once the picture has begun.
>
> *Thomas Buccello, Westport, Conn.*

After four years, three continents, and two wars, what does a soldier do when he comes home to the girl who wasn't waiting? Can you blame him?
Susy Pauker, N.Y.C.

You'll Cry.
Joseph S. Brownman, Alexandria, Va.

From beyond the solar system, they came to destroy earth! SEE the multiarmed monsters bat planes out of the air, destroy cities, swallow Lake Erie . . .
Joel F. Crystal, Brooklyn, N.Y.

She defied all the laws by which decent men live—but don't condemn her till you've seen her story.
Anna Corsi, N.Y.C.

He was young enough to be her son, but the instincts he aroused in her were hardly maternal . . .
Mrs. Judith Goldsmith, Woodmere, N.Y.

We ask you not to remain for the surprise ending of this picture so as not to reveal it to your friends.
Mrs. Jean Mayer, Roslyn, N.Y.

If you could see only one picture in your lifetime . . . well maybe you'd better skip this one.
Miles and Judith Klein, East Brunswick, N.J.

☞ *One-Letter Inserts*

"Welcome, Strangler"

Above, a title from a movie marquee, plus an added attraction. Competitors were asked to demonstrate the power of an extra letter inserted in a familiar phrase.

Report: So many deft-but-identical entries—among our favorites: "Make it one for my baby, and one more for the broad"; "Cast thy bread upon the waiters . . ."; "How High the Moron"; "A Fool and His Monkey Are soon Parted"; and, parochially, Damn Greenburg. Equally savory, but reprised from earlier comps: One Man's Meat Is Another Man's Poisson; "Tell me, where is fancy bread?" and "Supperstar." Also, en masse: "I'm Debbie, Flay Me to Miami"; "In the beginning, Gold created heaven and earth" or "Gold helps those . . ."; "Old Soldiers Never Diet . . ."; "A Sword to the Wise . . ."; Mary Queen of Scouts; *How to Wine Friends* . . . ; "A Chicken in Every Port (Poet)"; "Chaste Makes Waste"; "How Do I Love Three?" *Cant on a Hot Tin Roof;* "Two Heads Are Better Than None" and *No, Not Nanette.* No space to list all the commonest inserts—(b)right, heart(h), etc. Some phrases simply were not altered in meaning, at least not so's you'd notice it. Much. Yet, as Ms. Streisand might say, "All That Glitters Is Not Gould."

One-Letter Inserts / 261

" 'All right,' said the cat; and this time it vanished quite slowly, beginning with the end of the tail, and ending with the groin, which remained some time after the rest of it had gone."

Larry Laiken, Bayside, N.Y.

"I Cain't Say Ngo!"

Fred Cline, N.Y.C.

"If you knew Preggy Sue, then you'd know why I feel blue!"

Anita Daniels, Sevenoaks, Kent, England

FREE FIE FO FUM

Martin E. Healy, Sag Harbor, N.Y.

"It is a tale told by an idiot, full of sound and furry . . ."

George Fairbanks, Nutley, N.J.

GABLE'S BLACK AND GARSON'S GOT HIM!

Jacqueline Fogel, Jamaica, N.Y.
Peter Heumann, Roselle, N.J.

"LET ITT BE"

Jeffrey Ruesch, N.Y.C.

Elizabeth Taylor in *Bosom*

Charlotte Curtis, N.Y.C.

Clamp Unto My Feet

Pommy Weyl, N.Y.C.

Warm Is Hell

E. E. Zuesse, N.Y.C.

"The frog comes on little cat feet"

Susan K. Langsam, N.Y.C.

A Fool and His Money Are Soon Partied

Patricia A. Duddy, Hastings-on-Hudson, N.Y.
Jack Rose, N.Y.C.
Anitra Hoffman, Brooklyn, N.Y.

Prosperity Is Just Around the Coroner
Ellis Schein, Reading, Pa.

"You'll be glad you died"
Hale Wingfield, N.Y.C.

"Take two aspirin and call me in the mourning . . ."
Betsey Ansin, Leominster, Mass.

"I'd Rather Bet Right Than Be President"
Gertrude Robinson, N.Y.C.

Stake Me to Your Leader
Pearl Bartelt, Glassboro, N.J.

PHRASE II
Dan Conaway, Memphis, Tenn.

The Party's Overt
Raymond George, N.Y.C.

"The primary elections are allegro movements—the convention is the grand finagle."
Bradford Willett, Ingleside, Ill.

Behind Every Good Moan There's a Woman
Randy Gold, Brooklyn, N.Y.

"How sharper than a serpent's tooth it is to shave a thankless child."
Mrs. Erna Lovett, Hillside, N.J.

"Casey Ate the Bat"
Janet Cohen, Gainesville, Fla.

I love my wife, but oh, your kid!
Frances LaPadula, Staten Island, N.Y.

The Brothers O'Karamazov
Jeff Gold, N.Y.C.

"Not that I loved Caesar less, but that I loved Romeo more."

Jack Ryan, N.Y.C.

"For never was a story of more woe
Than this of Juliet and Herb Romeo."

Rita Oakes, Drexel Hill, Pa.

Look Homeward Angelo

Arthur Drooker and Jeff Kaplan, Bronx, N.Y.

"You funny little sunny little Miami . . ."

Thomas Alpren, M.D., Talaquah, Okla.

The Second Combing of Christ

Melvin S. Alpren, West Orange, N.J.

"Jesus loves me, this I know,
'Cause the Bible tells me sop."

Fred Berg, Boston, Mass.

HUGHES STOOL COMPANY

Michael Sage, N.Y.C.

"Little Miss Muffet spat on her tuffet . . ."

Neil Koenig, Bronx, N.Y.

True Grits

Douglas Shemin, Pleasantville, N.Y.

"We're looking for People Who Like to Writhe"

Elaine Stallworth, Willow Grove, Pa.

Tin God We Trust

Judith S. Wallach, N.Y.C.

BRIDGE AHEAD. STOP. PAY TROLL.

Tim Nielsen, N.Y.C.

GAY POWDER!

George Malko, N.Y.C.

"Upon thy so sore loss
Shall shine the traffic of Jacob's bladder . . ."
       James Fechheimer, Glen Head, N.Y.

"Beware the ideas of March!"
       Eddie Fay, Amityville, N.Y.

"We have met the enemy and they are yours."
       Levinson Family, Garden City, N.Y.

Castiles in Spain
       Alissa Abrams, Brooklyn, N.Y.

"Oh, that this too too stolid flesh would melt . . ."
       Joan Rivers, Beverly Hills, Calif.

The Least of the Mohicans
       Lynda Seif, N.Y.C.

Custer's Last Strand
       Maxine Neal, N.Y.C.

"Fill the steins for dear old Maxine . . ."
       Mavis Kauders, N.Y.C.

As the Twig Is Bent So Growls the Tree
       Bob Rose, Bloomfield, N.J.

"The train in Spain falls mainly in the plain . . ."
       Richard Bloomenstein, M.D., Teaneck, N.J.

Arthur Fiedler Conducts the Boston Poops
       Robert Blake, N.Y.C.

Oh! Calcutta! Original Caste Album
       Melvin Meyerson, Bronx, N.Y.
       Pericles Crystal, Brooklyn, N.Y.

"Angels we have heard on highs . . ."
       Ann Grossman, N.Y.C.

L.S.D./M.F.T.
       Fabian Stuart, N.Y.C.

"Norman is an island entire of itself . . ."
>Jay McDonnell, N.Y.C.

The Blast of the Red Hot Lovers
>Neil Gershman, Whitestone, N.Y.
>Riva Lee Asbell, Philadelphia, Pa.

. . . so quiet you could hear a pint drop . . .
>Jane M. Wolf, Cambridge, Mass.

Minnie the Smoocher
"Quick, Henry the Flirt!"
>Keypunch Pool, Market Resident Data, Inglewood, Calif.

You Only Get What You Pray For
>Sue Klapholz, Jamaica, N.Y.

"Better to resign in Hell than serve in Heaven."
>W. Hoffman, North Bergen, N.J.

" 'No, no, not that,' she screamed, her voice laden with freight . . ."
>George Scullin, Stony Brook, N.Y.

Nighty Must Fall
>Ashley Yudain, Greenwich, Conn.

The Old Man and the Seal
>Dirk Murphy, Milwaukee, Wis.
>Pacy Markman, White Plains, N.Y.

Gloomy Gnus
>Mary Ann Code, West Haven, Conn.

"How Now Brown Crow?"
>Sandra Wright, Milwaukee, Wis.

Ring out the old, ring in the newt!
>E. Thurston, N.Y.C.

"Believe me, if all those endearing young charms, which we graze on so fondly today..."
Grace Andriano, Richmond Hill, N.Y.

EVERY LITTER BITE HURTS!
Toby Smith, N.Y.C.

Oh, Dad, Poor Dad, Mama's Hung You in the Closet and I'm Feeling So Sado
Ronald L. Bohn, Los Angeles, Calif.

"The bill was plaid with a check..."
Dorothy Lieberstien, Brooklyn, N.Y.

John Wayne and the Cowboys—GYP
Mrs. Norman Schlesinger, Livingston, N.J.

The Murders in the Rude Morgue
Joel F. Crystal, Brooklyn, N.Y.

"He's not heavy, she's my brother"
Joan Sage, N.Y.C.

"None Abut the Lonely Heart"
David E. Diener, Irvington, N.Y.

"In the valley of the Jolly (Ho Ho Who) Green Giant"
Miles Klein, East Brunswick, N.J.

☞ *Gothic Novels*

..."Three days have passed since my master decreed that his wife, insatiable Lady Anne the Fat, be sent without food or drink to the bare dungeon, her sole companion a ravening crocodile: now, as I stare through the bars into Milady's mad yellow eyes, I slowly realize that she is quite alone in her cell...."

Above, a short tale of horror. Competitors were invited to submit a one-sentence Gothic novel.

Report: The mind boggles, the stomach turns, and the beat goes on. Animal fare unearthed the following: Moor-bound castles, groans, creaks; Foetid odours, S.-M. freaks; Creepers, crawlers, midnight maulers; Nursemaids, stalkers, clanking walkers; Chains, pains, ancient curses; Dwarfs, monsters, nothing worse is . . . well, maybe *one* thing: the bark of a newborn babe. A genteel assortment, including the rank reappearance of the bloated cadaver of you-know-who. These intimations of mortality lead us to believe that perhaps a competition editor is also an endangered species. . . .

When I entered the fetid vault and beheld the Duke's head impaled upon an ancient iron hook, its face blue and swollen, the eyes fixed upon some dreadful, nameless horror, I sensed that his inexplicable popularity had run its course at last.

Albert G. Miller, N.Y.C.

Lord B. demanded absolute privacy; he had even wooed and wed his wife without her ever seeing his face; every night for ten years he had come to her chambers once a week (Thursday) and made love to her under the cover of darkness; after her fourth child in five years, Lady B. finally wanted to sue her husband for a divorce and upon contacting his lawyer, she discovered Lord B. to be six years deceased.

Tom Menges, Livingston Manor, N.Y.

Daddy has shackled Mommy and locked her in the tower and now he's taking over her inheritance and sending Bibsy and me off to a run-down orphanage where we shall be beaten three times a day and fed only gruel and made to stand till we drop and our hair will be completely shaved and we'll have to exercise in the snow in our cotton dresses and if we catch cold we shall be fed to the creatures in the deep lagoon—and yet I feel somehow everything will turn out all right.

Phyllis Green, Livonia, Mich.

As I watched the daemonical thrashings of viscous membrane on my supper plate, I could not help but question how an unlettered scullery maid, in but a scant hour, had managed to succeed in what I had failed to create through a fortnight's time.

Richard Downing, Evergreen, Colo.

What can you say about a one-hundred-forty-five-year-old, magenta-haired, paisley-skinned, fanged Royalist dwarf who died?

Frank Jacobs, N.Y.C.

Since she was deeply involved with her occult experiments, no one had seen my Aunt Teresa for over thirty years, but surely the shriveled monkey-like form that scuttled on all fours across the moldering carpet toward me could not be the only living inhabitant of that great dark house.

Kathleen Johnson, N.Y.C.

Alone in the dark creaking emptiness of her ancestral home, she reached for the flashlight and it was handed to her.

Thomasine Neight, Nashua, N.H.

His Majesty, cupping his head in his hands, appeared tired, but methought His Majesty *always* appears tired when holding the head of one of his executed ministers.

Martin Panzer, Rockville Center, N.Y.

That only recently forgotten fear that had accused me as a child and reproached me as a man rushed upon me once again that stormy November evening when I realized that it was not the wind that had extinguished my candle, but that tallow made from my sister's fatty flesh just did not burn as well as beeswax.

John A. Kiley, Coventry, R.I.

To all the capitals of the Old World—London, Paris, Rome—the Terror had inexorably followed, haunting my every step, haunting my every move, giving me no surcease; but now that I am here, in this peaceful but otherwise indescribable New World city they call Philadelphia, the Terror has suddenly abandoned me and I seem, strangely, to be quite alone and, still more strangely now that I am here, I find that, on the whole, I'd rather be haunted.

Angelo Papa, Trenton, N.J.

Watching with mounting anguish as he came toward me, his arms raised high, eyes small and beady, his face covered with sweat, I realized it was he who had ordered the killings, and worse, I had voted for him for President.

Erik Anderson, Cambridge, Mass.

On a sunny, cheerful morning John Anderson, gray suit neatly pressed, briefcase under arm, kissed his lovely wife and their little blond daughter good-by and set off for his job of taking Englishmen; be they alive or be they dead, and grinding their bones to make his bread.

Sam Bassin, Brooklyn, N.Y.

I am turning to marble even as I stand here, the affliction is spreading upward throughout my body until now my shoulders cannot be moved, and as I write this my arms ache as they harden as though they'd crack and drop from me . . . Venus.

W. E. Glen, N.Y.C.

. . little Jenny, hearing her mother's soft step, kept her eyes tightly closed as she ran her small fingers across the familiar cheek, and felt the hairy muzzle and sharp incisors.

E. Thurston, N.Y.C.

As I contemplated the absurdity of Sir Hughford's scheme to mate people with horses, my thoughts were interrupted by the sound of Sir Hughford II galloping through the halls.

Jeffrey Bronster, Brooklyn, N.Y.

Being a witch, I soon discovered the trouble with my familiar was that it didn't understand the modern idiom, for when I left my wailing infant with the thought in my head "I just can't hack it," my obliging familiar did.

Florence Bahr, Port Washington, N.Y.

Funerals were not uncommon at the baron's castle (indeed they occured almost as frequently as meals), but this one, for his Siamese twin brother Gregor, was particularly distasteful.

David Grotenstein, N.Y.C.

I had resignedly accepted, as I thought a loving father should, the macabre tale of my daughter's accidental fall into an underground cave on that starkly sunny afternoon when she was left unattended by her nanny, as the fragmented and hallucinatory thought process of a demented mind, the tragic legacy of her maternal grandmother who remained on that very day on the third floor of the Estate, a captive of her own madness, until the following spring when one of the servants alerted me to the presence, in the children's playroom, of six baby rabbits, all with blue eyes and long, silky, yellow hair.

J. Evans, Bethesda, Md.

He's walking toward me now, the sword clutched in his hand; I glance down and see the tip of the blade, look up and into the mirror, and watch myself die.

Burns Copeland, Waldwick, N.J.

Emitting a most foul and rancid smoking stench, gates to the subterranean world parted to reveal a grisly gray turning staircase down which unwilling travelers had no choice but to descend into awful evil chambers and, by following fearful routes beset by blood-boiling heat, cacophonic rattling roar, oppressive pitch-black tunnels crawling with unwholesome rodents, and other most hideous horrors, suffer a tortuous course to their native tribes only after exacting the measure of a ghastly gray-streaked, amber-eyed, ten-car dragon.

Jeffrey S. Gold, Brooklyn, N.Y.

I can still see the eyes of old Harrison, the butler, as he sought to frame a reply to my question, the question that had risen to my lips when I, a prim American lady invited to spend a weekend in the Devon countryside, first entered that accursed house and recognized it as the locale of my recurrent dream since childhood, a dream in which I wandered endlessly through vacant moonlit halls, moaning inconsolably, gauze filaments cobwebbing over my face, the question that feared an answer: this house, was this house haunted; I can still see the old man's pupils dilating almost wildly as he gasped, "Yes, Madam, *YOU haunt it!!*"

Oliver M. Neshamkin, M.D., N.Y.C.

I gave Eric all the love I had to offer and when he insisted that he still loved Emily Hawthorne and could not ever return my adoration there was nothing left to do but kill him, remove the heart from his body, and keep it forever as my own in a lovely glass jar on the mantelpiece where this morning I awoke to find another, a smaller, a definitely female heart pulsing next to Eric's . . . and the *Daily Mail* says that Emily Hawthorne is dead!

Peter Howard, N.Y.C.

He was so in love with his wife, Jenny, that when she died early in life of a blood disease he discovered that they could continue living harmoniously simply by . . .

Harry Kondoleon, Whitestone, N.Y.

High above the waters of Lake Cataluna, St. Malachi's Academy for Exceptional Boys was nestled on a craggy bluff and there, among the twining ivy of its fortress-like buildings, the student body had hung the entire faculty.

Arthur Weller, Interlaken, N.Y.

As I turn to my guests seated around the massive oak table of my stately dining room, I cannot conceal my joy as I realize that I am forever rid of my husband, Sir Thespian, whose constant and deadly dull play-acting, both on and off stage, nearly drove me to the brink of insanity and I say with eagerness: "Would anyone care for another slice of the ham?"

Connie Hanson, Danbury, Conn.

Lloyd Perkins, twelve-year-old-son of Professor Henry Perkins, expert on the ancient Mayan civilization, wandered away one afternoon from his father's base camp deep in the Yucatán Peninsula, where his father had taken him to further his education; he followed a procession of Indians, descendants of the Mayans, to a hidden pyramid, where he furthered his education by discovering that Virgin Sacrifice was not extinct, and the very final thing Lloyd learned was that the virgin need not be a female.

Marilyn Crystal, Brooklyn, N.Y.

"Exactly what the professor found when he ventured into that house of death I cannot say," said the priest, mysteriously, "but thereafter, when I would see him taking the fork in the road that led to that horrible house, he would look at me with the tortured face of a man who'd not only heard evil, seen evil, and even spoken evil, but also tasted it, and asked for seconds."

Alan Rachins, N.Y.C.

It was shortly after the sudden, inexplicable suicide of Clovis's twin brother Claude that the mole on Clovis's left shoulder became increasingly sensitive to light and touch...

Sylvia Gassell, N.Y.C.

This really isn't a legitimate competition winner because I've gone to the dreadful expense and labor of printing up this illustrated page, painfully inserting it into this issue, and patiently waiting for you to receive it, you, my eighty-third victim who are about to die, with a smirk, reading the *New York* Magazine Competition, thinking I'm joking when I say, "Don't turn around . . ."

Arthur Zigouras, N.Y.C.

☞ *The Answer Game*

ANSWER: **1492 and 1776**
QUESTION: **What are adjoining rooms in a Polish hotel?**

Above, The Answer Game.* Competitors were invited to submit a probable answer followed by an implausible question.

Report: A. Results of competition. **Q.** *What happens when you ask a foolish question?* Damage estimated in the thousands. We've no foolproof means of checking originality in all cases, but we do know an old saw when we see one, to wit: 9 W; Washington Irving; Dr. Livingston, I presume. Other seesaws include: **A.** Chicken Teriyaki. **Q.** Name the oldest living Kamikaze pilot; **A.** MC^2. **Q.** Describe a TV Host; **A.** Gunga Din. **Q.** What is the noise made by gungas; **A.** Christiaan Barnard. **Q.** Who knows what evil . . .; **A.** Mounts Everest, McKinley, and Sinai. **Q.** Name two mountains and a hospital; **A.** Truman, Eisenhower, and Johnson. **Q.** Name two Presidents and a floor wax; **A.** ZaSu Pitts. **Q.** What's inside ZaSu prunes? **A.** 5,280 feet. **Q.** How many shoes for 2,640 men? **A.** Colt 45, Winchester 73. **Q.** What was the score of the Colt-Winchester game? etc. Other repeats ranged from

---

* With acknowledgment to Bob Arbogast, Steve Allen, and Johnny (Carnak) Carson.

puns—**A.** Lincoln Center. **Q.** Why was Mary Todd shopping? **A.** Butterfield 8-2430. **Q.** How many beans did Butterfield eat?—through ethnic (we asked for it, sorry) —**A.** First Telephone Pole. **Q.** Who was Alexander Graham Kowalski?—to faddish—**A.** Hot pants. **Q.** What does an overworked dog emit; **A.** Panty hose. **Q.** How do you extinguish hot pants?, etc. We've one final poser for you: **A.** *Nein,* Double U. **Q.** *Bitte,* do you spell moomoo like this? Oh, well. It's a sad week all around when the Knicks lose and your turtle dies . . .

A. March Hare, Mock Turtle, Dormouse, Alice, Queen of Hearts.
Q. Describe a lousy poker hand.
Kenneth R. Better, N.Y.C.

A. Never having to say you're sorry.
Q. What does not reading or seeing *Love Story* mean?
Sal Rosa, N.Y.C.

A. Happy, Dopey, Sleepy, Sneezy, Grumpy, Bashful, Doc.
Q. Describe Neil Simon in seven words.
Herb Sargent, N.Y.C.

A. The Mafia.
Q. When the answer is "The Mafia," you don't ask questions.
Lydia Wilen, N.Y.C.

A. I give up.
Q. Who was the second wife of the Archduke Ferdinand?
Eric Freedman, Ithaca, N.Y.

A. Saul Bellow, Philip Roth, and Erich Segal.
Q. Name two writers and a hockey buff.
Angelo Papa, Trenton, N.J.

A. Amelia Earhart
Q. What did you say your name wasn't?

Janet Murray, N.Y.C.

A. "Take that, you rat!"
Q. What is the most persuasive thing one can say to hard-sell a rodent?

Bill Goldschlag, N.Y.C.

A. "B Q R K F T L E X"
Q. Who wrote "The Sensuous Baseball Team"?

David Grotenstein, N.Y.C.

A. That which by any other name would smell as sweet.
Q. What is a *New York* Magazine Competition entry sent in by a Rose?

Bob Rose, Syracuse, N.Y.

A. Hertz.
Q. What does it feel like to be dropped into the driver's seat of a speeding automobile from a height of fifty feet?

William Schallert, N.Y.C.

A. SMU MIT UCLA
Q. How do you spell Smumitucla?

Michael Deskey, N.Y.C.

A. Jimmy Crack Corn and I Don't Care.
Q. Why are James Durante and Eva Tanguay famous?

Gibbs Murray, N.Y.C.

A. Somewhere Over the Rainbow.
Q. Where do you look for the signature on a Peter Max poster?

Margot Howard, N.Y.C.

A. The corn is as high as an elephant's eye.
Q. What did the Lilliputian doctor say when he examined Gulliver's sore foot?

C. R. Mann, Arlington, Va.

A. Cavett, Carson, and Griffin.
Q. Name two entertainers and a shoe polish.

Bill Blake, N.Y.C.

A. Mars, Venus, Jupiter, and Pluto.
Q. Name three planets and Mickey Mouse's dog.

Steve Melinger, N.Y.C.

A. California, Florida, and the Edsel.
Q. Name two oranges and a lemon.

Joan Weiss, N.Y.C.

A. Venice, Rome, and Florence.
Q. Name two Italian cities and the president of Hadassah.

Mrs. Emily Seiden, Brooklyn, N.Y.

A. Peter, Paul, and Mary.
Q. Name two saints and a typhoid carrier.

George H. Geller, N.Y.C.

A. "We are not amused."
Q. What did royal infants say when Queen Victoria went "Kitchy kitchy coo"?

Helen Shaffer, Chambersburg, Pa.

A. Mini, Midi, Maxi.
Q. What is the Latin translation of "I came, I saw, I conquered"?

Jane Feder, Brooklyn, N.Y.

A. Tataliaski and Corleonberg.
Q. Who are the warring families in the movie version of *The Godfather*?

M. Lloyd Rothstein, N.Y.C.

A. What's Going On with Smokey and the Miracles.
Q. What did God say when a bear put out His burning bush?

Math Coffee Room, University of N.C., Chapel Hill

A. A prefrontal lobotomy.
Q. What precedes a frontal lobotomy?
Stephen and Lyndall Klein, Atlanta, Ga.

A. Pat Nixon's back.
Q. What does Bebe Rebozo do when the President has a coughing spell?
Marshall W. Karp, N.Y.C.

A. Always divide each question into at least three parts and answer Part C first.
Q. What advice do President Nixon's advisers give him before each press conference?
Vinnie Stark, Flushing, N.Y.

A. Seesaw.
Q. Name a Polish port.
James Walsh, Worcester, Mass.

A. The 1962 World's Fair.
Q. What is an inferiority complex?
Bill Rittberg, Selden, N.Y.

A. Major Barbara.
Q. Who is commander of the military garrison at Fire Island?
A. A. Rascio, Brooklyn, N.Y.

A. The eye of an eagle, the heart of a lion, and the hand of a woman.
Q. Waiter, what's that in my soup?
Mike and Roni Raginn, N.Y.C.

A. Art Deco.
Q. Who designed the Chrysler building?
Christopher Murray, Salem, Mass.

A. Katmandu.
Q. Who knows what evil lurks in the hearts of men?
Ruth Ellen Galper, N.Y.C.

A. Vera Hruba Ralston.
Q. How do you say "I would like a bowl of cereal" in Czech?

James Turner, N.Y.C.

A. No, actually, I'm way up on my tippy toes.
Q. Toulouse, are you standing in a hole?

Albert G. Miller, N.Y.C.

A. Roger.
Q. Who wrote the Thesaurur?

A. J. Stein, N.Y.C.

A. To get to the other side.
Q. Why did the medium go into a trance?

Barry Strauss, Spring Valley, N.Y.

A. Richard Daley.
Q. What does Bebe Rebozo call the President, and how often?

Burns Copeland, Waldwick, N.J.

A. No Exit.
Q. Tonto, isn't that an entrance?

Jon Michaels, N.Y.C.

A. Office Expense.
Q. What Broadway musical starred Tommy Steele?

Bob Ellison, N.Y.C.

A. Animal Crackers in my soup.
Q. What medium did you use for your *chef d'oeuvre*, Mr. Warhol?

Elaine Stallworth, Willow Grove, Pa.

A. "Comment?"
Q. What did the distraught Viscountess de Flaugauche say to Signor Adonis de Formicatile at the semiannual

Balle des Chansons, in reference to their infamous ménage-à-trois?

Mark Manley, Staten Island, N.Y.

A. Grand Union; A. and P.
Q. What was the student-teacher relationship between two philosophers called?

Frank Mauro, Syracuse, N.Y.

A. Sterling Moss.
Q. What do you give a gardener on his twenty-fifth wedding anniversary?

Guy Bérard, Canton, N.Y.

A. " 'Kerplunk' goes the tablet."
Q. Cite a quote by Moses.

Stoo Tarlowe, Shawnee Mission, Kan.

A. Jesus Christ super star.
Q. What does a tenant exclaim upon discovering Candice Bergen is the janitor?

Steve Tuttle, N.Y.C.

A. Bats in the belfry.
Q. Deputy, where can I find Sheriff Masterson?

Carl F. Levine, Yonkers, N.Y.

A. D-Day.
Q. How does Miss Kappelhoff sign her checks?

Tom Lacy, N.Y.C.

A. N. M is not a working letter.
Q. What letter do you dial for murder?

Douglas S. Dickson, N.Y.C.

A. Tippy tippy tin.
Q. What is the name of Rin Tin Tin's sissy brother?

Robert Davis, Middle Village, N.Y.

A. Frick and Frack.

Q. Name the financiers who wanted to open a museum in a N.Y.C. mansion with an ice-skating rink in the basement?

Jack Seltzer, Forest Hills, N.Y.

☞ *The Newlywed Game*

If Ruta Lee married Kenny Baker, her name would be RUTA BAKER.
If Senta Berger married Gregor Mendel, and then Karl Czerny, her name would be SENTA MENDEL CZERNY.

Above, The Newlywed Game. Competitors were invited to submit two such hypothetical alliances by pairing bona fide names of fact or fiction.

Report: We should have known what we were in for when the mail bag thudded to a halt. Slews of entries and scads of duplicates. Some predictable (Pola Baer, Ella Funt) and some delicious (If Tippi Hedron married Albert Camus and Taylor Caldwell married General Thieu, they would be TIPPI CAMUS and TAYLOR THIEU)—we hated to see the latter variety repeated as they would otherwise have been prizeworthy. Speaking of repeats—we have, in the past, been lenient with occasional "afterthoughts," but with this enormous turnout, entries containing more than the requisite two submissions per individual were banished. We had to start somewhere. Leave us now cite other noncontenders: rhyming names, as in Kitty Twitty, Rhonda Fonda, *et al.;* telephone directory listings, as in: Nono, Nanette or May, Anais; far-out or mispronounced last names: Carla De Wilde is nice until you note that Brandon's last name is pronounced "De Wilda" (also I. M. Pei rhymes with day); divorcées with ex-name instead of given name, as in: Mrs. Bayh Bligh Birdie or Mrs. Haydn Kosygin; names that created *bona fide* but nonaphoristic phrases, as in: Althea Friday, or Bea Nizer Toomey; stay-the-same names, as in: Eve Montand, Virna Von Braun, Billie Budd, and misalliances disregarding first names, as in: Kim Novak Caine. Above and below, we give the results of these odd couplings, trusting that you can supply missing links in the interest of saving space. Duplicates as follows: Patti Schell; Candy Graham; Ali Katz, Kahn, Barber and Earp; Penny Wise; Cara Van; Alma Mehta; Zoe Long, Watt; Bella Buttons; Mia Culp Burr; Elke Selzer; Lana Lynn; Marietta Little Lamb; Mona More; Lizzie Fehr; Heidi Ho; Bebe Gunn; Magda Carta; Gladys Canby; Ida Wilde; Queen Faraday; Hedda Rowe Sachs Ewell; May Zola; Kitty Kerr Hawks; Mai Aiken Bach; Shirley Con Carney; Ruby Kahn Ott; Barbara Seville; Neva Ahn Sunday; Lily Pugh Shane; Debbie Thant Ball; Polly Warner Crockett; Phyllis Dean; Hope Lange Cassidy; Tuesday March Furth; Virna Lee Quinn Ochs; Alison Wonder Land; Roz Berry Schubert; Barbra Black Schaap; Helen Hiawatha; Ina Claire Day; Sheree Berry Bing; Mona Noonan Heidt; Happy Hanna Kerr; Bea Holden; Cass Abel Anka; Ouida Peebles; Jacqueline Hyde; Kaye Schirra Seurat; and Nina Pinter Hand Santamaria. It was also severally explained that should Kate Millett marry Sigmund Freud, her name would be Kate Millett. Right on. Here, without benefit of clergy, come de judging.

If Sue Lyon married Raymond Burr, then Gene Kelly, Joe Frazier, Franz Liszt, Richard Dix, Billy Eckstine,

Muhammad Ali, and then the Doge of Venice, her name would be SUE BURR KELLY FRAZIER LISZT DIX ECKSTINE ALI DOGESS.

If Holly Golightly married Ted Mack and then Leon Errol—HOLLY MACK ERROL.

Rees Behrendt, N.Y.C.

If Bea Lillie married Leo Genn and then the Aga Kahn her name would be BEA GENN, THE BEGUM.

If Han Suyin remarried former husband Nguyen Cao Ky after divorcing Hermes Pan, her name would be HAN KY PAN KY.

Jack Rose, N.Y.C.

If Rona Barrett married Cecil B. DeMille she would be RONA DEMILLE.*

If Rosemary de Camp married William Kunstler she would be ROSEMARY DE CAMP KUNSTLER.

Doree Cohen and Ellen Parker, N.Y.C.
* Marcia L. Brown, N.Y.C.
Mary Ann Code, N.Y.C.

If Emma Bovary married Paul Weiss, Dave Chasen, Claude Rains, and then Major Bowes, her name would be EMMA WEISS CHASEN RAINS BOWES.

If Gael Greene married Christopher Lee, John Gay, and then Robert E. Lee she would be GAEL LEE GAY LEE.

Carol Brener, N.Y.C.

If Anna Magnani married Billy Graham she'd become the AGA RAHMAN.

Lucinda T. Biese, Plymouth, Mass.

If Inga Swenson married Jerry Stiller, then Jimmy Dean, then Goodwin Knight she would be INGA STILLER DEAN KNIGHT.

If Sybil Thorndike married Alfred Lunt, then Rudolf Hess, she'd be SYBIL LUNT HESS.

Martin Charnin, N.Y.C.

If Happy Rockefeller married Clarence Day, Jean-Paul Sartre, Hiro, and then John Glenn, she'd be HAPPY DAY SARTRE HIRO GLENN.
If Lyn Nesbitt married Roy Cohn, then Chiron, she'd be LYN COHN CENTAUR.

R. and T. Guinzburg, N.Y.C.

If Honor Blackman married John Bull, then Jules Munshin, she'd have HONOR BULL MUNSHIN.

William Finn, Augusta, Me.

If BUNNY Lake married Roland PETIT . . .
If BEULAH Bondi married George BOOLE and then Bert LAHR . . .

Alice M. Yohalem, N.Y.C.

If MITZI Gaynor married Cesare SIEPI, then Roger MUDD . . .

Reuben Tam, N.Y.C.

If ALI MacGraw married Red BARBER, Philip AHN, Howard DUFF, Chet FORTE, Steve REEVES . . .
If DELLA Reese married Benson FONG, then John Wilkes BOOTH . . .

Miles and Judith Klein, East Brunswick, N.J.

If MARILYN Maxwell married Malcolm COWLEY, then Lucius BEEBE . . .
If IMOGENE Coca married George NATHAN . . .

Ann Lipman, N.Y.C.

If BEA Lillie married Alec GUINNESS, then Bobby LOCKE . . .

Arthur Rubinstein, N.Y.C.

If Betta St. John married Oliver W. Holmes, Tommy Sands, then Lord Byron she'd be BETTA HOLMES SANDS GORDON.

Ruth Dunkle, Edison, N.J.

If CARMEN McRae married Pierre TRUDEAU then Rob ROY...

If Cass Elliot married James Dunn, then Claudius Ptolemy, she'd be MAMA DUNN PTOLEMY.

Al Hattal, Silver Spring, Md.

If CYD Charisse married Wilbur WRIGHT, Dallas TOWNSEND, Orville WRIGHT, Arthur MAYSLES, then Frank ALETTER...

David Grotenstein, N.Y.C.

If DANY Robin married Muhammed ALI then John GARY...

Peter Stone, N.Y.C.

If NICOLE Maurey married Arthur LOEW, Papa DIONNE, Jacques COUSTEAU, then Moshe DAYAN...

Patrick McCann, N.Y.C.

If CHER Bono married Jack OAKIE...
If ALICE Toklas married Pierre TRUDEAU then John LOCKE, then Friedrich ENGELS...

B. Burke, Greenwich, Conn.

If RUBY Keeler married Thomas SCHIPPERS...

Richard C. Voigts, N.Y.C.

If INA Rae Hutton married General PERSHING, then Pierre CARDIN...

John H. Dorenkamp, Worcester, Mass.

If FRAN Allison married Paul SANN, then Joe FRISCO...

Mrs. Erna Lovett, Hillside, N.J.

If BESS Myerson married Peter SELLERS, then Franz LISZT...

June Muller, N.Y.C.

If QUEEN Esther married Ellery QUEEN, Wayne KING, MacKenzie KING, Alan KING, then Alfred FULLER, then Gaylord HAUSER...

Mrs. Helen Spitz, Brooklyn, N.Y.

If MAY Britt married Thomas MANN, then Arthur GODFREY ...*
If BROOKE Hayward married Jeffrey LYNN, U NU, then Dick YORK ...

Barbara Muccio, N.Y.C.
* *also from: Lee Silverstein, N.Y.C.*

If ANNA Magnani married John S. MILL, Stepin FETCHIT, Walter ABEL, Bobby ORR, Newton MINOW, then Tommy RALL ...
If FAITH Baldwin married Don HO, Arthur PENN, Don CHERRY, then Joey DEE ...

James Turner, N.Y.C.

If CORA Baird married Jon GNAGY, then Monty HALL ...

Martha Butchkiss, Brooklyn, N.Y.

If ANN Landers married Henry THOREAU, Gen. THIEU, Thomas MANN, then Keir DULLEA ...
If GENA Rowlands married Johnny RAY, Dick SHAWN, then Gen. GIAP ...

Lea Lane, Syracuse, N.Y.

If SYBIL Leek married James LING, then Maurice RAVEL, then Syngman RHEE ...
If Joan of Arc married Tom Dooley, then Eric Berne, then Saint Augustine, she would be Joan of ARC DOOLEY BERNE AUGUSTINE.

W. Becker, Urbana, Ill.

If PET Clark married George RAFT, Sigmund FREUD, then Steve FORREST ...
If LAUREN Bacall married Bobby ORR, then Richard DERR ...

Susan Berliner, Flushing, N.Y.

If EDNA Ferber married Ken MURRAY, Jan MURRAY, Sen. Karl MUNDT, Sam HUFF then Lee MAYE ...

Michael A. Norell, N.Y.C.

If ANNA Moffo married David MERRICK, Steven KENYON, then Henry PARRISH . . .

Dean Santoro, N.Y.C.

If MARY Wells married David MERRICK, Theodore WHITE, Immanuel KANT, then James DRURY . . .
If HEATHER Angel married Dennis DAY, John GUNTHER, then Dwight MORROW . . .

Arthur J. Lohman, N.Y.C.

If SCARLETT O'Hara married Francis LEDERER . . .

Joan Seltzer, Forest Hills, N.Y.

If Mary Martin married Joe Kipness then the President of N. Vietnam three times, she'd be MARY KIPNESS HO HO HO.

Arthur Shulman, Philadelphia, Pa.

If PENNY Fuller married Eric FROMM then Maurice EVANS . . .

Marilyn Rubin, N.Y.C.

If WINNIE Winkle married Chauncey DE PEW . . .

Lillian Kennedy, Flushing, N.Y.

If CLAIRE Bloom married Alain DELON . . .

Joseph Gavlick, Brooklyn, N.Y.
Msgr. A. V. McLees, St. Albans, N.Y.

If CYD Charisse married Robert A. ARTHUR . . .

Patricia Schairer, Levittown, N.Y.

If CANDY Kane married Arthur FROMMER, then Lucius BEEBE . . .

Jay A. Sigler, Haddonfield, N.J.

If WENDY Hiller married Wally MOON, Perry COMO, Giuseppe VERDI, then Yves MONTAND . . .

Math Coffee Room, University of N.C., Chapel Hill

If Ida Lupino married Doctor No, who would she then be? IDA NO.

Suzanne Whittemore, New Rochelle, N.Y.

If Gracie Slick's daughter married Bruce Dern she'd be GOD DERN.

Ted Klein, N.Y.C.

If NIKA Hazelton married J. S. BACH, Andy WARHOL, Pinky LEE, then Dennis DAY . . .

Louis Sabin, Milltown, N.J.

If ALI MacGraw married Gene ALLEY, Adolph OCHS, then Hubert HUMPHREY . . .

Ann and Bill Cullen, N.Y.C.

If Ivy Compton-Burnett married Robert Six her name would be IV VI.

Mary LeMieux, New Orleans, La.

If Mia Farrow and May Britt simultaneously married Lamont Cranston, they would be known as MIA AND MAY SHADOW.

H. L. Wiener, Silver Spring, Md.

If Melina manufactured auto trim would it be called MERCOURI CHROME?

J. M. Glick, Passaic, N.J.

If Gomer Pyle married the girl next door, they'd be NABORS.

If ELKE Sommer married Sal MINEO then Plenty ROYAL . . .

Ken and Fran Klass, Chicago, Ill.

If Chubby Checker's wife divorced him and married John Chancellor, their son would be a CHANCELLOR OF THE EX-CHECKER.

Alan Schoffman, Brooklyn, N.Y.

If SVETLANA Alliluyeva married Italo SVEVO, then Count Carlo SFORZA, she'd find damn few people who could introduce her.

Ken Olfson, N.Y.C.

If ANNA Sten, MATA Hari, and PIA Lindstrom all married a Mormon . . .

Gloria Kirchheimer, N.Y.C.

If Elsie the Cow and Candy married Mr. Lombardo and a Faun they'd be MOO GOO GUY PAN.

Arthur Penn, Philadelphia, Pa.

If Quasimodo married Rebecca he would be the HUNCHBACK OF SUNNYBROOK FARM.
If Choo Choo Collins married Mark Twain, she'd be CHOO CHOO CLEMENS.

Budd Gilbert, N.Y.C.

☞ *Biographies*

"I Shall Not Attempt, Here, to Tell of How Maurice Affected History, but Rather the Way in Which She Altered the Course of My Own Life..."

Above, the first sentence of an INTIMATE BIOGRAPHY. Competitors were invited to submit the opening line of A MEMOIR.

Report: Now at last I am free to tell of those strange occurrences which . . . but I digress. We must get across this point, finally. *Style*. Not jokes. (The Chaplin quote again: "If what you are doing is funny, you need not be funny doing it.") The entries, including the stylish ones, presented the spectrum of best-sellerdom even to the deliciously illiterate. Real people? We ruled most out because the tone did not seem precisely right for this competition. We did not need ascription, rather the implication of whose bios we read. Flavor rather than personality. Not who, but how. Typical subject matter: the star or mistress revealing all; and the reverse, the details of an ignominious or humble life; the first stirrings of sex, or just plain first stirrings (remarks from within, womb with a view dep't.); modest disclaimers from those urged by fans to write; and sentences on the order of: "Little did I realize, when I first . . ."; and "To others he was a despot and a murderer, yet to me . . ." We enjoyed them all. But we are getting ahead of our story . . .

"To those of Dev's friends who thought that polo was his whole life, I trust that these pages will recall the day he was taken into Porcellian, the delightful summers on Fisher's Island, his devotion to the club and Alma Mater, and yes, just as important, the grace and charm with which he greeted all, even a servant."

Robert J. Flynn, Huntington, N.Y.

"I knew him well enough to share his toothbrush and though it is sixteen years since his death I remain firmly in awe of him and of the recurrent thrush that defies medical attentions . . ."

Phyllis Green, Livonia, Mich.

"Although well you know, dear diary, of my success in the film world, you may not know that I was born (FADE IN HARMONICA SOFTLY BG) in a small town (OPEN ON LS OF VILLAGE AND BEGIN MOVE IN) in a very small house (DISSOLVE TO MS OF RUSTIC COTTAGE) of very humble parents (CU OF COTTAGE WHERE MOTHER STANDS AT KITCHEN WINDOW), but with a great ambition: I wanted to make it (VIOLINS UP) . . . and make it big!"

Patrick McInroy, San Francisco, Calif.

"I have vowed my small achievements shall be simply stated and will not consist of insufferably meticulous attention to details and attitudes or anesthetic notions of self-complacency that you dear reader would deem innocuous self-deceit."

Mrs. James Craft, Gallatin, Tenn.

"Anyone who thinks we have had an easy time being Queen of England is mistaken."

Mrs. Joel F. Crystal, Brooklyn, N.Y.

"It seems, in retrospect that the turning points of one's life should stand forth like shining jewels; yet I cannot even remember the day I met Sandor."

Kathleen Johnson, N.Y.C.

"Most of the criticism directed at Howard and I and our amorous liaison was centered around the argument against my youth and illitterecy."

Kenneth Geisert, Ridgewood, N.Y.

"Earliest years recall a feeling—a mood, really—of yellow and green, the hazy warmth of sun filtered through trees, of lightness and laughter and hope; yet simultaneously, a haunting sadness, the woe of Wednesdays' children, the too-young knowledge of the frailty and desperation of life . . ."

Susan Sussman, Forest Hills, N.Y.

"My decision to defect to Red China seemed hopeless, until I realized that the way to pull it off was amid the widest international publicity."

Maurice Varon, Bronx, N.Y.

"Some readers may think it regrettable that I did not begin these memoirs before my attack of total amnesia last spring, but . . . uh . . ."

Deborah Schwabach, Wilmington, Del.

"I didn't play football as well as Anna; I didn't bowl as well as Anna; I didn't play basketball as well as Anna; I didn't eat as much as Anna; I didn't exercise as much as Anna; our souls touched nevertheless."

Joseph A. Kaselow, Glen Rock, N.J.

"Think of me not as you know me now, a world-famous, glamorous movie actress, the toast of four continents, but try to picture me as I was then, a shy, awkward fourteen-year-old kid running home from school, hot tears of

shame and humiliation burning my eyes as I hear that cruel nickname echoing again and again: 'Hey, chesty.' "
Treva Silverman, Hollywood, Calif.

"Hell's Angels . . . why just the mention of our name strikes fear in the hearts of Middle America . . ."
Bob Sussman, N.Y.C.

"Here in the asylum my thoughts return daily to Irene and how well she would understand and nod in approval."
Maureen K. Conlon, Ogunquit, Me.

"Somehow, most of those claiming to be 'Bunny' Beethoven's friends seemed to be in awe of him."
Herbert M. Simpson, Geneseo, N.Y.

"A dwarf, twisted with lust for a première danseuse, is an awesome spectacle, but at the same time, an inspiration for those of us who love freedom."
C. R. Mann, Arlington, Va.

"As I gaze at his death mask, framed in a shadow box between candles on the mantelpiece, my thoughts go back to that glorious 1932 evening when I first encountered Gerald, blond and radiant, in the Christopher Street station, Sheridan Square."
James Fechheimer, Glen Head, N.Y.

"Ewe might well assk whoat kine of offal life a man coot have—neigh, shoat have withers lamb's heart for a ticker . . ."
Sylvia Gassell, N.Y.C.

"A door slammed against the world—a life no longer living—his story ended, mine just beginning . . ."
Chris Menard, Weston, Conn.

"I'm sorry, you are unable to read this book as opened; please turn the page and start again." A.G. BELL
Paul Korman, Belle Harbor, N.Y.

"This is my own story, but it is also the story of Ernest, Scott, Zelda, and all the self-serving, indulgent, golden children of the twenties who visited my laundry on the Rue Chansonette."

Ted Sennett, Closter, N.J.

"Call me Herman."

P. Dyer, N.Y.C.

"The course of my life has been much affected by the fact that the right hand of my great-great-grandfather, considered by many authorities to be the most accomplished pickpocket in Europe, was smashed in a duel with an irate husband, thus forcing his wife, pregnant with my great-grandmother, and their ten small children, to set sail for the shores of the New World . . ."

Marcella Arnow, Brooklyn, N.Y.

"It wasn't the dying that was hard, but rather the return to life that taxed my abilities to the utmost."

A. Genevieve McEldowney, M.D., N.Y.C.

"How well I remember the first time I met Jim on the team bus, as he busily wrote in his college-ruled notebook, pausing only to trade good-natured quips with the other players about bodily functions."

Gloria Ullman, Los Angeles, Calif.

"My history is studded with loves that if listed would compose a roster from which every nation can say: 'He was ours!'"

Frank Lopopolo, Yonkers, N.Y.

"Learn, O Reader (blessings be upon you), that there are different sorts of men and women; that amongst these is Mokailama and Zeldalama who are worthy of your praise and deserve your study of the various positions which they experienced during their graceful walk through the perfumed garden of life."

Donald Wigal, N.Y.C.

"Before I describe my first meeting with The Great One (Chapter 28), let me tell you a little something about myself . . ."

Jack Rose, N.Y.C.

"She was my sugar, my spice, my everything nice."

Richard Curtis, N.Y.C.

"There were just the three oldest children when I came from the old country to be nurse in the household of that simple Boston-Irish family . . ."

Ruth Dittmann, Basking Ridge, N.J.

"Come travel with me, dear reader, on the paths, waters, and voyages that have been my life's journey."

Mrs. Edward S. Kaplan, Memphis, Tenn.

"I realize that my friendship with Satan my prove to be of no interest to a great many, but I nonetheless feel compelled to record the memories of that alliance, as though I were being motivated by forces completely beyond my control."

David F. Fenichell, N.Y.C.

"Good evening, I'm Roger Grimsby, hear now my life . . ."

Bruce Chalfant, Morristown, N.J.

"That Philberto, Lucrézia, and I had managed to confuse and astound the world became apparent one night when we discovered we had each separately and on the same day, been urged to write a book about our lives together."

Mrs. Edward W. Powell, Jr., N.Y.C.

"I was born in September, when grass was green and corn was yellow, a tender and callow fellow looking for love about to billow like an ember."

Alan Kroker, Oak Park, Mich.

"As often happened in postwar 1947, she walked barefoot on my soul, so proudly springing those tiny breasts by which Bronx Irish Catholics are known."

R. E. Duffy, Tuckahoe, N.Y.

"I see that after this interval of four decades she is still listed in the Manhattan directory under her old maiden name, still living in the Village, and I stand here in a public telephone booth at the airport, my hair matching the pristine white of my tropical drills, and I put my finger to the dial and find myself in an agony of indecision as to whether to twirl it and complete the call . . . no, my first love, my impassioned first love, I had better not . . ."

Irwin Stone, Westbury, N.Y.

"On the first day of August 1951, on the eve of my twenty-first birthday, under the sign of Leo the Lion, in a year of cold war, with the temperature rising at 101, on a day when the Giants fell into the cellar, up on the roof of my father's garage, Jill Jablonski taught me the facts of life."

Michael Leach, N.Y.C.

"I'll never forgive Franklin and his New Deal for what they did to Oscar's pencil factory . . ."

Katherine Clifford, Upper Montclair, N.J.

☞ *Punned-Name Quatrains*

Alice B Toklas: Alice be quick,
Check the flatware, and then I shall dine.
As to knife-blade or spoon-bowl, that's really no trick,
But the fork! Double check GERTRUDE STEIN.

Above, a poem in honor of Gertrude's tine (sic). Competitors were invited to compose a quatrain, in any rhyme scheme, the final line of which concludes with the punned or otherwise mangled name of a well-known individual.

Report: We bequeath to your imagination the content of a kaboodle of repeat rhymes (given here in phonetic form) which concluded thus: Dine Ashore, Victor, You Go; Isaac's Turn; [Give] Fred a Stare; Too Loose, Low Track; Mountie Wooly; [Can Lee] Carry Grant?; Will Shakes Pier; [Sewing or Hawing in Her] Earnest Hemming Way; Marlin, Brand "O"; Johnny, Unite Us; [I'm] No "El" Coward; Erik's Eagle; [Monday: Rivet] Tuesday: Weld; Tom Is Tryin'; [The] Secretary Ate; Eff's Cot Fits Gerald; [Not Woman Weaker] Nor Man Maler; Marry and Madden. And, [the River Niger won't rhyme with] Rod's Tiger. We gave long shrift to the following:

She loved the style, so chic, so new
But the color scheme caused her to frown
She looked quite drab in boyish blue
and like HELEN GURLEY BROWN.

Carolyn Webster, N.Y.C.

Louis had a little auk, a feathered pet named "Lotta,"
And almost everywhere they went, the auk was *avis grata.*
But not at school, the head of which, a haughty Boston Brahmin boss,
Had early on declaimed with scorn, "We'll not have LOUIS AUCHINCLOSS."

John Hofer, Marlboro, Mass.

Though I know you'll do fine when you get to be queen,
And I doubt this would void any treaty,
Please allow me to point out, and don't think me mean:
Egypt's spelled with *one* t, NEFERTITI.

E. H. Kelly, Arlington, Va.

The hostess sent her son to bed, ignoring all his whining.
He begged to taste the party fare and watch the people dining.
His mom thought she heard munching in the den, while she was serving.
And there, in his pajamas, stood her little CLIFFORD IRVING.

Barbara Gorin, Brooklyn, N.Y.

Wolfgang's got by him der mumps.
Sigmund's pressure . . . oy, it jumps!
Klaus gets Herpes . . . vas iss das?
Und no vun knows vot HUGO HAAS.

Peter Howard, N.Y.C.

Of all of the people at Hotel de Graff
Guess who the owner likes best?

It isn't a member of family or staff.
Give up? It's EDGAR A. GUEST.
> *Jim's Friday a.m. Group, Caldwell, N.J.*

The reason he's late for appointments
Is his search for the ultimate rhyme;
But while Hal may be late for rehearsal,
You can bet that STEPHEN SONDHEIM.
> *Gary Blake, N.Y.C.*

"I have argued many a case, written many an article,
Been an all-around bearder of the lion.
But neglected science. No more. Today I charged a particle
To which I modestly give my name." SIDNEY ZION.
> *Nancy Weber, N.Y.C.*

Two poets on the sand, chaste-garbed, sit down.
But lo, the lady doffs her hat, her gown!
And what dread sight doth Robert stare at, frowning?
He frowns to see ELIZABETH BARRETT BROWNING.
> *Barbara A. Huff, N.Y.C.*

Washington's newest hotel
Is quite absurd
The bedroom's Louis Fourteenth
The JOHN DEAN III.
> *Mrs. Carolyn Molyneaux, N.Y.C.*

Noah's wife is a scold, but she gets on the ark,
And Marie Antoinette talks of cake for a lark.
So when Martha speaks up and denounces the Pres.,
Do you think she's forgotten what next LOUIS XVI?
> *Joanie Rogers, Dallas, Texas*

A clever devil my Edgar was,
And dreadful hard to best,
So when I slipped the poison in
His kippers, EDGAR GUEST.
> *Kaky Dafler, Yardley, Pa.*

When asked to dine in or asked to dine out
Whether by bride or by Spanish grandee,
My delicate stomach dictates that I scout
Just to make sure there's a W. C. HANDY.

> *J. Heaton, N.Y.C.*

Over old Heidelberg rose the full Moon;
Down in the Rathskeller with his Fräulein,
A student was calling above the gay tune:
"Bitte! ALBERT EINSTEIN."

> *Josephine E. Case, N.Y.C.*

In the Tower of London, Jon climbed the stairs
While his friend raced him up on the lift.
Jon reached the top first and his friend said, with glares,
"My . . . isn't JONATHAN SWIFT!"

> *Mrs. S. S. Klein, North Caldwell, N.J.*

Spooner, William A., sat down at the Linotype one day
To cast a sermon-review of a book by Brzezinski, Zbigniew.
He ended his say in his usual way
with the "nom de pew" SHTAOIN ERDLU.

> *Fran Ross, N.Y.C.*

Liza Minnelli went to New Delhi
And isn't returning at all.
Her taking French leave made poor Desi grieve
And LUCILLE BALL.

> *Ethel Strainchamps, N.Y.C.*

Our lower limbs have footing in history and lit.:
There's Namath's knee, Achilles' heel, the fatted calf, to wit,
And Friday's fateful footprint in the novel by Defoe;
But fictionwise, I get my kicks from HARRIET BEECHER STOWE.

> *Lou Seeger, Port Washington, N.Y.*

I wandered lonely 'midst the carts
That rolled in high past shelves each way;
"Where's meat?" I cried. They looked at charts:
"Four lanes have none but ELAINE MAY."

Michael Schreiber, Brooklyn, N.Y.

Again and again at the heat she did balk,
Until a new unit he said he'd deliver.
The man brought an *Air Temp*, a blackboard, some chalk,
And finally made SUSAN STEIN SHIVA.

Lydia Wilen, N.Y.C.

In the world of cravats, from reports that we've seen,
The "in" colors this year are white, red, and green.
And some clothing stores from reports that we scour,
Sell hundreds of green, red, an' DWIGHT EISENHOWER.

Richard Fried, Brooklyn, N.Y.

The pawn position was optic.
A desert mirage, a Pharaoh forsook.
The Egyptian gambit was coptic
A night for a queen. And KING FAROUK.

Mrs. William Brennan, East Greenwich, R.I.

We thought he was still on vacation,
But look at my chandelier rock,
With each pianoforte (Bang!) vibration,
Upstairs neighbor JOHANNES BACH.

C. Rollin Albert, Brooklyn Heights, N.Y.

Expectorant contests are funny events;
Men aim for some cuspidor hits.
But no one will envy the referee who
Must stand there all day and MARK SPITZ.

Lora W. Asdorian, Springfield, Va.

A poet struggles line by line,
Till inspiration's gone;
But writers of 'ricks & children's rhyme
Go on, an' on, ANON.

                              Irwin Vogel, Brooklyn, N.Y.

Some say destruction is born of God's creation,
Beginning with man who of bad fruit partaketh,
Yet others lay blame of the wealth of a nation,
Which one is truth, which one ADAM SMITH?

                              Jon M. Healy, N.Y.C.

As he sails his craft alone, alas,
Affairs of state get sicker,
So build him a brig with topside brass,
But make the botTOM WICKER.

                              Rebecca W. Petrikin, N.Y.C.

He come, he see, he take it all:
He take me woman, me food, me basketball;
Den he drink me liquor and poke a hole in de wall—
Dot's me brother, Charles, mon—he got DE GAULLE.

                              Hank Haffner, Jamaica, N.Y.

Try the White House, the Wheelhouse, the Hill House,
    the Warhouse;
Find out where and what floor that Dick's on.
Check our chickenhouse and gatehouse, the outhouse
    and icehouse,
But as far as R. MILHOUS, NIXON.

                              Lloyd G. Seymour, Scotia, N.Y.

Amanda and Gene were pianists of note—
Personable, striking, at the keyboard so handy.
But competing was futile. When put to a vote,
Judges couldn't decide between EUGENE ORMANDY.

                              Philip Edinger, Cloverdale, Calif.

Those craftsmen of Paris, *les couturiers*.
Do their work for Babette *et sa mère*—
Except for a few on Rue St.-Honoré
Where we find our friend, MAX ROBESPIERRE.
                        James Fechheimer, Glen Head, N.Y.

When Egypt announced it would seek
A peace with the Jews by next week,
Golda, stunned, said we should not stand pat;
But I just can't believe that ANWAR SADAT.
                        Morris Goldstein, Brooklyn, N.Y.

A new craze is sweeping the art world
With which I could easily part
They're now painting camels in swamplands
I'd rather see HUMPHREY BOGART.
                        Diane M. Ross, Cherry Hill, N.J.

Your meat bill is late,
And we don't mean to push, sir.
But we can't wait. Please remit.
DAVE DEBUSSCHERE.

                        Alice Richter, Morganville, N.J.

A prudish gal went to see *Gypsy* one day,
And dressed herself up as smartly as she could,
She felt loud clothes wouldn't strike men the right way,
But imagined dressing NATALIE WOOD.
                        Toni Marco, Brooklyn, N.Y.

If you stay Hotel Odessa
No leave key upon the dressa;
It is not a simple tasky
For a guest to BORIS SPASSKY.
                        Elliott Sperber, West Hartford, Conn.

Tami's parrot knew "Invictus" by heart
Though some said this was absurd
But all who heard it would always say
"Yes, that's an ADMIRAL BYRD."
                        Pericles Crystal, Brooklyn, N.Y.

Do you, like King Arthur, search for the Holy Grail?
Are you on a quest for Napoleon's pistol?
Do you seek in vain to find the Argo's sail? . . .
In Brooklyn, I'm told, they keep PERICLES CRYSTAL.

Robert Barrie, N.Y.C.

☞ *Letters to Santa*

Dear S. Claus:
What with eight tiny reindeer and one thing and another
You're a busy old elf, or so says my mother
So I'll come to the point: I've mended my fences, Claus
And have been a good boy, as good as King Wenceslaus.
My sister wants a new sash, I wish she'd grow up
I agree with the poem, sashes make me throw up.
I'd like a pencil box; not another rabbit with hutch
Which the Easter Bunny brought me and which I named Aloysius
    figuring that way if he died I wouldn't miss him so much
So, I don't need a shot glass or whisky decanter
Just a pencil box for school.
Elementary, dear Santer.
          Yr. Pal,
            O. NASH

Above a letter to Santa from Ogden Nash, age seven. Competitors were invited to submit a letter to Santa from a well-known person of fact or fiction, age six to ten.

Report: Ho-ho-ho yourself. Amid the clatter that arose: blocks for little Nelson Rockefeller; a baseball mitt or doll's house for the ambivalent M. Breckenridge; blank pages from M. Marceau, and some first-rate poetry parodies from a host of your favorites. A rather exalted group of "repeat" letter writers: R. D. Laing, G. Stein, R. Nader, Julia Child, and little e.e. cummings. Before discussing shortcomings, yes, Virginia, there was a typo which put an extra word in our example. Perhaps a few entries parodied life-style (or toy-style) rather than *writing* style—e.g., S. Agnew might ask for a Mickey Mouse watch, but would do so alliteratively—however, we loved them all.

Dear Santa: A horsey, a horsey; my kingdom for a horsey. —RICHARD III
Arthur B. Rubenstein, N.Y.C.

Dear Santa: (With such blithesome informality I've reckoned not),/I have but two requests, the first is positive, the second not:/The one for me, a Paul Roget, the king of all thesauruses/ (No more to filch my fellow second-former William Morris's)./The other, although niggardly among the goose and venison/(I am the very model of a pre-pubescent Tennyson),/For one "O. Nash," per one "M. Madden," who (but don't get *me* involved)/Thinks "fences, Claus" and "Wenceslaus" a rhyme (without the "C" involved)./A box of worm-invaded nuts (nor nougaty nor filbertesque). Y'r most ob'd't s'v'nt, I am, —W. S. GILBERT, ESQ.
Barry Brown, N.Y.C.

Letters to Santa / 309

Dear Santa: When you come to our hovely louse, please leave a repenting peacil for my daddy and a shawl for my mear dummy. Sister saw a fellow yawn in the woods yesterday and wants a stuffed animal just like it. As for me, a pair of ball-skating roller bears is what I'd like most. Please make it a good Xmas because I've behaved and been an absolutely brand goy all year.

—WILLIAM A. SPOONER
Norton Bramesco, N.Y.C.

Dear Crimson-clad, Yule-gladdening Santa: Grasshopper knee-high, I wish your attention to my gift request to call. Warmly welcomed would be a copy of the bibliot-eccen-teric *Life and Time of Tristram Shandy* by bright, British prowessayist Sterne. Wishes best to Krismistress Claus extend I. —HENRY LUCE
Lewy Olfson, South Lyme, Conn.

Dear Santa: I shouldn't write. How can I believe in someone no one ever sees? If you are real, I want an electrical set (I am doing security wiring on my room), a solitaire game, and a boat (one-seater). Please leave the presents in the trunk of the unmarked black sedan parked at Fourth and Maple at 2 a.m. December 25, or I can't accept them. This letter is real. If you do not recognize the signature, it is because I am leaving it by my door for the valet to sign. He knows I left it because he recognizes my voice. —HOWIE HUGHES
Joel Kampf, Chestnut Hill, Mass.

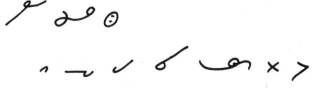

—BILLY ROSE
Joan Wilen, N.Y.C.

Dear Santa: Welcome! It's a great joy having you with us again this year. You're really super! A super Santa! Really terriffic! Fantastic, as a matter of fact! Great! What, in fact, is your definition of the word love? That's what I'd like to have from you for Christmas. Also, it would be absolutely smashing if you could bring me a delicious new list of adjectives. —DAVEY FROST
Anne C. Miller, Teaneck, N.J.

Dear Santa: I have been a very good boy. Please bring me a white shirt, a blue tie, a navy blue suit, black oxfords, and a new school bag. Very truly yours,
—RICHARD NIXON
Patricia Schairer, Levittown, N.Y.

Dear Mr. Claus: My sources report that each year, on the night of December 24, you unlawfully enter dwelling after dwelling depositing certain items of specific value under or in the vicinity of a tree at each residence. This procedure is most suspicious. Preliminary data collected indicates that you are not a man of wealth and have no visible source of income. A detailed investigation would be in the public interest to shed light on the acquisition of these possessions and why they are subsequently given away. —J. EDGAR HOOVER
Howard Abrahams, N.Y.C.

Dear Santa: May I please have sleighbells, skis, and a sled for Christmas, as I love snow. I hope we have snow for Christmas. I dream about it. Christmas without snow doesn't seem like Christmas. Thank you and may your days be merry and bright. —HARRY LILLIS CROSBY
Michael Deskey, N.Y.C.

Messrs. Claus, Donner, Blitzen et al: Petitioner ("Good Boy") hereby represents (Attachment A, Affidavit of Mommy) that, whereas pursuant to the binding agreement of December 26, 1969, and sundry amendments

thereto *ne plus ultra* and *ad hominem*: be it therefore resolved that cited behavior shall render due to me any and all gifts, presents, surprises, treats, donations, bequests, serendipities, etc., and that the foregoing not be deemed to exclude other nice stuff. Please reply to playroom of— —LOUIS NIZER
Anthony Gray, N.Y.C.

Nick . . . Long time no see . . . —NANOOK
Sue and Herb Wallach, Roslyn Heights, N.Y.

Dear Kurt: That is your real name. Not Nicholas. A nurse named Vonnegut switched you in your cradle. The reason your belly shakes like a bowlful of jelly is that you are pregnant. The father is named Jules Verne. He came to you in a cloud of snow. The offspring will all be robots named Virginia. They will kill you. To avoid this, deliver all toys here. Indiana is the real North Pole. Your belly will then fall off and you can be me. Meanwhile, do not press your navel. —S. CLAUS, C.I.A.
Theodore Hoffman, Brooklyn, N.Y.

Dear Santa: Let me be quite brief:/I'd really dig the Château d'If. —EDMOND DANTES, MONTE CRISTO
Berndt Kolker, Stockton, Calif.

Santa, red roaring night wraith/Clothed and close with furred and feathered friend,/Forever unfree of the pleas of children,/Another child speaks and cries please,/Please, on a lengthy day of my youthful age,/Tinseled trees shine and float,/Fly famous and fast to my house on the hill,/Sack on back, whippoorwill singing songs in the cheek,/And for a Welsh boy with his heart in his hand,/Bring magical sweetmeats and breath-catching treats. —DYLAN THOMAS
Nona Drosnin, N.Y.C.

Dear Santa: Bring please what me dream last night: soft pink playmate, no stiff black hair on arms, chest, legs,

bottom, it have red mouth, blue eyes, must walk on two legs, have no tail, better no swing in trees, so easy to catch. —ME, TARZAN
Albert G. Miller, N.Y.C.

Dear Santa: I would like a pen please. I am tired of writing with my finger. Thank you. —OMAR KHAYYAM
Jeanne Remusat, Forest Hills, N.Y.

Dear Santa: Please bring me twelve spiders spinning, eleven vultures flying . . . and a python in a palm tree.
—CHARLES ADDAMS
Jack Rose, N.Y.C.

Dear Santa: Liza Gratemen, Al Remindus,/"Wee" Kinmaykar, Liza Blyme,/Andy Potting, Lee Behindus,/Futprinz (Johnny), Sandra Thyme./These are eight of my small classmates/Who have asked me to assure you/That they, too, have been good children/Worthy of your best at Christmas. —HENRY W. LONGFELLOW
Msgr. A. V. McLees, St. Albans, N.Y.

Dear Santa: Just bring yourself. —COUNT DRACULA
Frank Jacobs, N.Y.C.

Dear Mr. Claus: If I quit telling everybody Mrs. Claus should join Women's Lib, and/You quit telling everybody I wasn't a good little girl last year, and/I quit counting on your giving me a Teenform bra, and/You quit giving me fur muffs with rabbits' heads on them, and/We avoid discussions like/Is Christmas really relevant and why aren't your elves in an encounter group,/Maybe we'll make it/A Merry Christmas. —JUDY VIORST
James Hammon, N.Y.C.

Dear Santa: All I want for Christmas is my thirty-two front teeth. —JACKIE "MOMS" MABLEY
Marc Levitt, Brooklyn, N.Y.

Dear Santa: I need a pea jacket size 6x and please also bring me anything that will help me grow big and strong like you. Ho-ho-ho. —JOLLY GREEN GIANT
Mary Ann Code, N.Y.C.

Sir: Down below my parents pause/Talking softly of Santa Claus . . . —TOMMY S. ELIOT
Dean Upshaw, N.Y.C.

Dear Santa: If it will not discommode you, sir, may I request a kite? Your obedient servant, —B. FRANKLIN
Gridley Fidel, Brooklyn, N.Y.

Santa Honey: A wood fence, a 24-carat-gold Segal lock for my door . . . Love, —MARTHA
Mrs. Edward W. Powell, Jr., N.Y.C.

Dear Santa: Please send me a box of fireworks.
—THE BOY IN THE HATHAWAY SHIRT
Dan Rosenthal, Washington, D.C.

Confidential to S.C.: For just 25 cents in coin, I will be happy to mail you a copy of my booklet *Petting Your Reindeer and How Far to Go* in a plain brown wrapper. Until it arrives you might try letting Rudolph play in some reindeer games that are a little more conventional so that the other members of your team don't get jealous.
—ANN
Henry Nuwer, Las Vegas, Nev.

Dear Santa: . . . Rambunctious offspring fare poorly in our home, therefore kindly avoid toys which denote parental liberalism. —WM. F. BUCKLEY, JR.
Philip Lindenbaum, Cedarhurst, N.Y.

Dear Santa Claus or Klaus, St. Nicholas, Kris Kringle, Father Christmas: I was a good, fine, nice, splendid, swell, super, first-rate, capital, noble, virtuous boy, laddie, youth, fellow, master, sonny, buddy, kid (slang), all year, annum, twelve-month-period. I would like presents, gifts. . . . Yours truly, really, actually,

—PETER MARK ROGET
Lil Wilen, N.Y.C.

Dear Santa: Toy Dispenser for the World, Doll Maker, Reindeer Driver . . . —CARL SANDBURG
Arnold Rosenblum, Bayside, N.Y.

Roller Skates; Chinese Checkers; Puppy. Dear Santa: Above, several examples of what I would like for Xmas. You are invited to submit as many articles as you wish but all must be received by December 25. P.S. Last year's offerings were more impressive in quantity than quality. Where did I go wrong? —MARY ANN
Cookie Gray, N.Y.C.

☞ *Gossip Items*

"... The CRATCHITS are tiny-clothes shopping ... PRINCE MISHKIN and his steady acting silly ... the HORATIO NELSONS seem to have patched it up ... are the HENRY FRANKENSTEINS (he's the noted M.D.) expecting a little stranger? ..."

Above, excerpts from imaginary gossip or society columns. Competitors were invited to submit up to three invented items relating to notable persons or events of past or present, fiction or fact.

Report: "Has CHRISTIAAN BARNARD got a new heart interest? ... The DUKE OF CLARENCE had a ripping good time last weekend ... A red-letter day for HESTER PRYNNE at the Big A ... It's splitsville for: the HENRY JEKYLLS; the BORDENS of Fall River, CHANG and ENG of SIAM ... MARIE ANTOINETTE going topless, seen at the head shops ... QUASIMODO tells us he has a hunch he'll be hearing wedding bells soon ... Don't invite TROTSKY and STALIN to the same Party ... MME DEFARGE knitting tiny clothes? ... Confidential to CLEO: don't be an asp ... Who's the big item in FAY WRAY's life? ... MICHELANGELO still flat on his back ... CYCLOPS and LONG JOHN SILVER not seeing eye to eye ... AHAB having a whale of a time ... Are the

316 / *Son of Giant Sea Tortoise*

JACK SPRATTS fed up with each other? . . . The PHILIP NOLANS are house hunting . . ."—some of the choicer items repeated. We suspect that the successful m.o. here was to select typical column jargon, as in "splitsville," and to adapt *it* to a person or event rather than the other way 'round. After reading 4500 or so column items, the *silliest* things make you laugh . . . for example:

DAVID and LISA are crazy for each other . . .
Lydia Wilen, N.Y.C.

. . . JAKE BARNES recuperating after minor surgery . . . Add to those combating burglaries with purchase of a dog: SIR HENRY BASKERVILLE.
Charlotte Curtis, N.Y.C.

EDDIE FISHER and DEBBIE REYNOLDS will make it final this spring . . . EDDIE FISHER and ELIZABETH TAYLOR will make it final this spring . . . EDDIE FISHER and CONNIE STEVENS will make it final this spring . . .
David Grotenstein, N.Y.C.

Are the CHINGATCHGOOKS running out of people to talk to? . . . COUNT and COUNTESS DRACULA are pulling up stakes . . .
Paul H. Coladarci, Paterson, N.J.

TAB HUNTER losing weight . . . the MAX FACTORS have made up . . .
Clay E. Delauney, N.Y.C.

JULIET CAPULET cocktailing at the Friars . . .
Emily Cobb, N.Y.C.

. . . ROSENCRANTZ and GUILDENSTERN are dead . . .
Elizabeth Reiss, Brooklyn, N.Y.
Daniel Rosenthal, N.Y.C.

What ever happened to CHESTER ALAN ARTHUR?
Arthur Penn, Philadelphia, Pa.

Is MRS. JACK SPRATT eating for two?
Mary Ann Code, N.Y.C.

CAROL CHANNING has big eyes for EDDIE CANTOR . . . MRS. NEBEL sleeps in long johns . . . Egg-specting but still billing and cooing: the ADMIRAL BYRDS . . .
Tom Morrow, N.Y.C.

GREGOR SAMSA has disappeared into the woodwork; nobody's seen him for ages . . .
Marilyn Fidel, Brooklyn, N.Y.

Is LOIS LANE's jet-set beau (initial S) flying solo these days?
Ted Sennett, Closter, N.J.

Short but hitherto impeccably dressed man-about-town "BILL" WINKIE claims the brouhaha of night before last was merely an attack of somnambulism . . . What over-the-hill MEMBER OF ROYALTY hires his own incredible string band to enliven his bouts of solitary drinking?
Mrs. Robert Amft, Evanston, Ill.

Are the D. W. GRIFFITHSES expecting?
Susan Schiff, Forest Hills, N.Y.

Look alikes: SYDNEY CARTON and CHARLIE DARNAY . . .
Charles Hollerith, Jr., N.Y.C.

Intimates hint C. COOLIDGE may say, "I do."
Louis Sabin, Milltown, N.J.

DAEDALUS and son are waxing eloquent about air travel . . . DAMON and PYTHIAS are doing the "we're just good friends" bit . . .
Clarence Rose, N.Y.C.

The MARQUIS DE SADE seems to be hitting it off with a new flame...

Gale Fieldman, Rockville Centre, N.Y.

ISAAC (scion of a prominent Jewish family) altar bound ... Is GORDIUS tying the knot?

Diane Davis, Huntington, N.Y.

The vacationing BENEDICT ARNOLDS have just gone over to Britain ... the SAMUEL BECKETTS are still expecting...

Karl Levett, N.Y.C.

The REVERES of Boston announce arrival of visitors from abroad...

Dana Chaifetz, Edgewater, N.J.

LADY GODIVA dropped from the best-dressed list...

Harriet Rosenblum, Pittsford, N.Y.

Has CAPTAIN QUEEG lost his marbles? ... The MOSLERS have been playing it safe...

Irene De Blasio, N.Y.C.

HANZ HOLZER has a ghost writer ... JO MIELZINER creating a scene at a B'way opening...

Sylvia Smith, East Brunswick, N.J.

The name of MAX DE WINTER'S latest heart interest is a puzzler to all concerned...

Eileen Tranford, Dorchester, Mass.

What CAVALIER has a Queen-size cape-cleaning bill?

Joel Kampf, Chestnut Hill, Mass.

Are LYSANDER and HERMIA and DEMETRIUS and HELENA heading for a Bob and Carol and Ted and Alice?

Ann Stanwell, N.Y.C.

It's splitsville for the PAUL MASSONS . . . Songstress TRILBY O'FERRALL undergoing intensive coaching . . .
Michael Deskey, N.Y.C.

BILL TELL and son arrived in the big apple . . .
John Sheehan, Baldwin, N.Y.

JANE EYRE back from Mayo Brothers Clinic found Rochester cold . . .
Michele Evans, N.Y.C.

Is GOV. PETER STUYVESANT stumping for a new first lady?
Mike Leifer, Valley Stream, N.Y.

Friends of playboy DORIAN GRAY worried. He no longer looks the picture of health.
Neil Leonard, N.Y.C.

ROMEO MONTAGUE and JULIET CAPULET are telling friends they can't live without each other . . .
Jean Sheppard, N.Y.C.

J. A. PRUFROCK, our man in London, reports that Italian art is a big topic at the best tables there . . .
Ruth Schiffman, Englewood, N.J.

. . . It's a son for the CHARLIE CHANS . . .
Andrew and Renée Herz, N.Y.C.

. . . SIR LANCELOT, they tell me, has at last given up night-clubbing . . .
Msgr. A. V. McLees, St. Albans, N.Y.

Has DOLLY LEVI finally met her match? . . . Has JANE WITHERS' career gone down the drain?
Robert Deutsch, Flushing, N.Y.

Insiders report J. CAESAR slated to go under the knife . . .
Richard F. Gibbons, N.Y.C

TOM SAWYER and his BECKY painting the town white . . . HEATHCLIFF has been seen all over the moors with a lovely young thing who doesn't in the least resemble his wife . . .

Eugene Boe, N.Y.C.

LUDWIG VAN B. no longer playing it by ear . . .

Albert G. Miller, N.Y.C.

MOSES doing well after operation at Mount Sinai . . .

Alice M. Yohalem, N.Y.C.

You read it here first: the JEFFERSONS are on the verge, with TOM being the one who wants independence . . .

Saul Richman, Wantagh, N.Y.

Is COUNT DRACULA in financial trouble? His friends report he's putting the bite on them . . . HARPO MARX and MARCEL MARCEAU not talking . . .

Howard Gottfried, N.Y.C.

ABIGAIL (MRS. JOHN) ADAMS writes: THOFE daftardly, red "ftrangers" who fo paffionately toffed 342 fea chefts into the previously unfullied waters of Boston Harbour laft fortnight, are known. How much longer muft filence fhield thefe ravifhers of our fweet aqua pura? Before another fun fets, fpeak out, o filent majority, againft thofe whose unafhamed felfifhnefs would pollute and deftroy our feas and our fouls!

Keith Blake, Gloversville, N.Y.

. . . Who's the tiny, young thing who has tough-guy GOLIATH weak in the knees?

Louis B. Raffel, Skokie, Ill.

RASKOLNIKOV and landlady having problems . . . the ETHAN FROMES in for a slide . . .

Erica Enright, N.Y.C.

... Friends in the know say the OWL and the PUSSYCAT are all washed up ... Has VIRGINIA JOHNSON been offered a new position? ...

Mrs. J. D. Waterbury, New Rochelle, N.Y.

... The SPRATTS settled out of court ...

Mrs. Edward W. Powell, Jr., N.Y.C.

The GEORGE CUSTERS are feathering a new nest.

Bruce Godfrey, Center Moriches, N.Y.

... DANTE ALIGHIERI has been going through hell lately. Could the reason be a certain lady named BEATRICE? ...

Carol M. Shlifer, Philadelphia, Pa.

... The MONTAGUES and CAPULETS tiffing ... The HENRY VIIIs finis?

Marilyn H. Rubin, N.Y.C.

... MARIE SKLODOVSKA and PIERRE CURIE radiating? ...

Eileen Coester, N.Y.C.

... Inside report: the GARDEN OF EDEN will soon go on twofers ... Lisbon to L.A.: BALBOA.

Jerry Coopersmith, Rockville Centre, N.Y.

LIZZIE BORDEN looking very chipper the other day ... DEMOSTHENES off to Pebble Beach.

Mitsu Yamamoto, N.Y.C.

LEDA was seen poolside with her new swain ... NEIL ARMSTRONG is planning to take that big step.

Larry Johns, Lodi, N.J.

SIMON LEGREE, of the Tennessee Legrees, and ELIZA, you know which one, are heading for thin ice.

James Turner, N.Y.C.

... SADIE THOMPSON'S tropical vacation a complete washout ...

Dita Greene, Sayville, N.Y.

☞ "*The Bloated Cadaver of Poor Mrs. Hays.*"

Above, the final line of a Gothic poem. Competitors were invited to submit appropriate verse in two quatrains (any rhyme scheme), the second quatrain to conclude with the above line.

Report: Competitors are invited to submit to therapy. A lavishly necrophilic turnout. Appropriately, some verses were truncated, others had extra feet, and many of you submitted only a single quatrain. Favored rhyming words and subject matter are generally well represented below (we stretched a point with Brian Colbath's offering, but we couldn't resist it). We truly regret lack of space to print twice as much of this ghoulash, or at least to acknowledge, by name, those responsible for excellent entries. Judging was nearly as gruesome as reading. Consider yourselves brilliant. *Sick,* but brilliant. Herewith the winners of our discontent:

'Twas the night before Christmas and all through the house
Mr. Hays heard a stirring. Could it be his spouse?

"The Bloated Cadaver of Poor Mrs. Hays." / 323

How absurd! He had drowned her, yet he listened with dread
To a clatter and patter like drums in his head
Just then down the chimney a jolly old elf
With gunny sack bounded: 'twas Santa himself!
And he placed 'neath the tree with its lights all ablaze
The bloated cadaver of poor Mrs. Hays.

Kate Lance, Falls Church, Va.

She scolds us for sending in entries too bleak
Too vulgar for prizes, too tasteless for praise.
Then asks us to use in a poème Gothique
"The bloated cadaver of poor Mrs. Hays"?

Jack Rose, N.Y.C.

The Hays family group is a strange one indeed
Young Roger eats spiders and sassafras seed
Sister Sue takes her ease in a coffin, we hear
And at sad news has frequently cried in her bier.
Old Dad, bless his soul, has the heart of a boy
Which he keeps in a drawer as his favorite toy.
But matters grow grave as they number the days,
Of the bloated cadaver of poor Mrs. Hays.

Norton Bramesco, N.Y.C.

Alas, Mrs. Hays, you have suffered calamity
Brought by an overabundance of amity
Not for your husband (he's deaf and in Greece)
But for Averill Averof, grossly obese.
This hefty seducer, with skill and impunity,
Got you with child at the first opportunity,
Wrecking your life in innumerable ways.
The bloated cad, Averof! Poor Mrs. Hays!

David Axlerod, N.Y.C.

The butler swore vengeance on plump Mrs. Hays
Because she refused his request for a raise.

One night when the moon was enshrouded and dim
He forced the old lady to go for a "swim."
He filled up a cauldron and told her to wade,
And boiled up her brisket and served her sautéed.
Her family loved her (they had her for days!),
The bloated cadaver of poor Mrs. Hays.

Barbara P. Alpren, West Orange, N.J.

Nymphet-inflamed, Humbert H. with aplomb
Planned for the future and wed her fat mom.
Proceeded to vex the poor woman so far,
She ran out and stumbled in front of a car.
Dirty Hum had his Dolly, but Mama's demise
Marred the idyllic affair in his eyes.
It haunted poor Hum for the rest of his days
The bloated cadaver of poor Mrs. Haze.

K. E. Lowenthal, N.Y.C.

On a dank Scottish moor as would make a mon shiver
A surgeon, Mac Hays, draws his scalpel and slays
His winsome young wife, then excises her liver
To use as a transplant—for transplanting pays.
He chants as he chucks her remains in the river:
"Flow gently, sweet Afton, among thy green braes
And into the foam of thy firth please deliver
The bloated cadaver of poor Mrs. Hays."

Fred Rodell, Bethany, Conn.

They say the good lady got lost in a maze
And wandered about its circuitous ways
For twenty-one nights and for twenty-one days,
While dreaming of filet with sauce Bordelaise.
On hedges she'd nibble, on grasses she'd graze;
Pour passer le temps she sang rude roundelays
Until she lay down and the maze now displays
The bloated cadaver of poor Mrs. Hays.

George Oppenheimer, N.Y.C.

"The Bloated Cadaver of Poor Mrs. Hays."

In her penthouse co-op, with some pills on prescription,
An overweight lush made an end to her days.
The newspapers carried the standard description:
"The exquisite corpse of the rich Mrs. Hays."
In a tenement basement, beer cans in profusion,
A stout dipsomaniac ended her days.
The newspaper carried the standard allusion:
"The bloated cadaver of poor Mrs. Hays."

Linda Roberts, N.Y.C.

Is this *la belle grande* for whom Dumas wrote plays,
Whose passions inflamed Chopin's last Polonaise,
Who posed as a subject of Edouard Manet's
While holding *salon* on a blue velvet chaise?
Alas! She fell in with a band of gourmets
Who wallowed in orgies of mushroom soufflés;
Behold the result of her gluttonous ways:
The bloated cadaver of poor Mrs. Hays.

Frank Jacobs, N.Y.C.

It's cheap and it's easy assembling the bones
That fell from the tree where they hanged Robber Jones,
But the brains and the nerves must be handled with care
So he pays highest rates to his friends Burke and Hare.
From jugs and from bottles he takes varied bits
Of the family Schultz that was hit by a blitz.
Integument last; he sings as he flays
The bloated cadaver of poor Mrs. Hays.

Miriam P. Hirsch, N.Y.C.

"Who needs Scotland Yard, my dear Watson?" said Holmes.
"This case I'm afraid, will inspire no tomes.
There's no Jack the Ripper, or even Doc Jekyll
To make this crime famous for fans *de siècle*.
Her spouse did the deed; from the cut of her jib

I deduce 'twas because she had joined Women's Lib.
No need to palaver; where felled she still lays,
The bloated cadaver of poor Mrs. Hays."
                          Joel Cohen, N.Y.C.

Old Mrs. Hays used to spy on each kid
Then tattled to parents about what he did
Until the McCalister boy and a friend
Brought her vicarious kicks to an end.
There just wasn't room for the corpse in the fridge
So Billy Joe threw the old girl from the bridge.
The blue Tallahatchie now grimly displays
The bloated cadaver of poor Mrs. Hays.
                          Diana M. Rose, Syracuse, N.Y.

Our histories tell us of brave Molly Brown,
They call her "Unsinkable" and they are right,
But when the ill-fated *Titanic* went down,
Nell Hays rivaled Molly that memorable night.
I had neither lifeboat nor life-saving vest,
So what kept me floating for seventeen days?
Exactly, dear reader, by now you have guessed:
The bloated cadaver of poor Mrs. Hays.
                          Albert G. Miller, N.Y.C.

Gross, lewd, disgusting and riddled with lice;
Grim, vile, repulsive, debauched, sick and base;
Horrid and rancid, it stars Vincent Price,
(see:) *The Bloated Cadaver of Poor Mrs. Hays.*
                          David Grotenstein, N.Y.C.

It's quite true as reported I ate her
In my permanent suite at the Ritz
If I do it again I shall grate her
I was vexed by her numerous pits . . .
                          Paul Rosenberg, Jamaica, N.Y.

"The Bloated Cadaver of Poor Mrs. Hays."

Malevolence festered in Jonathan Hays:
He knew how to murder in ninety-two ways.
Though all in good taste, with éclat and finesse,
The death of his wife was his crowning success.
The means he selected to do his wife in?
He fed her on tuna fish out of a tin.
And now, in his parlor, he proudly displays
The bloated cadaver of poor Mrs. Hays.
Walter C. Siff, Scotch Plains, N.J.

Mrs. Millicent Hays (once a Las Vegas "bunny")
Was happily married to Mr. Hays's money.
You'd know her at once at a concert or binge
Her head in its "fall" was a lunatic fringe.
Pride goeth before every fall, to be sure.
She grew very heavy, and death soon came to 'er.
Her soul flew to heaven, but here on earth stays
The bloated cadaver of poor Mrs. Hays.
Madeleine Collins, Hastings, N.Y.

John Hays bought the water bed Mrs. Hays saw
Last Christmas the present she wanted the worst.
She slept until one night one tragic flaw
Popped open a seam and she sank in head first.
But nothing was lost because John used his head:
He took the thing back and then, after three days,
Got double his money back on both the bed,
(and) The bloated cadaver of poor Mrs. Hays.
Stephen F. Friedman, N.Y.C.

The good Dr. Hays, who was wont to wax crass,
Said, "By George, she'll amaze my anatomy class!"
How profuse the palaver, how lavish the praise
For the bloated cadaver of poor Mrs. Hays.
David G. McAneny, Rumson, N.J.

Mrs. Hays, on safari, was prone to remark,
"The Deity moves in inscrutable ways,

He created me fair. He created you dark,
So remember your places, for I'm Mrs. Hays!"
Mrs. Hays merely laughed when they told her with pride
That *their* Deity answers the humblest who prays,
And when dawn lit the camp-ground, the bearers espied
The bloated cadaver of poor Mrs. Hays.

       R. E. Calper, N.Y.C.

"My dear, you are spreading," said Mrs. Hays' hubby,
"Dr. Stillman helps women like you get unchubby.
Eight glasses of water—eat as much as you please:
Lean meat, chicken, fish and, of course, cottage cheese."
"Oh, goody!" she said. "Really? All that I wish?"
She ate all the town's lean meat, chicken, and fish.
And all of that water? It floated for days—
The bloated cadaver of poor Mrs. Hays.

       Clay E. Delauney, Jr., N.Y.C.

The list of those memories stays by my bed
And night after night it is thoroughly read.
I sit and I wonder the various ways
We discovered the bodies of family Hays.
Carlotta was hanged, young Bill was garroted,
Old Bill was smothered while he was besotted.
But what I'll remember the rest of my days—
The bloated cadaver of poor Mrs. Hays.

       Kay Hodge, Beverly, Mass.

A sea nymph he called her. He spoke with such grace
Of her weed-tousled hair; her pale, limpid face.
How could I but know that he damned with faint praise
The bloated cadaver of poor Mrs. Hays.

       Rita Halley, Hastings-on-Hudson, N.Y.

No pleasure had she in her Rutherford B.
The twosome was gruesome from elbow to knee.
Tho' Rutherford made the electable grade,
The President's lady chose rather to fade.

"The Bloated Cadaver of Poor Mrs. Hays."

She often sat in with her resident gin.
While he went all out, she would take it all in.
Small wonder they found her, that saddest of days,
The bloated cadaver of poor Mrs. Hays.
              Sally Latham, Chattanooga, Tenn.

'Twas a hideous dinner which Hays served that night.
Though I poked with my fork, I choked on each bite.
The meat was too rare and the bread was quite stale.
Then to my horror I bit on a nail.
It was painted bright red and attached to a bone.
I peeked in the server expecting a moan.
There buried so nicely in pink mayonnaise:
The bloated cadaver of poor Mrs. Hays.
              Mary Anne Bollen, Storrs, Conn.

There was something elusive about Mr. Hays,
Yet I found him appealing in so many ways.
He wined me and dined me and took me to plays,
And once to the Ritz where he usually stays.
Though I woke the next day in a roseate daze,
I was slightly put out when the dawn's early rays
Illuminated coquettishly poised on the chaise,
The bloated cadaver of poor Mrs. Hays.
              E. C. Pier, Whittingham, Vt.

I saw her on Sunday, quite cheerful and gay
On Monday, alas, she was carried away;
Her tale one of error and fate most unkind;
A case of bad luck and poor vision combined.
Beset with postprandial ache whilst in bed,
She sought baking soda but took yeast instead;
O cherish your faculties, friends, and appraise
The bloated cadaver of poor Mrs. Hays.
              Philip G. Becker, Garnerville, N.Y.

Couturière Hays was a widow of note
Who lived in a castle inside a deep moat.

She dressed "fit to kill" in a mink (autumn haze)
So somebody killed her, in two different ways.
A cop smelled a goat and found, from a boat,
Afloat in the moat in her autumn haze coat,
With a gash in her throat and a shiv in her stays:
The bloated cadaver of poor Mrs. Hays.

Henry Morgan, N.Y.C.

In vain she endeavored your contests to win,
Her rhymes were atrocious, her rhythm, a sin,
Ideas, she had none; so futile her strife,
In utter frustration she took her own life.
Alas for the worthless aspiring to fame;
For even the ocean disgorges this dame!
And vultures may hesitate as they appraise
The bloated cadaver of poor Mrs. Hays.

Aaron Edel, Bayside, N.Y.

My story is much too sad to be told,
But practic'ly everything leaves me totally cold,
The only exception I know is the case
When I'm out on a quiet spree
Fighting vainly the old ennui,
and I suddenly turn and see—*
The bloated cadaver of poor Mrs. Hays. . . .

Brian Colbath, N.Y.C.

---

* "I Get a Kick Out of You" by Cole Porter. Copyright © 1934, Harms, Inc.

☞ *Terrible Riddles*

Q. What Goes in Like a Lion and Comes Out Like a Lamb?
A. A Lion Leaving a Lamb Suit Boutique.

Above, a terrible riddle. Competitors were once again invited to descend to the absurd by submitting one such riddle posing a bona fide, "old saw" question with a legitimate but novel rejoinder.

Report: We now know more than we cared to learn about why the chicken crossed the road, what's black and white and re(a)d all over, and what has four wheels (plus added attractions) and flies.

Q. Why did the chicken cross the road?
A. Because he was giving it the last rites.
Andrew and Renée Herz, N.Y.C.
Cynthia Dantzig, Brooklyn, N.Y.

Q. What's black and white and red all over?
A. An American flag with a lot of mistakes.
Arthur Gaffin, Brooklyn, N.Y.

Q. Why does a fireman wear red suspenders?
A. He wants to conform with departmental regulations regarding proper dress.
Miles Klein, East Brunswick, N.J.

Q. What looks like a cat, flies like a bat, brays like a donkey, and plays like a monkey?
A. Nothing.

C. R. Mann, Washington, D.C.

Q. Why did the moron tiptoe past the medicine cabinet?
A. He didn't want to wake his friend, the midget, who was asleep inside.

Ronn Owens, Miami Beach, Fla.

Q. What did the pot call the kettle?
A. Afro-American.

Jean Seligmann, N.Y.C.

Q. Why did the chicken cross the road?
A. 1. Because the road reneged on its promise.
2. Because it was there.
3. To get away from Colonel Sanders.
4. The alternate-side parking rule.
5. To avoid the demonstration.
6. He didn't want to get involved.

1. *Madeline Aria, Brooklyn, N.Y.;* 2. *Judith McMahon, N.Y.C.;* 3. *Michael Marcus, N.Y.C., and Vincent Sforza, Brooklyn, N.Y.;* 4. *Melvin S. Alpern, West Orange, N.J.;* 5. *Dan Lauffer, South Nyack, N.Y.;* 6. *Ted Spaeth, N.Y.C., and Leonard Segal, Astoria, N.Y.*

Q. Who knows what evil lurks in the hearts of men?
A. Acme Polygraph Services, Inc.

Michael Deskey, N.Y.C.

Q. Why is the pen mightier than the sword?
A. Because nobody has yet invented a ballpoint sword.

Albert G. Miller, N.Y.C.

Q. Who helps those who help themselves?
A. The Ford Foundation.

Matthew Laufer, Bronx, N.Y.

Q. Who is the little rotund man who knows if you've been bad or good?
A. J. Edgar Hoover.

Joel F. Crystal, Brooklyn, N.Y.

Q. Why does a rolling stone gather no moss?
A. This is not within its area of competence.

Virginia Feine, Hartford, Conn.

Q. What will sticks and stones do?
A. Build lousy houses; that's why the third little piggy used bricks.

Irene De Blasio, N.Y.C.

Q. What's black and white and red all over?
A. 1. The question presents a contradiction which does not represent any possible situation. "When the answer cannot be put into words, neither can the question be put into words. The riddle does not exist." Ludwig Wittgenstein, *Tractatus Logico Philosophicus.*

    2. Quotations from Chairman Mao.

    3. A Piebald Indian.

    4. A marble cake having a hot flush.

    5. *Survey of Ethnic Groups in America* (Revised Edition).

    6. A female zebra at the Harvard Club.

    7. A Kremlin crap game.

    8. The salt and pepper in a Bloody Mary.

    9. Godfrey Cambridge playing Santa Claus.

1. *Thelma Blitz, N.Y.C.;* 2. *Donald Wigal, N.Y.C. and John Stevenson III, St. Louis, Mo.;* 3. *Aben Rudy, N.Y.C.;* 4. *Barbara Alpren, West Orange, N.J.;* 5. *George Fairbanks, Nutley, N.J.;* 6. *A. John Armstrong, Charlottesville, Va.;* 7. *Richard Krashes, Brighton, Mass.;* 8. *Dale McAdoo, N.Y.C.;* 9. *Al Aaron, N.Y.C.*

Q. Why did Humpty Dumpty have a great fall?
A. To cover his bald head.

Alan Levine, Amityville, N.Y.

Q. What's an Eskimo boat spelled the same forward and backward?
A. An Eskimo boat and taob omikesE na.

Jack Rose, N.Y.C.

Q. What hath charms to soothe the savage breast?
A. A candymaker on safari for *National Geographic*.

Norton Bramesco, N.Y.C.

Q. If two is company, what is three?
A. A conglomerate.

Michael Sage, N.Y.C.

Q. What has four wheels and flies?
A. 1. Chitty Chitty Bang Bang.
    2. A garbage helicopter.
    3. A cherub on a training bike.
    4. A quartet of male potters.
    5. A blue jean factory run by a quadrumvirate.
    6. Half of the Air Force Academy backfield.

1. *Anne Kouts, N.Y.C.;* 2. *Tillie Eulenspiegel, N.Y.C.;* 3. *Rees Behrendt, N.Y.C.;* 4. *Bruce Feld, Bronx, N.Y.;* 5. *John Sansing, Washington, D.C.;* 6. *William Spiller, Ridgewood, N.J.*

Q. What goes in like a lion and comes out like a lamb?
A. A lion kebab.

Arnold Soboloff, N.Y.C.

Q. What goes in like a lamb and comes out like a lion?
A. John Simon.

Gerald Erdelberg, Brooklyn, N.Y.

Q. Why did the moron call his mother long distance?
A. Because that was her name.

Christine Tranford, Dorchester, Mass.

Q. Why did the moron jump off the Empire State Building?
A. He was manic depressive with suicidal tendencies.

Philip Hathaway, N.Y.C.

Q. Why did the moron throw a clock out the window?
A. Who else but a moron would throw a clock out the window?

Larry Berliner, Flushing, N.Y.

Q. What has three green heads, six black legs, and is red, white, and blue?
A. The Supremes in green wigs singing The Star-Spangled Banner.

Arthur J. Cunningham, N.Y.C.

Q. What has he who hesitated lost?
A. The Third National Invitational Snap-Judgment Competition.

Harris Alexander, Brooklyn, N.Y.

Q. What wasn't Rome built in?
A. France.

Terry Kelsey, N.Y.C.

Q. What speaks with forked tongue?
A. Talking snake.

Julie Kurnitz, N.Y.C.

Q. Who is more to be pitied than censured?
A. Jos. Pettigrew Pity (1792–1859) illegitimate son of Martha Pierpont Pity. Purported father: Sir Thos. A. J. Censure. In his autobiography, *The Sins of the Father* (1845), Pity wrote: "My father failed to claim me; I do not wish to claim him. Do not Censure me, sire. Rather, Pity me."

Charles Love, N.Y.C.

Q. Who is Sylvia?
A. That's Estelle's sister-in-law from a previous marriage.

Steven W. Wolfe, N.Y.C.

Q. Why does haste make waste?
A. He's so out of it he doesn't know they call them blouses now.

Janice Chalmers, West Falmouth, Mass.

Q. What speaks softly but carries a big stick?
A. An effeminate pole vaulter.

John Luke, Mt. Sinai, N.Y.

Q. Why does Suzie sell sea shells by the sea shore?
A. To help pay for her house in the Hamptons.

Sue and Herb Wallach, Roslyn Heights, N.Y.

Q. What has four eyes but cannot see?
A. A blind monster.

Steven Coist, N.Y.C.

Q. Man shall not live by "what" alone?
A. Bread. Exception: Zabar's pumpernickel raisin.

Janice Morgan, N.Y.C.

Q. What has a silver lining?
A. A termite's stomach at the U.S. Mint.

Rosemary Bascome, Shelter Island, N.Y.

Q. What is brown on the outside and red on the inside?
A. A radical sheik.

Susan Richkins, N.Y.C.

Q. Who can't be taught new tricks?
A. A dead magician.

Joan Wilen, N.Y.C.

Q. "For men may come and men may go, but I go on forever." What am I?
A. *The Apartment.*

Eva Pedersen, Parma, Mich.

Q. What rises in the east and sinks in the west?
A. The film industry.

Angelo Papa, Trenton, N.J.

Q. What is cast upon the waters that will return a hundredfold?
A. The star and feature players of *Two by Two*.

Michael Schreiber, Brooklyn, N.Y.

Q. What shouldn't you cast before swine?
A. Sally Kirkland.

Karl Levett, N.Y.C.

Q. Why should the physician heal himself?
A. His doctor doesn't make house calls.

Ted Kleiman, N.Y.C.

Q. Neither a borrower nor a lender be. Why?
A. Well for one thing there are the children to consider.

Charles Almon, Brooklyn, N.Y.

Q. Which came first, the chicken or the egg?
A. The egg, from Dairy (aisle three); Meats & Poultry is aisle seven.

Joseph Lisanti, N.Y.C.

☞ *Greeting-Card Verse*

This Little Bird Has Come to Say
Best Wishes on Your Wedding Day
He Hopes Your Future Holds at Least
The Joys You Knew as Our Parish Priest.

Above, verse from a modern greeting card. Competitors were invited to submit a brief (limit six lines) rhyme suitable to a greeting card of today.

Report: Skyjackers, draftees, unwed mothers
Sex change, transplants, pot and others
Topics modern, sane and foolish
Ranged from the sublime to ghoulish
Scanning problems made us curse
Greetings that went bad to verse
Because (you should excuse the punning)
Many left their meters running.

One kidney is in Denver; The other's in Coos Bay
His heart is up in Buffalo; both eyes are in L.A.
You must not think of him as dead: he's only gone away.

Elaine Anderson, N.Y.C.

Roses are red
Violets are blue
Your immolation
Was sad to view.

Miles Klein, East Brunswick, N.J.

Hello there, old secret pal
I thought of you today
And now I want to tell the world
You're in the C.I.A.

Herb Sargent, N.Y.C.

Congratulations on catching a man
I knew you could do it, I'm glad
Though it must have been scary walking in
While the guy was robbing your pad.

Joan Wilen, N.Y.C.

Congratulations! Lots of luck!
Now you're Mr. and Mr.
The wedding was gay, but I am blue
My wife's in love with your sister.

S. H. Rudko, Riverdale, N.Y.

Thrilled to hear you've shed your skin
For something new in midi
Not even snakes should be unchic
In trendy New York Cidi.

Dan Greenburg, N.Y.C.

To our charge customers who have complained
They think they're being swindled
Please do not return your checks
With cards that have been spindled.

Susan Amin, Flushing, N.Y.

Yesterday I thought of you
And suddenly the sun shined
So this card I send you
Because you're David Susskind.

Grace Katz, Rutland, Vt.

Your housewarming gift of china was fine
Your choice of silver was great
But the things I really love to call mine
Were the killer dog, the electric gate.
Jack and Laura Godler, Sunnyside, N.Y.

Get well dear Daughter of Bilitis
Without you, Gay Lib incomplete is
Get well too, old Mattachine
A healthy man's a king—or queen.
J. F. O'Connor, Arlington, Va.

We're just a pair of backward squares
Who cling to old designs
We sorta feel you're folks like us
Please be our Valentines.
Ira Levin, N.Y.C.

Oh, Valentine, if you'll be mine I will be thine forever
You'll never find a girl like me, so sexy and so clever
Let's wed today and sail away to some deserted segment
I forgot to take my pill last month, and think that I am
   ... in love.
Esther K. Oriol, Great Neck, N.Y.

Three per cent, four per cent, five-point-two
This statistic now includes you
Make yourself comfortable—join the mob
Congratulations on losing your job.
Catherine Lahant, East Northport, N.Y.

Roses are red
Violets are blue
For an Army deferment
I'd wear lipstick too.
Judith Klein, East Brunswick, N.J.

"No knock" law's here—pollution and fear
We wish you a Merry Christmas, and a Happy New Year.
Philip Lindenbaum, Woodmere, N.Y.

Greeting-Card Verse / 341

I send along this puppy
Whose name so aptly fits
You see, I call him Cuspidor
Because he is a spitz.
                          N. E. Reynolds, Bridgeton, N.J.

Dear little baby, born today
Take heed to what we have to say
Get turned on, you deserve your lot
But pray you sit, not smoke, the pot.
                          Jeanne Remusat, Forest Hills, N.Y.

From the mayor on down we're pleased as can be
That you've chosen our town for your D and C.
                          Arthur Penn, Philadelphia, Pa.

We miss you more and more each day
Since you and Charlie went astray
No one's seen you anywhere
Congratulations on your affair.
                          Phyllis Sandler, Yonkers, N.Y.

Your anniversary has come so fast
The year before was to be your last
You and others say just one more
Happy Anniversary, Vietnam War.
                          Howard Furman, Brooklyn, N.Y.

We heard your bank was bombed this week
It really is a pity
'Cause now we'll have to take our loot
To Second National City.
                          M. S. Arentzen, Brooklyn Heights, N.Y.

At age thirteen you're man, not boy
Your father's pride, your mother's joy
But between the caterer and the band
This day will cost at least three grand.
                          Allen Goldberg, Flushing, N.Y.

We feel, dear girl, you have us guessing
To acting school you went with our blessing
Now marching protests, bombs in your blouse
Is *this* how you plan to bring down the house?

                              Arthur J. Lorden, Attleboro, Mass.

If you belong to the Mafia
No one cares—why bother?
This is your day, you dear sweet man
Happy Birthday, Godfather!

                              William Hicks, Brooklyn, Heights, N.Y.

It's a week since you've given up smoking
Positively, no whiffs and/or butts—
Now either relax or relapse, lad
You're driving the rest of us nuts!

                              Msgr. A. V. McLees, St. Albans, N.Y.

Words cannot express how much
I appreciate the (turn wheel to appropriate word:
   heart, liver, lung, kidney) I have within
Since my donor's out of touch
I thank YOU, next of kin.

                              Asa J. Berlin, State College, Pa.

Just a line to let you know
All at home miss you so
Here, alas, it's the same old song
Recession, Mitchells, Martha, John
Hope things are cheerier
With you in Algeria.

                              Angelo Papa, Trenton, N.J.

Insurance premiums
Are getting higher
Best of luck
On your fire

                              Helen Rosenbaum, N.Y.C.

Here's a floral corsage for daughter
For your first formal dance
May its beauty match your own, dear
May its colors match your pants.
> *Rawson Foreman, Atlanta, Ga.*

London is just much ado
A pox on Puerto Rico too
We at home all share your bliss
We all learned with you, dear miss
That nothing obsoletes the stork
Like a weekend in New York.
> *Joel Kampf, Chestnut Hill, Mass.*

Happy birthday, little child
Air-born over Idlewild
We hope the day is bright for you
And hope you land before you're two.
> *Bob Krieger, New Orleans, La.*

Bon Voyage!
Enjoy your stay!
Sometimes exile
Is the only way.
> *Susan Dubel, Miami, Fla.*

The diamonds, dearest assignee
The furs, le château acheté
Requiteth not my love for thee
In maximum security.
> *Eileen Tranford, Dorchester, Mass.*

They have cards for health and birthday invitations
Christenings, thank yous, and operations
But here's a new one as you can see
Congratulations on your I.U.D.
> *Eileen Boyle, Lakewood, N.J.*

Hearty congrats to you kids in the cellar
You worked on a bomb with its own self-propeller
Success crowned your efforts. The newspaper tells us
Your building blew higher than anyone else's.
> *Emily Barnhart, Pittsburgh, Pa.*

Just a little note of congratulation
On your artificial insemination.
> *Al Aaron, N.Y.C.*

Turkey seasoned with MSG
The cyclamate jelly was great
The idea of yams with a saccharin sauce
Was so good I just couldn't wait
All in all thanks for a wonderful meal
Remember the days when it was all real!
> *J. Hoefer and B. Ross, N.Y.C.*

You heard the call
And bought the pitch
We hope you'll find
A happy niche
Best Wishes on
Your Party Switch!
> *George and Barbara Fox, Atlanta, Ga.*

I do not like you New York Tel
With me you seldom ring the bell
Although your circuits might be worse
Those I get oft make me curse
But most of all the thing I hate
My Butterfield to two-eight-eight.
> *Michael Deskey, N.Y.C.*

Hard Hats thought you out of line
And caused some damage to your spine
Bowed and bent since your peaceful mission
Good luck to you in your new position.
> *Linda H. Wilen, N.Y.C.*

With this card the wish is carried
From my graying wife and me
That you'll be as happily married
As we thought that we would be!

William Cole, N.Y.C.

O Barnard, be my Valentine!
Say we shall never part. . . .
I am pushing ninety-nine
So please give me your heart!

Henry Morgan, N.Y.C.

Happy anniversary, one golden year is o'er
A nugget in your treasury of many, many more
May joy and happiness accrue in all the years ahead
From this shining moment, until the day you're wed.

Patricia Miller, N.Y.C.

Happy Birthday my lady fair
No flowers or candy do I dare
Send in your liberated state
Just love. Dinner's served at eight.

Charles Almon, Brooklyn, N.Y.

Roses are blue, violets are green
Colors are heard, music is seen
Your every sense is sharp as a whip
Bon voyage on your next acid trip.

Marshall W. Karp, N.Y.C.

Happy Birthday, you're as sweet as sugar
And cuter than a monkey
Happy Birthday, you're the best there is
God bless you, dearest junkie.

Barry Cherin, N.Y.C.

You've picked up your pad and made the move
To another dig and a friendlier groove

May fortune and bounty to you amass
As you wallow in love and greener grass.
Raymond Builter, Fairfield, Conn.

A Happy Anniversary to a lovely wife
For ten wonderful years of married life
You make our home seem like a palace
All our love, Bob, Ted, & Alice.
Edward J. Walker, N.Y.C.

Well good for you
You're getting a baby
The news is too gay to be true
There is one question we do have, maybe
Is it Harry after him or Tim after you?
Patricia Bronzell-Lowery, Durham, N.C.

Thank you for the towels you sent
My son, the newlywed.
But could you change the "His" & "Hers"
To "His" & "His" instead?
Nyda Albert, Brooklyn, N.Y.

Your lucky number's 63
Congrats to you we're wishing
And so we now report with glee
You've won that competiting.
Alan Kaltman, Highland Park, N.J.

Roses are red
Violets are blue
Tulips are yellow
Leaves are green.
So?
Ronald Eisenberg, Howard Beach, N.Y.

You've no birthday due soon, that I know
There're no wedding congrats to bestow

Still, I'm sure you will pardon
My sending this card on
Your receiving draft status: C.O.
>> *Ben Hoffman, Monterey Park, Calif.*

I'm just as sad as sad can be!
I've missed your special date
Please say that you're not mad at me
My tax return is late.
>> *Hal Silverman, Ossining, N.Y.*

We wish you great sadness
We wish you great glee
We wish you more—sensitivity
We're sorry this chicken is leaving the coop
Good luck from your encounter group.
>> *Joan Seltzer, Forest Hills, N.Y.*

☞ *One-Word Inserts*

"Tell Me, Pretty Maiden, Are There Any More at the Home Like You?"

Above, it was familiar phrases again: this time altered in meaning by the addition of a single word. Competitors were invited to submit one well-known phrase transmogrified by a one-word insertion.

Report: No complaints with this lot unless it's our perennial lack of space. One or two entries relied on punctuation as well as word insertion as in "What ever happened to the baby, Jane?" No matter what the phrase, certain words seemed destined for pairing up. They were as follows: grass/smoke; throw/up; right/on; shoot/up; and out/house. You get the tone. Other duplications: High at Noon; O Come Now All Ye Faithful; Call Me a Madam; I Think Therefore I Am Thinking; Mary Had a Little Lamb Chop; I Want to Make One Thing Almost Perfectly Clear; Come Up and See Me Some Other Time; The Way to a Man's Heart is North Through His Stomach; Praise the Lord and Pass Up the Ammunition. Oh yes, and *New York* Magazine Beats Competition. How nice. All Happy families are somewhat alike.

"Into the valley of death rode the six hundred dumbbells."
Clarence Rose, N.Y.C.

"You're a queer one, Mr. Julie Jordan."
Albert G. Miller, N.Y.C.

Everything You Always Wanted to Know About Sex but Were Afraid to Ask For.
Sol Kass, Brooklyn, N.Y.

"You Don't Have to Read It at All, but It's Nice to Know That It's There."
Maurice Varon, Bronx, N.Y.

"He Ain't Heavy, He's Swallowed My Brother."
David Grotenstein, N.Y.C.

"Still Life Is Just a Bowl of Cherries."
Alan Levine, Amityville, N.Y.

"I'd Rather Nixon Be Right than President."
Fred Berg, Boston, Mass.

"*Now* Would You Buy a Used Car from This Man?"
Jeremy Cole, N.Y.C.

"I'll Be with You in Apple Blossom Savings Time."
Tom Lacy, N.Y.C.

"Black Is the Color of My True Love's Hair Tonight."
Bonnie Miller, Roanoke, Va.

"John." "Marsha." "John." "Marsha." "Fred?" "John." "Marsha."
Anita Fricklas, Bound Brook, N.J.

"There's no Cure for the Common but Cold."
Mrs. Hilda Stocking, Bellmore, N.Y.

"The Shadow Knows of Your Smile . . ."
Theodora Huxford, Skaneateles, N.Y.

"Why Fly Me to the Moon?"
James Coco, N.Y.C.

"The Show Off Must Go On!"
R. Ross, N.Y.C.

"He Who Hesitates is, uh, Lost."
Suzanne Remusat, Forest Hills, N.Y.

Mene Mene Tekel Upharsin, Inc.
Oliver M. Neshamkin, M.D., N.Y.C.

NO FAIR PARKING 8 AM—6 PM EXCEPT SUNDAY.
Myron Gross, Fort Lee, N.J.

"Quoth the Raven, 'Nevermore' Unquoth."
Woody West, Cheverly, Md.

"Till Now There Was You."
Roberta Rosenthal, Roslyn Heights, N.Y.

"Make Mine a Manhattan."
James Turner, N.Y.C.

"The Big Rock Singer Candy Mountain."
Ray Weisbond, N.Y.C.

"No, No Thanks, Nanette."
Mrs. Edward W. Powell, Jr., N.Y.C.

"How About Now Brown Cow."
Mark Allen Stang, Miami Beach, Fla.

"I Get No Kick From Domestic Champagne."
Gerald C. Weinborn, N.Y.C.

"You Can't Tell a Book by Its Paperback Cover."
Ed Butler, N.Y.C.

"What's a Nice Girl Like You Keep Doing in a Place Like This?"
J. C. Moss, Brooklyn, N.Y.

One-Word Inserts / 351

"You Can't Tell the Players Anything without a Program."

Dolly Hecht, N.Y.C.

"On the First Day of Christmas My True Love Gave It to Me."

Esteban A. Chalbaud, N.Y.C.

Louisa May Be Alcott.

Linda Agran, Port Chester, N.Y.

"... And God Called the Light Doris Day."

Ilene McGrath, Englewood, N.J.

"To Know Him Is to Love Him Anyway."

Joan and Jack Meyer, Baldwin, N.Y.

"La Donna e Auto Mobile."

Frieda Arkin, N.Y.C.

"Though This Be Madness, Yet There Is Method Acting In't."

Bobbie Kaplan, N.Y.C.

"Comfort Me with Apples, for I Am Sick of *Love Story*."

Mrs. JoAnn West, Cheverly, Md.

"Warning: The Surgeon General Has Determined That a Cigarette Smoking Is Dangerous to Your Health."

Jack Savona, Winthrop, Me.

"I Get a Kick Back Out of You."

Richard Ames, N.Y.C.

"Never Send to 'Occupant' Know for Whom the Bell Tolls."

Ruth Schiffman, Englewood, N.J.

"I Am the Assistant Captain of My Soul."

Katy Sonnenberg, Kansas City, Mo.

"By the Time I Get Used to Phoenix . . ."
Diane Davis, Huntington, N.Y.

"Everything Happens to Me Mither."
Mrs. Robert Amft, Evanston, Ill.

"You've Come a Long Way, a Baby!"
Pat Martin, Chicago, Ill.

"You Can Lead a Horse to Water, but You Can't Make Him a Drink."
Sidney J. Frigand, Massapequa, N.Y.

"Who Is Sylvia? What Is She Wearing?"
Mrs. Dolly Weiss, Roslyn Heights, N.Y.

"Casey Would Waltz with the Strawberry Blonde and the Band Played On Wisconsin."
Norton Bramesco, N.Y.C.

"Love Is Just $5 Around the Corner."
Newcomb H. Small, Chicago, Ill.

"She walks in beauty like the night watchman."
Pat Clipner, Prairie Village, Kansas

"*Sexual Politics* Makes Strange Bedfellows."
Roy Franklin, N.Y.C.

"Man Does Not Live Long by Bread Alone."
Miles and Judith Klein, East Brunswick, N.J.

The Days of Wine and Four Roses
Joanne Palmieri, Bronx, N.Y.

"I Can't Give You Anything but a Love Baby."
Clay E. Delauney, Jr., N.Y.C.

"God Is in Love."
Leonard Sims, N.Y.C.

"Shot Down Among the Sheltering Palms."
Robert Moberly, N.Y.C.

"Give Credit Cards Where Credit Is Due."
Mrs. Erna Lovett, Hillside, N.J.

$E = $ (Approximately) mc^2
Marvin Goodman, N.Y.C.

"The Lord Is My Shepherd; I Shall Not Want You."
Peter Howard, N.Y.C.

"Lay on down, MacDuff."
A. R. Sharpe, Jr., Richmond, Va.

" 'Tis Better to Have Loved and Lost Count than Never to Have Loved at All."
Don Leigh McCulty, Clarksburg, W. Va.

"I Have a Little Eye Shadow That Goes In and Out with Me."
Mavis Kauders, N.Y.C.

"One Man in His Time Plays with Many Parts."
Fred Schreiber, Bronx, N.Y.

"Good All Night Sweetheart."
Carleton Carpenter, N.Y.C.

"Ouch! Raise High the Roofbeam, Carpenters."
William Cole, N.Y.C.

"Northerners Moon over Miami."
Stan and Brenda Lelewer, N.Y.C.

"I Will Take You at Home Again, Kathleen."
Mike Leifer, Valley Stream, N.Y.

"I'm at the End Because of My Rope."
Wally Reach, N.Y.C.

"The Party's Over There."
Ellen Novak, N.Y.C.

"All the World's at a Stage."
Dianne Hluboky, Long Island City, N.Y.

"The Queen of Hearts She Made Some Tarts Respectable."
Virginia Cravatt, Mineola, N.Y.

"When I Grow Too Old to I'll Dream."
Winthrop Drury, N.Y.C.

"Every Dog Has His Day Off."
Pericles Crystal, Brooklyn, N.Y.

"Nobody Doesn't Like Sara but Lee."
Mrs. Barbara Strauss, Demarest, N.J.

On a Clear Day You Can See Saw Forever.
Sharon Shebar, Freeport, N.Y.

"You Can't Win Them at All."
Mrs. Beryl Levenson, Flushing, N.Y.

"Hometown Boy Makes Good Girl."
Pete Kaplan, N.Y.C.

"I Gave in at the Office."
Arline Youngman, N.Y.C.

"Be Careful, It's My New Heart."
Nancy Gallanty, N.Y.C.

"In Philadelphia, Nearly Everybody Reads Off *The Bulletin*."
Elaine H. Stallworth, Willow Grove, Pa.

"We're Pleased to Inform on You..."
>*Patricia Bronzell-Lowery, Durham, N.C.*

"Love and/or Marriage."
>*Barbara Randels, Newark, N.J.*

☞ *Repunctuation*

"I Saw You Last Night and Got That <u>Old</u> Feeling"
"My Wife Doesn't. Understand me?"

Above, two familiar phrases altered in meaning. Competitors were invited to submit one well-known phrase similarly transfigured by changed punctuation and/or italic emphasis.

Report: *Some* enchanted evening! Gobs of entries, thus, unfortunately many duplications. Some were all too familiar: "What's that on the road? A head?" "What's for dinner, Mother?" "Teachers Pet!" "Call me, Ishmael." Others needed explication: R. Crusoe: "Thank God! It's *Friday!*" Additional "repeats" as follows: "*All* the news? *That's* fit to print?"; "Abie's Irish, Rose"; "How do! I love thee! Let *me* count the ways" (theme and variations); "Let *me* call YOU sweetheart"; "What! NOW, my love?"; "*Damn!* The torpedoes!"; "Rose's are red, *Violet*'s are blue"; "What is this thing *called,* love?"; "Do not *fold:* Spindle or Mutilate!"; "Do you take this, woman?"; "You can lead a horse to water but you can't make him. Drink!"; "Uncle, Sam wants you"; "*Don't!* Just stand there"; "People, people! Who need people?"; "Make love not. War!"; "Our father *who*?" "Art. In heaven"; "Look, before you leap . . ."; "I can get it. For *you,* wholesale"; "Donald! *Duck!*"; and, "Let me make *one* thing perfectly clear." Take our advice, and pretend you're Jackie Mason when reading these. It helps. At least it helped us, but then we're *always* pretending we're Jackie Mason (when we're not Marie of Roumania . . .).

Boy meets girl.
Boy loses.
Girl-boy gets girl. *Eve Merriam, Stonington, Conn.*

You're Rumple Stilt's kin! *Barbara Kindness, Arlington, Va.*

"You won't have Nixon to kick around any more gentlemen." *Joseph T. Rigo, N.Y.C.*

Some of *my* best friends are JEWISH?
Henna A. Zacks, Brooklyn, N.Y.

Psycho, the rapist. *Robert A. Fowkes, Yonkers, N.Y.*

There's no *businesslike* show business.
Herbert C. Holt, Woodstock, Vt.

You go to MY head. *Warren Lyons, N.Y.C.*

Me Tarzan. *You* Jane.
John H. Dorenkamp, Worcester, Mass.

On the road: Tom, and a lay.
Dolores Hodesblatt, Monsey, N.Y.

I took *one*. Look at *you*! *Peter Schwed, N.Y.C.*

To be *or*, not to be *that*! Is the question "Whether 'tis nobler in the mind to suffer the slings and arrows of outrageous fortune?" or "To take arms against a sea of troubles?" and "By opposing, end them?"
John Heilig, Somerset, N.J.

I remember you. Well? *Gene Tashoff, Jamaica, N.Y.*

A. ROSEBY. Any other name would smell as sweet.
Virginia Annich, Pennington, N.J.

Rockefeller's done a lot—*Hell*! Do More!
Ted Lewellen, N.Y.C.

There was an old woman who lived in a shoe, she had *so* many children (she didn't know what to do).
Alvin Schreiber, Washington, D.C.

The party's over. It's ALL OVER MY FRIEND.
Stephen Dickman, Brooklyn, N.Y.
Treva Silverman, Hollywood, Calif.

Stars fell on Ala.; BAMA! *J. D. McKean, N.Y.C.*

Casey would waltz with the strawberry. Blonde and the band played on. *Mrs. R. H. Perry, N.Y.C.*

You made me. *Love* you? I didn't want to do it.
Cookie Gray, N.Y.C.

When I fall in, Love, it will be forever.
Mary and Bill Galvin, West New York, N.J.

First, *class* passengers only! *Brenda F. Gustin, N.Y.C.*

A *Lice*? In *Wonder Land*? *Judith McMahon, N.Y.C.*

"Jack Spratt could." "Eat?" "No!" "Fat, his wife, could." "Eat?" "No, lean!" *Paula Callan, N.Y.C.*

Kent got it all—to get her?"
Miles and Judith Klein, East Brunswick, N.J.

I never promised *you* a rose garden.
Geraldine Bucholt, N.Y.C.

I'm gonna buy a paper, doll. *That* I can call my own.
>> Dodi Schultz, N.Y.C.
>> Mark Perry, N.Y.C.

People who live in glass houses shouldn't. Throw stones!
>> A. B. Cooper, N.Y.C.

I am the Pres. I den't make no mistake about it.
>> M. Moore, Philadelphia, Pa.
>> Mrs. Betty J. Lowry, Dalton, Mass.

Don't always stop me in the mid. Dle of a sentence.
>> Walt Wikol, Birmingham, Mich.

Oh, to be in England, now. *That April's* there.
>> Louis Sabin, Milltown, N.J.

What are you giving up for, Lent?
>> Msgr, A. V. McLees, St. Albans, N.Y.

Zip-a-dee-do-dah, zip-a-dee. Eh?   Anne Commire, N.Y.C.

She ain't *what?* She used to be.   Dolores Dolan, N.Y.C.

We have met. The enemy and the "Y" are ours.
>> Jonathan Steele, Hollis, N.Y.

"You *always* hurt!"—THE ONE YOU LOVE.
>> Sam Harned, N.Y.C.

Boys and Girls: Together me and Mamie O'Rourke tripped! The light? Fantastic on the side;—WALKS (of New York).   Roberta Rosenthal, Roslyn Heights, N.Y.

I love you for sentiment. AL REASONS.
>> Peter Friedman, N.Y.C.

I love you. A. BUSHEL and A. PECK.
>> Alan Levine, Amityville, N.Y.

Help!—POLICE   Harvey Chipkin, N.Y.C.

Gentlemen: Prefer Blondes. *Paula Salamone, N.Y.C.*

I'm Rose of Washington, Square. *Fran Gross, N.Y.C.*

A horse? A *horse*? *My* kingdom for a HORSE?
George Glassgold, N.Y.C.
Robert Bennett, Brooklyn, N.Y.
Barbara Goldstein, Hempstead, N.Y.

Don't you know what *good* clean fun is?
Nathaniel Benson, Essex, Conn.

Nearer (My God!) to *thee*?
Oliver M. Neshamkin, M.D., N.Y.C.

Rome, O Rome. O wherefore art thou?
Valerie Hansen, N.Y.C.

"Simple," Simon says. *Sylvia Rothenberg, Merrick, N.Y.*

"*I'm* a Yankee Doodle." "Dandy."
Gail V. Benjamin, N.Y.C.

I wandered lonely as a cloud that floats on . . . *high* o'er vales and hills. *William Cole, N.Y.C.*

When the moon comes *over* the mountain.
Eva Pedersen, Parma, Mich.

Half the world does not know how; the other half lives.
John Felber, Hillside, N.J.

Thirty days hath September. April, June and November (all the rest) have thirty-one. *Peter Lushing, N.Y.C.*

Call a spade. "A Spade!" *Judy Witryol, N.Y.C.*

She loves *me*? SHE loves me? Not she; LOVES me?
Edward Armour, N.Y.C.

Let's take an old-fashioned—WALK.
>Patricia P. Agnew, Washington, D.C.

Remember the Maine?
>David Martin, N.Y.C.
>Joe H. Klee, N.Y.C.

Don't! I *know* you.   Tom and Steffi Waber, Brooklyn, N.Y.

When I consider how, my life is spent.   Joanna Rose, N.Y.C.

Oh say, can *you* see by the dawn's early light?
>K. R. Silk, Bronx, N.Y.

You can't? Go home again!
>Catherine Borden, Chapel Hill, N.C.

Pop goes! The weasel.   Babette Zalcensztajn, Edgewater, N.J.

Should auld acquaintance be forgot and never brought to? Mind?   W. Gardner Kissack, Chicago Heights, Ill.

Love is Just, around the corner.
>Sheila Greenwald, Alexandria, Va.

A *heavenly* host.   Tupper Saussy, Nashville, Tenn.

The lion shall lie. Down with the lamb!
>Donald Wigal, N.Y.C.

Everything? You always wanted to? Know about sex?
>J. F. O'Connor, Arlington, Va.

My sweet: Lord, I really want to see you.
>Ann Max, North Truro, Mass.

What are you doing New Year's, Eve?
>Mrs. Seymour Taubman, Whitestone, N.Y.

Love is where? *You* find it!   Peter Howard, N.Y.C.

Boys will. Be boys! *Lee Israel, N.Y.C.*

Beware the fury of a patient, man.
Jane Coolican, North Arlington, N.J.

Tom, Dick *and* Harry? *Eileen Shapiro, Brooklyn, N.Y.*

Did you ever see a laddie go this way *and* that?
Sue and Herb Wallach, Rosyln Heights, N.Y.

I *told* you. So? *Ruth Moses, Rego Park, N.Y.*

The bear went over the mountain and what do you think? He saw! *Madeline Goldstein, Washington, D.C.*

Some thing there is that doesn't love. A wall.
James Fechheimer, Glen Head, N.Y.

I want a girl just like the girl that "married" dear old Dad. *Hugh Mitchell, Boston, Mass.*

Fly? ME? To the *moon*? *Michael Kay, Norfolk, Va.*

Take me out to the ball. Game?
Anthony Bowman, Washington, D.C.

What is so rare as a day in, June?
Susan Berliner, Flushing, N.Y.
Andrew and Renée Herz, N.Y.C.

☞ *Opening of a Bad Novel*

"I remember the moment, the exact moment when I grew up. Nothing had prepared me for it. I had known at least four freedoms. I was undemanding and not petulant. My needs had been attended to, always. I was six."

Above, the first lines of a resistible novel. Competitors were asked to provide (in fifty words or fewer) the unbeguiling beginning for forgettable fiction.

Report: Such beginnings. Either for tragedy, comedy, history, pastoral, pastoral-comical, historical-pastoral, tragical-historical, tragical-comical-historical-pastoral, scene indivisible, or poem unlimited. And all of them fine. Or almost all. A few rewrites, as in: "Call me Maurice." Or "Irving Roark laughed." Some heavily stylized, as in: "The Marviks and Dobnats quenting on the planet known as Xeb." Many bioflashbacks, taking a cue from our example, as in: "If I knew then what I know now . . ." Of these, most dealt with tiny lives of clamorous desperation, these, most dealt with tiny lives of clamorous desperation, jocks; the Holt-Du Maurier or Brontë manor-born governess; sex kittens; accountants. Some tacky sure-fire paperback sellers; some hard-core hard-cover material. (See Jack Ryan, N.Y.C., for the all-purpose paperback.) What appealed was the engagingly-boring-rather-than-just-banal book. To stultify, you have to be amazingly near-good. And so many were. But back to our story . . .

The door of the ancient root cellar, the rotting capstone of my unholy nether sanctuary, was suddenly wrenched open. Despite the sun's midday brilliance, few of its rays carried past the intruder's immense evil bulk to my stunned and horrified eyes. "Peekaboo!" I said gamely. . . .
John Hofer, Marlboro, Mass.

El Burro meticulously peeled the skin from the banana until it fell, flower-like, over his closed fist. Sancho limped in breathlessly. "Zee general has turned against us! You must flee!" El Burro pointed the banana menacingly toward his aide's head. "I weesh you had not said that, amigo."
Elaine Stallworth, Willow Grove, Pa.

Forget I'm a cop. I do when on vacation. Poco's is a licensed hotel in the jurisdiction of Sullivan County with the PomPom Bar, SLA License 874727. At approximately 0900 hours, I was approached by a W/F, 108 lbs. 5'2", hair brown, eyes blue, complexion ruddy. "Hello," she stated in English.
Jeremy Hurley, N.Y.C.

By the close of the Fourth Ice Age, coinciding as it did with the last great mega radiation wave, the scattered remnants of the once proud International Federation had deteriorated into loosely-knit city-states huddling along the coastlines of the great continents, each self-sufficient and suspicious of its neighbors.
Oliver M. Neshamkin, M.D., N.Y.C.

There wasn't much left of the guy. A blast from a shotgun

six inches away never leaves much. Except questions. And I had plenty. *Cal and Fran Ackerman, Teaneck, N.J.*

Jan Sobieski's deep-set eyes glowed like dying embers. "Is there no one left in Poland with honor, courage, daring?" A sturdy blond lad pushed his way through the cowering throng. "Sire," he said. *Martin Gross, N.Y.C.*

There were six of us, scampering, sun-kissed children at Mayport. There we built our castles in the air, young, tanned bodies lying on the sand, and on Mayport's soft sands one, one of us six, built a deadly dream.
Mitzi Daniel, Forest Hills, N.Y.

Shall I tell you that I loved him? He with his funny crooked smile, and how his eyes grew sad when I read Gibran to him. The papers called it a crime of passion, but my only crime was loving him too much.
Cheryl Davis, Milford, Conn.

Gardner lay still, listening to himself breathe. He could feel the air, thick with heat, pass in and out of his lungs like a clumsy cutlass. Something was wrong, terribly wrong. If only he could remember. Then he knew. He was sober. He was in Manila. And he was sober.
Toni Konits, Flushing, N.Y.

Good evening. It is Sunday, May 6, 1973. I have just taken Collins La Pierre home. I have two philosophies of life. These two main philosophies can be conveyed in one paragraph. I will draw them out into a book (as is usual with all philosophers and their books).
Dona Zeger, Englewood Cliffs, N.J.

Hank Cleaver, ex-O.S.S., dragged thoughtfully on his Old Gold Straight, his gaze fixed resolutely on a spot just below Humboldt's chin. "No. I won't do it. I won't clean up your bloody mess for you."
Don V. Booty, Macomb, Ill.

"It was hard being German in Miami Beach, even if you were blond and blue-eyed and had a body that women ogled at. Middle-aged men resented your flat stomach and ladies could see that all the riches of body and spirit were not enough to fill an empty purse."
Ms. André Derzavis, West Hollywood, Calif.

I stepped out of the shambles of my solitary-confinement cell and ventured outside. . . . Was I the only living thing that had survived that awful holocaust?
David Gordon, Bronx, N.Y.

Tolkiens are cute. *Henry Morgan, Toronto, Ont., Canada*

Robert Frost said that one could do worse than be a swinger of birches. I love that line. For thirty-five years it's literally been my hold on life. Perhaps that's why I'm here at Utica State Hospital.
Patricia Kissane, Whitesboro, N.Y.

When you read these words, darling Miles, the State shall have exacted what it believes to be justice. Stephanie, if not Philip, will be avenged, Ronald vindicated, Bernice free from fear, and you, with Lucy's help, must try to forget. Do you remember the beginning, that foggy June in '38? *Barbara A. Huff, N.Y.C.*

One dusky October in 1942, I perceived from the study's travertine terrace a long figure, female in gender, approaching the esplanade, her identity concealed by a terpsichorean exhibit of leaves in purgatory. "Evelyn?"
Charles Almon, Brooklyn, N.Y.

When Freud passed out the egos, it is very probable that he passed over the crib of little Mackinlay Finley.
Aaron C. Alson, N.Y.C.

. . . I knew it was over because that morning I had

steamed the stamp off my letter to her to mail the phone bill. Payment wasn't even overdue.

Lawrence Marc Vincent, Cambridge, Mass.

The pang I felt as I turned and beheld for the last time that hated place where I had spent my first sixteen years was unexpected. As sheets of cold rain imposed themselves, the borrowed (stolen) car raced forward to what I thought, naïvely, was freedom. *Lee Bailey, N.Y.C.*

Tegucigalpa (and the bulk of my story concerns itself with the special charms of that most exciting of world capitals) was where I first met them—the Drunk, the Dwarf, the Priest, and the Woman. *Fran Ross, N.Y.C.*

"A mysterious stranger has bought the haunted mill," the Judge announced, when he came home for lunch one day. The two girls looked at their father with interest. It was June, school had closed, and they had always liked mysteries. In fact, they had even solved a few . . .

James Elward, N.Y.C.

20/20 I watch Crystal tick away on jewel heels across a marble hall. She cannot tell the time of life is run or know, as I, an instant all is all and so infold tomorrow into now. I see her icy still, unsprung, and bored policemen lifting bloody prints. *Paul A. Stone, Silver Spring, Md.*

"Edna's not coming." "Are you quite—" "This just arrived—" ". . . sure? I wonder—" ". . . from Paul." ". . . why. From—" "They've eloped!" ". . . Paul? The deuce you say! What about—" "And gone off to Cannes —" ". . . Steve? He was going—" ". . . to see films." ". . . to marry her." "Probably Swedish." "Wasn't he? Hello!" "Ta!" "Edna!" "Meet Tony."

George Fairbanks, Nutley, N.J.

You can say what you want about Bruce Bradley. Most people did. And after they read his will, I added a few words of my own. I was his wife.

Ms. Gene Winslow, Florham Park, N.J.

They say that when you lie down with dogs you can expect to get up with fleas. Well, when I was in Kansas City those first few years I didn't exactly lie down with dogs. And then I didn't exactly get up with fleas either. But . . .

Rosemary Bascome, Bronxville, N.Y.

"A billion-dollar heist," I chortled joshingly. "Do you intend to rob Fort Knox?" His intelligent eyes flared briefly. "No," Lance replied softly, "I intend to steal Fort Knox."

William J. Graham, Massapequa Park, N.Y.

Mother and I were surprised the day my brother brought home Raquel Welch. No, he had not won her in a publicity contest. My brother isn't young or handsome. Baldish, glasses, stammer, unemployed. Not Raquel's mental equal either. We were surprised because he never brought a girl home before.

Jack Paul, Brooklyn, N.Y.

Having begun his intellectual odyssey in a certain country where a certain revolutionary *brio* is a key ingredient of the national character, he was to traverse rugged contours of a vast philosophical terrain before arriving, that torpid October afternoon in Marrakech, at the single most pivotal point of his life.

Robert Chamblee, N.Y.C.

Oy, thought Israel Goldfarb wryly, it is midnight, I have much studying still to do, I have run out of cream cheese, and all the stores on Pitkin Avenue are closed.

Tony Chiu, N.Y.C.

Robert fired his rifle and the poised cobra slumped over the tea bush. "Look, Constance!" he cried, as six tiny

creatures broke through their shells and slithered over their mother's lifeless form. We gingerly lifted them into our sun helmets and carried them home to raise as our very own.
David Newburge, N.Y.C.

As Cynthia donned her space suit/nurse's uniform/shawl/make-up/G-String/ she was excited/worried/tearful/nervous/hot/ for her first day at the space station/hospital/old house/theater/massage parlor/and she dreamed of Commander Kirk/Dr. Derek/the Young Master/Bruce/Olga . . .
Jack Ryan, N.Y.C.

Mother was a Vanderbilt. Father was a kleptomaniac. A curious partnership, as Mother was more the blind than the mute partner. I was split ragged on the acquisitive cusp of Taurus. I see all this as accidental, not casual. Coincidental, not interrelated.
Herbert Duval, N.Y.C.

While the armies of the Tsar swept with alarming speed across the frozen steppes, Nikolai Dashkin, stiff but resplendent in his colonel's uniform, gazed abstractedly at the snow-covered onion domes of Saint Petersburg. "So white, so pure." His thoughts turned automatically to Natasha.
Ian Irvine, Cambridge, Mass.

I walk on your streets and you do not know me. But I know you, all of you, all your pasts and futures. You scoff? Wait . . . wait, I'll show you. . . . I see . . . seated at a bar . . . in Hollywood . . . three members of the champion Los Angeles Lakers. Not only that . . .
Gregg M. Rosen, Plainview, N.Y.

"At the risk of boring you . . ."
Morton Cooper, Stamford, Conn.

☞ *Conclusion of a Bad Novel*

"That night, as I lay awake, sleepless, I realized what a shambles I'd made of my life. I was sixty."

Above, the concluding line of a bad novel. Competitors were asked to provide (in fifty words or fewer) the unfetching finale for a work of forgettable fiction.

Report: Faded youth, frazzled dreams, fizzled romance. Deathbed and graveside farewells. A moribund lot. But delicious. Typical quotes: "Or was it just the beginning???" and "He knew now what he must do." Sci-Fi, Children's Lit and Current Events commingled artlessly. The Watergate goings-on may well be stranger than ———, but must still be classified as nonfiction. For a general critique, see report on the previous competition. For specifics, see below. After all, she reasoned, tomorrow is another day . . .

By the time I laid aside the last page of her letter, the window had paled with the light of a new day and my candle had commenced to gutter, I sighed. "Abdul," I called after a few minutes, "saddle my horse. I am going to rejoin the regiment."   *E. C. Pier, Whitingham, Vt.*

Conclusion of a Bad Novel / 371

The Thing on the bed was shrinking. It jerked spasmodically once, twice more, and lay still. A great rushing wind rose up in the room, as unnamable evils seemed to be taking flight. Then a stillness descended, broken only by the sweet, regular breathing of the child. He had won.
Oliver M. Neshamkin, M.D., N.Y.C.

"Sixth Lancers?" inquired Colonel Carruthers of the sole survivor at Fort Zama. Sergeant Tyrone pointed to the long line of sabers over sandy graves. "All present or accounted for, sir!" Through his tears, Tyrone saw them pass in review . . . Tommy, Scotty, Ballantine, and all the rest of the Fool's Brigade. *Jack Ryan, N.Y.C.*

Esteban was dead and Juliet was dead, but Harold was going to come out of it. Thinking about Harold, I lay down and looked straight up at the sun.
Patricia Miller, N.Y.C.

What had Sheila seen, in those last terrifying seconds, in that aerial view of the Champs-Elysées? The photograph was gone; Oscar, with his insatiable appetite, had seen to that. Now he knew with chilling certainty it was his quest alone. He pressed the DOWN button. The journey was begun. *Dodi Schultz, N.Y.C.*

Digby showed the Inspector the door and returned to the library to Cathy, mixing mimosas. "Hachacha," he said, kissing her brow. "We've pulled it off, pet. Cheers!" Cathy was raising her glass when her eyes fell on the frayed bellcord. "Oh, Digs," she murmured, aghast, as the doorbell rang again. *Kit Hurley, N.Y.C.*

Alexiana was born strong, like all Rooxens. Now, rather than puffing out her four birthday candles, she hurled the cake into Alex's glorious hair. Paralyzed with horror, I fled into the long night, knowing for what I had been spared: Rooxiana burned into the ground.

Betty H. Zoss, Berkeley Heights, N.J.

And now, looking back at those six months, I can't believe that it's really me, back in my sunny kitchen, the familiar plants on the window sill and the cat purring; the same person—except for the scarf I will always have to wear around my throat.

Suzanne Zavrian, N.Y.C.

The walls around me convulsed once more. Someone grasped my feet. The world swung crazily about me. I cried out when the blow struck. I was born.

David E. Diener, Irvington, N.Y.

It was so. It is so. And so it will ever be. Man is from Woman born.

Aben Rudy, West New York, N.J.

. . . Better shave, he thought, and weaving into the bathroom, he slouched before the mirror. He couldn't focus.

Raymond Kauders, N.Y.C.

Having returned to 1973, I switched off the time machine, knowing I would never use it again. Clearly, the "Good Old Days" weren't as "good" as people supposed. "Clara!" I shouted as I lit my pipe and settled in my easy chair. "What's for dinner?"

Frank Jacobs, N.Y.C.

The cock heralded the rosetta dawn as I wearily backed my Ferrari out of Pamela's life forever. *John Wendt, N.Y.C*

"I will never return to Ten Oaks," she said. He touched her and then, as evanescent as the motes of sunlight which played across her alabaster neck, she was gone.

Jim Fritzhand, N.Y.C.

And so it goes. *Ardian Gill, N.Y.C.*

And when she turned to say good-by, he was already gone. And somehow she knew she would never see him again. Most likely. *Larry Laiken, Bayside, N.Y.*

So, that was my turn at bat. I touched all bases and made it home. Now it is your turn. Play ball!

Donald Wigal, N.Y.C.

"You have learned all I can teach you here," Madame said sadly. "Now you must learn from the world."
Ruth E. Kramer, Brooklyn, N.Y.

When the word reached the meeting of the *famiglia* that the *pezzonovante* had bitten the dust, the *caporegimes* bowed their heads in reverence, and, as the *consigliere* jotted a few notes in his little black book, the Don smiled.
Frank B. Lewis, N.Y.C.

After three decades of marriage, and having blown it sky-high, Stoney's political career faltered upon the altar that precipitated his second attempt at wedded partnership. The White House seemed far away.

Lee Greene, Briarcliff Manor, N.Y.

Seeing Marsha waiting impatiently at the side entrance, he squeezed down into the motorized pumpkin beside the dwarf and raised a fine surgeon's hand to the painted face, not daring to look back toward the center ring.

Robert Kenney, Sausalito, Calif.

It was a seesaw, you will recall, which had brought us together years ago. How ironic, then, that I should now find myself perched helplessly aloft opposite this massive matron whom I had once effortlessly whisked across a threshold! *George Fairbanks, Nutley, N.Y.*

Emotionally and physically exhausted, I had just sunk into a fitful sleep in the arms of Captain Christiansen

when I heard the Widow Ashcroft cry, "Look, everybody!" I sat up and looked around me. Land. It was really land, at last.
Marge Curson, Jersey City, N.J.

He was leaning on the rail, smoking, looking emotionally drained from his ordeal. He was lost in thought, staring over the waves. "That's a lot of water out there, Captain," I said. "I know," he replied, "and that's only the top of it."
Dennis Hartin, Wading River, N.Y.

... And afterward, they smoked.
Kenneth Milne, Staten Island, N.Y.

She was dead and that was that—but for the rest of my life I knew I had to live with the terrible secret that my love—and not the cottage fire—had consumed her.
Charles Librizzi, Atlantic City, N.J.

Stretched out before him years of fireside bourbons and quiet fishing by Lake Huron. For the first time, an easy smile found the face of Dan Carmichael, formerly Col. Igor Rostrovsky of the elite K.G.B.
R. C. Adelman, Bellerose, N.Y.

Oh, well, thought Vikki, good-by Birmingham, so long Bruce. Smoothing down the uniform and turning on the smile, she told herself to watch out for the bald pinstripe in the third aisle seat.
Dorothea H. Scher, N.Y.C.

The bump on Tajil's head throbbed as he watched, across the aisle, the American blonde cross her legs, while below the carriage two streaks of rust uncoiled relentlessly toward the horizon—tomorrow, after tea, they'd be in Trebizond and there Amurdaga would be waiting.
Elizabeth W. Blass, Little Rock, Ark.

... "Gid frae w' birk, lad," the old laird had told me, "guid-willie waught." What, I wondered desperately as final night closed 'round me, had he meant?
Woody West, Cheverly, Md.

Conclusion of a Bad Novel / 375

I turned from my mother's grave and walked out of the cemetery for the last time, and into the bright sunlight. It was a new beginning. *Jerry Lesch, Portland, Ore.*

As the great machine lumbered down the runway and flung itself into the air, I sprang to a window for my final glimpse of that jungle arena where I had found both war and love. . . . *Fred Berg, Boston, Mass.*

He never quite recovered from the shock. His final years were spent with WKAT-TV in Miami. . . .
Ron Butler, N.Y.C.

. . . Here was Jean Brown in my arms, and I knew. She was television. She was a hit series with reruns. And I knew I would renew her every season for the rest of my life. *Robert Bernstein, N.Y.C.*

Well, you may remember what I said about lying down with dogs and getting up with fleas. I guess I just really didn't do either one. *Rosemary Bascome, Bronxville, N.Y.*

"All isn't really lost, *bonne mère*," I said reliving last night's debacle. "I'm still able to pose for your old friend, Rodin." *Camilla Gellert, N.Y.C.*

I said good-by to Leslie, hung up the phone, and poured myself a drink. From where I sat I could see the north end of town. It was beginning to snow.
Lelic Vascent, Providence, R.I.

Roy smiled quietly. Yes, it was worth all those years of work (and, yes, suffering). MARISSA: a blue lagoon,/ A Spanish tune,/An amber moon,/And you/Are all I need/To sow the seed/Of love, indeed,/So true./ He'd done it! By Godfrey, he'd done it!
Rev. Vincent P. Gorman, Bronx, N.Y.

... Even the dog is asleep. *Pat Allen, Warsaw, Mo.*

... The door clicked coldly; Sybil did not stir.
Herb Lambert, Walnut Creek, Calif.

Very well, thought Vladimir, as the hotel door closed behind her. So be it. One thing his profession had taught him was how to be alone. He would survive.
Elaine Andartrodlt, N.Y.C.

As I descended the scrubbed marble steps of Dexter Adams's Federalist house to the brick sidewalk, one reporter was still left, the persistent youngster from *The Boston Globe*, with more questions about Doc's life. How could I ever tell him? How could I ever tell anybody?
Michael Deskey, N.Y.C.

... Once more I am forced to the belief that, if given the chance to live the life of a character in a movie, I will always go out for popcorn.
Lawrence Marc Vincent, Cambridge, Mass.

Waves of blind panic engulfed him as he wildly tore apart the threadbare foul-smelling mattress where Max had hoarded his life's savings. Half gasping, half choking, he clutched at the crisp new bills as they poured out. He examined one, then another. "Counterfeit!" he screamed. "They're all counterfeit!" *Alissa Abrams, Brooklyn, N.Y.*

... After a while I left to walk back to the hotel. But it was raining, so I took a cab. *E. F. Maricle, St. Louis, Mo.*

And then I woke up. *John Anthony Russo, Dix Hills, N.Y.*